BOOK ONE OF THE HALLOWED WAR

THE PAGAN NIGHT

TIM AKERS

TITAN BOOKS

THE PAGAN NIGHT
Mass-market edition ISBN: 9781789090208
Ebook edition ISBN: 9781783297399

Published by Titan Books
A division of Titan Publishing Group Ltd
144 Southwark St, London SE1 0UP

First mass-market edition: September 2018
2 4 6 8 10 9 7 5 3 1

A CIP catalogue record for this title is available from the
British Library.

Printed and bound in the USA.

For Jennifer.
Forever.

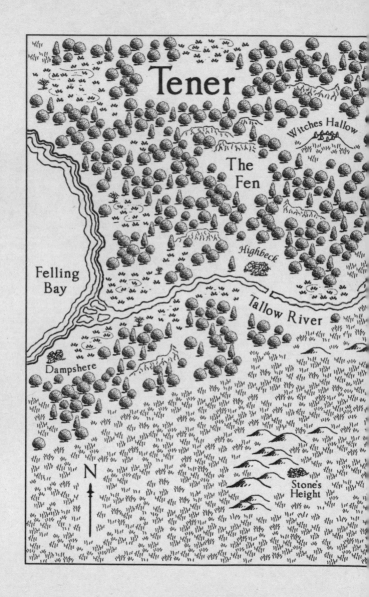

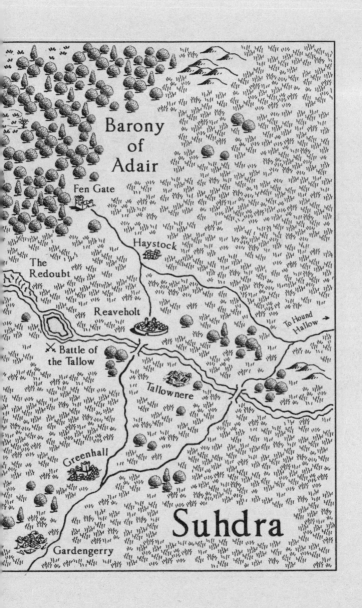

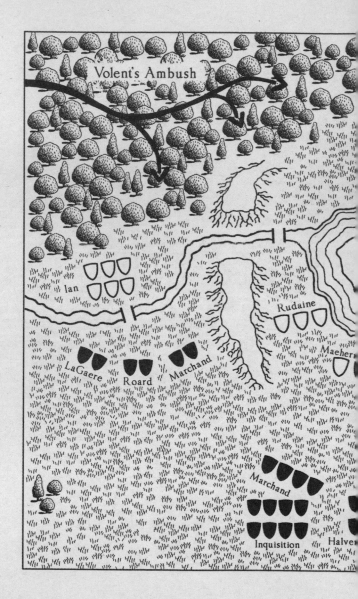

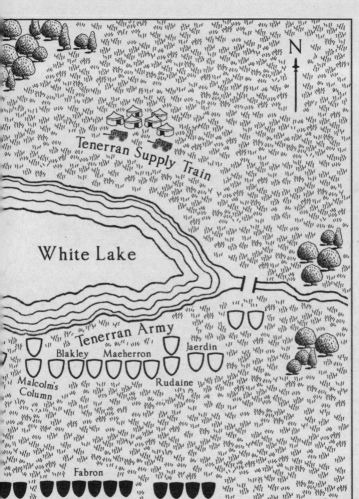

N

Tenerran Supply Train

White Lake

Tenerran Army

Blakley   Maeherron   Jaerdin

Malcolm's   Rudaine
Column

Fabron

Inquisition

Halverdt

Suhdrin Army

1

A GATHERING OF HERETICS

IRON IN THE BLOOD

1

THEY WAITED IN the gloom. Six men in a small stone hut, warming their hands over the fire pit in the middle of the floor, well armed, well frightened. They didn't look at one another.

An unexpected cold snap, not uncommon this far north even in the heart of summer, gave them a morning more like autumn. Their breath fogged the air, mixing with the smudgy wood smoke to fill the closed hut with haze. Each man's face was stitched in the traditional tattoos of the Tenerran spirit warriors of legend. The markings were painted on, muddy blue ink that wrinkled and flaked when they talked.

They were on the south side of the border between Suhdra and Tener, the wrong place to be wearing the ink. They all had friends who had died just for being Tenerran, and family, cold and buried in the mud, who had been murdered by the duke of Greenhall's men. All risked the same with that ink on their face, even if it was false. A last vestige of the crusade that had taken their religion from them and replaced it with the church, unifying the island under the celestriarch's rule, putting a doma in every village and priests of Cinder and Strife at every altar.

While the rest of the island had settled into uneasy

peace, the marches still saw more than their share of blood and hatred.

"Later than usual," one of the men said. He was thick, with little neck and an excess of beard.

"He's always late. You be calm, Tunnie."

"I'll be calm when he's here. Till then, I'll damn well be what I please."

"You nag like my mother."

"Your mother nags like she screws, Mancey," Tunnie replied. "Everyone."

They laughed, but it wasn't a settled laughter. Their voices were blunted by their accents. Deep Tenerran brogues muddied their vowels. They were dressed like farmers, but there was a bundle of clothing on the ground between each man's feet. A sword lay across each bundle. They didn't look at those, either. The freshly sharpened steel of the blades danced in the light of the fire.

The men waited, and they stared at the flames.

The door opened, revealing a cloaked man. When he came into the room, they all started to stand, then remembered themselves and settled back onto the bench. He was tall and thin, with delicate wrists and long, narrow fingers, each tipped with a musician's callus. The man who had grumbled before, Tunnie, spat into the fire.

"Late enough," he said.

"Early enough, you mean," the newcomer said. His voice was crisp, the twist of the rural accent more like the notes of a song. It was the kind of voice women loved, and bards cultivated. "Moon's only now up—and we're about the moon's business."

"You talk like a priest," Tunnie said.

"No need to be cruel," the newcomer said. "Now.

Let's get about it, shall we?"

Grumbling, the men stood and lifted their bundles, revealing cloaks like the newcomer wore. All but Tunnie. He kept his hands to the fire.

"I mean it, Allaister. You talk like a priest." He looked up. "The place we're going, we don't need priests."

"You accuse me of something, Tunnie, but I don't know what." Allaister picked up his own bundle and began to unpack it. "Are there things you feel need saying?"

"Just this. You've been here four months. We don't know anything about you, other than that you escaped from Greenhall's dungeons. We don't even know what put you in there, much less what broke you out."

"I broke myself out," Allaister said. "The gods broke me out. What does it matter? And what does it matter what I was doing there?"

"No one breaks out of that place," Mancey mumbled, but Allaister ignored him. Tunnie nodded.

"People don't go to Gabriel Halverdt's prison for nothing," he said, "and people don't just walk out. You could be anyone. A murderer, a rapist… we don't know enough about you, Allaister."

"Oh, I assure you. I am a murderer," he said with a smile and a nod. "Isn't that what you want?"

"I've never seen you at the Frostnight keg. Never seen you drink at the Allfire, and yet you're the one leading us. I wonder how that happened."

"You wonder? Have I been anything but honest with you?" He threw back the hood of the traveler's cloak that he'd been wearing. Allaister's face was a maze of traditional Tenerran markings, his name and the promises of the Seers etched in woad across his cheeks. True ink, permanent and profane. His face was handsome under the crude markings. His goatee was well trimmed, and his eyes were black. But his voice was calm.

"You've been grumbling against Duke Acorn for how long? Years? How often have his men raped your wives? Your daughters? How many of your harvests have gone to his stores, how many young calves pitted for his table? While you starved?" He turned from one man to the next, and then stopped. "This land is occupied, Tunnie, held by a Suhdrin lord when it's good Tenerran blood that works its fields. We were born on the wrong side of the border, and for that our brothers have died. I came, and I've done something about it."

"Something. You've gotten a lot of us killed. We've spilled a lot of our own blood for you."

"Blood is the price," Allaister answered. The other men nodded and whispered the same phrase in response, like a prayer. It was an old phrase from the liturgies of the shamans—mystical words, words that carried meaning down from the ancient days, their edges worn smooth by repetition and hope. Tunnie grimaced. He had walked into that. Still, he rubbed his hands over the fire and made no move toward his bundle of clothes. By that time the other men had donned their cloaks and penitent's masks, to hide their ink and identity.

"I know the words, priest. My family has been bleeding into this ground longer than anyone here. Longer than the church. Don't think you can preach to me."

"Tunnie." Allaister tightened the cord of his belt and picked up the simple sword at his feet. "We go tonight to clean the land. We have bled in different soil, you and I. Our families have knelt to different

16

spirits, but they are honest spirits nonetheless, and not the bookish gods these bastards put over us after the crusade. So I ask—" he raised the sword and fitted the tip of the blade into the scabbard, then slapped it home "—what the hell is your problem?"

"I don't know you," Tunnie said. "I haven't prayed with you. Your fathers didn't sit the midnight vigil with my fathers, nor your sons with my sons. I don't know what sort of man you are, nor how you bleed when the spirits call."

"My brother, tonight you will know." Allaister fastened the blade and scabbard beneath his cloak, and then raised his hood. The weapon disappeared completely beneath the pilgrim's robes. Allaister folded his hands into the sleeves of the robe and stood up straight. "Though you must judge the Suhdrin blood I will be spilling, and not my own."

The others laughed. Tunnie sighed, but he stood and started to put on his cloak.

"I damn well hope so," he muttered. "My brothers have sacrificed much since you showed up."

The others ignored him, though they finished their preparations quietly while he got dressed. Allaister stood by the door, staring out into the night. When everyone was ready, they flipped their hoods up over their heads and filed out into the darkness. The last man dumped sand onto the fire, leaving darkness and ash and the stink of fear in the air.

Gilliard stood atop the guardhouse and looked down at the moon-washed ruins at Gardengerry. The banner of House Halverdt, a triple acorn and a cross, stirred sluggishly in the breeze over the gate. This place had been old when the first Suhdrin traders had found it, shunned by the tribes of Tenerran savages—stone walls surrounded by offerings of burnt flowers and totems of pagan power.

The water here was fresh so the traders had settled and Gardengerry became a major stop for the pilgrims on the road to Cinderfell, populated entirely by faithful Suhdrin and their kin. They had never fully repaired the ruins, however. In the moonlight, Gilliard imagined he could see the old city that had once stood here, tall and bright under the starry sky.

"You're looking the wrong way." The voice came from below. Gilliard turned around. There were pilgrims, seven of them, standing outside the gate. They were wearing full mendicants' robes, hood and mask covering their faces. In the darkness it was impossible to tell more about them.

"Ah, sorry," he said. "It's a beautiful place." Gilliard scratched his head and started the slow walk down the outer stairwell. He was wearing heavy chain mail and a pair of awkward plate gauntlets, along with boots of good steel. The whole kit was heavy, though, and made him nervous when he had to take the stairs in the dark. "Bit late to be outside, don't you think? You're close to the savage lands," he said, gesturing broadly to the north, where the border between Tener and Suhdra lay.

"Really?" the lead pilgrim said a bit tensely. "I was under the impression that most Tenerrans were friendly to the church." Something about his voice sounded odd. "Hard to walk all the way to Cinderfell without crossing through a few Tenerran fields, hm?"

"It's Tenerrans from here to the winter god's shrine, boys. The tame type, mind you, but still. Stick to the godsroad and you'll be fine. Stray far, and it'll be mad gods and murderers for you." Gilliard smiled beneath his helm. "But surely you know that. This your first time traveling to Cinderfell?"

"It is," the pilgrim answered. The rest of them were awful quiet, and Gilliard still didn't like this fellow's voice. He leaned against the wall and peered down.

"Like I said. Bit late to be out, isn't it?"

"Travel from Pilgrim's Rest has taken us longer than we expected, but we're glad for your hospitality."

"Ho, now. Let's not get ahead of ourselves." Gilliard paused at the cupola that overlooked the road. This outer wall wasn't much good in a siege, but it served well enough for collecting tolls and keeping out vagrants. The guard rested his spear against the wall and leaned down for a better look. "Healthy lot, for pilgrims."

The men looked among themselves, and the lead one shrugged.

"Should we have been starving ourselves?"

"Traditionally, yes," Gilliard said, "and Pilgrim's Rest is quite a distance from here, if that's how you came. Where'd you stay last night?"

"Doonan. Came up the godsroad."

"Doonan's a good walk, but aye." There was something about these fellows that Gilliard didn't like. Only one of them talking. "The rest of you taken some kind of vow of silence, then?"

"Uh, yes. They have... and loving kindness, as well. Which is why we're willing to keep standing here and chat politely, when you really should have opened that door by now."

"Oh, aye. *You've* taken no vows then, have ya?" Gilliard smiled broadly. "But you're not worried about running into any Tenerrans, I don't think.

Because you're of the tribes, aren't ya? I can hear it in your voice."

The man sighed. When he answered, the brogue was distinct, though certainly less heavy than the filthy rural types who lived in the outer villages.

"Aye, the sun and moon blessed us with that name, but we're good little kneelers, my lord. We're going east, to practice bending the knee in Cinderfell for the Allfire."

"And why do you travel to the moon's temple to celebrate the festival of the sun, hmm?" Gilliard liked this group less and less. There were few tribesmen inside the walls, but it was still more than he preferred. "I'm not going to let you in here if you don't start talking your station. Now, first, why is a group of Tenerran converts traveling through Pilgrim's Rest? Up Dunneswerry, by the river, that's the way for lads like you. Thought you lot avoided the 'Gerry."

"We aren't from the grasslands, nor the lakes. We live in Lac Leure, down Heartsbridge way," the pilgrim answered, a hint of anger appearing in his voice. "Just as if we were real people."

"Not with an accent like that, you don't. You know," Gilliard stood straight and snatched up his spear. "I think you can sleep outside. Just for tonight. Lord Cinder will appreciate your sacrifice."

"Bloody Suhdrin and their bloody accents," the man mumbled, exasperation leaking through his tension. "Tunnie?"

The big pilgrim in the back, who had kept his head down for the entire exchange, glanced upward, and then rolled his shoulder. His arm came up in a lazy arc, like he was stretching, and then four inches of cold iron dart was sticking out of Gilliard's forehead.

The guard collapsed, clattering down the remaining stairs and out of sight of the seven nervous men. His limp body struck the wall and pitched over, landing with a crash at Allaister's feet. He made a terrible commotion as he went, all that chain and plate, battering against the stone.

"Not ideal," Allaister hissed. "Joer, get up there. Tunnie—" he turned to the man "—that blood enough for you?"

"Not near enough," Tunnie rumbled.

"Good," Allaister said.

Joer clambered smoothly up the wall, finding finger holds in the vine-cracked stones. The defenses hadn't been maintained well enough to keep men out, hadn't even been built for such a mundane purpose— something the Suhdrins had never really recognized in their rush to settle the ancient ruins.

A minute later the gate swung open.

"Surprised no one heard that," Mancey said.

"Oh, I'm sure someone did," Allaister answered. "Which is why we need to keep moving." He hurried the six of them through the gate, then lingered over the fallen guard. Allaister knelt beside the corpse, drawing a blade from his sleeve.

"My apologies, brother. Your sacrifice will be remembered, and your blood counted. Go now to the quiet house." Allaister muttered something quietly under his breath, using one hand to draw the blade across Gilliard's neck while making the sign of the moon with the other. A plume of frost whispered out, melting quickly in the summer night. The blood on his blade was sticky and black. Allaister used it to draw a symbol on the dead man's forehead, smearing blood around the wound.

Gravel crunched behind him.

"You coming?" Tunnie called from the open gate. Allaister closed his eyes in frustration, but hopped up and trotted inside.

"Of course, of course. Making sure the bastard was dead," Allaister said as he passed the big man. "Didn't want him talking."

Tunnie stared at the dead guard and the smear of blood on his forehead. For a second he thought it might be a Celestial death rune, the kind of thing their priests burned into the skin of the departed.

Surely not.

Torches appeared on the upper wall, and the voices of guards drifted down. Grimacing, Tunnie gripped the sword beneath his robes and hurried after the others.

These men were farmers. Their work was the earth, mud and stone and water, the slow cycle of the year's planting and harvest. They were not born to killing, but some of them had acquired a taste for it.

The doma at Gardengerry was dedicated to Lord Cinder in his aspect as judge and the long winter. At the festival of the Frostnight, the flood of pilgrims traveling north to pay homage to the gray lord brought crowds of ash-robed worshippers through its doors. The door to the temple was polished frairwood bound in silver, a testament to the doma's wealth. The torches that illuminated the passage were fine silver, the tapestries silk and cloth of gold. The twin-horned altar of Cinder and Strife at the building's center was carved from a single block of marble.

The blood that spilled from Allaister's blade soaked into silk robes. The skin the blade parted was soft, unaccustomed to hard work. The frair stood in front of the altar, calling down judgment on them. He clung to his staff, somehow staying upright as Allaister put a sword into him, over and over again. The frair eventually settled to the floor and was quiet.

The celestes put up more of a fight, screaming as Allaister's men cut them down. The stone walls of the doma were thick and quiet. No alarm was raised.

When they were finished, Allaister's men gathered around the altar, their chests heaving. Crimson spotted their robes. Tunnie's eyes were wild and free, a bloody sword gripped in each fist, one that he had brought and one plundered from the ceremonial instruments of the winter god. The others were a little more hesitant, unsure if they were excited or terrified, or simply scared of how much they enjoyed the blood.

They had a lot of potential, this group. Allaister looked around the room, at the slumped body of the frair, the celestes all crumpled in one corner, blood streaked on the granite floor and pooling beside the altar.

A good night.

"Well done, lads. A fine harvest," he said with a smile. He kicked the frair's staff, sending it clattering across the room. "We're almost done."

"Almost?" Joer gasped. "We have to get out of here. There were horns sounded when we were at the wall. It's only a matter of time before they come here. We need to leave."

"We can't go empty-handed, my friend." Allaister swept a hand across the doma. "The priests are dead, but the church can send more. It would just be a matter of days before prayers are said again, and blessings are given. Seems a waste, don't you think? To come this far, and leave so much behind?"

"Not part of the plan," Tunnie said, but his eyes were eager.

Special potential in this one, Allaister thought. "Not part of your plan, maybe," he said aloud, "but I've thought this through. There's good silver in these cabinets, and jewels in plenty." He pointed at an ornate knife that lay upon the altar, its handle ivory and jet. "How many pigs will this buy, do you think?"

"They catch us with these things, it'll be our lives. Our families," Joer said nervously. "They'll grind our bones and salt our fields."

"There's already blood on your hands, friend. Why not gold in your satchel as well?"

A short wave of concern went through the group, but Allaister had them. Even if they ended up dumping most of it in the river, there was wealth enough here to see them in comfort for the rest of their lives, and theft was an easier crime than murder. Allaister sent them into the doma's outer chambers to scrounge what they could. Anything that would burn was brought to the altar.

He kept Tunnie at his side.

"How're we to get this stuff back home?" Tunnie asked as the pile of loot grew. The men were falling to their task with enthusiasm, splintering the wooden rings of the orrery, prizing sconces from the walls while leaving enough to light their way. It was considerably more than they could carry.

"Let them have their fun," Allaister answered. He plucked the frair's staff from the floor, using a silk cloth to wipe the blood from its icon, then leaning it almost reverently against the altar. "Do you know why we came to Gardengerry?"

"To kill priests."

"Yes, but there are priests throughout Tenumbra. Hell, there are priests in Tener itself—we could have crossed the border into Adair's land, or Blakley's, and done our reaving in relative safety."

"Halverdt land is our land. It was taken from us." Tunnie was watching him with a measure of confusion. Allaister shrugged.

"Yes, yes. All true," he agreed, "but really, the whole island was taken from the tribes—Gardengerry was just taken most recently. No, my reasons are older than that. The old city, the one that was here before, was unoccupied when the Suhdrin lords came north. The ruins of a grand temple. Empty."

"It's a cursed place," Tunnie said. "Cursed by the gods."

"No, not exactly. Even the few shamans who remain in the north have forgotten the story of this place."

"What are you getting at, Allaister?" Tunnie asked. The twin swords in his hands hung limply now, the thrill of killing ebbing away.

"There was a henge here—a temple, to a different god. One the pagans saw fit to lock away."

"Here?" Tunnie looked around.

"*Exactly* here. This room." Allaister swept a hand over the doma. "A shrine before it was a temple. Holy before it was sanctified." They were alone, the rest of the men scattered to the outbuildings. The town guard would arrive soon. He had to be fast. "It was a place of sacrifice long before the Celestial prayers haunted the air." With that he swept the ornate knife off the altar and put it into Tunnie's heart. The blade, thin and sharp, punched straight through.

"Gentle, now… gentle." The dying man struck out, but his blows were weak, and Allaister fended them off. He eased him to the stone floor, supporting his neck until Tunnie's eyes were sightless. It was a quick death. *Better than the celestes were allowed.*

"My apologies, friend. This is a complicated time in my life," Allaister whispered. "I have a lot of things I'm trying to figure out."

The holy knife snapped, the blade buried in Tunnie's body. Allaister dropped the handle and took a hatchet from his belt. He used it to split the man's chest open. The ribs cracked one at a time, until the heart and lungs appeared. Whispering an endless stream of prayer and invocation, Allaister drew out the organs, arranging them on the ground.

There was a sound behind him.

"What the fuck are you doing?" Joer gasped. He had just come into the room, a double armful of candlesticks pressed against his chest. These clattered to the stones as he drew his blade. "What the hell is going on?"

"Something holy," Allaister answered. "You should be happy about this."

Joer didn't have an answer. He started to call out… then stopped, horror stealing the voice from his throat.

Allaister rocked back on his heels, squatting over Tunnie's steaming body. He sprinkled a handful of dirt, gathered at another henge, blessed by certain heretics he knew.

Something happened to the air. The shadows that hung beneath the altar, trapped there by the flickering light from sconces, grew heavy. They crawled between stones, leaking as black as ink through the cracks, until they gathered against Tunnie's still form. The shadows stitched together and spread like a web over the dead man. They reached into the cavity of his chest. Allaister took a step back, a smile ghosting over his mouth.

Tunnie stood. His veins pulsed with shadow, and his eyes leaked a greasy fog. He turned to Allaister, dragging the wreckage of lung and heart across the floor, dangling from his chest like afterbirth. One hand still held a blade.

"Hunt," Tunnie's mouth said, but his voice was grinding bones and tearing flesh.

"Hunt," Allaister answered, "but first, this place must be sanctified." He stepped aside, gesturing to Joer. "These men have profaned your holy ground. They must be cleansed."

Tunnie turned to Joer.

"Cleanse," he said in that unholy voice.

"I would run," Allaister said to Joer. "Though there's little point in it."

Joer ran.

Tunnie took a single step toward him, and the shadows that flashed through his veins splashed down into the cracked stone. They sped across the floor like lightning, tangling into the fleeing man's feet. Joer screamed. Tunnie's blade ended that. Then the tendrils of shadow swirling through doorways and crawling up the walls, seeking out the others.

A scream echoed in the distance. Tunnie lumbered toward it, dragging his heart behind him.

Allaister waited by the altar as his servant-god cleansed. And then it was time to hunt.

2

THE ROAD TO Gardengerry was quiet. There was no other traffic but Artur's fruit cart, and no sound but the birdsong from the woods and the creaking of the cart's wheels. Little Marie sat on the bench next to him, humming quietly to herself. The cart was full of apples and not a few peaches.

They were on their way to the Allfire festival, hoping to make a little coin before the summer turned, but Artur had left a little early, and was riding a little fast, because no one in his hamlet had heard anything out of the 'Gerry for more than a week. Artur had a brother in Gardengerry, and he was worried. So he loaded the cart, made some excuses to his wife Catha about getting in before the competition, and set out.

Along with the fruit, he hid the rusty old wood-splitting axe under his seat, wrapped in burlap to keep his wife from seeing it. Didn't want her to worry, which was why he didn't have an excuse for not bringing Marie. The wife had promised their daughter that she could go to the next Allfire, and Artur had no way of breaking that promise.

He kept telling himself that he was being silly about nothing, that Gardengerry had a good, strong doma, that gheists didn't go near holy ground, and certainly not this close to the Allfire. Holy days made for safe roads, the priests always said. Still. He would rather have left the girl at home.

Marie was oblivious. She hopped off the slow-moving cart and plucked a handful of wildflowers from the side of the road with her chubby hands, stuffing some of them behind her ears before she clambered back up onto the cart. The rest she piled into her lap, twisting the stems and tying the tiny flowers together into random shapes, humming all the while. Artur looked down at her and let his nervousness soften.

"What ya got there, lady love?" he asked.

"My favor. I'm going to give it to a knight at the market, and he'll be my lord husband and kill bugs for me." She had a thing about bugs, putting them at about the same threat level as wildfire and bad pudding. "We'll live in a castle, like Uncle Teodre."

Uncle Teodre was Lord Hastings Teodre, Artur's sworn master, though to be honest he was just a minor baron in a minor holding, and his castle was a motte in the mud. Marie treated him like the celestriarch in Heartsbridge. Teodre, for his part, treated his sworn men like family, especially during the holidays. Artur patted her on the head and smiled.

"There'll be no knights at this market, love. Gardengerry has no tournament to bring them in. Just peasants and merchants and maybe a priest or two. Do you know who *will* be there?"

"Uncle Connor?"

"Yes, Uncle Connor, but also the sweets man. Do you remember the candy apple you had last Allfire?"

Marie nodded enthusiastically, the flowers forgotten in her tiny fingers.

"Well, if you're good and quiet, there will be

another. What do you think of that?"

Marie stared at him, her mouth firmly clenched shut, her little cheeks quivering.

"Well, you don't have to be quiet yet, lo—"

"I would like that very much!" Marie yelled in a burst of childish joy. Artur erupted in laughter, leaning over in the seat and shaking, until he realized that the cart was slowly drifting off the road. He corrected the mule and then gave Marie a warm hug with his free arm.

"Well, love, we'll see to that. Now, you've dropped all your flowers on the road. Gardengerry is close, and you wouldn't want to get there without the proper favor to give your lord knight, would you?" He gave her a little shove and she squealed. "Better mend that."

Marie squirmed off the bench and hopped down to the road to look for more. When they had started their trip, it had been a muddy track through the woods, branches hanging down to brush against their faces. This close to town the road was hard-packed dirt and pebbles, with a verge of grass that pushed the forest far from the cart. They were going uphill, near the summit, so the mule strained against even the half-load of fruit.

There were no good flowers here, just a scattering of budding clover that made terrible favors. Marie peered into the forest, then saw a patch of goldengem up near the top of the hill, just on the border of the forest. She ran ahead, ignoring her father's shouts to stay close.

Goldengem was a beautiful flower. One of her mother's favorites. Maybe, if she got enough of it, Marie could make a necklace to give her when they got home. She could tell Mother that it was a gift from a handsome mage that they met at the market, who had given it to Marie in exchange for three kisses, three promises, and three songs. She had started to pull the flowers up by the stem, tearing great patches of golden flowers up out of the ground, when she looked up and saw that they really were quite close to the town.

Her memory of the place was fuzzy, but Marie wondered why so many of the townspeople had pulled the roofs off their houses, or why they had blackened the stones of their walls with ash, like the hearth of Uncle Teodre's magnificent home in the mud. Town folk were silly, she decided.

There was a rustle among the trees to her right. Marie ignored it at first, and when she turned to look, she gasped and dropped the golden petals to the ground. She could hear her father yelling as if he was at a great distance. He was off the cart and fumbling with a bundle of burlap as he ran toward her.

There was a man of shadow and darkness crouched sternly by the edge of the woods. He was barely there at all, a mere shell of dark lines like the veins in a leaf, wrapped into the shape of a man. Marie could see through him to the forest beyond, could see trees and goldengem and the bright sunshine. He pulsed with dark energy and stared attentively down at the town, his hands wrapped around a short staff that was tipped with a cruel blade. A cloak like a spider web shivered on his back, writhing in a gale that Marie couldn't feel.

Finally he glanced down at her. The shadowman looked as startled as the little girl.

"Have faith, child. The lord of winter is with you." His voice was like the echo of tombs, and when he hunched toward her a chill ghosted across Marie's face. The flowers at his feet glittered with frost. Marie took a step backward. "There is a little girl here," the shadow said to no one in particular. "Are you from Gardengerry, my dear? Is this your town?"

Marie stood shivering.

"No, I'm not frightening her," he said. "You're not... little girl, don't be afraid, I'm a priest of your Lord Cinder, husband of Strife, and the light of winter." The shadowman peered carefully at Marie, as if measuring her reaction. "She doesn't seem to understand me... hello?"

Artur came roaring up, the axe half-unwrapped in his fists, his face red and furious. The shadowman spared him a glance, then sketched a shape in the air between them. A wispy blue knot appeared, trailing behind the priest's rapidly moving fingers. When he was done, the shadowman breathed into the knot. It frosted like a window in winter, and the air around him crystallized into dark frost.

Her father stumbled to a halt, his fingers turning blue. It was so cold that Marie was afraid her nose was going to fall off, as her mother often promised it would when she went out in the snow without her hood.

"Know the servant of Cinder, your god and judge, sir," the shadowman snapped, a hint of irritation leaking into the bone-deep echoes of his voice. "Doesn't anyone go to church, anymore? Cinder and Strife, man! Are you citizens of Gardengerry?"

Marie and her father stood shivering in the sudden iciness, the flowers at her feet withering, the cart behind them creaking forward. The shadowman grimaced and turned back to his view of the town.

"Never mind. It's at least as bad as we thought." He became distracted, tracing the air with a ghostly finger, as though he was running it across the ruin of distant Gardengerry. "I'm coming back."

He disappeared without a sound, the warmth and light of summer returning with a violent snap. The strands of the shadowman's form, the dark veins of his shell, writhed and then slithered together before they evaporated. The ground where he stood, glittering with frost, was the only evidence the strange apparition had been there at all. The circle of white shrank rapidly, leaving only the crushed imprints of two boots, the mud beneath them tinged with ice.

Gasping for breath, Artur dropped his axe and gathered Marie up in his arms. He felt her all over for wounds, for patches of cold, for anything out of the ordinary. The child was struck dumb, staring at the withered flowers on the ground. Once he was sure his daughter was as safe as she could be, Artur glanced down at the town.

It was ruined. Huge swathes of the town were blackened by fire, the roofs burned away, the stones dark as coal. Wisps of smoke drifted through its streets. At the center of town the doma stretched stony steeples over the wreckage. Every wooden shutter and stained-glass window had burst open, the glass like brittle teeth in the sunlight. Only the dome appeared intact.

Artur tucked his daughter against his chest and ran back to the cart. They wouldn't get home until near dark, but he didn't want to waste another moment of light. Behind him, Gardengerry sat quietly and waited, smoke twisting in the breeze between fire-blasted walls and the wreckage of ash.

Frair Lucas, inquisitor of Suhdra and holy brother of the celestial church, hung limply against his darkwood staff, the blessed linen straps wrapped loosely around his arms and chest, his elbows resting on the crossbar of silver and darkly polished wood.

Lucas was a weathered man, old but still spry, his limbs strong from seasons on the hunt, though the years were starting to take their toll. His hair was as white as the snowy crown of the winter god, shot through with gray and black. He was handsome and humble, sacred and strong.

He leaned his forehead against the symbol of the moon at the junction of the crossbar, the crescents leaving dimples on his skin. He looked asleep, or in deep prayer. His robes, wine-red and decorated with ancient knotting that indicated his position in the court of the moon, swam with shadows that defied the bright sun of summer. The fingers of his right hand twitched, and his mouth moved.

"I'm coming back," he whispered.

A dozen men were gathered around him. Three stood in a tight circle, facing away from his relaxed form, swords drawn and at guard, eyes on the surrounding trees. They wore the colors of Cinder's sect, black and gray, their closed helms decorated in the symbols of winter. The other men stood nervously to the side, tending their horses or leaning on ashwood spears, all but one dressed in the generic black and gold of the Celestial church.

A woman wearing the gold and crimson armor of a vow knight stood casually in front of the frair, arms folded. Taller than the other guards, thick at shoulder and hips, she wore plate-and-half that had been traced in gold and set with matte red stones the color of dying embers. The tabard tied loosely over her breastplate was inscribed with the holy symbol of the winter sun—a gaunt, black tree, branches twined around a sun in eclipse, with stars instead of leaves and roots twisted and grim. Her sect, the knights of the Winter Vow, was dedicated to bringing the light of Lady Strife into the dark places of the world, to serve as a reminder that even in the darkest days of winter, the dawn still comes. Her face was laced with scars along the cheekbones in the pattern of a lightning strike, and her hair was brown twined with gold, the color of harvest heavy and ready to be gathered.

Her name was Sir Elsa LaFey, hunter of gods and scourge of heretics throughout Tenumbra. Her blood had forged the armor on her back, and her sword was tempered with the souls of darker spirits.

The air around Frair Lucas grew cold, and strands of black naether twisted into existence around his shoulders, vibrating like a spider web with a fly at its center. For a brief moment the frair was the center of a storm of black lightning and ghostly frost, and then all the tendrils slithered into his still form. He jerked upright like a man waking from an unpleasant dream.

"Are you well?" Elsa asked. Lucas was pale, even more than usual, and his fingers trembled on the staff.

"Yes, yes. That was just on the edge of my range. I am heavier in my body than when I was younger."

"Did you frighten the girl?" Elsa asked.

"How would I know? Children scare easily," Lucas said as he began to unwind the linen cloth, reaffixing it to the staff in intricate knots. "I assured her of the faith of the church, and then her father tried to strike me with an axe."

"It's a wonder these people go to church at all. You didn't kill him, did you?"

"Tried to strike me, Elsa. Tried. I put the fear of

Cinder in him, I did." Yet Frair Lucas grimaced at the memory of his encounter, as if he had been forced to eat something sour.

"So what of Gardengerry?"

"There's nothing left. The scryers were right enough. There was a gheist, at least, maybe more than one."

"This close to the Allfire?" Elsa asked.

"Don't let the calendar blind you," Lucas said. He stood and rolled the staff between his palms. "The demon's path leads north. Nearly straight north, in fact."

"We should send a rider to Cinderfell."

"No, not yet." Lucas looked around the road, counting his men and weighing his options. "Greenhall is in much greater danger than the 'Fell, and there are the survivors of Gardengerry to consider."

"There are survivors?" Elsa asked. Lucas shrugged.

"Perhaps," he said. "I don't know." He turned to the column of guards in their Celestial colors. These men were little more than soldiers, armed with blood-wrought steel and a handful of prayers. "Sir Grie, take your men into Gardengerry. Find what survivors you can, secure the doma for sanctification, and then send a rider to Cinderfell requesting support. High Inquisitor Sacombre will want a report."

Lucas had run afoul of the high inquisitor too often for comfort. The frair valued his independence, and if it took sending riders all the way to Cinderfell to keep Sacombre happy, he would do it. No matter how inconvenient it was.

"And what of us?" Elsa asked. "Are we to kick our heels in the forest, hoping this demon comes back?"

"Not at all. Take a spare horse and ride hard for Greenhall. You will need both mounts to make it in time. Warn them of what's coming, and prepare to defend the city in case the gheist strays in that direction. Halverdt will have a few vow knights on hand, but I doubt he'll want to let them out of his walls, especially if there's a gheist on the prowl. It will fall to you to protect the surrounding villages."

"Halverdt's guardians are weak, cowed by the fear of their master. I will enjoy humbling them."

"Try to avoid the politics of the situation, if you can. Kill the rogue god and get out."

"Easily said, delicately done," she answered. "What will you be doing?"

"Hunting the gheist from here. You will be able to travel to Greenhall faster by the roads, but I want to stay on its trail, in case it turns, or can be caught before it reaches the innocent."

"You can't do that alone."

"I can, I have, and I will." Lucas pulled off his robe of office and folded it into his saddlebag. Beneath the vestments he wore simple colors, the drab clothes of an itinerant priest. "Now, go. This is a dangerous spirit. I know of no pagan god given to manifesting in this land, nor in this way. We mustn't delay."

Elsa bowed and turned to Sir Grie and his men. She gave a few simple instructions, reminding the soldiers of their responsibilities and tasks, then mounted her horse, reined the spare mount beside her, and rode back down the road the way they had come. She never once looked back.

"A woman of duty," Lucas said quietly. He secured his staff across his saddle, then mounted painfully and with much complaint. By the time he was settled, the column of soldiers was already riding toward the ruin of Gardengerry.

"Now to hunt," he said with little enthusiasm.

37

He turned his tired courser toward the woods. She nosed delicately between the trees. It was only a few minutes before he came upon the gheist's path. The ground was trampled and torn, charred by the demon's passing. With a sigh, Lucas wrapped himself in bindings of sight and deception, then followed the mad god into the woods.

3

THERE WASN'T MUCH of the log left. The leather overwrap was shredded, and the heart of the wood was badly splintered. Ian adjusted his grip on the broadsword and swung in, hard. The blade buried itself deeply into the wooden frame of the target, and then stuck. He wrestled with it for a few seconds, trying to free the blade, but the steel of the sword wouldn't budge.

"You're too damned earnest, boy," Sir Dugan, master of guard to Blakley's keep, muttered quietly, so the impromptu audience that had gathered around the training yard couldn't hear. "You miss that first stroke and the fight's over."

"Well, I didn't miss the first stroke! I hit the damn stroke, but now the blade is stuck!" Ian paused, jerking hopelessly on the hilt. The log creaked, and the sword settled deeper into the soft, splintery wound of the wood. "Damn it all, Dugan, how is this supposed to help? A man isn't made of broken wood, is he?"

"No, but a *man* would object to you practicing on him. Especially with a blow like that." Sir Dugan looked uncomfortably up at the balustrade, where Ian's mother and sister were waiting. The women were elegantly dressed, in anticipation of the guests who would be arriving soon. "To hell with your honor, boy, get that sword free."

Ian grunted irritably. He wasn't small for his age, but he was no brute, either. His shoulders were starting to hurt with the effort. The elegant scrollwork of his birthday tattoo wrinkled as Ian scrunched his face in concentration. Lifting a boot, he planted it against the log, and then heaved back. His fingers slipped free of the hilt and he began to fall. Horrified, he scrambled for a better hold, but his hands went too far forward and fell against the blade.

Hot pain arced up his arm.

With a gasp, he let go and fell backward.

"Damn it!" he yelled. A titter went up among the audience, and Ian scrambled to his feet. "Damn it all, Dugan, your damn sword bit me."

"A sword is born to bite, my lord," Dugan said smoothly. "Are you hurt?"

"I'm fine," Ian said crossly. He held up his hand to look at it. The chain mitt of his practice glove was bent, several of the rings burst and digging into the flesh of his palm. Nothing serious, but painful. He shook the glove free. One of the rings had broken the skin, and he sucked the blood off his hand. "It's these damned gloves, Dugan. I can't get a proper grip with them."

"Those damned gloves just saved your fingers, my lord. Now..." Sir Dugan took the sword in hand and, with a twist and a shake, drew it from the target. "What is the lesson?"

"To not practice the blade when there are women watching," Ian muttered. Dugan chuckled and shook his head.

"There will be greater stakes than a woman's notice, my lord." Dugan rested the tip of the broadsword in the dust and leaned the hilt toward the young man. Ian took it, his face flushing. "Now, tell me what went wrong?"

"The bloody sword got stuck. I'd imagine that if that happens on the battlefield, it will be more my opponent's problem than mine." Ian rested the sword against his chest and started fiddling with the chain gauntlets. "I think it's the grip I've got wrong. Third finger of the left hand over the first of the right." He left the tip of the sword on the ground as he wrapped his hands around the hilt. "But when I transition to the back stroke, it's the second finger, and I'm not sure what to do with my thumbs. Does this look right to you?" he asked, glancing up.

"I have no idea, my lord. I never think about it."

Without warning Sir Dugan stepped back, smoothly drawing his own sword and presenting a high guard. Ian looked puzzled, but then Dugan's blade was coming at his head. A gasp went up from the audience.

Ian backed away, lifting the broadsword into a high guard. Dugan's weapon skittered off the steel of Ian's blade, then danced around and came at him again. Ian shifted his stance, holding the tip steady but sliding the cross-guard to meet the arc of his instructor's attack.

Steel met steel, and as Ian thrust forward, Dugan skipped back. The older knight came at him with a quick series of overhead blows, and it was all Ian could do to keep his steel in the way. Finally, he saw an opening. He shuffled forward, putting Dugan off his balance, then swung the broadsword over his head, gathering speed and chopping across his body.

Sir Dugan jumped aside. The heavy blow of Ian's sword struck the target log squarely. He twisted it, leaned against the hilt and then drew it free in a long, rattling cut that sliced off the top of the log.

Dugan sheathed his sword and nodded.

"And what did you do with your thumbs, my lord?"

"I'm not sure," Ian said. He was gasping from the effort of the assault, staring at the wide gash in the log. "I would have to think about it."

"I strongly urge you to not do that, my lord. You're a fine swordsman, when you leave your head out of it. You're too serious. You study the blade too much. Leave your mind out of it, and let the blade find its path."

A smattering of applause came from the audience. Ian had forgotten about them, and turned to see his sister and her friends beaming down at him. His mother looked less amused.

"You'll catch hell from my mother for that," Ian whispered to the knight. Dugan shrugged.

"Better that than catching hell from your father for not giving you the training a duke's son deserves," he said. "Better than sending you into battle unprepared, my lord, and watching you cut down by some lordless knight who practiced the blade every day. As a knight should."

"There's more to a lord's duty than the blade, sir," Ian said.

"If you say," Dugan replied. "I would not know, as I am not a lord." He drew his sword again, picked up an oiled cloth, and ran it down the length of the blade. "You aren't either," he added.

"When my father dies, I will be duke of Houndhallow, and lord of the Darkling March," Ian said sharply, forgetting the audience. "Best that I prepare for that day, don't you think?"

"Perhaps. Though for now you are merely the son

of a duke, and the heir to a throne. There are worse things for heirs to prepare for than battle."

Ian was about to respond when a horn sounded from the battlement. Dugan glanced up at the gate.

"Our guests will arrive soon, my lord. Your mother will want you properly dressed."

"There's no time," Ian said. "I will meet the high elector in my sweat and in my blood, as befits a lord of the north."

Dugan chuckled. He drew the gloves from his hands and tucked them into his belt.

"I can train you for battle, my lord, but I cannot advise you on a mother's anger. Time is no excuse. The high elector is a large man. It will take his wagon an hour to make the approach. A lord of Tener should be able to change his shirt in that time."

Ian didn't say anything, but slid the long blade of the broadsword into its sheath and hung it over his shoulder. Then he glanced up. His mother had already disappeared from the balustrade, leaving Ian's sister and her friends alone. Doubtless the duchess of Houndhallow was on her way to the training field, to have words with Sir Dugan.

Best to be gone before that happened.

"I do not love this blade, Sir Dugan. It's too large, and too clumsy. Next time I will practice with the dueling steel, I think."

"That is the Suhdrin style, my lord. You are Tenerran born."

"And what do you mean by that?"

"Just what I said," Sir Dugan answered. He sheathed his sword and grimaced. "That sword is the blade your father carried into battle, and his father before him, going back to Black Kirk of the tribe of hounds. It may not fit your hand, but it fits your blood."

"These are not the days of Black Kirk, sir," Ian countered. "Times have changed."

"As I am constantly reminded, my lord," Dugan said, sounding tired.

"Tomorrow we will practice with the dueling steel," Ian said.

"Yes, my lord," Dugan answered. "Now be on your way. The high elector will be here. Eventually."

"And my mother will be looking for you. Best we both make ourselves scarce."

"I will not run from my battle," Dugan answered, a sharp smile on his face. "Though your mother is a harder foe than the high elector, I'd imagine. Go on. Find your books. Leave the sword in the armory. Tomorrow we'll see if we can make the dueling steel into a real weapon, and not just a nobleman's toy."

Ian snorted and hefted the heavy sword higher on his shoulder, then left the field. When he looked back, Sir Dugan was collecting the pieces of the target dummy and muttering to himself.

Ian was unbinding the locks of his hair from the leather strap that kept it out of his eyes, shaking out the few thin braids that he had earned, when his mother swept out of a corridor and fell on him. Her blond hair, unusual in Tenerran blood, flowed around her head like a torch. She was much angrier than even Ian expected.

"What were you thinking?" she said sharply, and he thought she might strike him. "What in the hells were you thinking?"

"Shouldn't you be yelling at Sir Dugan?" Ian asked. "After all, he's the one who attacked me."

"Attacked you? Attacked? You idiot, you could have killed him. How would that have looked, with your sister watching, and the high elector on our doorstep? And look at your hand!"

"I was trying to get a quick practice in before the high elector arrived," Ian replied, a hint of anger in his voice. "Just because the church is visiting…"

"Hush," Sorcha Blakley answered. "You need to get that temper of yours under control, child. What would your father say to Dugan's family if you had put that damn sword through his gut, rather than into the log? Hmm?"

"Oh, I think Dugan was in little enough danger from me," Ian said. "Besides, that was the point of the exercise, wasn't it?"

"Little enough danger? Gods, what an idiot you can be." Sorcha grabbed the sword belt and twisted it off her son's shoulder, lifting it with ease. "This is not a dummy blade, child."

"I am well aware what sort of blade it is, Mother."

"Are you?" Sorcha clattered the tip of the sheath to the ground and grabbed her son's hand. With a yank she freed his hand from the chain mitt and then drew four inches of blade from the scabbard. Before Ian could react, she laid the meat of his palm against the blade. His flesh parted like fine silk before shears, and blood washed across the steel.

Ian yelped and snatched his hand back.

"What in hells is wrong with you?" he cried out. Sorcha sheathed the sword and then, stepping forward, slapped Ian across the face.

"It's blood, child. Tenerran blood." She grabbed his wrist and held the wound in front of his face. "Become accustomed to blood. There will be more, unless you start taking those lessons seriously. Pray the next time it isn't yours."

"But…"

His mother shook her head. "Enough. Go and dress properly for our guests." Then she swept away, leaving Ian alone in the hallway. She stormed down the corridor toward the training yard, probably to tear an equal chunk out of Sir Dugan. Ian wrapped a loose cloth around his hand.

"Too serious, not serious enough," he muttered. "At least Sir Dugan lets me fight back."

He sighed and pulled the cloth tighter. The high elector's visit had everyone on edge. The Allfire was approaching, the highest holiday of Lady Strife, goddess of sun and summer and war. Tension along the border between Suhdra and Tener—never soft—had grown in intensity. His father's court was filled, day after day, with common folk complaining about abuse from Gabriel Halverdt, the duke of Greenhall, to the south.

He smiled, knowing Halverdt's court was likely choked with complaints of untrustworthy peasants and pagans in the night. On top of that, the summer had brought another drought, and the fields were yellow with dry wheat and ashen soil.

The celestriarch had invited Ian's father to celebrate the Allfire in distant Heartsbridge, holy seat of the Celestial church, and Malcolm Blakley had declined. None of the Tenerran lords had accepted that invitation, but quickly thereafter had come word of the visit from the high elector.

The timing was more than coincidence. Ian was certain of it. The church was always willing to let the Suhdrin nobility run roughshod over the north, but recently the people had begun talk of calling banners and riding south. It was half of why Ian had wanted to practice that morning. He wanted to greet the high elector with blade in hand.

The blood from his hand was running in rivulets down his fingers, spotting the floor in crimson. Again Ian pulled the linen tighter, cursing his mother's will. He would need to visit the apothecary before he dressed.

He hoped the high elector didn't ask the source of his wound.

Malcolm Blakley waited patiently in the courtyard. The massive wains of the high elector's caravan rumbled through the front gate, surrounded by men-at-arms dressed in the colors of the church, joined by a few vow knights. There were a lot of blades inside his castle that had no loyalty to him. Even though they were all gods-sworn men and women of the church, it made him nervous.

His own guard spread out behind him, their armor bright and spears tipped in bloodwrought iron. His wife, Sorcha, stood at his side, and the rest of the family lined up beside her. Ian looked nervous, almost anxious, his fingers plucking at the place on his belt where a sword usually hung. Even Nessie appeared cross. He would have to speak to them later about their manners.

As for Malcolm himself, he wore the armor of his station. Dukes in the north always carried the threat of war, even in a council of peace. He was a heavy man, the muscle of his younger days just beginning to fade away into fat. His braids of coarse black hair were shot through with silver, and the naming day tattoos that ringed his eyes were obscured by wrinkles. The heavy hands that rested on his scabbard were scarred from years on the hunt and the tournament, not to mention the violence of the Reaver War and the unkindness shown him in the court of Halverdt in the days before. He was a gentle man in eye and voice, but his body spoke of war.

The wagons rumbled to a halt and their esteemed passengers got out. The first wagon was full of lesser priests and administrators, their fingers stained with ink and blood. The second wagon disgorged the higher servants of the church, clustered around the bulk of the high elector, his own little court of scryers dousing the air with frairwood incense before he descended. The stinking smoke made Malcolm wince. Did they really trust him so little, that they would sanctify the ground before they risked their precious elector's skin?

The high elector himself was a large man. In another life he would have been a farmer's son, the kind of boy who was good at baling hay and lifting stones, but not much good at the finer things in life. But Marcus Beaunair was born to the Church of Strife, and the path of the bright lady suited him well, a path that led him from initiate to frair to high elector before the first white hair graced his thick skull. His hands, born to do hard and thankless labor, were instead as smooth as silk and ringed with gold and silver. When he saw Malcolm standing stiffly to attention, his face broke into a grin as bright as sunshine.

"Do people still call you Reaverbane, Duke?" he asked with a laugh and a clap of those wide hands. "I think I would encourage it, if I were you. Such a fine name. A fine name!"

"Not often, your holiness," Malcolm answered. "I prefer the titles the gods were good enough to give me."

"Yet it's a title you've earned," Beaunair said loudly, his voice echoing off the high walls of the courtyard.

"A name given to you by the blood of your enemies and the wailing of their widows." He took Malcolm's hand in his own, and slapped the duke heavily on the shoulder. Malcolm winced. "And not just your enemies. Our enemies. The enemies of the church!"

"Yes, your holiness, and we are blessed that you would visit our home. You may find our doma quite humble compared to your seat in Heartsbridge, but I hope you'll do us the honor of the evensong."

"There is no truer doma than a humble one," Beaunair said. "The golden walls of Heartsbridge always seem a bit much to me, don't you think? I know the builders meant it as a tribute to our Lady Strife, but it's foolish to think any damned metal could truly stand beside the beauty of dawn's first light, eh?"

"Perhaps, but doesn't the light of the sun glimmer more beautifully off gold than any other metal?" Malcolm asked. "Isn't that the goldwright's meaning? That we should be as gold, glimmering in the light of our lady's love?"

"Ha!" Beaunair barked, clearly delighted. "A theologian. A poet! Gods know what I was expecting, but you're much more than I could have hoped. You should have been a priest, Duke. You might have made something of yourself."

"Something more than a Tenerran lord, you mean?" Ian muttered to himself, a bit too loudly. Malcolm flushed, but Beaunair smiled more broadly and went to Ian's side.

"This is the one... This one!" He prodded Ian's chest with one thick finger before grabbing the boy by both shoulders and shaking him like a sieve. "I have heard much of you at court, Lord Ian! A hunter to rival the wolf, and a swordsman as swift as the wind and twice as kind. Ah, boy, when I was your age I wouldn't have ventured into these woods for all the peaches in the choir eternal!" Ian fumbled around with the phrasing, finally blushing furiously when he realized what the high elector was implying. "Look at the two of you. Heroes! A family of heroes."

"Thank you, your holiness," Malcolm said, "and we are truly honored by your visit. My men will unload your luggage and show you to your quarters."

"We have little luggage. We are only briefly in Houndhallow."

"Oh? Then where do your travels take you?" Malcolm asked.

"Back to Greenhall, as soon as you are able to leave."

"Leave, your holiness? Do you mean to give me Greenhall's throne as an Allfire gift?"

The high elector laughed, his great chest and belly bouncing under his vestments of gold and red.

"A foul gift that would be, Duke. The getting of which might kill you." His eyes twinkled, but something harder came across his face. For the first time since Beaunair had gotten out of his carriage, the smile on his face seemed false. "We have some business for you, Malcolm Blakley. Something that needs to be done in Duke Halverdt's court."

"Something, your holiness?"

"A task. A peace. A bit of a sacrifice for you, I'm sure," Beaunair said, "but you'll do fine."

He turned to Sorcha and Nessie, and continued with his jokes.

4

THE HIGH ELECTOR moved away, surrounded by his staff and led by Ian's mother. Nessie tagged along, contentedly eating the sugar bun Beaunair had produced from the pockets of his robes. Ian stood nervously beside his father.

"What do you think he means?" Ian asked.

Malcolm's eyes were distant, though looking in the direction of the departing group. He was tapping his teeth together and swaying slowly back and forth.

"Father?"

"Sorry. Yes—what does he mean?" Malcolm's voice was bitter. "He'll let us know soon enough."

"Another tax, do you think? We've already given mightily to the church's coffers, to feed their destitute." Ian sighed heavily. "Gold that should have gone to Tenerran poor, not Suhdrin. Their crops fail and our vaults empty. I swear, if they mean to bring a levy…"

"It's not that," Malcolm said. "Or probably not. They wouldn't send the high elector to grub for gold. You heard him. They mean us to travel with them… somewhere. Perhaps declining the celestriarch's invitation was a mistake." He looked meaningfully at his son. "Be grateful that we have the stores to give. Suhdra has been caught in the grip of this blight for

51

too long. If their people starve, the Circle of Lords won't be content to sit in their castles. They will come north and take whatever they please."

"I did not learn the sword to better my charity," Ian said. "If Suhdra comes north, they will find steel in these forests."

Malcolm snorted, then rubbed his son's loopy hair and gave him a shove.

"You've been listening to too many ballads. Go, find your mother, and see that Nessie doesn't spoil her dinner."

"Where are you going?" Ian asked.

"Council. I need to speak to Sir Dugan before the high elector summons me. He'll have made it to the kitchens by now. That will keep him occupied for a while." Malcolm started to march off briskly, then paused. "Ian, don't let this worry you. This kind of talk comes around every Allfire. Sleep soundly this night, son."

Ian's cheeks burned as he watched his father walk away. He clenched his fists and his jaw, then spat into the dirt.

"Sleep I will, but not in your trust," he muttered. "I can do more than hope for sweet dreams. I *will* do more."

A servant pushed open the door that led out to the council yard, backing into the private space while balancing a tray of selected meats, fruits, and a jug of mulled wine. The men who had been talking cut off abruptly.

"Pardon, my lord," she said, sketching as much of a bow as she dared without endangering her tray. "My lady thought our guests could use some refreshment."

The duke of Houndhallow was seated on a campstool on the trimmed grass of the yard, his hands folded lightly on a wooden table in the center of the open space. There were five other men gathered around the table. Three of them wore the red and gold of Strife's zealous sect, flanked on both sides by the master of hearth and master of guard, Master Tavvish and Sir Dugan. The men of Houndhallow looked grim.

The wall around the yard was solid stone, rising twenty feet up, but the yard was open to the sky. An old superstition, tracing back to the days of the Tenerran tribes. Even in the dead of winter, the Blakleys of Houndhallow did their most important business under the open sky.

"Thank you," the duke said, not disguising his sarcasm as he gestured to the table. "The lady is always considerate in these matters. It wouldn't have occurred to me to provide food until one of us collapsed from hunger."

"Hardly fear of that," High Elector Beaunair said. "Your hospitality has been outstanding. And fresh air! I can hardly get enough of it."

"The air, or the hospitality?" Tavvish whispered into the duke's ear. They watched the high elector tucking an ear of charred corn into his mouth. The man was capable of incredible feats of consumption, as had already been demonstrated during the long walk to the council yard. Malcolm had to wonder how such an appetite didn't lead to a flabbier man. The high elector must have a furnace burning in his belly, he mused.

"Both!" Beaunair agreed, and Tavvish straightened his back. "Both, indeed, but I did not come all this way from Heartsbridge to discuss fatty pork."

"No, your holiness."

"House Blakley has been a friend to the church for a very long time. They were the first to lay aside their pagan ways during the crusades. When the reavers came to our shores, it was House Blakley who led the fight to join the faithful of Tenumbra together to throw them off, and when war has threatened between our two countries, it has been House Blakley who has brought us to the common table of understanding."

"My father felt strongly about his faith," Malcolm said stiffly. "I try to follow his wise footsteps, where I am able."

"Yes. He was the one who sent you to Greenhall, was he not? To treat with the Circle of Lords, gathered there to repel the reavers, should their incursion break free of Tenerran borders." Beaunair leaned forward, hands on his precipitous knees. "It nearly cost you your life."

"Our houses have not always seen eye to eye. I spent some time as Greenhall's unwilling guest, and from there was fortunate enough to lead our combined armies, when it became clear that the reaver threat wasn't merely a Tenerran problem."

"When they sacked Galleydeep and the Burning Coast, you mean. When their steel-prowed warships trawled through the canals of Heartsbridge. When Halverdt and his allies didn't have a bloody choice, you mean?" The high elector cracked another rib of pork, but didn't eat it. He seemed genuinely upset.

"When the Suhdrin Circle of Lords realized the depth of the problem, yes. I was given my freedom," Malcolm agreed, "and the opportunity to prove my worth."

"Yes. Not bitter about that, I trust."

It was Master Tavvish who spoke. "We all made

sacrifices in that war. House Blakley more than most."

"As you say—but look, it made a hero of you! You enjoy the love of all of Tenumbra, those who remember that far back."

"I do not like to think of the death of my father as something to be celebrated. I wasn't prepared to ascend to his throne, any more than I was ready to bury him," Malcolm said tightly. "That war is behind us. If people think well of me, simply because I fought when others ran, then so be it." He stood, taking a glass of wine from the tray and walking around the yard to stretch his aching legs. "People are quick to forget details. It's the grand gestures they remember."

"Which can be good, and can also be bad," Beaunair said. He settled back on his stool, the wood creaking under his bulk. "It is a grand gesture we ask of you now, Duke."

The two priests at his side shifted awkwardly. They hadn't spoken a word since the high elector introduced them as Frair Momet and Frair Freu, and named them as trusted advisors to the celestriarch. They were unremarkable men, men who looked perpetually uncomfortable in their skin and with their station. Their presence at the side of the jovial high elector was as drab as rain clouds gathering around a sunrise. They pushed a little closer to the table, leaning forward to take over the conversation.

"Duke," Frair Momet said, "we understand that things have sometimes been difficult along the border. Relations between your house and that of Halverdt can be fragile, and even those difficulties pale when compared to the troubles between Greenhall and Lord Adair." He was an extraordinarily thin man, his voice delicate and precise, each word formed with all the care of a master craftsman, their sound light in the air. "There is a history of misunderstanding. Mistrust."

"Death," Malcolm said. "Murder. A history of war and crusade and pogrom, often incited by members of your church."

"*Our* church, Houndhallow," Momet said carefully.

"Our church," Malcolm agreed. "But when the crusade came north, the lands that comprise the duke of Greenhall's demesne belonged to Tenerran tribes. They were awarded to the newly established House Halverdt in recognition of Yves Verdt's service (by which I mean his hand in the murder of those tribesmen). So you can see how there would be some lingering feelings of mistrust."

"History that has passed," Freu said. "The wound only weeps because certain members of your blood keep picking at it." Unlike Momet, his voice was like a rushing wind clattering through dry weeds, a tumult that barely contained meaning.

"Or perhaps the wound is infected, and threatens to take the flesh with it," Master Tavvish said stiffly. "Our complaints against Gabriel Halverdt are nothing new. Generations of Tenerran people have suffered under his family."

"Which is why this current trouble is so dangerous," Momet broke in. "There is already a sickness in the land. The fields of Suhdra are consumed with blight. The forests of the south are bare of game, and the waters off the Burning Coast are more treacherous with each season. Tenumbra has fallen ill. We cannot let the patient become... agitated."

"You are reaching for metaphors," Malcolm said. He was tired, and a little drunk. The cranking aches and pains in his legs were making him restless. He walked over to the table and set down his glass. "Say what you mean, as clearly as you are able."

"You are a hero. A man recognized in Suhdra, and loved in Tener." Momet spread his hands in the air. "Heroes can be helpful."

"Gods!" Dugan hissed. "Never go to the church for clear words or peaceful nights."

"What my brothers are trying to say," Beaunair said, reentering the conversation, brushing Momet and Freu aside, "is that the church has need of you. Specifically you, because of your history. You are a man who has opposed Gabriel Halverdt in the past, but you have also made peace with him. The other Tenerran lords respect you. Admire you. I would go so far as to say that they trust you."

"And in Suhdra?" Malcolm asked. "What do they think of me there? Am I their favorite tame barbarian?"

"You have earned their honor. Not all of them feel that way, surely, but enough to make a difference."

"A difference in what?" Malcolm asked. He settled into his chair, suppressing a grimace as his legs and back groaned in protest.

"If things do not improve between the duke of Greenhall and Lord Adair," Momet said, "the church is worried it could lead to a larger conflict."

"Another war," Malcolm said.

"Let's not use such a term," Momet said stiffly. "Not until banners are called. But we are worried."

"This sounds like the business of diplomats and soldiers, high elector. Why is the church getting involved?"

"When Gaspard Bassion, king of Suhdra and last of that title, drew his lances together and started the War of Three Crowns, it was the church that stepped in. When Lord Martiniere broke his pledge to the Circle of Lords and cut the Pilgrim's Road with his tolls, it fell to the church to break his gates and drag the gold from his coffers," Momet said. Warming to his subject, the frail priest gestured grandly to Malcolm's banner. "And when the reavers descended on Heartsbridge, it was the church that commanded Halverdt to release its hostages and band together with Tener to repel the invasion."

Malcolm sat quietly, chewing the dry, flaky bread that the servant had brought. There was more wine on the table, but he had lost his taste for it. When the priest had finished his declaration, Malcolm dusted his fingers over the grass and sat back.

"Gaspard was last of his name because the church broke the throne beneath his back and hung his royal head over the Celestial dome. You ended Suhdrin kingship for time eternal, formed the Circle of Lords, and gave them just enough power to have something to argue about among themselves—enough to keep them biting each other rather than defying the church's power."

"The north has never had a king. What do you care if we destroyed a royal line in the south?" Beaunair asked with a laugh.

"Just this—that the church intervenes when it pleases the church."

"And so it pleases us now," Beaunair answered. "Is that not enough for you, Duke?"

"It would have been, if you had been pleased to intervene earlier. Gabriel Halverdt sits upon his throne like a tyrant. His people die, not from pox or hunger or the gheist's ravaging, but because Greenhall wills it. This is not news. He and I have argued more than once. His peace with Lord Adair is half as safe, and twice as bloody. So something has changed." Malcolm folded his arms and stared a nail through Beaunair's forehead. "Why are you involved now?"

The priests on either side of the high elector glanced at each other and at their leader, looking flighty and nervous. Only Beaunair seemed calm.

"There is movement in the Circle, Malcolm," the high elector said. "Suhdra is stirring."

"Bassion or Marchand or Galleux are always clattering on about something," Malcolm said dismissively. "They are no concern…"

"Not in the chamber," Momet said quietly. "In the corridors beyond. In hallways and bedrooms." He paused, weighing his words carefully. "Among the shadows."

"They are making plans," Beaunair rushed in, "and searching for excuses. Cinder has claimed another crop from Strife's bounty. The farmers in the field are tilling dust and reaping blight. Not even Halverdt has escaped this time around."

"You can't be asking for more donations," Dugan hissed. "Our own harvests have been shallow. It's better the farther north you go, but there the season is so short, the lack of blight matters little."

"Peace," Beaunair said. "This cannot be solved with food. The fever of the land will burn out, but in the meantime, the people are mad, and madness leads to war."

"You are a priest of Strife, my frair," Malcolm said carefully. "Surely war would please you."

"War pleases none of us—not in this case—but if the north lets itself be bullied into a fight, they will pay dearly. Especially along the border. Especially the houses of Adair and Blakley."

"So we line our border with steel, and our banners with Suhdrin blood," Dugan said sharply. "If that is what they seek, they will have it."

"I am not asking you for war," Beaunair said. He plucked an apple from the table, admiring its shine before eating half of it in one bite. His teeth snapped like a trap into the flesh. "I am asking you for peace, and leave the madness to us."

Malcolm nodded slowly. He watched the high elector finish the apple and begin another, drumming his fingers on the table. His masters sat beside him, tense, waiting for the response.

"Peace, then," Malcolm said. "What must I do?"

As soon as the procession ceremonies were over and the high elector's lesser staff was all that remained, Ian left his sister in the care of one of the ladies-in-waiting and went to find his father. The lord of Houndhallow had disappeared into the council yard, along with the high elector and everyone else who was important or interesting in the castle. Ian wanted an ear in that meeting.

Ian followed the cloister wall around the doma, away from the droning voice of Frair Daxter as he guided the lesser priests through the shrine's many icons and dusty artifacts of the faith. The castle servants had descended on the high elector's train of carriages, and was quickly dissecting his luggage and carrying it off into the waiting chambers of the guest tower. For only staying a night, Frair Beaunair carried a lot of clothes. Ian dodged around that procession, afraid of being wrangled into helping, sneaking around the stable yard to reach the keep beyond.

He watched the passing of the guard from gate to garrison. Dugan had left the guard in some lesser sergeant's care, meaning that even he was in council. Surely if Dugan were included, the matter was important enough to include Houndhallow's heir.

The great hall was as busy as a honeyed apple dropped on an anthill. The kitchen servants were swarming through the room, adjusting place settings and straightening tables. The air smelled like smoked sausage and stew, and a cauldron squatted over the fire pit, bubbling deliciously. On the dais above, the family table had been shoved to the side to make room for the visitors and their retinue. The wall behind was hung with the Blakley seal, flanked on one side by the smaller tapestry of his mother's family and on the other by the holy banner of celestial Tener, the cluster of stars beneath a slivered moon, all swallowed by the sun's embrace. It harkened back to the land's icons from before the crusades, subsumed into the symbolism of the twin deities of Cinder and Strife. The hound of Blakley, standing rampant against the field of white and crowned in the holy symbols of the sun and moon, loomed over the hall like an angry god.

"Are they coming?" a startled voice behind him asked. "Is it time? It can't be time, we're not finished! We haven't even *begun* to be finished. We've barely started!"

Ian turned to greet the master of the chamber, Phillipe Castagne, one of the few Suhdrin in his father's service. The man stood nervously beside the stew, his hands clutching an ink-stained parchment and the remnants of a quill.

"Not yet, Phillipe. I have stepped away early, to monitor the situation with my father. The others will be along in due time."

"You skipped out early, you mean," Phillipe said sharply. "First your father packs himself away in the council yard, and then you slip away because you're bored." He made some notes on his parchment, as though he was calculating the degree of insult that had been done, and what he would have to do to balance the account. "The duchess will be in a fine mood, after that."

"She'll be in a fine mood once she sees what a grand job you've done with the feast, Phillipe." Ian snatched an apple from a passing tray and smiled. "And I'm sure the high elector will just be glad to be off the road and at a proper meal."

"You set the standards so high, my lord. How can I fail when the alternative is gruel, cooked beneath a wagon in the pouring rain? Honestly. As for the high elector…"

"As for the high elector," Ian said, biting into the apple. He immediately made a harsh face as the juice, thick and sweet as syrup, dribbled down his chin. "What is wrong with these apples?"

"They have been infused with hartlife and sugar," Phillipe answered without looking up from his ledger. "They were a specialty of my father, handed down to him by his father, and on down the line. Very popular in the court of King Bassion, in his day."

"Well, his day is long past." Ian dropped the apple into the fire, where it hissed and burst, filling the air with the pungent smell of burning sugar. "I hope we're able to find some regular apples, as well, or I may starve to death."

"You should really broaden your tastes, my lord. There is more to being the lord of Houndhallow than hunting elk and eating cheese pie. Your father has done much to edify himself in the ways of his wife's family." Phillipe finished with his calculation, then sniffed at the stew and gave it a stir. "You should do the same."

"Speaking of my father…"

"The duke is not to be disturbed. He is discussing a matter of some importance in the privacy of his council yard." Phillipe looked down his thin nose at Ian. "I believe I already mentioned that."

"Yes, but if it's a matter of the realm, don't you think I should be informed?"

"It doesn't matter one jot what I think. You've all made that perfectly clear in my time in this…" He paused, fixing a smile on his face. "What matters is that your father has not chosen to include you in his council. If you have trouble with that, you should take it up with him."

"I will. Immediately, in fact. In the council yard, you say?"

"Where he has demanded absolute privacy."

Ian grimaced but looked away from the older master. Phillipe was not the sort of man to be persuaded, especially in matters where he had received direct orders from the lord of the estate. Ian would have to wait.

"Priests never bring good news," Ian muttered.

"They bring the light of Strife and the judgment of Cinder," Phillipe said stiffly. "No need for heresy."

"But what could he want? Why would the high elector come all this way, only to depart the next day?"

"It is not my privilege to know such things, Master Ian, as it is not my responsibility. I am charged with the running of the house, which today includes the proper presentation of this feast. To that end,"

Phillipe said, bowing and backing away, "I must be about my business."

Ian leaned against one of the tables, chewing his lip nervously as the servants buzzed around him. He was still standing there, thinking about the sort of trouble the high elector could visit on his house, when his mother cleared her throat. He turned around to discover that the servants were gone, the feast was prepared, and the delegation of lesser priests had arrived. Sorcha Blakley stood just inside the door to the great hall, Nessie, and a half-dozen men and women of the church standing awkwardly behind. His mother fixed her son in her gaze, a look of disappointment on her fine face.

"Dear Mother," he said stiffly, straightening up and fixing his collar. "I have been overseeing preparations for the feast. I am pleased to announce that Phillipe has done his job with exceptional skill, as is his custom."

The duchess of Houndhallow rolled her eyes and marched past her son, taking him by his braids and dragging him to the dais. Nessie was tittering hysterically. When they reached the dais, and without the presence of the lord of the castle, the duchess called for the rest of the attendees to be let in, and for the feast to begin.

5

DARKNESS FELL AND the minstrels played on, but it seemed as if the feast would never end, and still the duke of Houndhallow didn't appear. The lesser priests of Strife, all holy men and women, were working their way up to the feast of the Allfire, a week-long debauch that marked the height of summer and the reign of Lady Strife. Ian stayed as long as he felt was proper, and then a good deal longer when his mother caught him trying to sneak off.

Sometime after Nessie had fallen asleep in her chair and the priests of Strife had sung the evening down, off-key and without half the words, he managed his escape. He went straight to the council yard.

There he found several empty bottles and a guttering lantern, but no council. His father was gone, along with the high elector. The guard at the door said that all but Malcolm and High Elector Beaunair had left hours earlier, and the duke and his guest had stayed and talked and drunk until just half an hour earlier.

"I'm surprised Father didn't come to the feast, then," Ian said. "Mother will be unhappy."

"His lordship seemed in no mood for feasting. The high elector saw to that."

"Trouble?"

The guard shrugged. Ian began the search for his father.

Figuring the lord of Houndhallow would head to his chambers, Ian rushed up the stairs to where his parents slept. The door was shut, and the guard on duty insisted that the lord had not retired for the evening.

Confused, Ian began to wander the castle. He couldn't very well return to the feast after having successfully slipped away, and his father probably wasn't there anyway. It worried Ian that his father had spent so much time alone with the high elector, and had come away burdened. What could the church want to discuss with the lord of Houndhallow that couldn't bear the company of Sir Dugan and Master Tavvish? And why hadn't either of them come to the feast?

This was all very peculiar.

Wandering both in mind and in body, Ian found himself on a curtain wall, overlooking the great hall and the yard before it. The wagons that had brought the high elector to Houndhallow were tucked beside the stables, taking up more than their fair share of the training grounds, and some of the kennel runs. The yard itself was trampled, and by the looks of the stables, there were more horses in the castle than Houndhallow had seen in years. He leaned against the wall, resting in the noise and business of the castle yard, watching the servants scamper around while the family and their guests ate their meal. He found comfort in knowing that the castle continued working, even when the Blakleys were occupied elsewhere.

Then he noticed the shadow looming on the castle wall not far away, leaning against the crenels, a bottle in his hand. His father, duke of Houndhallow and lord of the Darkling March, looked like the town drunk as he rested his elbows against the stone wall and swilled wine. He was facing away from the castle.

"The council is over? I thought you would be in your rooms," Ian said as he approached his father.

"I knew you'd come looking for me, eventually. You or your mother… and I needed some space," he said, quietly. His breath stank of wine. Ian wondered how much his father had consumed while the council was still going on.

"Should I leave you here in peace, then?" Ian asked.

"Too late for that." Malcolm looked his son over blearily. "You've cut your hand?"

Ian ducked the bandage behind his back. "It's nothing."

Ian leaned on the wall next to his father and looked out. Hallowton rested below them, across the river that served the castle as a moat. Beyond, the forest stretched for a great distance, farther than either of them could see even in the daytime. Malcolm offered his son the bottle. A harsh wine, black on the tongue and bitter, it was a welcome change from dinner.

"What business did the high elector have?" Ian asked. "Is he really only staying for the night?"

"Aye."

"Does he travel north?" Ian asked.

"He travels to Greenhall. He means to celebrate the Allfire with Gabriel Halverdt." Malcolm took the bottle back from his son and drank from it, grimacing as the wine hit his throat. "He means us to go with him."

"Go with him? But the Allfire is less than a week away. We'll be hard pressed to make it in time."

"Which is why we leave in the morning. Early," Malcolm said. "You should find your way to bed."

"But why?"

"Because bed is where we sleep, Ian. Unless you mean to pass out here on the wall." Another drink, then a smirk. "Which is sounding pretty good right now."

"You know what I mean. Why are we going to Greenhall? Preparations have already begun for our own celebration. Mother will be furious to miss the feast Phillipe has prepared, and Nessie…"

"They aren't coming with us. It is you, and me, and a small contingent of knights. We mustn't threaten Greenhall with our numbers."

"He would be threatened by our ladyfolk?" Ian asked with a grin.

Malcolm looked sideways at his son. "We mustn't give him a way to threaten us, either. Mother will be safer here. Any woman who travels with us will need to carry a sword, and not a gentle one, at that. We'll bring Sir Doone. She can enter the lists."

"If it's so dangerous then why are we going?"

"We go because the church asks us to go. That's all you need to know."

"Surely there's more…"

"That's all you need to know," Malcolm repeated, almost angrily. "Now give your father some peace. Night has fallen. I have my prayers to say."

Ian shook his head and grimaced.

"How do you expect me to learn anything if you won't let me inside these sorts of meetings? If I'm to be the next lord of Houndhallow…"

"If you're to be the next lord, then I'm to die first, and you'll forgive me if I'm not anxious to play that out," Malcolm said sharply. "Besides, you're still a boy. What counsel do you expect to give?"

"I'm a man of sixteen, grown enough to take the vow if I chose, and yet…"

"A boy of sixteen, and grown enough to know he knows nothing." Malcolm finished the bottle and tossed it out into the river. It disappeared from sight long before it reached the raging waters below. "Honestly, son, you have enough to worry about without adding these things to your table."

"What? What have I to worry about? I spend my days practicing the sword, riding the lists, and dancing. It's ridiculous, and while it might be enough for a child of the south, groomed to walk the courts of Heartsbridge, I'm not interested in that life. I want to be a lord of the north, Father, like a man of the old tribes. A leader! And I can't begin to be that if you don't let me learn to be a lord."

"You can learn the way I learned, boy. The same way you learned to fall off a log—by falling off a log." Malcolm rubbed his face. "It's just, you understand, that I was as anxious as you, when I was your age. Anxious to be about my business."

"Then why do you keep pushing me back?"

"Because my father never did," Malcolm said sternly. "Because he took me to every council meeting, sought my advice on matters of state, taught me how to dance with a lady and greet the ministers and address the Celestial throne. And then, when he died and I was the one truly in command, it was all..." He stared down at his hands. "It wasn't enough. It was worthless. They never teach you what you need to know."

"Then teach me that," Ian said, after a moment of silence. He didn't like seeing his father like this. "Whatever it is, whatever grandfather didn't teach you. Teach me that. That's what I want to learn."

Malcolm laughed, a low, rolling chuckle that

seemed to be rooted in the stone of the castle. He clapped his son on the shoulder and smiled.

"That cannot be taught," Malcolm said. "You can't be prepared for what this throne requires of a man—not until you're on the seat. Not until it's your word that ends a life, or saves it. Not until it's your decision that can lead to war—" His voice caught, and Malcolm looked out over the forest, his eyes glassy under Cinder's harsh light. "Nothing can prepare you for this life."

The two stood there awkwardly. Below them the castle's inhabitants continued on their frantic pace, ignoring the duke and his heir.

"So what am I to do?" Ian asked.

Malcolm didn't answer.

"Live," he said after a time. "Live and be a child. The weight of a man will be on you soon enough. Perhaps sooner than you hope. Perhaps sooner than we *all* hope."

"I mean tonight," Ian said.

"Ah. Go to bed. Sleep. Morning is not far off."

Malcolm gave his son an affectionate cuff across the face, then pushed past him and shuffled down the battlement to the main tower. Ian watched him go, wondering what in the names of both gods might be on his father's mind, what news the high elector brought, and why Beaunair was insisting they travel south for the Allfire. Especially to that bastard Halverdt's court.

He looked out over the forest, staring south to distant Greenhall, and wondered what was waiting for them in the night.

Morning came, and with it the cost of that bottle of wine, harsh in Malcolm's skull. He woke before it was light and slipped from his bedchamber, shutting the door on his wife's gentle breathing. Sorcha would never forgive him if he failed to say a proper goodbye, but he would rather not trouble her with his discomfort.

He dressed in darkness, then snuck down to the doma. There he prayed twice, once to each of the gods in the doma, and once more, before dawn came, hidden in the hallowed shrine from which the castle took its name.

The dome of the shrine was low and arched, the rough stone barely taller than a man at its highest point. The air was dank and still. A low wall ringed the icon at the center of the shrine, and a runnel in the solid stone of the floor led to the icon, a memory of the time when a natural stream ran through to wash the blood away. As with all holy things of the old days, this shrine had once been open to the sky. Generations past the Blakleys bricked it over as the first sign of their devotion to the new religion. Since then the castle called Houndhallow had been built above the dome, to be the seat of House Blakley's modest realm.

In the center stood the shrine itself, an uncut block of dark stone, and perched on that was the head of an enormous hound, forged from blackest iron. The jaws of the hound gaped open, larger than a man's chest, and the eyes were black pits. Oil lanterns sat in the hollows of the eyes and flickered, while thick, inky smoke smothered the air. The jaws were stained in ancient blood, stains that continued down the rock and onto the floor. The first Blakleys had been vicious men, brutal in their zeal for the dark spirit that the iron hound represented.

The head was surrounded by a dry moat that had in the past served as both a fountain and a fire pit.

The stone wall of that moat served as a kneeler, worn smooth by generations of supplicants, all of them praying to different gods for different reasons.

And there, his head in his hands, knees bent before the symbol of his family, Malcolm Blakley, duke of Houndhallow, prayed.

"I expected you to still be in bed," Sorcha Blakley said from the door. She was dressed in a simple robe, her long brown hair laced in gold and amber, bound in a thick braid that reached to her waist. The hound's flickering eyes struck sharp shadows across her tired face.

Malcolm relaxed into his pose of supplication, the sound of his wife's voice draining tension from his shoulders. Still, he didn't stand.

"I have too much on my mind for sleep," he said.

"A tired mind makes mistakes," she murmured.

He sighed and then, creaking, turned and sat on the kneeler. He laced his fingers together. He looked like a hunter taking a breath in the woods, resting before he moved on. Nothing like one of the greatest heroes of the Reaver War, duke of Houndhallow, faithful son of the Celestial church.

"I have little enough choice in the matter," he said. "I can't make sleep come, no matter what I try."

Sorcha sat beside her husband and put a gentle hand on his shoulder.

"You must try to rest, my love," she said. "This trip will ask much of you. Your body is not what it once was, able to sleep in the saddle and fight in the morning."

"Oh, gods, woman. I know my limits. My knees won't let me forget the price they've paid in my service." He stretched out his legs, rubbing life into them. "It's my heart that seems to have found its limit."

"Nonsense. I know of no deeper heart," Sorcha whispered.

Malcolm sat quietly, staring at the sooty wall, rubbing his hands together. Eventually, he turned to his wife.

"I do not like the taste of this task," he said simply.

"No?" she said. "You go to Greenhall, to celebrate the Allfire. What is distasteful about that?"

"You know as well as I. Greenhall has never been friendly ground. It's no kinder during the Allfire." Malcolm sighed and rubbed his face. "To Tenerrans, at least."

"Surely you won't be alone. Many Tenerran knights make the journey to Greenhall. I believe a MaeHart won the lists last year."

"The Tenerrans who go are only spoiling for a fight. More blood is drawn in the streets than on the melee ground. Three years ago a brawl broke out during the evensong. The frair's nose got broken."

"And Gabriel Halverdt got a new frair out of it. So everyone is happy," Sorcha persisted.

Malcolm laughed and shook his head. "Always the bright side with you," he said. Sorcha shrugged but didn't answer. After a few breaths, Malcolm's countenance fell. "He knows what he's doing. Halverdt breeds that kind of conflict. The Circle of Lords will only protect him as long as they believe the north is on the verge of rebellion. He baits us. He baits me."

"He does no such thing. You have to get that out of your head, that he does the things he does just to provoke you." She took her hand away from his knee. "Gabriel Halverdt is not so unlike you, Malcolm. He is a lord of his land, plagued by problems that an average man could never hope to understand, and an average wife can only help him bear. His problems are not your problems, granted, but don't try to make his solutions your worry."

"I sometimes think you practice these speeches," Malcolm said quietly, "so smoothly do you employ them."

Sorcha smiled weakly. "The duke of Greenhall is often on your mind, husband. The things I say to you, I have said before. Sometimes I wonder if you're really listening."

"I listen," he said. "I hear. I consider, and sometimes you're right. Sometimes, however, the trouble is deeper than your advice can provide for."

"I don't know what else to say, love."

"Exactly. And so I can't sleep. Because there's nothing else to be said."

The two of them sat there quietly for a while as the oily smoke from the hound drifted around them. Finally, Malcolm stirred.

"If I do not return from Greenhall..." he started. Sorcha swatted his hand.

"Don't talk like that. Don't even think those thoughts. You go under the banner of the church, to bring peace to a troublesome lord. The high elector needs you—he will see you safely there and safely back." She rubbed his temple lightly, brushing a smudge of soot away. "You needn't give your wife further worry."

"If I don't return," Malcolm bulled on, "it will fall to you to defend the hallow. Nessie isn't old enough, and Master Tavvish won't know what to do."

"And Ian? You won't trust the lordship to him?"

Malcolm paused nervously. "He's coming with me," he said.

"With you?" she said, suppressing a gasp. "Why ever would he need—"

"Because he's a boy no longer, yet still too much a child. Because he needs to see that sometimes a war can end with the stroke of a pen, rather than the glorious charge and the letting of blood." Malcolm turned slightly away from her, gritting his jaw. "Because he dreams too much of honor, and not enough of the lives that his honor would cost."

Sorcha sighed but didn't argue any further. There was no point in it. She stood and gathered her robe around her shoulders, shivering.

"I never liked this room," she said, "and that thing. I can't believe the church lets you keep it."

"Tradition," he said. "The church doesn't mind a little tradition. It was the price we demanded for our allegiance to the first celestriarch. The trappings of the old way, and the faith of the new."

"It seems to me more like heresy," Sorcha answered. "Then again, I'm not a priest."

"Thank the gods for that," he said, then reached over and pulled her into his lap. Sorcha had the decency to shriek, but she rolled herself into Malcolm's arms, resting her head on his shoulder. "Thanks again," he said.

"For?"

"Making an honest hero of me. I could have become an insufferable bore after the war. Too full of myself. Of my glory."

"Who's to say you haven't?" she asked with a smile. He squeezed her, and they stayed there for a while, silent in the presence of the old god, listening to the torches sputter and watching their shadows dance across the walls.

It wasn't long before a servant came to fetch the lord and prepare him for his journey. Malcolm slid his wife to the bench beside him and, without looking back, left her there.

He was off to end a war before it started.

6

"THIS TOURNAMENT IS a waste of time," Ian grumbled. He rode beside his father at the head of their column with the banner of House Blakley shifting lazily over their heads and a dozen good knights and their attendants following. Sir Doone and Sir Dugan rode to either side, hands loose on the reins, their backs as straight as pikes. To them, Greenhall was enemy territory.

"You have no interest in glory?" Malcolm asked.

"I can find glory enough without riding all the way to Greenhall. There are tournaments in Dunneswerry, the Fen..." Ian leaned closer. "There's no reason for us to get Suhdrin dust on our boots. I don't know if you noticed, Father, but they were making preparations for the Allfire at Houndhallow as we were leaving. We could have stayed home, maybe ridden the tilt against Master Tavvish."

"Tavvish would not have ridden an honest tilt against you, boy," Malcolm said dismissively. "A lord's knights would never embarrass the heir on his own field. It doesn't matter, though. You will not be riding the lists. That hand of yours is excuse enough. There will be no dishonor in sitting out the tourney."

Ian flexed the injured hand. "It has nearly healed. I am

certainly well enough to ride against Suhdrin knights."

"Do not underestimate the southern blade, son," Malcolm said. "Nor my will. There will be no tournament for you."

"Then why am I here?" Ian asked.

"To watch a war end before it starts, in ink, rather than in blood."

Behind them, Sir Dugan gave a short laugh. He nudged his way forward to ride beside Malcolm. Houndhallow's master of guard was cut from the old cloth, with hair in thin braids and ink around his eyes. He sat slouched in his saddle, more huntsman than knight. Ian always thought his father kept Sir Dugan around to remind him of the house's heritage, of the tribe they used to be and the history they shared. The rest of the court treated Dugan like a feral child, curious and dangerous in equal parts.

"Be glad, young Ian. At Greenhall you'll find more than a challenge," Dugan said. "Be happy if one of Halverdt's tame monsters doesn't try to run you through in your sleep."

"That's not helpful, Sir Dugan," Malcolm muttered. "Try to keep that sort of talk to a whisper while we're the duke's guests, and please don't run anyone through yourself."

"If my honor..." Dugan began.

"Honor? You're starting to sound like a true knight," Ian said with a smile. "Will you be in the joust, finally?"

Sir Dugan grumped and sank deeper into his saddle.

"No matter," Malcolm interjected. "The point, Ian, is that we are here to improve relations with Greenhall. The Reaver War brought Tenerrans and Suhdrin closer together, and the high elector has asked us to remind Halverdt of that heritage. Let's not ruin all that with misplaced honor or an impatient blade."

"And keep your prick buttoned," Sir Doone added from over Ian's shoulder. For a woman and a knight, Sir Doone had many opinions about the buttoning and unbuttoning of pricks. A ripple of laughter went through the column behind her.

"Well, yes," Malcolm agreed, and his voice caught. "Yes, that as well."

Ian had no answer for that, nothing beside a blush and muttered assurances. They rode in awkward silence for a few miles, passing by the icons that kept the godsroad safe from the gheists, the graven images of Lord Cinder and Lady Strife watching them with stony eyes. When they passed the high henge that marked the border between Tener and Suhdra, Blakley and Halverdt, Sir Dugan leaned over and spat eloquently.

"Keep it to yourself, sir," Malcolm rumbled.

"We should have brought the dogs," Dugan answered.

Malcolm gestured to the banner over their heads.

"We brought the hound," Malcolm said. "Let's do it justice."

Greenhall lay before them, in all of summer's glory. A young castle, it had been built in the Suhdrin style after the last crusade. It was both a promise and a threat. A promise that this was as far north as the Suhdrin lords would try to reach, now that the holy site of Cinderfell was under the protection of the Celestial church, and a threat that any attempt to reclaim this march would be met with all the violence the south could muster.

The shining stones of the castle walls were hung

with banners of green and gold, the colors of House Halverdt fluttering over the fields of the tournament grounds. Beneath the keeps but still embraced by the curtain wall, the city breathed and rippled like an old oak, raising its arms to summer's light.

"That's a hell of a sight," Ian whispered. The column behind him was tired, the end of it stretching out of sight, but the sight of the city put some fire in their blood. The same breeze that moved the hundreds of Halverdt banners reached across the plain to lift the hound. Pride swelled through Ian's heart. He looked behind him. The whole rumbling caravan, from the men-at-arms to the several dozen knights, twisted back up the road as far as Ian cared to look. They had brought an army to Greenhall, even if half their number were cooks and servants.

"No prettier time in the old march," Dugan said. His family had once come from the hunting grounds around Greenhall, before the Suhdrin legions had pushed them north, and his tribe had joined with Blakley. He often spoke as though he had been born there himself, even though the loss was generations past. "If you must be in such a place, now is the season for it."

Malcolm snorted and spurred his horse to a trot.

The word passed down the caravan that the city was in sight, and a collective murmur washed through them as wagons stopped and windows opened to catch that first glimpse of Greenhall's famous doma. The Celestial faith had already spread throughout Tener, but that dome had been the first built by a Suhdrin lord on land taken from the pagans, and Halverdt had built it to impress, its snowy white bulk rising above the jagged skyline of the city, its towers hung in pennants of summer. Several men slid from their mounts to say a prayer.

"It's not that bad," Malcolm allowed, "once you get used to the politics and the smell."

"Both of which are closely related," Dugan muttered.

Ian ignored them. His visits to the seat of Halverdt's power had been rare. Though a steady peace had ruled the border for longer than any of them had been alive, it wasn't until the Reaver War that relations improved between Tener and Suhdra. Certain relations, at least. Generations of crusade and atrocity left deep wounds and bitter memories. Because of that, most of Ian's memories of the city were gilded in the fog of youth. To him, it was a place of stuffy rooms and stern conversations, full of quiet gardens and avenues lined with rank after rank of nervous guards.

His father had brought him south for some negotiations, something to do with farming rights along the border, and the visit had stuck in Ian's mind. The Suhdrin builders made their castles as beautiful as they were functional, something that was rare in the north. Ian felt that the bleak walls of Houndhallow seemed dull in comparison, an opinion he tried to hide. Yet on the wide approach to the city, on these fields that had seen so many battles, it was difficult for Ian to hide his awe.

"Enough gawping, the pair of you," the duke called over his shoulder. "We've a pavilion to establish and lists to enter, and we should present ourselves to our host. Let him know we're not here to reave."

"*You're* not here to reave," Dugan grumbled. Malcolm ignored him.

"Why do we have to stay in a pavilion, Father?" Ian said when he had caught up with the elder

Blakley. "Surely the duke will provide us with rooms in the castle?"

Malcolm didn't answer for a minute. He went a little faster, until there was some space between them and the rest of the train. When he spoke, he looked straight ahead.

"Sir Dugan is not all wrong in his warning," Malcolm said. "I would feel safer in my own tent than surrounded by Halverdt stone."

"And the duke won't take offense?"

"He may. He well may."

The first sounds of the city reached them. It was a great tumult of horses and livestock and wagons and the unending sound of voices in the streets, arguing and yelling. Above that, weaving in and out of the clatter and chaos of the city, came the sky hymn. It rolled out from the cloud-white dome that dominated the skyline at the top of the terraced streets, its arches and smooth white towers looming over the lesser mass of the citadel.

The hymn came and went as the winds shifted and the chorus drifted, but Ian was sure he could pick out the chords of summer mixed with autumn's melancholy, and on the edges of the harmony was the dirge of winter, the first trace notes of the coming court just starting to weave themselves into the hymn.

"Gabriel Halverdt is a painfully holy man," Malcolm said, marking his son's attention. "He employs the finest choir outside of Heartsbridge. Perhaps finer."

"I had forgotten about the hymn," Ian said.

"Hard thing to forget, boy, but you'll stop hearing it after a while."

"No," Ian said. The hymn was weaving its way

into his mind, even as they moved toward the gates. "I don't think I will." The city gate loomed just ahead of them, but Malcolm directed the column away from it, to the tourney grounds, which lay outside the walls to the west. The knights who had come with them, and many of the men-at-arms, unraveled themselves from the caravan.

Ian could see a canvas town, several villages' worth of tents huddled in the shadow of the city walls. The sounds coming from that direction were louder, happier, somehow more joyous than anything coming from the city proper. The perimeter of the tourney grounds was guarded by a rope fence, hung with the icons of the summer court and blessed by clerics of Lady Strife. A number of priests of Cinder were circling the fence, checking it for doctrine and scrutinizing the icons their brothers of summer had chosen to use. Ian marked this, and leaned over to his father, pointing.

"Do they truly need to ward against gheists this close to the Allfire?" he asked.

"Need? No, there is no need. But the duke of Greenhall is... cautious, when it comes to gheists."

"He's scared shitless of shadows," Dugan said. "He keeps a cadre of torchbearers in his room to ward off the pagan night."

"Not exactly true," Malcolm said, allowing himself a grin, "but he does spook easily. Of all the things you might fear in Greenhall, we can be sure there will be no gheists under the bed."

"There will be danger enough, without your pagan gods," Beaunair called out. Ian and his father twisted to see the high elector riding slowly toward them, his shining face leaning out of the lead wagon. The priest's column of wagons had fallen behind as soon as they left Houndhallow, creating an intentional gap. Beaunair and Blakley had agreed that they shouldn't arrive at Greenhall hand in hand. Even their arriving on the same morning would put Halverdt on edge. The high elector waved happily to the city, the pavilion, the sky itself. "But there will be joy as well. Find the pleasure of the bright lady on the Allfire, Duke. Your task here is to join the church together."

"My task here is to prevent a war," Malcolm muttered. "I'll take my joy in that."

Beaunair laughed but rumbled past. At the sight of the high elector's banners, horns sounded along the castle walls, and a general sound of welcome and joy raised up from the city.

Malcolm snorted. "I don't imagine they'll be giving us the same greeting," he said. "Come. Let's find some peace and quiet. I've had enough of priests for the day."

Malcolm led the column to a patch of grass at the periphery of the tournament grounds. The lesser melees had already started, and the sound of pitched battle hung over the grounds as Ian and his men started to unpack. There was empty grass around them, with pavilion sites still to be filled. The Allfire was imminent, however. By the time the first lance was broken, this entire field would be full of pavilions from many of the southern houses and lesser tents for their vassals and various petty lords. There would be few Tenerran banners, despite Greenhall's proximity to the border, and the other Tenerran pavilions would house a rougher sort of knight than the Blakleys brought to the joust.

Once the tents were up and the pavilion festooned in the harsh black and white heraldry of House Blakley, the knights split up to find their rest. Most headed to one of the dozen makeshift taverns that ringed the tournament grounds, or into the city to try their luck with the Suhdrin women. Sir Dugan and Sir Doone wandered away to watch the early melees—these were fought entirely between unlanded lancers hoping to catch the eye of some noble house in need of a squire, or a mercenary company searching for recruits.

Ian and his father were left alone in the breezy expanse of the pavilion. Malcolm undid the straps on his armor and let it fall onto the ground before unfolding a camp chair. He eased himself into the chair, hissing and wincing as his bulk settled into the fabric. Ian stood awkwardly by the door.

"Father, listen…"

"No conversation that we have goes well when it begins like that." Malcolm rested his face in his hand and sighed. "There must be a bottle around here somewhere."

"A bit early, don't you think?"

"We are at the end of half a day in the saddle, son, and nearly a week on the road. No time is too early."

Ian cast through his father's baggage, finally producing a bottle of whiskey and two tin cups. The drink tasted like burning moss in the back of his throat. They sat quietly, wincing into their cups.

"Father," Ian began again. "I need your permission to ride in the joust."

"No, you don't," Malcolm said.

"Maybe," Ian admitted. "But I want it."

"The joust will take any man's mark, as long as he has his own horse and the heraldry to fly." Malcolm tossed another finger of whiskey into his cup but then held it between his hands, rolling the cheap tin back and forth between his palms. "You have a horse. You have a name, and the honor to go along with it, and I'm fairly sure Frair Daxter taught you how to make your mark."

"If I enter the lists, you will bless that entry? You will toast my victories and honor my defeats?"

"No, lad. I forbid you to enter the joust." He drank a little, grimaced, and finished the cup. "But I am lord of Houndhallow, and we are in Greenhall. My word is not law."

"I won't defy you," Ian said sharply.

"Good for you. Wait for next year."

"How old were you when you first rode in the lists?" Ian asked.

"Two years younger than you, and at my father's insistence. I was nearly maimed and lost my favorite horse when Ewan Thaen dipped his lance and tore a hole through her ribs." Malcolm shook his head. "I shouldn't have been up there."

"So I am two years older than you were, and twice as prepared. I ride the joust at home all the time. Sir Dugan says I'm as fine a lance as any in your service."

"Sir Dugan flatters his master's son, though he's not far wrong. As I have already said, we are not at Houndhallow." Malcolm leaned back in his chair, old joints creaking, back aching. "This is Greenhall, and I will not have my son ride his first joust under Halverdt's baneful eye."

"Then why am I here?" Ian snapped. "Why did you bring me along on this fool's mission?"

"This fool's mission was brought to us by the church, and blessed by Strife. If we fail in this, your first lance may splinter in a heavy charge, rather than in the lists." Malcolm sighed. "Though that may be no less deadly."

"You think it's dangerous?"

"What I know is that farmers along the Tallow are robbed more often than the countryside has thieves. That Sir Calmorte and Sir Hamon beat a Tenerran boy near to death when he dared strike them at the Frostnight duels, and that the boy's father took it upon himself to burn Calmorte's tent to embers by morning." Malcolm rubbed his face and tossed the empty cup clattering to the ground. "I know that every time Tenerran knights gather to bless the gods and turn the seasons at Halverdt's court, they're half as likely to end the week in a drunken brawl."

"I'm not afraid of a fight," Ian said.

"Neither am I, but fights become wars sometimes, and I'd rather not be the start of one." Malcolm raised himself slowly to his feet. "Enter the archery contest. Wrestle with your friends. Flirt. But there will be no joust for you."

"Flirting with Gabriel Halverdt's daughter would do just as much to start a war, don't you think?"

"Well…" Malcolm shrugged. "That might be worth it. Now go. I need to rest for a moment before I speak to Gabriel Halverdt."

"If I can't join the joust, then I don't understand why I came at all. What's the point?" Ian asked. He rushed out of the tent, the flaps billowing behind him.

Malcolm sighed and sat back down. The heat of his son's anger filtered through the room.

"Because a son stands by his father's side," Malcolm said quietly. "And if it does come to a fight, I would rather have your sword beside me than any other."

Ian spent the rest of that afternoon cleaning the armor he was convinced he would never get to use. All that hard work, close on the heels of his long journey, left him sapped and sour by the time the evensong mingled with the choir's constant hymn.

Most of the host returned to the camp just long enough to change out of the clothes in which they had traveled, before heading once again into the city. Malcolm never reappeared from his visit to the castle, so Ian was left in an empty tent as dusk passed into night. Restless despite his fatigue, and too hungry to take the time to wrestle a meal from their supplies, he buckled a blade to his belt and went into the torch-lit lanes of the tournament city.

The air smelled of incense, ale and sizzling meat. The lanes, marked by rope lines and already muddy from traffic, were filled with crowds that flowed between the tents. They were vibrantly dressed in the colors of summer, they were happy and loud, though most of them smelled like they had been living in the forest for the last month. There was an air of desperate joy to the festivities. The Allfire was Lady Strife's highest day, the longest sun before the slow descent toward winter's harrowing. Most of the celebrants were determined to squeeze every last drop of joy from the season.

Ian paused at a food cart and purchased a hot pie of steaming meat and onions, then found his way to the melee grounds. The last skirmish of the day was winding up, the shadowy figures at the center of the field struggling in the flickering light of the dozen torches. Fatigue made them move with dream-like slowness, battering at shields and helms with blunted swords, the armored men and women staggering back to fall gracelessly to the ground. It looked to be a hard fight, mud and shadow combining to give the combatants an otherworldly appearance, like soldiers made of earth and arcane power.

Ian was just finishing with his pie when another figure, a man who had been walking around the outside of the melee, noticed him and walked over. In the shadow and his armor, it was some time before Ian recognized Martin Road. Mud obscured the copper tint of his plate, and the tightly tied tabard around his chest was a spattered ruin, but his smile and the brightness of his eyes were unchanged.

Martin was an effortlessly handsome youth. He was dark of hair and complexion, which was unusual among the Suhdrin houses. Martin's family held the hard lands to the southeast, along the rocky coast of the Defiant Sea. He and Ian had known each other since they were children, their fathers having fought together at the battle of the Henge, though they only rarely met in person these past few years.

"As I pray and sing," Martin said brightly. "Ian bloody Blakley! I heard the banner of the hound had gone up beside a particularly grim and dreary sort of tent, but I wasn't sure you'd make the trip. Good to see you, brother!"

"And you," Ian answered, clasping arms with Martin and then wiping his hand clean on his robe. "Have they already beaten you out of the fight?"

"Not at all. I've passed my round and have until the morning to drink and woo and make merry. These poor blighters are in the elimination round."

"Why in hells do you enter this thing, anyway? The proper tourney hasn't even started yet. Is there a single nobleman out there?"

"Besides me, you mean? No, I don't think so. It's mostly masterless lances and squires hoping to catch an eye. Maybe some of gentler blood, entered under a false name, but who can tell in all that mud?" Martin rubbed the muck from his chest and shook it from his fingers. "It's not a noble fight."

"Then why are you out there?"

"Because, my dear friend, this is what war looks like. These men are desperate for the win, desperate to come out on top. They're poor, they're hopeless, they may have nothing more than the horse they rode here and the armor on their shoulders. Winning this tournament could change their lives for the better."

"Then you mean to ruin that?"

"Not at all—I mean to learn from it. In true battle, lives are on the line, and there are no stewards circling. If I spend my life in the lists, Ian, I will only know how to fight noble men, in noble tradition, and I may not always be fighting noble men. I would rather dip my honor now, and keep my head later."

"As always, you have thought this through more than is necessary," Ian said. "I just assumed you like to wade in among the peasants and hit people with your blade."

"There is that as well," Martin answered wryly, "but I have to give Father a better excuse than that, if he's going to let me risk my noble neck."

"Well, that's a glorious plan you have, but I think I'd rather practice against men who know which end of the blade to wield."

"It's your funeral. Is Halverdt's field too dangerous for your likes, or will you be joining the lists?"

"Not this year. My father won't allow it," Ian answered. "He's afraid some Suhdrin knight will put his spear into my skull, or that I'll mistakenly kill the wrong southern bastard. No offence," he added hastily. "I keep telling him that we're allies now, Suhdra and Tener. It's a pity we're having this tournament under Halverdt's banner, but if we're to make peace with the likes of you, I suppose we must make peace with the likes of him, as well."

"I do wonder about that." Martin gazed thoughtfully on the muddy fight beyond the barrier. "But your father isn't far wrong to keep you away from certain spears. There are more lords here that lean Halverdt's way than you might think. I know our fathers are close, Ian, but you will find your share of enemies on these fields."

"You're sounding like Sir Dugan, bless his name," Ian said. Martin laughed, though with little joy. "You're serious?"

"There's always trouble to be found." Martin looked his friend over with a smile that seemed almost condescending. "Things are simpler in the north, I suppose, but a smile doesn't make a friend. Not here."

"Then you shouldn't smile when you say that."

Martin laughed, then wiped more mud from his chest and looked at it distastefully.

"I think I'm done here. Have you eaten?"

"Some, but it's been a long trip. I could do with more."

"Then let us eat, and drink, and let me forget that I'm going to spend the morning getting beaten into the mud by some lumbering clout from Halfton who traded his hoe in for a hammer and likes nothing better than using it on fancy noblemen's sons."

"Fancy noblemen's sons who should know better than to enter the melee," Ian corrected him. "Let's not forget that."

"Yes, yes, I should know better—but we'll see how it shakes out. Now, to my tent, to my clean robes, and then to my favorite house of bad intentions. Come!"

7

THE WAY AHEAD was dark and crooked. The gheist's path left the wreckage of Gardengerry and traveled north, twisting from river to road and beating back the thick oak and elm trees of the forest like a trail of broken bones. The shadows of its passage lingered in the sun, clinging to the dirt in scraps of night and nightmare.

Frair Lucas followed this trail as much in his dreams as during the day. Each night his mind conjured the shape of the following day's journey, tracing the widening damage the gheist was doing to the naetheric paths of Lord Cinder.

There was something awful about this newborn god, unlike any demon Lucas had hunted before. A gheist manifesting on the verge of Lady Strife's highest holiday, it wrenched the life from the land, leaching the vital energies from trees and soil, leaving them ashy and soft. Bark crumbled under Lucas's hand, and his boots sank deep into the ground. The air in the wake of the gheist tasted like charred incense.

Nothing about this was right. Nothing about it was sacred.

Lucas was three days from Gardengerry when he

woke one morning with the distinct feeling that one of his dreams had found its way into the daylight world. He lay perfectly still, listening, blinking up at the eaves of oak leaves that had sheltered him through the night. His breath was slow and tired. His bones ached from another night on the road, another lifetime far from home. Lucas was just starting to sit up when something stirred at the edge of his hearing. It sounded like the dry shuffling of leaves, though autumn had not yet robbed the trees of their clothes.

Lucas eased his legs beneath him, then sat up. His staff lay across his lap.

The gheist was at the opposite edge of the clearing. A field of dew-tipped grass glistened between them, crowned by midsummer glory, trees and shrubs as bright and green and swollen with life as Lucas could imagine. Even the sunlight was heavy with golden energy.

When Lucas had fallen asleep last night, this clearing had been gray and sullen, leached of greenery, prey to the passing demon Lucas was tracking. Something had changed. Everything had changed.

The gheist lumbered out from the trees and into the clearing, a shambling mass of muscle, a bear with fur that glimmered amber and sunlight, tall as a horse and as wide. It snuffled among the grasses, and the blades of grass writhed around it like eddies of water in a turbulent stream. The fur on the bearlike back rippled in response, and then the individual hairs blossomed and grew, each one twisting open into a dandelion seed. A wind rose, and a cloud of seeds wafted off its body, drifting in the shafts of sunlight, gliding to earth to sprout new growth and new life.

It was not the gheist he hunted.

"Drawn by the corruption..." Lucas whispered to

himself, but the gheist heard him, and rose onto its hind paws, towering over the clearing like a mountain of sunlight and life. Its face was not that of a bear, but more like an eel, a wide mouth of scything teeth that gaped open, slick with blood. Black blood and bile.

"...and corrupted yourself," Lucas added. He had hoped to leave this gheist alone, to let it go about the business of renewing the forests of the north, repairing whatever damage the rogue god from Gardengerry had wrought. Most of his brother inquisitors would never have considered such a mercy, but Lucas had spent enough time in both Suhdra and Tener to know that total suppression of the gheists could harm the land. He suspected that the church's rigid suppression of the gheists in the south was at the root of the current blight, an opinion that would have gotten him branded a heretic in Heartsbridge. So if this one had been drawn by the corruption and sought to repair it, that was all the better.

Yet the corruption had tainted the god, and so the demon it had become had to be culled, the land set back to rights.

The gheist gasped out a long, mournful sigh, and the sickness of its jaws flooded the clearing. The grasses withered at its breath, the sweet air turned sour, and the dappled light that danced through the trees shivered and dimmed. Lucas drew his staff in front of him, then called upon Lord Cinder's gift of naether.

"I will break no peace with you, demon," Lucas muttered, "and ask for none in return. Return to your realm, and you will find no argument with me."

The gheist dropped to all fours and charged toward Lucas. Its slow, rolling gait shook the ground. The haze of its fur, now floating in the air, streaming behind it like a banner, squirmed with embers that danced through the seeds and stitched the air in lines of amber and gold. Lucas planted his staff and twisted the air around it, lacing shadows together, binding his flesh to the fog-thick essence of the naetherealm.

Lucas's blood chilled as his spirit left the mortal world. The gheist's fiery charge brushed Lucas aside, but instead of crushing the priest, it passed through him as if he were a wisp of smoke.

Once the bear was past, Lucas threw aside the skeins of shadow, leaving them to ground harmlessly into the forest like dark-veined lightning, kicking up puffs of ash and silt where they struck. He whirled on the gheist, pulling power from the naetherealm and attempting to bind it to the rogue god. Shadows snapped against the demon's flesh, scattering the downy spore from its back, catching on its limbs and snarling its gait.

Slowly the gheist turned, lazy, heavy, its slabs of muscle and fat breaking the bonds Lucas summoned. Lucas could see the god's eyes, saucers of golden light shot through with dark veins, as if the corruption that had claimed its jaws was slowly working its way into the brain.

The demon lowered its head and lumbered again into a thunderous charge. Its gaping jaw dragged through the grass, leaving a trail of pitch-black spittle that bubbled and hissed in its wake. Its back rippled with the rolling gait of its muscles.

Lucas assumed a stance of meditation, balancing his frail frame on one foot and leaning against his staff. He touched his forehead to the staff's focusing icon, then dropped his mind into the naetherealm, leaving his body dangerously exposed in the mortal world. Yet he had no chance of defeating this beast with flesh and blood. His strength was of the mind, and his hope for victory lay in thought and deception.

The world changed around him, and time slowed down. The clearing lost its amber sheen, the vibrant life replaced by the cold weight of the naether. Lines of force and energy, the inevitable charge of the gheist, arced out from its body, etching a path that would tear through the frair in a matter of heartbeats.

Untethered from his body, Lucas examined his attacker.

"Nature spirit, as I thought," he said to himself. "Restorative. Some aspect of spring, come to undo winter's damage." His spirit floated past the gheist. "But it is not winter that has broken this land, and so you are driven mad." The demon's form was like fog, insubstantial in the naether, shot through with its own magical energies as well as the darkling tendrils that had corrupted it.

"A spirit of unrest has settled on your mind," Lucas whispered. He traced the presence from the gheist's jaws into its skull. The black strap of darkness writhed and bucked. "And there is little I can do to save you— even if that were my calling. And so, I must find some way to end you. Or perhaps help you end yourself."

With a steadying breath, Lucas reached into its mind. It was a realm of chaos, so unlike the minds of blood and light that he was used to fighting, a tumble of instincts and urges that nearly swept the old priest away. Lucas bore down, focusing on his task, reminding himself that the gheist had nearly reached him. He untangled the beast's senses and found its vision, stained by corruption but still bright, holy in the pagan way, seeing the world in terms of life and death, health and decay.

Vertigo swept over him—it came with seeing himself through the eyes of this creature. He barely recognized himself, and felt a flutter of revulsion go through him. And then Lucas pushed through. He bound the gheist's eyes to the naether, surprised at how quickly the corruption welcomed the binding, how weakly it surrendered.

Then he pulled free of the gheist's mind.

"Gods, but what a madness this one holds," he muttered. Tethers of shadow trailed from his hand, linking his will to the gheist's vision. Exhausted, he took a moment to still his own mind…

…then returned to his body. Lucas gave a startled gasp as air filled his lungs and the warmth of the sun scorched his eyes. He stumbled back, but was able to glimpse the fragile threads of shadow that strung between his hand and the gheist.

Only a moment had passed, and the demon was thundering forward, a bellowing, rampaging, terrible force of nature. Lucas fell to the side, jerking the shadow threads, pulling at the bear spirit's perception and balance. It rumbled past him, folding to the ground with a gasp. It struggled to its feet, turned and charged again, but now Lucas had it well in hand, drawing it to the side whenever it got close, bending the gheist's vision to baffle its mind, to make a maze of the grassy clearing.

As the gheist stumbled around, letting out droning bellows of confusion, frustration, and despair, Lucas slowly sapped its strength. He drew shadows from the forest to entangle it, formed increasingly confusing puzzles in its mind, spiked shadowy darts into its thick hide. With each step the gheist weakened, its divinity dissipated, like light from a guttering candle.

Finally, pitifully, it fell.

The gheist lurched forward, front limbs buckling, snout and shoulders plowing into the ground. It dug a trench with its bulk, coming to rest at the center of the clearing. A final cloud of firefly seeds rose up from its back, floating aimlessly in the shafted sunbeams, before disappearing into the everealm. Lucas stood at the beast's shoulder. He untangled the deception of naether, clearing the god's vision. The gheist stared up at him with one eye, a shimmering pool of wet, golden light, shot through with dark corruption.

"Such is the cycle, my friend," Lucas said, patting its shoulder. It was warm and thick, the muscles twitching with exhaustion. "Such is the way of your life. Whatever drew you to this clearing, I must escort you out. Have peace, little god. Go home."

He raised his staff and struck the gheist a sharp blow between the eyes. He was an old man, and such a blow would never hurt a creature of this size if it didn't carry with it the banishment of Lord Cinder, the god of winter and death. The gheist's body collapsed, folding open like a split purse, bleeding light and heat and the thick, musky stench of new spring growth.

Lucas stepped back and watched as the creature's body melted away, sinking into the ground as though it were water. The grass sprang to new life, the air cleared, and a wave of vibrant energy washed out from the gheist's dying breath. The trees all around the clearing grew a little, the grasses rustled and sprouted, suddenly reaching Lucas's waist. He couldn't help but laugh at the change in the air. It was like stepping outside on the first day of spring, the first birdsong in your ear, the promise of summer in the air.

"And so it goes," he said. "You return to the

everealm, and I return to my search." He rubbed his face, a momentary revulsion shivering through him as he remembered how he looked in the eyes of this little god—the revulsion it felt. He shook it off.

With his staff, Lucas parted the grasses at the spot where the gheist had fallen. The vegetation was incredibly green and hearty, little spears, broad of leaf and sturdy. It took some effort to find the ground.

There, shivering in the dirt, was the flat black strap of corruption. Like a snake in the vines, it hissed as the sunlight found it. Lucas raised his staff and crushed its head, grinding the shadowy tendril into the dirt. It writhed against the darkwood shaft, whipping through the grass and trying to find purchase on Lucas's boots. Finally, something cracked, and the corruption dissipated. It broke apart and bled into the dirt. The grasses sickened and died at its touch.

Before he left, Lucas made sure the ground was sanctified in Cinder's name.

Something dark was growing in the trail of this demon from Gardengerry. Something Lucas didn't understand, but something he was learning to fear.

The next day found Lucas well down the trail, and staring at a fork in his path. A second gheist had manifested, either alongside the demon from Gardengerry or in pursuit. Now two trails burrowed through the forest. There was no way of telling which belonged to the original quarry.

The first trail turned sharply east toward Greenhall. It was good that Sir LaFey had traveled on ahead, to warn the duke and prepare the defenses, though she would be hard pressed to arrive before the fast-moving gheist.

The second trail turned north. Straight into Tener. Straight for the Fen Gate.

Content that Elsa could manage things in Greenhall, Lucas turned his feet toward the pagan north. His path led to the Fen, and House Adair.

8

MALCOLM LEANED HIS head against the cool stone wall of the doma and breathed deeply. Night had fallen, and he wanted nothing more than to curl into bed and sleep away the pain of travel. His spine felt like a cooking rack, searing the muscles of his back with each step, and the pain in his hips, his knees, even his feet, would not relent.

The feet seemed like a particularly cruel joke. If Malcolm had walked from Houndhallow he could understand his feet hurting. His head was already pounding, and he hadn't even spoken to the duke of Greenhall yet.

"This is what it's going to be like from here on out," Dugan said. The knight was standing in the center of the doma, hands crossed over the hilt of his sword, staring up at the painted frescoes that described the movement of the stars and the seasons of the twin gods of the Celestial church. "Waiting in their holy places."

"Our holy places," Malcolm answered. He stood by the door, resting against the lintel. "I see you at every high day, and hear your prayers at the solstice."

"The wine is good," Dugan said. "Never fault the Suhdrin for their wine."

Malcolm shifted his weight to the opposite foot and

settled against the wall once again. Dugan smirked.

"What's that for?"

"You," the master of the guard replied. "You look like my grandfather, right before he forgot all of our names and wandered off into the forest."

"Show some respect for your elders," Malcolm said. "I could still beat you in the joust."

"The joust is a sitting man's game. Try me in the melee, and see how we measure up."

"I'm tempted to try you in a court of law for such insubordination," Malcolm snapped. Standing was no good. He tottered over to the altar and pressed his palms against the cool ivory. "I am still your liege lord."

"And I will follow you into the depths of hell, my lord, but if we get to the point where someone needs to help you with your toilet, I may have to reconsider."

Malcolm laughed. He was about to turn and give Dugan a good whack on the cheek when a priest appeared at the door. He was dressed in the black and gray of Cinder's anointed.

"The duke has been delayed," the priest said, giving Malcolm a disapproving glare. Malcolm slouched casually into a standing position, removing his hands from the altar and clearing his throat.

"He certainly has," Dugan said sharply. "Though I mean the duke of Houndhallow, not your master."

"My master is Cinder, lord of winter and—"

"Yes, yes, he meant nothing by it," Malcolm said, cutting in. "I only wish to offer the duke of Greenhall my blessings and respect. As you know, I am here at the invitation of the high elector."

"The high elector does not rule in Greenhall. It is the duke's invitation you should have sought," the priest said stiffly.

"And to whose whims do you attend?" Dugan muttered to himself. The priest bristled, but Malcolm stepped sharply between them.

"I would hope that the word of the high elector would be honored in Suhdra, as it is in Tener," he said. "We share a common faith, my frair."

"Your faith is common enough." The man sniffed.

"Will you please just fetch the duke?" Malcolm said, ignoring the slight. "We only want to offer the visitor's gift, and secure the promise of honor from his lordship."

The priest bowed and exited without another word. Malcolm spoke to his master of guard without turning.

"You have to be kinder than that," he said.

"I don't feel that I do," Dugan answered. "The priests the church sends north are decent enough, but this lot Halverdt keeps in his walls need a good punching."

"I think Halverdt may be more to blame for that than the church. Speaking of which..." Malcolm eased his way to one of the pews and began to lower himself. "If he's going to treat us like servants, I'm at least going to have a seat while we wait. And see if there's any wine."

A distant sound echoed through the doma, drifting down from the shuttered windows. Malcolm stopped himself.

"Was that..." he said.

"War horn," Dugan finished for him, rushing to the door. Malcolm followed, the pain in his back forgotten. He threw the door open. The walls were alive with torches and the sound of soldiers. The horn sounded again, a low rolling blast that echoed through the canyons of the city and filled the air with dread. It was a familiar sound in the north, the universal warning given when the old gods stirred.

Malcolm just never expected to hear it during the Allfire.

"Gheist," he whispered.

The horn brought Ian running, along with the rest of the occupants of the tavern. The mud streets of the tournament village were filled with drunken celebrants, most of whom were rapidly tipping into panic. Torches lined the city wall above them. The gate, held open due to the Allfire celebrations, boomed shut.

"What the fuck is going on?" Martin shouted. His face was flushed with the wine, but even through the glaze of his eyes, Ian could see his fear. Before he could answer, the horn came again. The rolling panic of the crowd matched the surging sound.

"Gheist, gheist, gheist..." Murmurs danced through the night. People began to run toward the safety of the castle gates.

"They'll never open up, not with a gheist out here," Ian said. "Do you see anything?"

"Nothing. Shouldn't there be priests, or..."

Hooves thundered behind them, coming down the street. Ian grabbed Martin and pulled him to the side of the road, up against the tent wall of the makeshift tavern. A trio of knights hammered past them, half-armored, half-drunk, flying the black spear and red rose of House Marchand. The crowd parted before them, though more than one reveler went to the mud with a horseshoe in his back.

"Bloody lot of good that's going to do," Ian said angrily. "Come on."

Still in a daze, Martin followed him as they ran to the Blakley pavilion. A few of his father's men were milling about, pulling on armor and splashing water in their faces. Sir Doone stood in the middle of the muddy lane, her face grim.

"Where is my father?" Ian demanded, dragging her around. "Where is the duke?"

"Not returned from the castle," Doone answered. "These damned Suhdrin aren't going to know what to do with this."

"No, they won't. Which is why the gods have put us here. Fetch my spear and kit, and my father's, as well."

"This is no hunt, my lord. They don't blow the horn for a lesser god."

"This is Suhdrin land, sir. They blow the gheist horn if one of their horses farts too loudly. Now get moving!"

Doone hesitated a moment, then nodded and disappeared into the pavilion. Ian started stripping down. Martin drew his sword, but didn't seem to know how to hold it.

"What are you doing?" he asked.

"Preparing," Ian replied. "You should stay here. You aren't exactly dressed for this."

"You aren't exactly dressed at all," Martin said as Ian's tunic dropped into the mud. Sir Doone ran up with two bundles of leather, and two spears. She handed one bundle to Ian and set the other on the ground.

The tree line at the edge of the tournament ground was alive with torches and the shouting of men. It was hard to see from among the tents, but Ian could hear the slow chant of priests and the hunting horn of the Marchand knights. He struggled into the pants Doone had brought him, then shrugged on the bulky shoulder armor and padded sleeves of his hunting gear. His chest he left bare.

"You mean to hunt it?" Martin asked. "You must be insane."

"Hunt or be hunted, friend. I haven't time for chain or plate, so this will have to do." Ian took the spear and held it to the light. The head was long and sharp, the metal dull and red as rust. A rune carved into the shaft marked the spear as Ian's, showed that it was his blood that had been used in the blade's forging and sealed the spells. "Bloodwrought steel. As close to magic as we'll get tonight."

"Leave it to the priests," Martin said. "There's no reason to risk your neck out there."

"Listen to you. Just this afternoon you were talking up the advantages of having peasants pound you in the head with hammers, so you could learn a little something about true combat—and now you want to hide behind the church?"

A terrible sound rolled out of the forest. It was a creaking scream, like trees torn asunder. Martin winced at the sound of it.

"I wouldn't call it hiding," he said. "Just clever positioning. Find a place of strength, and depend on it."

"I'll be my own strength, thank you," Ian answered. He motioned and a few soldiers from his father's company followed him, each in various states of preparedness. Their column clanked and clattered as they strapped on armor, and belted scabbards to their waists. Sir Doone was at their head, her face grim in the flickering torchlight.

A crowd was gathered at the perimeter of the camp. Most of the people were just as unprepared as the Blakley party, standing around in piecemeal armor, many of them drunk or half-asleep. A ring of priests stood by the warded fence that surrounded the tourney ground. Ian looked them over. By their dress and nervousness, he pegged them as common frairs, untrained in the mystic powers of the Celestial church.

In the woods beyond the barrier, the light from the perimeter torches faded and the trees dissolved into shadow. Here and there distant spots of light danced between the trunks: scouts, darting along hunting trails, looking for the source of the alarm. The horn on the city wall droned on, the sound echoing through the night. Above, Cinder shone his silver light, crowded on all sides by his host of stars.

Ian forced his way to the fence's edge and leaned over.

"Did Marchand ride out?" he asked the closest priest. He was an older man, wrapped in the crimson robes of Lady Strife and wearing a costume of cheap brass. He blinked slowly in Ian's direction before answering.

"On horses, yes," he said. His voice was slushy. "I tried to stop them."

"How many vow knights does Halverdt command?"

"The knights of the winter sun are not under the command of any mortal…" the frair began. Ian waved him off and hopped the narrow picket fence that the priests had set up to keep the nervous Suhdrin hearts safe from the frightening woods.

"Never mind," he said, and he turned. "Sir Doone, you and the rest stay here. I'm sure the vow knights will be with us soon enough."

"Not bloody likely," Doone muttered, climbing ponderously over the fence and dropping into the mud. "If your father hears we let you walk the gheist hunt alone, he'll have our bones for batons before morning. It's not like we can leave you in the care of Marchand's clan, can we?" A few more men followed her example.

"All the faithful are to remain behind…" the priest began. Ian ignored him.

"Three good knights have ridden out, and we can't leave them to gather all the glory on their own. Besides, they're southern boys. Probably have no idea what to do with a proper gheist."

"I'd wager it's a false alarm anyway," Doone said, though she didn't sound convinced. "Creepy sounds in the night, and the watchmen have their tits in a twist."

"Hopefully," Ian answered. "I don't like to think what sort of gheist could break into the Allfire." With a nod to Martin and a condescending glare for the priest, he led his little band into the woods. He was more worried than he let on. The gheists were the gods of the old religion, the spirits of stream and forest that the Tenerrans had worshipped for generations before the crusades. Now deprived of their sacrifices and abandoned to the quiet places of the forest, many of those spirits had gone mad. They manifested in strange and unexpected places, sometimes demanding tribute, other times taking their sacrifice in blood and fire.

One universal truth, though, was that the Celestial church held sway over them. The sanctified godsroads that crossed the forests and connected south to north were almost always free of their profane incursions. The blessed ranks of the vow knights and the priests of the inquisition could break the gheists with their gods-given powers. The divine calendar of the Celestial church could track their manifestations and predict their intrusions into the mundane world.

The Allfire was the height of Strife's power, as Frostnight was the apex of Cinder's worldly rule, each set at a solstice. During the equinox, when Cinder and Strife were most briefly in the sky, that was when the gheists were most likely to roam the land.

Ian stood at the forest's verge and listened to the distant roaring of this forgotten god. It was almost unheard of to see any kind of manifestation this close to the Allfire. Whatever was out there, it was either extremely weak, oppressed by Strife's abundant power, or it was so powerful that it didn't fear the bright lady.

Either way, he meant to face it.

A lesser horn sounded in the forest, a hunter's call. Ian lifted his spear in that direction.

"Marchand and his men," he said. "They have sighted it. We'll beat our way in their direction and hope they flush out the beast. How many of you carry bloodwrought weapons?"

"We're no hunters, my lord, but we carry good steel," Sir Doone answered.

"If this is a true gheist, good steel won't be enough," Ian said. "If this thing is larger than a dog, stay away. Form a funnel and try to beat it toward me, or at least away from the city. If it comes for you, to hells with your honor. Run."

"Aye, my lord," a nearby man said, and others mumbled with different degrees of enthusiasm. Sir Doone didn't answer at all.

The woman would never run.

"Fine," he said. "Then form on me. Stay tight and fast, and may the gods watch your blood." With that Ian held the spear aloft and trotted into the forest, Doone close on his heels. His cadre followed in a clanking line. The shadows swallowed them quickly. The forest was loud with vibrant insect life and the eerie creaking of wind-whipped trees. Only the drone of the gheist horn stayed with them.

They tromped through fallen branches, squinting into the darkness, the ghost world of trees and flickering leaves slowly dissolving out of the shadows as their eyes adjusted to the gloom. The gheist horn's drone warped the air around them, only slightly louder than the chattering bugs, the forest floor alive with scampering creatures that only stayed in sight long enough to startle the increasingly nervous men. Ian was afraid they had lost their way when Marchand's horn sounded again, very close.

It was followed by the short scream of a horse, a clatter of armor, and then meat and metal tearing. The column stumbled to a halt.

"So," Sir Doone whispered in Ian's ear, "bigger than a dog."

"Aye. Draw the men together and take them back to the camp."

"Not going to happen."

"You're no good out here. None of you are. Spare my father the pain of your burial cost and return to the camp. Halverdt will have summoned the vow knights. You can give them some direction."

"A very practical suggestion, my lord," the knight said. She made no move.

"Well, if you're hells bent on getting killed…" Ian said with a shrug. He looked down the column behind him. All were scared, but none were leaving. "When we see the beast, have the good sense to stay away from the killing bits. Spread out, draw it close, then let me do what needs to be done."

"Any idea which sweet god we might be facing?"

"This close to Greenhall? The Darkhenge is beyond the horizon, and the river Grehl can only draw its spirit once a season."

"Vow knights put her down just after the equinox," Doone said. "Too regular, that one. Could be the hound?"

"It is not the hound," Ian said with more confidence than he felt. His family's totem spirit had a history of dangerous predation along the border of Halverdt's lands. Ian could never bring himself to lift a spear against the great beast, though he had seen its furry back flickering between trees ever since he was a child. "And this close to the Allfire, it's probably not one of the regular manifestations."

"Aye," Doone agreed. She looked up and down the column. "Let's get about it, my lord, before the men lose their cool."

Before I lose my cool, you mean, Ian thought, but he gripped his spear tighter and crept forward.

They crouched at the edge of a broad clearing, grass and stone limned in Cinder's light. At the center of the clearing were the remains of a horse and rider, armor a splintered shell of steel and leather. Of the rest of Marchand's knights there was no sign. Cinder was in half aspect, his cloak drawn across his face. Yet there was still sufficient light to see. Ian crept to the clearing's edge.

"Do you see anything?" he whispered.

"Dead knight," Doone answered.

"Besides that. It's close, you can taste it in the air." Ian breathed deeply, and his nose filled with the murky stink of swamp and tombs. *Not natural. Not godly.* He prayed a quiet prayer to Strife for strength, and Cinder for clarity of mind. Then he stepped into the clearing.

"My lord," Doone hissed. Ian waved her off.

"Your steel may do some good, but only if you take it by surprise. Wait here. I will draw the beast."

"That is a terrible plan."

"You shouldn't speak to your lord's son this way, Doone. I will speak to Father of your impertinence." He gave her a smile that none of them could see, then walked slowly into the clearing.

There was no sound from the trees, of insect or god. Only a handful of breaths brought Ian to the dead knight in the center of the clearing. The man was beyond help. With the butt of his spear, Ian snapped the knight's visor back and recognized him: Grandieu, a knight from the dusty hills around Heartsbridge. He had ridden with Ian's father during the Reaver War. The knight had been opened from crotch to heart, his ribs cradling a ruin of pulped organs. A chill went through Ian's chest, shivering the sweat on his chest. He tapped his spear against the ground and scanned the tree line.

"I think it's gone," he called back to Doone and her men. "The other riders must have led it away." *Or been chased to their death, somewhere between these trees*, he thought.

The loose line of Blakley soldiers followed the knight into the clearing. The far tree line shattered and shook, and delivered a god into their midst.

It unspooled from the trees like a ribbon of darkness, lightning fast threads of liquid night that slumped out of the forest and pooled on the ground. It was huge, two horses wide and bristling with legs and arms that stuck out of the tangle of its body. The shape of a man fell from its front and crawled forward, his body bound in cords of shadow. The mass of the gheist was dragged along behind, rising and falling on half a dozen other legs, hands, and other unidentifiable body parts.

He saw the bundled form of a woman whose whole body was being used as a leg. The god looked like a tumor of bodies, tied together by satin ribbons, glowing with malevolent, purplish light.

"Much bigger than a dog," Ian whispered to himself.

The demon slithered toward them, sometimes slow, then as quick as fog in the wind. A single torso sat atop the body of bodies, broad shoulders and thick arms grasping at the air. It strained against the dark cords that held it in place. White, tattered robes stuck out between the shadows, and a pilgrim's cowl hid the man's face.

The gheist opened its mouths and howled.

"Fuck this," Ian said, and ran. He passed Sir Doone and her men, grabbing at them as he went by. They followed, those who had not already taken flight. The ponderous thumping of the gheist's pursuit disappeared, replaced by slithering wind. Ian dared a glance behind him, just in time to see the beast arc its body like a twilight rainbow, bounding over him to land with a thunderous crash at the forest's edge.

Ian skittered to a halt, staring at the roiling mass. Doone and the rest clustered around their lord's son, gripping their weapons in quaking hands. The beast howled again.

"Or we could make our stand here," Ian said.

The demon fell on them, arms and mouths and grasping ribbons of night.

9

As THE BROKEN god howled across the field toward them, its myriad of teeth gnashing and shattered arms tearing the ground, Ian knew terror. His limbs froze, his blood stopped, his breath and lungs went solid in his throat. The spear at his hip trailed forgotten through the grass. He watched the gheist come, action forgotten, bravery fled.

He should have died.

The beast crashed forward, and Sir Doone responded. The knight struck with her sword, gripping it in both hands and screaming as she thrashed the blade against the gheist's coiled limbs. Something cracked, the beast howled, and then slid to the side.

On the ground between them, lying at Ian's feet, was an arm. It was thin and wasted, the product of a life of deprivation and hard work. The gnarled fist was lined in dried blood. The tattered remnants of a mendicant's robe wrapped the flesh, the edges charred and grimy.

The gheist circled like a wolf, snapping its jaws, growling in many voices. Ian looked from the arm to the demonic figure, then raised his spear.

"The bodies break!" he shouted. "Destroy them, and only the gheist will remain!"

The soldiers raised their voices and their swords, then broke into a stumbling charge with Ian at the fore. The gheist clenched tighter into itself. Ian felt a thrill at cowing such a large abomination. His men fell on it, hacking and breaking and cleaving it into pieces.

The gheist struck back. It seemed to break apart, bodies flying from the core, the black cords that bound it together straining against skin and bone until the bare flesh of the possessed showed through the binding. They clawed at the Blakley soldiers with fingers broken open, their bones tearing at armor and flesh, shattered wrists punching past chain mail and drawing blood. Ian saw two men go down, then another, overwhelmed by enemies who would not falter when their bones were broken and their flesh cut.

Ian drew close to Sir Doone, weaving the tip of his spear through the air. The gheist avoided the bloodwrought tip of his weapon, slipping away whenever Ian tried to bring it to bear. He used this to clear some space around the knight, who was hard pressed by the gheist's remaining limbs.

"Grim business," Doone spat through clenched teeth.

"Aye," Ian agreed. "We'll need to break soon."

"No breaking. There's nowhere to break to."

Ian looked around the field of battle. The knight had the truth of it. The gheist's tendrils were circling their increasingly tight perimeter, diving in and snapping one or two of the Blakley men down before circling again. They were penned like cattle. The massive creature moved fluidly, a handful of possessed bodies pressing Ian's position while the rest moved past to attack the flank. Ian watched with horror as it coiled around them, tighter and tighter.

"That one remains," Ian said, pointing at the torso that seemed to stick out of the center of the slithering mass, broad shoulders and a head like a boulder, split by a wide and horrific smile. "The others move around it."

"Head of the snake?" Doone asked.

"Maybe. Maybe not, but it doesn't seem to care about the rest of its bits."

Sir Doone didn't answer, occupied as she was with hacking apart one of the gheist's slender forms. It turned out to be a woman. Her head fell from the tendril-laced mass of the god, rolling between Ian's feet. She wore the silver-and-gold-twined circlet of a celeste. Ian's mind wrestled with that, wondering at a gheist made up of the bodies of dead priests and penitents.

Doone drove back the demon, aided by Ian's spear and her own maddened fear. Two of the Blakley men remained, and those bleeding from many wounds. Only Ian was unharmed.

"It's afraid of the spear," he said. Then he made a hard decision. "Stay here. Whatever you do, don't follow me."

"My lord?"

"The hound! The hallow!" Ian yelled, the ancient battle cry of his tribe. Ever since he was a child, he had dreamed of giving voice to those words in some great battle. Half-expecting to die beneath the gheist's assault, he'd be damned if he would pass up the chance to bellow it now.

He dived forward, straight at the big man at the swirling center of the gheist. His spear cut the air. The gheist fell back and then, when it realized it couldn't get completely away from this unexpected charge, collapsed into his path to try to stop him. Suddenly

Ian was flooded with black-coiled arms and legs, blunt teeth gnawing at the thick leather on his arms and breaking the skin of his chest. Something tore through his face, ragged bones plucking at the soft skin of his cheek and raking his jaw.

Blood poured into Ian's eyes, and still he fought forward. He vaulted over one body, grimacing as shadowy tendrils wrapped around his ankle and sucked him down, struggling toward his goal in spite of the storm of pagan energy that lashed against him. The gheist tried to fall away, the tendrils of its presence straining as the core rolled and the rest of the bodies threw themselves at their attacker.

He fought through them.

With a final push he jumped clear of the attack and plunged his spear into the heart of the core figure. The bloodwrought blade of the spear sizzled as it cut through the shadow coils, into flesh and grated bone. Ian buried the weapon in the chest of the mad god.

Then there was silence. Everything was still.

The corrupted god gave voice to a dozen mouths. Howling.

Then its presence wilted like a vine in drought, the dark tendrils of power slithering back to the core, lashing limply against the ground as it abandoned the myriad bodies, each falling loose-limbed to the ground as the god left them. The ribbons of the gheist's true body coiled in a tangle around Ian, battering his skin and burning his spirit, flailing in one final attempt to be free of the spear's grip. They pulled away from him, wrapping around the wound, and then slumped to the ground, a loose knot of broken power.

Ian sagged to his knees. The spear was sunk to the shaft in the chest of a burly mendicant, his robes stained with blood and dark ichor. As the corpse folded in on itself, the dead man's cowl fell back from his face. He had the pagan ink, though it was drawn in paint rather than tattooed into his skin. A wave of hatred washed over Ian, traveling through the spear and into his arms, his bones, his heart.

And then it died, dissipating into the air like the memory of a dream, cut away by morning's light.

"Gods… damn," Doone said from behind. Ian looked back. The survivors—Sir Doone and two others—knelt before the fallen god, leaning heavily on their swords to keep from toppling over with exhaustion.

"Damn that god," Ian agreed. He tried to stand, but his knees were weak and his strength was gone. "Never thought I'd break a gheist."

"Really? Then why the hells did you lead us out here?"

Ian shrugged. He settled onto his ass, laying the spear across his knees.

"Well, someone should get back to the camp. Let them know what we've done. Send someone out to gather Sir Grandieu and…" His voice trailed off. He looked over to the dead knight. A tangle of blackness was gathering against the man's shattered chest. As Ian watched, the pale white of Grandieu's ribs was eclipsed. With a sound like grinding marbles, Grandieu knit himself back together and rose again, knight and horse bound together with bands of night and heresy.

"Oh, seriously, what the hells?" Ian said. Exhaustion beat against his chest. He unfolded slowly, struggling to his feet. Doone and the survivors closed around him.

The body of the knight and the corpse of the horse

wove together into a grotesque hybrid of armor and flesh. The broken length of the knight's spear wrapped tight with the gheist's strange ribbons, shattered and broke again, given life by the fallen god to become a prehensile limb, tipped with scything jaws of splintered wood.

The gheist turned toward Ian, snapping those narrow jaws together. It sounded like swords clashing.

"Well. We made a hell of a try," Ian said.

Sir Doone stepped in front of him, raising the notched length of her sword and bellowing her fury.

"*The hound!*" she yelled.

She was answered from the tree line. The shadows of grass and young trees swirled as though caught in a sudden wind, and then a lone rider burst into the clearing.

"The hound! The hallow!" the rider called, full plate glinting in Cinder's light, shield and spear lowered for the charge. He thundered across the clearing and crashed into the gheist at a full gallop. There was a shattering of metal and bone. Bits of armor and flesh tore free of the gheist's grip, spraying across the grass of the field like broken pottery. The rider rode straight through, turning near the tree line and presenting his spear to the gheist. He rose in his saddle, slapping his visor up.

Malcolm Blakley glared across the field at his son, the moon illuminating the hound on his shield and the blood on his spear.

"Run, you idiot!" he shouted, then he lowered his visor and prepared for a second pass. The swirling mass of shadows at the center of the field seemed shocked by Malcolm's attack, but largely unhurt. It squared itself up to face the charge, shadowy tendrils rising from its shoulders like wings.

At that moment a new sun broke among the trees, coming from the direction of Greenhall. As Ian watched, a knight of the winter sun hovered into the clearing. She wore the ornate plate-and-half crimson armor of her sect, traced in gold, marked with the sanctified runes of the Lady Strife. A tabard tied loosely over her breastplate showed the gaunt, black tree of the winter sun. With the Allfire so close, the bright lady's power was near its apex, and that power shone through the armor. Runes burned with an amber light, molten gold and blood flowing through them in a never-ending circuit.

She wasn't riding a horse, as most flesh would singe in the presence of the full manifestation of the goddess. Instead she drifted over the ground, her toes barely grazing the grass beneath her. A field of heat sheathed her, the air shimmering, the trees shrinking away as though trapped in sudden drought. She held a sword in front of her, as bright as a shard of the sun, the gold runes along the blade flashing like lightning from a summer squall. Hair as black as midnight rolled down her shoulders. Her eyes were the color of splintered copper.

"In winter, in darkness, in the night," she intoned, her voice stiff with ritual, more song than declaration, "I shall bring the sun."

"Run!" Malcolm bellowed again, tucking his spear beneath his arm and spurring forward. His horse leapt at his touch, and lord and mount rushed through the clearing.

Ian lingered just long enough to see the bright lady manifest, her presence a blinding spear at the heart of the vow-sworn knight. It left the taste of copper in his mouth.

And then he ran, stumbling through the night, blinded by Strife's presence and the knight's glory. Behind them a storm broke through the forest, tearing through shadows like lightning.

Ian woke in pain. A deep fire burrowed through his head, simmering behind his eyes like pots of boiling oil. When he tried to sit up, nausea forced him back down. He heard a groaning sound, and realized it was coming from his throat.

"The dead have risen," his father said. Ian cracked his eyes. Even the dim light that filtered through the canvas of his tent made them water. Malcolm sat at a camp table near the tent's flap, his hands wrapped around a mug of coffee.

"Food?" Ian asked.

"We'll get you something to eat as soon as you are out of bed, and dressed, and the worst of the stink is washed off your body." Malcolm toed a bucket and sponge, the water frothed with soap. "Not necessarily in that order."

"I stood firm in the face of a gheist," Ian said. "Doesn't that earn me a little breakfast in bed?"

"If you were a wet-eyed Suhdrin lord with a poet's quill in your trembling hand. But you are heir to one of the greatest houses in Tener. The blood of hounds runs in your veins, the horns of ancient ruin echo in your voice." Malcolm stood with a sarcastic smile. "And your father is a damned hero. No son of mine is going to lie in bed just because they got a little god-touched the night before."

"I am wounded!" Ian pled.

"You are hung over," Malcolm answered. He scooped the bucket up in one hand and sloshed it over his son's bed. Cold, soapy water splashed into Ian's face, and he yelped. It stung his eyes and took his breath away. "They're going to pretend you're a hero out there, Ian, but let's be honest. You were too drunk to know any better."

He dumped the rest of the water onto Ian's head.

Ian sat bolt upright, sputtering and nearly knocking his father to the ground. Malcolm's laughter boomed through the tent. He bounced the sponge off his son's chest, then went back to the camp table and his coffee. Ian stumbled around the tent, rubbing grit into his eyes with the sponge and trying to find a towel. His father's rumbling laughter chased him.

"I'm serious, Ian," Malcolm said as he settled onto the stool. "Caris Doone and her men have been telling stories. Your name is on the lips of half the knights in this camp, and all of the women. They're going to hang a lot of titles around your neck, but you need to keep your head about you."

"Titles?" Ian asked. "What sort of titles?"

"Forget about it. Keep your heart in your chest, young man."

"Easy for you to say." Ian wrapped a towel around him and began fumbling around for his robes. Even at the height of summer, it was chilly in the tent. "They still call you Reaverbane in every court under the Celestial throne."

"Not to my face," Malcolm said, and he sounded tired. "Though I have no doubt it will end up on my tomb. But listen to me for a minute, son." He stood and took Ian by the shoulders. "You did well, but it was foolish. Your sister would make a fine duchess, but she has no love of court, and no interest in the Hunter's throne. For her sake, if not for your mother's, have more sense before you risk your blood next time."

"You rode out," Ian said.

"Once I had a vow knight at my side, and we knew what we were facing. Lord Marchand raced back to the wards as soon as he saw the beast, though not soon enough to save Sir Grandieu." Malcolm paused, his eyes lost in memory. "A good man. A good soldier. And you lost five of my sworn blades, none of them even properly armed to face that thing."

"How many more would now be dead if I hadn't acted? If the gheist had found its way to the tourney grounds?"

"Fewer. Maybe none. The wards were strong, and the vow knights were gathering. You will lose men if you mean to lead them, but that's no reason to be eager for their deaths."

Ian remained silent for a moment.

"I am sorry, truly," he said, "but I told them to run."

"They would follow you anywhere," Malcolm said. "That is their duty. That is their oath to me as their lord, and to you as their future leader. You will march the dirge at their wake, and deliver the wergild to their families. On foot. In ashes."

"Father..."

"No," Malcolm snapped. "They marched with you to their deaths. Their souls are bound to the quiet house. It is your burden."

Father and son stared silently at each other. Beyond the tent, the camp was stirring with life, yet Ian realized the world had grown quiet as they argued. He was used to having these kinds of disagreements behind cold stone walls, high in the keep and away from his father's men. He cleared his throat.

"Of course, Father. It will be an honor to wear their ashes."

Malcolm stood stiffly, then nodded. He set the mug of cold coffee on the table and left the tent. A quiet chorus of "m'lord" followed him as he tromped away.

Ian sighed and wiped the last of the soap from his eyes. He got dressed quietly, careful of the wounds he had earned and the ones he had hidden. When he was ready, he buckled a sword to his belt and went to find some breakfast.

10

DAWN WAS STILL hours away when Gwendolyn
Adair shook herself awake. The young huntress
lay in bed, listening to the hectic preparations in the
hallway outside her door, the shushing rush of silk
robes and slippered feet, the muffled clink of cheap
nails being driven home, the murmuring voices of
the servants as they prepared the secret feast of Lady
Strife, goddess of summer and sun and joy.

It was the morning of the Allfire, the longest day
of the year, and the castle Fen Gate was alive with
quiet activity.

Gwen propped herself up on one arm and blinked
at the window. Still dark. She wondered if her parents
were up yet, making ready. Traditionally, the servants
woke the lord and lady of the castle before rousing the
children, but as huntress of her clan, Gwen lived apart
from her parents, younger brother, and their host of
attendants. Her rooms were beside the kennels, below
the watchtower that held the gheist horn. Still, her
mother would want her to be part of the family's
procession into the doma, to offer their prayers and
their praises to Lady Strife.

Someone should have come for her by now. Gwen
was about to get up and poke her head into the

hallway when her door creaked open and Mab the Older appeared.

"My lady," the elderly woman whispered in a voice that was as rough as bark. "The bright lady calls you to…"

"Yes, yes, Mab," Gwen replied. "I'm awake. Lady Strife calls me to this and that, but first I have to make ready." She sighed and put her feet on the cold floor. Even in the heart of summer, the mornings in northern Tenumbra had a chill to them. "I'll be along shortly."

"Your mother says…"

"My mother says something about a dress. I know. You have done your duty, and shall not be held accountable for whatever I end up wearing. Thank you."

"Yes, my lady…" Mab said, leaving quietly. Gwen rubbed the night from her eyes and turned to her wardrobe.

A dress, indeed.

She got up, splashed cold water on her face, and pulled her hair back into a band, out of her eyes. She was tall, tan and strong from nineteen summers spent in the saddle and nineteen winters on the hunt. Her dark hair was streaked black and rusty red, unusual for Tenerrans of noble birth, and her wide eyes were a brown that was nearly black. She wore her hair short in the summer, something that drove both of her parents to distraction, but long hair had no place in the brambles of the wilderness. She had cut it the day her father appointed her the huntress of House Adair.

Gwen spent her days among the dogs, beneath the sun, on the hunt. Protecting her family's land from the mad gods that roamed the forests, gheists keening through the night for the worship that the Celestial church had stolen from them. However, today was the Allfire, Strife's holiest day, and the height of her power. The bright lady would keep the gheists at bay.

Gwen fumbled a lantern to life and by its flickering light began to pull dresses out of her wardrobe. Mother had expressed an opinion on the day's attire, but that held little interest for Gwen. She would submit to wearing a dress on a day like this, but if she was going to appear in such impractical clothing, it would be of her own choosing.

The noise in the castle grew as more of the household woke up. Two men held an angry conversation in the courtyard below, their voices rising until the distinct gravelly growl of Mab the Older shut them up. The hunting pack, no more aware of the significance of this day than any other, began yipping at the gate of their kennels, looking for breakfast and hopeful of the hunt.

Gwen gave her collection of dresses a dispirited look, then quickly buckled on her leathers and went up the stairs to the watchtower.

Aine MaeCliff was sitting against the wall, his arms crossed over his spear and a flask in his hands. He had the temerity to blush when Gwen tromped up the stairs and into his watch station.

"Bit early, Aine?" she asked.

"Bit late," he said. "I'm expecting relief."

"Quiet night."

"The Allfire," he said, then offered her the flask. The whiskey was fiery and sharp. Gwen took just enough to wash the dreams out of her mouth. "You have your own duties this morning, I think."

"Aye," she said. "Wanted a moment with the sky before prayers."

Aine smiled and leaned his spear against the parapet.

"Then let's call you my relief, and let me get a nap in before the festivities." He started down the narrow stairs that led to the barracks. "Edra will be along shortly."

Alone on the battlement, Gwen leaned over the wall and breathed in the morning air. The sun was still below the horizon, Lady Strife making ready for her glorious day. Lord Cinder, god of night and winter, hung low above the trees, the last of his silver light brushing their leaves like frost. The wind was cool and clean, sharp with the night and as fresh as the streams that laced their way through the forest below.

Gwen was glad for her day of peace. Each solstice celebration marked the height of the Celestial church's influence. The old gods rarely stirred on those days, or even in the weeks leading up to them. It was only as the equinox approached that these lands would be plagued by the remnants of their forgotten faith.

Well, mostly forgotten. Some still held the rites close to their hearts, hidden away in deep forest covens, lighting the flames that kept the old gods alive. Gwen cast her eyes through the lingering night, the iron-gray trunks of the trees reflected in the torchlight from the castle walls. Somewhere in that darkness, the pagans still said their prayers.

That Gwen said those prayers as well, along with the rest of her family, was a secret tightly held and deadly to know. Her father explained their double faith as two sides of the same coin, paying the church to preserve the new gods, and curbing the old gods to keep the church out of their business. The inquisition would be less understanding, however, if they discovered the truth behind House Adair's heresy.

Gwen kept her prayer short and quiet. In the doma behind her, the first bell of the Allfire struck. The call to prayer and preparation. A foot scuffed on the stairs.

"Aine. You've done something with your hair," Edra said. There was already a curl of drunkenness to her voice. The guardswoman smiled as Gwen turned around.

"Stow it." Gwen released her prayer into the morning, then handed the watch-spear to her relief. "I'll be checking on you, Edra. Don't think you have the day off just because it's the Allfire."

"Wouldn't imagine," she said as she clumsily hid her bottle in the too-short sleeve of her jerkin. From down the stairs a whisper stole its way up. A boy. The guard blushed and shrugged.

"At least take turns watching the forest, 'Dra," Gwen said. "I'm sure you can manage to keep one of you facing out, hmm?"

Edra stuttered an unintelligible response. Gwen passed the boy on her way down, a baker's son from the village, arms strong from lifting racks of bread, but with a face as soft as dough. Too young to be spending time with the likes of Edra. But it was the Allfire. The whole day was dedicated to making interesting mistakes.

Back in her rooms, Gwen selected a modest dress of deep red, trimmed in black. The colors of House Adair, without any of the uncomfortable iron ornamentation that so often went along with the name. When she felt as awkwardly acceptable to her mother's expectations as she could manage, Gwen snuffed the lantern and then went out into the hall and across the courtyard to her family's quarters.

The whole house was awake and, it seemed, rushing through the hallways and to the doma at the foot of the great hall. No one was talking, other than to apologize for getting in her way, or to wish her a bright Allfire, or compliment her color. Gwen bore it all, grateful that she wasn't expected to answer.

The doors to the doma were still firmly sealed, symbolically shackled in chains daubed white to represent winter's distant grasp. The crowd outside the sanctuary stood in silent reverence, shuffling back and forth in anticipation. Many more stood on the walls around the courtyard, the wall walks crowded with pilgrims and peasants, all in their holiday best. Most of them were looking down on the doma, but some faced east, waiting for Strife's bright face to find the sky.

The doma would wait. There were still minutes to pass before the Allfire officially began, and other rites were waiting for Gwen. She turned aside toward the crypts.

The way down was dark and crooked. None of the servants said anything to her as she passed, winding past the kitchens and cold storage, nestled in the cool damp stone, finding her way to the torch-flickered path that led deeper into the earth. Past the ranks of Adair dead, each holding silent to the secret kept by every heir to the Sedgewind throne. Gwen would join them one day, and find peace in that silence. The burden of secrecy troubled her—she didn't like its weight.

She didn't like its dishonesty.

Beneath the crypts there was another chamber, hollowed out in ancient days, crafted by the first tribes that would eventually become the House Adair. Abandoned when the Celestial church came north and built their domas. It was the hallow of the Fen, the holy place of the House Adair, once the tribe of iron.

Gwen stepped inside. Her witch was waiting.

"Cutting it close, Huntress," the woman whispered.

"The sun will wait," she replied. The room was cold and dark and damp. Water seeped from the walls, gathering in a clear pool at the center of the shrine. Three torches flickered on the walls. Gwen gathered her skirts and knelt before the pool. The ground there was smooth, worn by generations of Adair knees praying their hidden prayers. "Have my parents been here yet?"

"They have," the witch answered. The woman was a stableman's wife in Fenton, just one of hundreds of tired faces in the village. Her callused hands moved smoothly over the instruments of her station, quiet and precise.

"And my brother?"

The woman paused, tilting her head toward Gwen. After a breath, she went back to work.

"They have decided to keep him holy for another year," she said.

Gwen felt a wave of relief go through her. Her parents had been discussing bringing Grieg in on the secret, adding his blood to the rituals and his soul to the crime of heresy. Gwen was glad he would have another year of peace, before the troubles found him.

"You should not smile at that," the witch said without turning around. "The more shoulders that bear the weight, the lighter the burden."

"I would protect him," Gwen answered, "for one more year."

The witch didn't answer. Instead she turned and placed her left hand under Gwen's chin, tilting her head back. With her other hand she loosened Gwen's dress, pulling it free of her shoulder. Gwen shivered, and then the knife rested against her ribs.

"The god of spring awaits you," the witch whispered.

"To renew me," Gwen answered.

"The season of rebirth calls to you."

"And I will always answer."

"Today is the Allfire. Spring has delivered summer, and summer has consumed the land. And now, bloated, fat, it slides toward winter." The witch drew the blade slowly across Gwen's chest. So sharp, so cold, the blood trailing down the runnel to drip quietly into the pool. "The season of dying."

"But spring awaits," Gwen whispered.

"It awaits." The witch rocked back on her heels, withdrawing the knife. The blood flowed freely down Gwen's chest for a second, and then she heard the gritty crunch of a poultice being rubbed over the wound. The smell of rose petals filled her nose.

The witch turned away.

Gwen quickly redid her dress and stood. She would have to hurry to make it to the doma without being noticed. She was turning to the stairs when the witch's voice stopped her.

"Do you understand your promise, Huntress?"

"Of course. Believe me, my father has been clear on this."

"He has," the witch agreed, "but I'm not sure it has settled in your heart. We have hidden the last true god of the north. Should something happen to your father…"

"You don't have to scare me into faith, witch. My heart is pagan. My god is buried in the Fen." Gwen drew her hand across her chest, where the blood had dripped. "My iron is yours."

"So be it—but pray that faith is never tested," the witch answered. Then she turned away, busying herself with the blade and the blood.

Gwen huffed, but had no time to argue. She hurried

up the stairs. Back in the castle, she went around to the private entrance, through the artifact hall and past the holy forge, and entered the doma in silence. Frair Humble, improperly named, was waiting by the altar. The altar was crowned by the symbol of the Celestial church, a blazing sun clutched by the grim sliver of a crescent moon. The sun was wreathed in flame, the moon in branching spears of frost. Humble was dressed in cloth of gold and crimson, the chains of his office heavy on his chest, his pious head bent and resting against his ornamented staff of gold and silver, bound with ivory and decorated with the iron icons of the Celestial faith.

On the pews before him knelt Gwen's family, and behind them the knights of the household and masters of chamber, hearth and guard. Only Gwen's mother looked up at her entrance, her face both impatient with her daughter and pleased that the girl had not somehow wiggled free of her finery and donned something inappropriately comfortable. Gwen closed the door behind her and hurried to her father's side.

Colm Adair, baron of the Fen Gate and lord of the Sedgewind throne, knelt humbly before the altar of the Celestial gods. Like his daughter, he was dressed in the red and black of his family, and wore a false pauldron and gauntlet on his left arm, made of thin metal and ornament. Like many men of Tenerran blood, Colm's skin was pale and his hair dark and straight, though his eyes were lighter than most, and his build was wiry and long. And like most men of Tenerran birth, Colm had a light scrolling of runes tattooed across his cheeks and over his eyes.

The traditional ink was a remnant of the pagan rites long banned by the church. He wore his hair short, in the Suhdrin style, with a neat beard and none of the braids or fetishes that some Tenerrans favored. Gwen bore much of his likeness, though her temper came from her mother. Lady Adair had done a turn in the legion of hunters before she caught the baron's eye, and the blood and passion of the hunt still lived in her.

Gwen's younger brother Grieg gave her a sly wink as she slid down the pew to find her place. There was already ale on his breath. Mother would find out who had given the boy a drink, for all the good it would do.

With Gwen properly in her place between her mother and brother, and the rest of the household aching on their knees, the frair of the Fen Gate raised his head and began the rite of summer.

"In ancient days, on heavenly roads, before Cinder quenched his flame and Strife claimed the brightening sky..."

Gwen's mind quickly wandered, tracing the way back to her most recent gheist hunt, two weeks past. Already her heart ached to be back in the forest. It had been a tight chase, the goddess of some old river rising up and flooding the mill in Fenton. Gwen and her men had chased off the demon, but not before a good bit of grain was lost.

The Allfire rest was nice, but Gwen couldn't help but wonder how long it would be before the gheist horn droned again.

"And so we rise, as she rose!" Humble proclaimed, and the congregation slowly shuffled to their feet. Gwen bounced up, feeling the first tickle of excitement for the day ahead. Whatever trouble hung in her heart, the Allfire was a day to be celebrated. To be happy. Tomorrow would come as it would come.

When she stood, Gwen caught a glimpse of the

roof of the doma. There, painted in black and gold, were the twin figures of Cinder and Strife. They were surrounded by the dozens of shuttered windows, each opened on one of the holy days of the Celestial church, to allow either Strife's warmth or Cinder's icy gaze into the sanctuary. Today's window, gilt in gold and hung with wreaths of false flame, creaked open at the hand of some hidden servant. Beyond it were gray skies and the few remaining stars of night. While Gwen watched, a line of golden light burst across the frame and fell on the far wall, illuminating an icon of the bright lady.

"We rise, and we live. Not today to the quiet house," the frair rumbled, his cadence finally getting into the spirit of a goddess of life and love. "We live, and fill the world with our light. As Strife lights us, so we light the darkness. As Strife loves us, so we love. Children of Strife! Blessed of the bright lady!" Frair Humble lifted the staff of his office and touched it to the altar. A flame leapt from the golden horn of the lady, to settle at the tip of the staff. Humble walked to the first pew, the faces of the faithful lit by the dancing, holy flame.

"Come out of the darkness, come to the light! Put tomorrow away. Forget the days that have passed. Today we live for the lady. Today we live for fire!"

The shackled doors of the holy doma burst open, again manipulated by servants hidden in the walls. Beyond them, the people raised their voices as one, howling as Frair Humble swept out of the doma with the flame aloft. The baron and his wife joined their voice to his, and the host of knights with them, rushing forward into the crowd to begin the festival of the Allfire. A shiver went through Gwen's bones, a thrill that pricked her skin and raised her heart. Forgetting tomorrow, forgetting the past, forgetting heresy and faith, she raised her voice and joined them, to live and love and worship the lady bright.

11

THE WALLS OF the Fen Gate were alive with flame. Torches crowned the old, black stone of the castle in flame. The people of Fenton had come out in the hundreds to worship the bright lady at the bottom of a mug, and their heat and their noise added to the hectic air of the day. The morning's chill had snapped, and the full heat of the sun beat down on the dusty walls of the castle and the village beyond. The lady was greatly pleased.

It was a humble castle, built as a lonely keep to guard a border that had seen more than its share of conflict between Suhdra and Tener. Since the Reaver War, however, and the peace that joining against a common enemy had brought to Tenumbra, the Fen had become a peaceful place. The major trade routes passed it by, the merchants and pilgrims keeping to the river Silveryn and continuing on to the Wyl, stopping in Greenhall and Houndhallow on their way to points south.

The harsh fens that surrounded Adair's lands offered little to the farmers who swore fealty to the baron. As such, the men and women who crowded the streets of Fenton were hard as iron and eager for joy, more willing than most to forget tomorrow. For this day, at least, the villagers and farmers were as happy as nobles and as drunk as poets.

Gwen walked through the village with her own flagon of red wine, carefully watered down to keep her senses keen, though refilled often enough from the passing carts that her face was flush and her tongue loose. Lady Adair had insisted that Gwen be accompanied, and so she walked along with her younger brother, Grieg.

His age was just beginning to reach him, in long legs and spindly arms, bony wrists that stuck out from shirtsleeves that fit a week earlier. The Mabs were always cursing his growth and the tangle of hair that no amount of well-meaning spittle could keep straight. They walked side-by-side, Gwen still trapped in her dress, Grieg wearing his best approximation of a hunter's leathers. They shared a leg of turkey and talked quietly.

"It's a good enough showing," Grieg said as they walked down the high road toward the small tourney ground that had been set up at the edge of the woods. "Not Heartsbridge or Houndhallow, for certain, but good enough." He took a greasy mouthful of turkey. "I heard that Blakley is celebrating the Allfire in Halverdt's court this year."

"Gods bless him. There's no way I would ever raise a mug in Greenhall," Gwen said. "There may be peace between Suhdra and Tener, but that doesn't mean there's any sort of love."

"Oh, I don't know. I've seen a few fine ladies take their turn at the gentle blade, the last Frostnight. I could learn to love."

"If you want your blade handled gently, then yes, it's Suhdrin ladies for you," Gwen said. She tossed her hand to her forehead, as though fainting. "My lord, my lord, how mighty is your blade? Forsooth!"

"Lady Charlotte would have a fine laugh at that, sis. Right before she put steel through your ribs."

"Charlotte Malygris can suck my tits," Gwen said. "And don't give me that look."

Grieg waved his hand and tried to hide his laughter, to little effect. His mug wasn't half as full of frothy beer as it had been moments ago, and had been filled more than once. Gwen snatched the crockery out of his hand and drained it.

"I'm tired of thin wine," she said, pushing her glass into his hand. "You drink this."

"Nah." He emptied it behind a barrel and shrugged. "There's more than enough ale for everyone. No need to waste good belly space on that swill."

They continued down the street, avoiding roving gangs of jugglers and the occasional prophet, all of them deep in their cups. Just off the road, a certain amount of indiscriminate lechery was happening, barely concealed beneath canvas tarps or half-open windows. Grieg's head was on a swivel. Gwen had seen her share.

She and her brother found a barrel of ale and refilled their mugs, then settled onto a bench overlooking the meager tournament grounds. Truthfully, this wasn't a proper tournament. There was no tilt to be run, no jousting lists to be entered or melee to be contested. The baron's master of the chamber had organized an archery match, and Sir Merret and Sir Dobbs were conducting a lancing demonstration, which was drawing a nice crowd. Gwen and Grieg sat and drank happily, watching the two knights pass slowly by each other, touching lance to shield to the cheer of the crowd. Though Sir Merret was the older by quite a few years, even in this mock tourney his skill at lance was clear. There was enough ale in the audience to keep the onlookers entertained, even if the competition wasn't fierce.

"I swear, if they go much slower they'll lame the horses," Grieg muttered as Merret's lance bounced off Dobbs' shield.

"It's all in fun, brother," Gwen said. "You wouldn't want our father's men to hurt each other, would you? Surely there's enough danger in the world without that."

"There's enough danger, all right, but if a knight of any real court saw this masquerade, I swear these two would be laughed out of any lists they might wish to join in the future."

"Little chance of that. The Fen Gate hasn't drawn much of a crowd, beyond the village."

"Oh, would that it were true," Grieg said, straightening his back and frowning. "We have company."

Gwen gave him an odd look, then turned to see what he was staring at. A pair of riders had entered the clearing. The first was a priest dressed in the drab colors of Cinder. He was a handsome man, if a bit old to be on the road still, with light hair and strong features, all of them very typically Suhdrin. He wore the robes and staff of a frair of Cinder, though none of the icons of the god of winter. The priest sat low in his saddle, shoulders slumped, his arms crossed casually over the staff. He looked like a wolf, if wolves could ride horses.

Beside him rode a knight, wearing a shirt of mail that was covered by a green tabard emblazoned with a golden triple acorn and cross. The knight seemed very young, his tabard and sword freshly bestowed. His face was too sharp to be attractive, too delicate to be admirable. Behind them followed a mule, laden with heavy baggage and the tools of war.

The knight watched the mock joust, a thin smile on his face.

"What's so unusual about a priest and a knight on the Allfire?" Gwen asked.

"I'm never happy to see an inquisitor in the Fen."

"Well, he's here, and we must make him welcome, Cinder or Strife," Gwen answered. She slid from her seat. "But it's not the priest who worries me. His fellow wears the acorns of Greenhall. Can't imagine what a knight of Halverdt's stable is doing in the Fen."

"Another pass, if you would, gentlemen!" the knight called out, just as Gwen and her brother approached. "Those are fine lances you carry, that they could stand such a furious charge without breaking."

Sir Merret ignored him, but Sir Dobbs clattered to a halt and raised his visor. His fat face was red, and his thick beard stuck out around his cheeks like fire.

"We only demonstrate, sir," he said. "There is no need for mockery."

"Crockery, you say? Yes, please, demonstrate some crockery! You seem fit for a potter's apprentice, though perhaps a bit too fat!"

"Good sirs," Grieg called. "Welcome to the Fen Gate. I greet you in the name of Colm Adair, baron of the—"

"Save the pleasantries, boy." The knight didn't spare Grieg a glance, but looked contemptuously around the meager fair grounds. In the distance, a small choir of drunken villagers broke out into a bawdy song, but around the visiting knight, the festival had grown quiet. "There must be more, mustn't there? Or did the pious Colm Adair travel to Heartsbridge, to bow his pagan head before the celestriarch?"

The priest at his side put a hand on the knight's shoulder, speaking in calm, quiet tones.

"Good sir, there is no need to antagonize these people. We hope to be their guests, after all."

"Shut up, priest," the knight said. He spurred his horse away from his companion, then the knight's eyes fell on Gwen, and his already wicked grin got sharper. "What is this? What lovely rose perches at the edge of this offal? By your colors, I mark you as an Adair, no? The daughter of our brave baron?"

Gwen stood still, her head swimming with the wine and a sudden anger that rolled up out of her gut to grip her heart. The knight trotted closer, leaning forward to look her in the face.

"Are you struck dumb, or born that way?" he said. "A perfect girl, I think, silent and yet beautiful. A perfect girl for certain things, at least. Does your mouth open, at least?"

Gwen couldn't help herself. She rolled her head back and let out a long and hearty laugh. When she looked back down, the young knight was turning every shade of red his face could muster.

"Oh, gods, what a charming and brave fellow you are," she said sharply. "Is it the custom of knights in Halverdt's service to ride far and wide, to offend the ladies that they meet and insult the good servants of the gods?" She leaned forward, squinting at him. "Or are you simple?"

"Do not think a sharp tongue will keep you safe, child," the knight hissed. "I've beaten prettier girls than you."

"With every word you add greatly to your honor,

and to the glory of your name," Gwen countered. "Perhaps I shall give you a title, to commemorate your many victories against the whores of your land. Why, we could even have a ballad written in your honor! What is your name, brave knight?"

"I will not stand here and be insulted by a girlish whelp!" the man said.

"Sir Standhere, yes, a fine name. Sir Standhere the Whore's Scourge. I like the sound of it. Now, how shall your ballad go?" Gwen cleared her throat and made a face to appear as if she was thinking deeply. "Sir Standhere was a mighty man, a wicked man, a childish man. Sir Standhere fought the ladies true, he beat them blue…"

The crowd that was gathering gave a polite and nervous laugh, until a smart bard behind the huntress took up the song on his lute and started adding his own verses. Soon the crowd was singing along, coming up with rhymes for "limp" and "bollocks," to a point that had Gwendolyn blushing. As the song rolled on, the priest dismounted and came to stand beside her and her brother, looking out over the crowd.

"I swear to the gods, I have never been treated this way by a child," the knight said, drawing steel. "You will learn the error of your—"

"Knave!" Sir Merret said, loud and plain. He had ridden to the edge of the tourney yard, and sat with his lance couched at his foot, his visor up. "That child is huntress of this clan, and the true heir of Lord Adair. Leave her alone, before she gelds you in truth rather than just in verse."

The knight raised his brow and turned to face Sir Merret.

"Whom do I address?" he asked.

"I am Sir Alliet Merret, knight-marshal of Lord Adair, and sworn to the lady's service." He tipped his head. "And you?"

The knight was silent for a moment, sawing his horse back and forth between Merret and Gwen. The fury had faded from his lips, but not his eyes.

"Sir Yves Maison. Knighted of Halverdt, and sworn to the holy celestes in Heartsbridge." The knight tilted his head, appraising Sir Merret as he would a prize calf. "There are Merrets sworn to Roard, I think, far to the south. A fine line of Suhdrin knights going back to the first crusade, brave men of proud blood. Are you of that noble line?"

"I have the honor," Sir Merret answered.

"And how did such honest Suhdrin blood come to be subject to filthy Tenerrans? What sin did you commit, to be banished to the pagan north, good Sir Merret?" Maison leaned back in his saddle, resting his gauntlets on the pommel of his saddle. "Or could you simply not cut it among the true knights of Suhdrin name?"

"I will not rise to your childish barbs, Sir Maison. If you wish to partake of the baron's hospitality, I would suggest you blunt your tongue, before I am forced to dull my blade with your blood."

"The pagan's dog has a bark! I have not come to partake in the hospitality of some mud-hut noble, if it can be called hospitality, and if you can call such as this—" he swung a hand at Gwen "—nobility."

"Colm Adair is the celestially appointed baron of the Fen Gate, and his blood has held this honor for generations," Sir Merret said tensely. "Longer than your name has spoiled the pages of the peerage, I assure you."

"I will not take lessons in nobility from a pagan's

pet Suhdrin," Maison spat. "Better that you change your name to reflect your station, jester-jouster. I think MaeMerret suits you better, don't you agree?"

"You have twice named Lord Adair pagan, and that is twice more than I will allow. The baron prays in the doma, serves the gods of heaven, and is a more faithful, noble and holy man than you will ever know. If you won't take lessons in nobility, perhaps you will take a lesson in steel?" Merret slid his hand to the hilt of his blade. "I have instruction here, if you are interested."

"Gentlemen, please," the priest said quietly, speaking with little urgency. "This is a festival day, and we are guests in Adair's realm. Let's not ruin the joy of the day with petty fights."

"It is the festival of Lady Strife, priest," Maison said sharply. "I can think of no better day to ruin with blood."

"Yes, well. I had to pretend to try, didn't I?" the priest said, giving Gwen a fatherly smile.

"Nor can I," Merret answered Maison, ignoring the priest. "If you are brave enough to insult a child, perhaps you can muster the steel to face me, as well? Or do they not teach bravery at Greenhall, these days?"

Sir Maison sat, his chest heaving, his fine face shading from red to black and back again before he answered.

"I have no second," he muttered.

"I will serve that function," Sir Dobbs answered.

"As if I would trust a Tenerran savage to tie my boots, much less my armor."

"Then your trust must fall to me," the priest answered. "Unless you doubt the faith of the holy church?"

Maison stared at the frair for several breaths, then nodded. The crowd grew, a muttering wonderment rising into the air as the fight began to form up. The strange knight rode to the far end of the field, drawing his mule with him. The priest sighed and turned to Gwen.

"I apologize for this," he said. "His business is not mine, nor his manner."

"Why do you ride with such a man, if you don't mean to support him?" Gwen asked the priest. He shrugged, an elaborate gesture that involved his shoulders, his face, and most of his chest.

"We met on the road from Greenhall, and were going in the same direction. The way was safer with me along, so I offered to accompany young Maison as far as your tourney ground. He is beyond my protection now."

"Don't you mean your way was safer with him along? Sure it is the duty of knights to protect the blood-sworn of Cinder?" Gwen asked.

The priest chuckled, gesturing to the blushing knight. "Do you feel safer with him around?"

"Should I instruct Sir Merret to go easy on him? We don't want an incident."

"This man needs humbling," the priest answered. He gave Gwen an appraising look. "You are the huntress here?"

"I am."

"Then my business is with you, once this nonsense is finished. You and your father. Speaking of whom, you should go find the baron and tell him what is happening. Then hide yourself away. This will go sour before it goes sweet."

"I am as safe here as hidden away," Gwen said.

"Perhaps, but I am trying to protect young Maison. Please."

The priest gave Gwen the barest push. Clenching her jaw at being sent on an errand like a servant, she hesitated. She would rather stay and watch the bastard get beaten into a pulp, but was deeply uncomfortable with the knight's constant accusations against her father. Someday, someone would ride into the Fen Gate and make that accusation with proof behind it.

Turning, she ran to find her father.

By the time she returned with the baron in tow, the two knights were facing off. The crowd was silent and tense, wondering what would come of this joust. There was a taste of great violence in the air, much worse than most tournaments Gwen had attended. She imagined this must be what a battle felt like, in the moments before the charge. Despite her trepidation, there was a thrill to it that made her heart sing.

She reached the front of the crowd just as the mysterious priest dropped the flag and the two knights charged. Merret, a veteran of the lists, surged smoothly forward, dropping his lance to meet Maison's shield. Both lances burst in the center of the lists, and a shower of splinters filled the air. When the horses had thundered past, Maison was on the ground, rolling groggily to his feet, and Merret was at the far end of the lists.

The crowd roared.

"I will save you the trouble of your duties, good priest," Sir Merret announced. "I forfeit the right of second pass. On your feet, Maison."

"I need no coward's shield to guard me, fool!" Maison roared. "Bring your steel, and we'll see who is better with the blade."

"We have settled that, or did you fall so hard you forgot having ridden? Shall we try again? I'm sure I could find a child to lower a lance for you, if you prefer."

"Enough of this!" Colm Adair shouted. He stepped

into the open ground of the lists, the fine silk of his robes muddied at the hem. The false steel of his ornamental armor flashed in the light of the morning sun. He carried a sword, the bright blade bare and sharp. He turned to face the fallen knight, and then Sir Merret, and finally his daughter. "No blood will be spilled on this ground!"

"Aye, my lord," Merret said tensely. "I beg your pardon."

"Given," Adair said. "And you, sir knight?" Colm asked, facing Sir Maison. "Will you seek pardon? Or do you have offense left to give?"

Maison stood quietly, his sword loose in his hand. He glanced around at the swelling crowd, the handful of knights who had gathered by their lord, and finally to Sir Merret, still in his saddle.

He shrugged. "I beg your pardon, my lord. The passion of the festival... I had the fire of Strife in my blood."

"Strife's pardon is not mine to give," Colm said, "but you are welcome to this festival, and to my house. Will you accept our hospitality?"

Maison paused again, then walked to his horse and, without assistance, mounted. He sheathed his blade and trotted to where his pack mule waited. The knight rode back into the woods without looking back.

"That went about as well as I could have hoped," the priest muttered at the baron's side. Colm Adair turned to the man.

"I hope you at least will accept our hospitality, Frair..."

"Frair Gillem Lucas, most recently of Cinderfell, though I have not passed through that blessed gate in many years."

"A traveler, then?" Grieg asked.

"Of a sort," he answered. "I am sorry for the trouble I've brought to your celebration."

"Not to worry," Gwen said. "Brave Sir Maison seems to have been taken care of."

"Oh, not that trouble, my lady." Lucas squinted up at the castle. "I'm afraid that I have tracked something quite dangerous to your lands. A gheist, making its way from Gardengerry and through Halverdt's territory. I believe it crossed into your lands last night."

"It's the Allfire, Frair," Gwen said. "This is not the season for gheists."

"Some heresies refuse to keep our calendar," Lucas answered. "Damned inconvenient, I know. But many have died." He turned to face Gwen squarely. "Call the hunt, Huntress. We have a god to kill."

12

DARK RAIN ON thatch. The walls of the little hut creaking in the wind, water pooling on the floor, and Father yelling in the other room. Smoke in the air. Henri squeezed his tiny eyes tight and counted the heartbeats between lightning and thunder.

Not our house, he thought, curled up in the scratchy dry straw of his bed. *They haven't taken our house, not tonight. Not yet.*

The sky rumbled again, and the sound of it echoed through the ground, shaking the hut. Henri whimpered, turning toward the wall and clenching his jaw. His father's yelling stopped for a minute. He was listening. Mother's voice slid into the silence, so quiet. Calm. When his father answered he was quieter, but Henri could still hear his father's words.

"It's just a storm. Another storm," he said.

"That's what you said the night they came for Jossie and her husband," Mother whispered.

"Nobody came for Jossie or her husband," Father answered. "You know that. No one knows what happened to them. Anything could have happened."

"Don't give me that. You know what became of them." Mother sighed, a long shuddering breath that was laced with tears. "We all know."

Father was quiet for a moment. The storm kept going outside, low, rolling thunder shaking the walls, keeping Henri awake. He wanted to sleep so badly. He wanted to squeeze his eyes shut as tight as stones and fall asleep, and then it would be morning and the storm would be gone. That's all in mighty heaven that he wanted, and he just couldn't do it.

"It mightn't've been the storm," Father said. "It was at least a week before Hadley went up there to gather wood. They could have been gone..."

"Please, just... just be quiet. I don't want to hear—"

A sudden crash of thunder washed over the house, followed by a short, sharp scream from outside. Henri heard his mother gasp, and his father's heavy footsteps went to the door.

"Was that—" he started.

"The Merrils," Mother said. "That was surely the Merrils. Jacque, you can't be thinking—"

"If we were out in the storm, you would want Jeb to come check on us. It could be anything."

"It could be anything," Mother agreed sharply. "Don't go out there, I beg of you. It could be nothing, you said."

"Never mind that. Martha, if it was us out there—"

Another sharp crack, this one nothing to do with the sky. Wood snapping, like a tree in a storm, but the wind wasn't that strong. Mother gasped and started to cry.

"I can't stay here," his father said. "I can't sit by while—"

"Please, no. Please stay here. Stay for little Henri, if not for me. You don't have to go out in that. It could be nothing. They might be fine, Jacque, please."

"Love, love, I'm sorry," Father said, his voice

muffled, as though his face was buried in Mother's hair. "I'm sorry, but I can't stand by."

Suddenly the storm was inside, the wind and rain whipping through the tiny hut, and then the door banged shut. Mother was left alone with Henri, and he could hear her crying—big, jagged, gasping sobs that she tried to swallow into silence. He gripped the blanket over his head, tighter and tighter, listening to the rain. Listening to the thunder, and the incredible quiet in the hut that his father had left behind.

Hours it seemed. Days. Surely it was morning by now. Surely he had fallen asleep and the sun was out. But the rain still fell, the thunder still rolled. Mother was by the hearth.

The door opened.

"Jacque, what was... Jacque? Jacque!"

Henri opened his eyes for the first time that night, since his mother had tucked him in after dinner. There was light from the main room, and something in the air. Something sharp like lightning struck close. He sat up, sliding his naked feet to the dirt floor. The storm was strangely quiet outside, though he could still feel the wind pushing on the walls and see the lightning flickering between the gaps in the roof. In the main room his mother was crying uncontrollably, her sobs caught between shrieks and breathless wailing. It sounded like madness.

Henri picked up the heavy wooden stick his father kept by their bed, nearly as tall as the child and heavy in his numb hands. His whole body felt numb, unreal, like he was walking through a dream. A dream, a dream, let it be a dream. He crept to the door to the main room.

His father, what was left of him, hovered in the doorway. He hung limply in the air, one arm outstretched, mouth slack. Something stood behind him. Something Henri couldn't look at, his eyes sliding to the side whenever he tried to fix it in his vision. Father came in, followed by the thing Henri could not see, came to his mother.

The floor beneath his father rippled like a pond. Small waves of dark energy, blue and crystal black, washed through the room, wave after wave. They lapped over Henri's numb toes. Something about his mother changed. She began to flow into his father, as if she was drawn up into him. The nothing-thing behind Father grew. It stretched, and the ceiling shivered overhead. Henri dropped the stick and covered his face, but he could still see. Father and Mother, and the unseen thing.

Henri cried out.

Well into the room now, the thing turned to him, and he could see it for a second. It was a creature bound in white and blue lightning, a spirit shaped like a mockery of a man, and beneath its skin was another man, and then another, each one smaller and deeper, buried just beneath the spirit-man on the outside. It was like an onionskin of lost souls, each spirit wrapped in another, and Henri recognized the spirit on the outside.

Old Jeb Merril, loose skin hanging from his cheeks.

While Henri watched, old Jeb sank deeper into the spirit, and a new form grew around him. *Father*. Jacque Volent shivered and looked at his son, reached for him. The air around the spirit's hand swirled with dark blue lightning, wrapped in a milky shroud. The bolt struck Henri, and his eyes and teeth felt frozen in his skin.

He screamed and ran, turning to the door and

stumbling out into the storm. The sound was back, suddenly, as if an invisible wall had been keeping the howling wind away. The child ran through the rain and the mud, his fingers tingling, his feet numb. He ran and he ran, and the rain fell onto his face, mingling with the tears and the snot, running into his eyes and mouth as he ran screaming into the night.

It was only later, huddled in the lee of a broken oak, that Henri realized he couldn't feel his face. That the skin was cold and dead.

Volent woke with a start, the memory of rain on his face fading as he sat bolt upright in bed, his breath coming in short, panicked gasps. He ran fluttering fingers over his cheeks, under his eyes. Nothing. He felt nothing, not even the damp of tears. The skin of his face felt like cold, stiff wax under his hands.

He struggled out of the twisted sweat-stained ruin of his bedding and went to the ceramic bowl in the corner of his room. A beaten metal mirror hung over the bowl. Henri stared into the smudged image as he splashed water over his head. Just a habit, the water. He never felt the chill until it reached his neck, ran in goose bumps down his chest, his arms. A sliver of light from the window illuminated the pale ghost of his body. He looked down at himself, trembling with the dream, the same dream, the every-night dream.

It was spreading. A blossom of icy dark veins flowered across his chest. A small area, hardly larger than the palm of his hand, but when he ran a blade across it there was no feeling, no pain. On his thigh, too, and inside one forearm. The veins crept up from the depths of his bones like spidery tentacles emerging from a still sea, stealing the feeling in his skin.

Volent splashed more water on his face, shivering as it froze the skin on his shoulders. His arms and hands were shaking as he raised the water to his head, matching the mad beating of his heart. *Silence, Henri*, he thought, staring at himself in the smudged mirror. Achieving calm, he dried off and got dressed. The numbness had spread enough that he could keep most of this shaking in his bones. The mornings were always the worst, with the dream and the fear fresh in his waking mind.

A knock. Volent shied away from the sound, then limped to the door and opened it a crack. There was a servant in the corridor. The boy looked terrified.

"Sir Volent? My lord has summoned you to his throne."

"What time is it?" Volent asked. His voice was as soft as velvet, his lips barely moving with the words.

"Nine bells, sir."

Volent nodded and closed the door.

He stood outside the great hall of Greenhall, waiting for an audience with his liege lord. He was making the other courtiers nervous. The court was already in a state of nervous shock, the gheist horn still echoing from the walls and in their minds, the avenue outside lined with the bodies of those who had died in the attack. He stood silently in front of the door to the chamber, his hands folded comfortably at his waist. Waiting. He wore dingy gray armor, the plate unadorned and poorly maintained, the sleeves of chain frayed and unraveling at the cuff. Even his blade was of poor quality—hardly what would be expected of the favored servant of a duke of Suhdra, much less the knight-marshal of his master's realm.

It wasn't those things that discomfited the other courtiers, in their bright robes and holy vestments. Nor was it his manner, calm to the point of death, so still that you might think him a statue. No, what caused the courtiers to avoid him, what left the priests muttering silent prayers as they passed, what gave the children nightmares and made the whores down in the village charge extra, was his face.

His pale, still, beautiful face.

He heard the whispers, knew the rumors. Ignored them. No one at the court was sure of his age, and there was nothing in his features to give any indication. He had the look of a young man, not yet reached his naming day, a face that would draw the girls and delight their mothers. The problem was that his visage wasn't natural. The skin was cold and soft. Dead. When he talked, nothing moved except the barest flicker at his lips. He never smiled, he never frowned, never showed surprise or fear or excitement. His face, pale and beautiful, was dead yet undying.

A plume of dark veins danced under the translucent skin like cracks in the icy surface of a frozen lake, hinting at the dark waters beneath. The spider web was centered just beneath his right eye, and traced its way across his cheek and forehead, fading gently as the fractured lines reached his jaw. Though they never seemed to move, those who watched the man closely claimed the shadowy veins were different from day to day, sometimes darker, sometimes wider, sometimes reaching all the way across his face and down his neck.

As for Volent, he was silent about his face, and the origin of his pain—as he was about most things. He kept the dreams to himself. Fear was never an honorable thing in a knight. Henri made a practice of creating fear in other men, and his numb face and quiet voice never betrayed the terror that crept beneath his skin.

Finally, the wide door to the great hall groaned open, and a wave of smoke billowed into the hallway. The duke was in the middle of one of his sessions, apparently. The smoke smelled of frairwood and damp grass, spicy and thick. A servant, his eyes watering, motioned for him to come inside.

"Sir Volent," he said, nodding, "his lordship awaits."

Henri Volent did not acknowledge the man, did not bow or nod, but walked briskly into the chamber. As he entered, a knight of the winter sun passed him on the way out. Her face was ruddy, the skin across her cheekbones pocked and red, as though she had recently been burned. The locks of her hair was twisted and crisp. As she passed, the knight gave Volent the barest of glances. Her eyes glittered copper and red.

The servant shut the door, trapping them with the smoke.

The duke of Greenhall sat at the center of the room, attended by a priest. His scryers, men of the Celestial church who had taken vows to Lord Cinder in his aspect as visionary, stood around a fire pit at his feet. Plumes wafted out of the pit, the fire stoked flameless, and the men talked in hushed tones. They waved their hands through the smoke, swirling curls in the air with their fingers as they made the holy signs of the gray lord.

Volent stopped at a respectful distance and dropped to one knee, peering at the floor but listening intently.

"Enough of that," Gabriel Halverdt said, waving his hand and fanning the smoke away from his face. "I have heard your signs and seen your scryings, old man. You didn't warn me of this, did you? It took a vow knight from Lady Strife to do that, and still there were eight lives lost—and during the Allfire, no less.

"What am I to make of that?"

"My lord, you must understand," the priest responded, "the sight of Cinder extends only so far and so clearly. His vision is best used for decisions, for clarity of thought, for reasonable—"

"I've had enough of being reasonable, Frair Julian." Halverdt flicked his cloak irritably over his knees, as if he was cold despite the stuffy, incense-choked air, and rested his head on one meaty fist. "As I have of your excuses. I bring you here to scry my life, to protect my realm. I expect more than this."

"It is summer, my lord, and the days are long. Lord Cinder's rule does not begin for nearly three months. Until then, we must make do with what power we can glean at night." The priest bowed his head. "I am sorry."

"Sorry will not do," Halverdt said. "It will not do at all. And must we have more of that?" he complained, waving as one of the priests dropped a handful of frairwood splints on the fire. A gray cloud of smoke blossomed into the air, pluming to the ceiling. "It's hard enough to breathe in here, much less think."

"No gheist can stand the frairwood's essence, my lord." The older priest crept forward, his hands cupped before him.

"Oh, enough… fine. What do you think of that, Deadface? Do gheists fear such a foolish thing as smoke?"

Sir Volent had spent this time on one knee. He didn't mind, as there was less of the pungent smoke near the floor. At his lord's question he stood and spared the priests a glance.

"Knowledge of such things is beyond me, my lord,"

he answered. His voice, much like his face, was still and soft around the edges. The limited movement of his lips gave his words a hollow sound. "If the holy men of Cinder say it is so, then I accept their word. They have always been faithful to a certain kind of honesty."

Halverdt smiled, but the priests looked distinctly uncomfortable. With a nod, Halverdt dismissed them and turned his attention to Sir Volent. The priests crept out, making holy signs as they retreated into the shadows. One of the priests paused at the door, the hood of his robe pulled tight to his head. Volent didn't recognize the man, and he thought he knew all of Halverdt's pet priests. The priest's face appeared briefly, shaded by the hood. Sharp features, dark hair and, surprisingly, the pagan ink across his cheeks. Volent was about to stop the man when suddenly he was gone, retreating into the hallway without a sound.

"You think I waste my time with them, don't you?" Halverdt asked when the holy men were gone. He stood and stared toward his knight-marshal, awaiting the answer.

"It is not my place to say, my lord, nor is it why you called for me." Volent paused, considering. "I would not speak against the church. Nor would you."

"Nor would I, indeed," Halverdt answered, smiling. "But I don't think they're listening now, Henri. You may relax."

Volent made no move to relax, nor was he tense. He just stood there, his hands at his waist, his head slightly bowed. Halverdt laughed, his voice booming through the smoke-filled room.

"Always the lively one, my friend," he said. "Always the jester." Volent tilted his head in acknowledgement.

"The vow knight who just left, my lord. Is she the

one who rode against the gheist?" Volent asked.

"Sir Elsa LaFey, yes. She rescued that fool Blakley child and then sought to destroy the god. To an unsatisfying result, if you ask me."

"She wasn't able to destroy the demon?" Volent asked.

"No, but she wounded it, and drove it away. It took flight, and she wasn't able to keep up."

"It escaped?" Volent said. "You have to travel fast to outrun the sun."

"Travel fast or be the night, eh?" Halverdt asked with a twisted grin. "But that isn't why I have summoned you, either."

"If the gheists aren't reason enough, then I worry at your purpose."

"More than gheists haunt my forests, Henri. Peasants haunt my forests. Peasants and pagans. You know how they are—put on a black mask and some antlers, rape some women, burn the grain that's meant to keep your family alive during the winter. Idiots." Halverdt leaned against his throne, his head tilted to one side. For a moment, the duke of Greenhall looked as if he'd been hanged and was twisting on the wire, like some snared rabbit. Volent shook the image off. When Halverdt continued, his voice was far away. "They don't need their gods to ruin my mood, do they?"

"No, my lord," Volent answered as quickly as his numb lips would allow. He wanted to shake Halverdt out of this mood. The duke was dangerous when he was melancholy. Even to a favored servant.

"No, but something useful has come of it. You have heard of the matter in Gardengerry?"

"A group of pagans attacked the city's doma. Killed the priests, the celestes, and disappeared into the night. Took the bodies with them, if the reports can be believed," Volent answered. "Did Sir LaFey think this attack had something to do with that?"

"Something, indeed. Everything." Halverdt paced around his simple throne, hands clasped behind his back. His cloak, heavily embroidered and nearly thick as a tapestry, dragged on the ground behind him. The cloak had been a gift from the holy Gaston LeBrieure, celestriarch of the church. Halverdt wore it as a symbol of his piety, and a ward against the shadows in the corners and the pagans at his gate. "Did you pass the bodies on your way in? Did you count their number?"

"A dozen, perhaps? Maybe more?"

"Yes." Halverdt held up his fingers and began counting them off. "The five fools of House Blakley. The scout who originally sounded the alarm. Grandieu and his horse are gone or not yet found. So who are the others?" Halverdt stalked closer, a mad look in his eye. "Do you know?"

"No, my lord."

"Priests, celestes, and pagans."

"The dead of Gardengerry?" Volent asked. Even in his dead tone, there was a hint of surprise. "How is that possible?"

"It is possible because there is more to the story than the church has been telling. That vow knight just gave me what she knew, but only if I swore to keep it quiet. The pagans who bloodied Gardengerry also summoned a gheist in the doma—it's the only answer. Few survived the attack on the town. Gardengerry is a ruin, I am told, but a farmer saw the demon as it fled. The church was quick to discredit him, but the man claimed something came out of the floor of the temple, and took the pagans and their victims with it."

"And then it came here?"

Halverdt nodded. Volent paced around the fire pit, unable to squint to keep the smoke out of his eyes. Tears streamed down his nerveless cheeks.

"But why?" he asked.

Halverdt shrugged. "The church knows nothing more about it—or they will say nothing more. I think it was just passing through. Heading north to find its pagan followers, perhaps."

Halverdt looked troubled, dragging his feet until he stopped beside the throne. Again he leaned against the stone frame, his hand resting on the carved gargoyle at its height. The carvings pre-dated House Halverdt, were older even than the Tenerran tribesmen who lived here before the last crusade had driven them out. Much of Halverdt's realm was scavenged from that forgotten past, buildings and ruins bent to the will of the Suhdrin conquerors and their Celestial church.

"Your land is full of trouble, my lord," Volent said. "The church trusts you to protect the faithful south, and that says much."

"My land is full of rebels!" Halverdt snapped, stepping forward, his face momentarily distorted in rage before he gathered himself. Turning away, he returned to his seat on the throne. "And pagans. And gheists. And *that* is why you are here."

"I am no hunter of demons," Volent answered. "You'll want a priest, my lord. Knights of the winter sun, and inquisitors to hunt the witches to their den."

"The church will do its duty, I'm sure. It's not the gheists I want you to worry about, Volent." Halverdt twisted his hands together, tapping his knuckle against his chin. "The church has asked for my patience, they have asked for my loyalty, and they have asked for my time. I have given all of it that I can. These Tenerrans bend the knee by day, and sharpen their knives at night."

"What would you have of me?" Volent asked.

"The church will send inquisitors and knights of the vow to destroy the beast, but there will be more. There will be others—an unending stream of gheists until the pagans who worship them are put down. The inquisition will question the peasants, search the forests." The duke waved a hand dismissively. "They may find something... in time."

"My lord has no patience for that?"

"Your lord does not," Halverdt said as he turned to grin at Volent. "Your lord does not require patience. Your lord has you."

Sir Volent sketched a bow and touched his forehead.

"I live to serve, my duke," he said. "What would you have me do?"

"The pagans who did this are dead, laid out like cattle in my courtyard, but they had families. They had companions, other pagans who might look favorably on what happened in Gardengerry. What happened here last night. The inquisition will ask its questions, separate the guilty from the innocent, and serve their cold revenge." Halverdt knotted his hands together, worrying the hem of his cloak. "I do not wish to wait for that."

"The demon must be traveling to its faithful," Volent offered. "Where it goes, we will find pagan blood."

"Yes, pagan blood that you must spill," Halverdt said. "I have no doubt that it was drawn here by those Tenerran bastards in the tourney camp. It's certainly no coincidence that the demon arrived the same day Blakley hung his banner outside my walls. It's like a godsdamned siege." The duke shivered despite the heat of the room and his thick cloak. His voice became murky. "Perhaps the Blakley boy was meant to draw it out and tame it. Still, I cannot act against them, not yet." His eyes cleared, and Halverdt turned his attention back to Volent. "The gheist will lead you to its witches."

"What have your priests said? Where should I start?"

"To hells with what my priests say. Start where you will, ask whomever you must. Bleed your way to an answer, Sir Volent, but don't come back here until this is solved."

"Care should be taken, my lord, to not upset the common folk..."

"The common folk can go to the quiet with the priests, and pray their way to heaven for all I care!" Halverdt shouted. He banged the flat of his palm on his throne, swirling the thick smoke of the air. "The common folk hide these murderers. They come to the doma on high day and pray to gheists the rest of the week. I will tolerate them no longer!"

"My lord, I think..."

"Damn you, man! Am I your lord or your bar mate, to care what you think? Find these men. Kill them! When the inquisitors of the damn church set foot in Greenhall, I will throw the heads of these pagans at their feet." He adjusted his cloak, his hands quivering. "Go, and do not return until my vengeance is settled."

Sir Volent bowed and backed away, not turning until he was by the door. The duke sat on his ancient throne, gnawing on his knuckle and staring blankly into the smoky, flameless fire at the center of the room. Clouds of gray and blue billowed around him, like a vision in the fog.

Volent went to gather his men. There was no reason to delay, no need to plan. A mission of this sort was second nature to him. When he rode out of Greenhall with his contingent of knights, the herald at Volent's side flew two flags; the three acorns of House Halverdt, above a cross in green and gold, and his own sigil, smaller. It was a field of black and a mask, white, shot through with lightning.

Like a mask of ice, shattering.

13

GWEN WAS FALLING behind her pack. She could hear their baying just beyond a copse of brambles, but she couldn't get her courser to muscle through the prickly shrubs and into the field beyond. It was driving her mad.

"Through, you ox! Through!" she yelled, kicking her horse on. "You damned broken nag, what would you do if we were pursued?" Missy, a big dapple-gray mare that was neither a broken nag nor an ox, was having none of it. She trotted along the muddy path, sniffing doubtfully at the brambles.

While Gwen was urging her horse to do something it was never going to do, the dozen riders of her hunting party caught up. They were all riding much larger horses, destriers, all in full barding to match their riders' plate-and-half. It was hardly the sort of thing to be wearing as you crashed through the forest, but the nature of the hunt called for it. Their column bristled with the dusty red metal of bloodwrought spears. Other than Gwen, the only rider in less than full armor was Frair Lucas. The priest seemed strangely at his ease, despite the danger the gheist presented.

"My lady, perhaps we have followed this trail long enough," Sir Merret said from the head of the column.

"Any god able to manifest so close to the Allfire must be too weak to bother with."

"Or too powerful to be faced," one of the men grumbled.

"Do you find your faith lacking, sirs?" Gwen asked. "Or are you simply tired of being in the saddle? Is that too much of a task for you?"

"My lady—" Merret started again. He was older than the rest, and had been in her father's service ever since Gwen could remember. He was one of the few Suhdrin knights in Adair's service.

The rest were all Tenerran, men her father had personally raised to titled rank from the various tribal villages that dotted his humble domain. The only thing that marked Sir Merret as different was his constant complaint about the dullness of Tenerran food, and his willingness to correct the baron's daughter. Not that either habit got him anywhere.

Gwen interrupted him before he was able to get any further in his excuses.

"I am sworn to protect these lands from the pagan gods," she said. "Not to protect them until it gets to be a dangerous business, or to run from the whispers of what a gheist might be without laying my own eyes on it." She gave him a stern look. "I will carry out my duty."

"Assuming you're able to defeat the demon of this bush," Frair Lucas said quietly. He was smiling and distracted, his eyes wandering from the company of knights to the forest around them.

What is he hiding, Gwen wondered, *behind that indifferent expression?*

"Frair, you are on this hunt as a courtesy to the church," Sir Merret snapped, pulling his horse level with the priest's tired-looking mare. "It's not your place to insult my lord's heir. The role of huntress is an ancient and honored tradition in the north. You would do well to offer the lady the respect she has earned."

"I'm sure her place as the daughter of Lord Adair has nothing to do with her place as huntress," the frair said, without either malice or conceit. Still, the whole company bristled.

"What are you implying?" Gwen said stiffly.

"Nothing. Simply that I have not seen you face the threats a huntress usually has to face." He smiled. "And I try never to judge someone until I've had their weight."

"How kind of you," Gwen said sharply.

"Not kind—just Cinder's nature." Lucas raised a finger, tilting his head toward the sky. "A moment, please."

"This is a dangerous task we're about, Frair. If you'd rather be having a theological discussion back at my father's castle—"

"Honestly, just one moment of silence," Lucas said. "I think…"

The baying of the hounds, once distant and filtering through the trees, switched suddenly, and Gwendolyn stood up in her saddle. They were getting closer. She looked excitedly to the knights beside her. None of them seemed afraid, and while that could well change, she was glad to see them perhaps as eager as her. Only the priest seemed discomforted.

"It's hardly a challenge if the beast comes to you, is it?" he muttered.

"I will take the hunt however Strife sees fit to give it to me," Gwen answered. "You will have your judgment shortly, priest of Cinder. Men, form on me and—"

Abruptly the copse of thorns shuddered, the tightly bound tendrils shivering loudly, and then they burst aside. In an instant the unholy creature was among them, howling.

Gwen caught barely a glimpse of it before Missy turned aside, jerking her away from the gheist. What she saw was a coiled bundle of bark and stone, loping out of the forest like a wolfhound. It was smaller than she had expected, but bristling with furious energy. Its howl was the sound of tree limbs snapping, and it had claws of stone that tore up the damp earth as it barreled past. When it was gone, the air smelled like the forest after a heavy rain.

"That is not the god I was expecting," Frair Lucas said with a tinge of disappointment.

"But a god none the less," Gwen answered, "and I mean to answer it."

"A second gheist in these woods?" Sir Merret said. "If Frair Lucas is to be believed, the tangled black creature that attacked Greenhall was seen on our borders. And now there are two."

"We can worry about the details later," Gwen said. "Merret, Hobbs, form the van. Everyone else spread out. We have to steer it away from the farms east of here. Frair Lucas, you had best stay with me."

"I wouldn't dream of being anywhere else," he answered.

"Very good. Lads, get riding."

Sir Merret drew his short hunting spear, tipped in bloodwrought iron from the forge-shrine at Hollyhaute, and rode off after the gheist, Hobbs close beside him. The other riders broke into the woods, crashing through bush and bramble with their armored mounts. Gwen waited until the sound of their passage began to fade. She turned to the priest.

"I am not used to having priests question my

ability, especially not in front of my men."

"And I am not used to huntresses dawdling over a matter of honor while a gheist escapes them," he answered.

"Have you been on many gheist hunts, frair?"

"A few," he answered, flicking his reins across his lap. "Fewer than you, I'm sure."

"I'm sure. It's convenient that you were traveling through just as the hunt was called, and that you knew what we should find out here."

"Well, apparently I was wrong about that."

"Yes," she said. There was a moment of strained silence, then she added, "Why are you here?"

Just then the hunting pack burst through the bramblewood copse, well behind their prey. The pack was Gwen's personal litter, dogs she had bred and trained from birth. They were cragshounds, the initial breeding stock a gift from House Malygris years ago as a sign of peace between the Suhdrin and Tenerran families. The dogs were broad of shoulder and long, with strong, muscular necks and jaws that could snap bone.

The pack flowed out of the forest like a tide of bright teeth and rippling fur, browns and blacks and whites flecked with mud. Without the scent they had fallen silent, but as soon as they emerged from the thorny bushes the pack raised a piercing cry that startled the priest, and filled Gwen with a thrill of laughter.

"Come, frair—the hunt demands our presence!" Gwen yelled. "We will talk later, rest assured." Then she galloped down the path after her pack. It was all she could do to keep near them.

The gheist seemed to be sticking to the path now. Merret's men had torn through already, snapping tree limbs and tearing up the sod. Gwen could see nothing of the creature's passing, but trusted in her dogs' instinct. As she rode, she assumed Lucas was somewhere behind her.

It struck Gwen as odd that the demon, after weaving through bramblewood and spearpines all morning, had suddenly taken the beaten path. The whole hunt had been a winding affair, with the riders working their way through marshy fens and around impenetrable hedges, trying to stay close to the prey and the pack.

Trees whipped past them, whistling in the breeze.

Something else started to twist through the breeze, a smell that Gwen had trouble identifying at first. Kitchens, maybe, or the close stone ceiling of the doma, during one of the holidays, when the priests swung their censers, trailing incense. She didn't give it much thought as she barreled ahead, but then the sound of her dogs took on a tone of confusion.

Before she knew it, Gwen caught up with the rest of the riders. They were milling about at the crest of a gentle hill that poked its grassy head out of the forest. Gwen pulled her courser up short, trotting until she was sitting next to Sir Merret. The knight looked concerned.

The dogs had fallen silent.

"What news, sir?" she asked. "Did we lose our prey?"

"We have not lost the prey. But I'm unsure if we should proceed, my lady," Merret answered, nodding down the hill, "on account of that."

Their vantage point gave them a good view of the surrounding forest, stretching away like a sea of leafy green. Not a hundred yards away, seemingly ahead of them on the path they had been following, was a plume of dark smoke. That was what Gwen had smelled, racing through the woods.

"A forest fire?" she asked.

"More," Sir Dobbs answered. He was a muscular, balding man. His accent was thicker than that cultivated by most of Adair's knights. "We're right on the Tallow, beyond the Highfen."

"That's a village," Gwen said. "Tallownere."

"Aye," Dobbs answered, "and listen."

Gwen had been so tuned to her pack's baying that once they were quiet, she hadn't really been listening to the rest of the forest. Now that she put her mind to it, though, she could pick out other sounds: metal clanging dully against wood, and men shouting.

"Someone else has found our gheist," Gwen offered.

"I don't think so, lass. I think our gheist has found someone else."

"What he means to say," Merret interrupted, "is that our gheist seems to have led us here."

"What? But why…"

"That line of trees, where there's the break in the canopy, do you see it?" Merret asked, pointing. Gwen saw the break clearly enough, just this side of the smoke. "That's the Tallow River, on the Suhdrin border. The border of your father's property, and the beginning of the lands of Greenhall."

"Halverdt," Dobbs muttered.

"Well, why does that matter? If those people need our help, surely the duke would want us to lend a hand, wouldn't he?"

"My blood's from around here," Dobbs muttered. "Ten generations, raised up here before there were any damn Suhdrins to speak of."

"No offense taken, Sir Dobbs," Merret said testily. "What he's trying to say is that this is a Tenerran village, Tenerran homes that are burning, and it's worth pointing out that this trouble, whatever it is, drew the attention of a gheist. They are the source of their own misfortune."

"You can't blame the people, man," Dobbs replied. "If them dying draws the eyes of the spirits…"

"That is very rarely the case," Frair Lucas said, still strangely calm. "I find it very odd, indeed."

"How do we know what's going on down there?" Gwen protested. "It could be bandits, it could be another gheist!" She took Merret's sleeve in her hand and tugged. "We don't know what could be happening to those people."

"That is a Tenerran village," he said stiffly, "in Halverdt's land, and none of our business. We are here to hunt gheists, and to protect the lands of House Adair."

"You may not feel the pull of blood, Sir Merret," Dobbs answered, "but I doubt Halverdt's men feel the same."

"I am new to these lands," Lucas said, rounding on Dobbs. "What exactly do you believe is happening below?"

"The gheist that you tracked here from Greenhall will have caused the duke much embarrassment," Merret answered for the slowly seething Dobbs. "The duke will want to assign blame for that. He will look for blood to spill."

"And he rarely cares if the blood he takes is truly guilty," Dobbs said, "as long as it is Tenerran."

"We are meant to be hunting gheists," Merret whispered into Gwen's ear, grasping her reins. "This is not our charge, my lady."

"Then perhaps it should be," Gwen snapped. She wrenched the reins from the old man's hand and spurred her horse forward. "What good is it to protect the people from mad gods, if we let them die at the hands of mad lords?" She looked among her men. They were in hunting gear. No tabards, no pennants, no colors of House Adair among them.

"Cover your faces," she said, drawing the cowl of her robe across the lower half of her features, securing it in place with a twist. "Say your prayers and follow me." With that she dove down the hill, her courser picking up speed as they reentered the forest canopy. Her pack of dogs began howling again, and followed after. The riders were close behind. She smiled and bent herself to the road in front of her.

The bridge across the Tallow came fast, little more than a clattering span of loose boards, the river itself brown and slow. By the time Gwen was across the dogs were with her, coursing around Missy's hooves and voicing their low, rolling growl. She heard her riders crash across the bridge seconds after she cleared it.

There wasn't much to the village: the low wooden wall was bound with the icons of Cinder and Strife, necessary this far from the godsroad, even at the height of the church's power. The wall surrounded a handful of small buildings. Half of the thatch roofs were on fire. The sound of yelling was much clearer now, and even from a distance she could see men moving around the village square, armor glinting. There was a great deal of screaming from what sounded like pigs in the midst of the slaughter.

A body lay in the middle of the road, just before the gate. It was a farmer, a threshing blade held across his chest. His head was caved in, pieces of skull and blood scattered across the road. She was past it before the violence of his death registered with her, Missy vaulting the fallen man's splayed limbs without a pause.

Then she was inside the wall. There was blood, such blood, and her mind reeled. Tallownere was little more than a collection of a dozen buildings clustered around a dusty common space, sprouts of browning grass in place of a lush yard, a tumbledown well of stone and graying wood. These were the saddest sort of wattle-and-daub hovels, this one on fire, that one caved in, a man's foot sticking out from the wreckage.

Two dozen soldiers stood in the courtyard. They were Halverdt's men, dressed in green and gold, armor bright under the noonday sun. They were gathered around a small group of screaming women and girls, most of them lying on the ground beside the well, their hands over their heads. A line of bodies, all men, lay on the other side of the square. Butchered. It was the screaming of the women that Gwen had mistaken for pigs.

There was nothing human left in their terror.

The dogs got there first, but didn't know what to do. They were hunting dogs, and there was nothing here to hunt. They ran around the circle of soldiers, barking excitedly, their tongues lolling. The soldiers were confused by this interruption, one of them spotting Gwen as she roared toward them. The circle parted and a man stood up from where he'd been crouched. His hands and pants were covered in blood, and a girl at his feet wasn't moving.

Gwen swung the hunting spear out from its quiver and raised it up. She wasn't thinking, wouldn't believe that what she was seeing was real, was even possible.

She drew the spear back and threw.

It slid down the man's arm, hooking into his greave and tearing flesh and chain. He roared and tore it free. Missy clattered to a stop in front of the men, trotting sideways to go around. The soldier lunged, the horse bucked, and Gwen was free of her saddle, rolling on the blood-soaked cobbles of the village square.

Her breath left her with a whump.

She tried to roll to her feet, but the impact had knocked the balance from her head, and she was reeling on one knee, struggling to stay upright while the whole world seemed to be tipping away from her. Her mask fell away, and her leg was on fire.

Then her riders were in the village. There was a great crash of metal and horse, and the remaining villagers scattered. Gwen slid away, crawling on her hands and knees to get clear of the confusion of crushing hooves and swinging blades. She found herself beside a trough and crawled over it, landing in a sty. The ground smelled, and the pigs were all dead in the mud, but at least there was no one here trying to put a spear through her head.

She watched the fight from the mud, saw Merret and Dobbs fighting side by side. One of the farmer's wives was killed by accident as she threw herself at them. Dobbs batted aside the shield of one of Halverdt's men and ran him through. One of her riders fell to a grievous wound, then another.

More than one of Halverdt's soldiers met their end, but her men were armed for the hunt, not for a sustained battle, and they were outnumbered. A knight came out of one of the burning buildings, flecks of ash on his black cloak. He had his hood thrown back, and wore no helmet. The gray locks of his hair were smeared with soot.

His face was incredibly still, as if he was watching a squabble between two children. He threw his cloak aside and drew his sword, a length of pitted metal that shivered in the light. He launched himself into the fight, and it became a murder, a slaughter of men and women and horses and dogs—whatever got in his way, even his own knights.

When Sir Merret saw him first, he yelled out.

"The Deadface!" he cried, and he backed away from the fight. The man killed Missy with a single blow across the mare's broad neck—Missy who was just standing there. Three dogs rushed him, sensing something in him that should be put down, and he cut them open like melons. Sir MaeDerry, a boy who had taken his sword and his oath just the previous summer, charged the Deadface, roaring and swinging away with that great mace of his. Halverdt's pet monster killed him with hardly a blink, MaeDerry collapsing to the mud with his belly the wrong way out, blood bubbling from his mouth.

Gwen backed herself against the side of a meager wooden building, then rolled around it, dragging her leg, though she couldn't feel it any longer. She looked it over, and found blood streaked down the torn leather of her hunting gear. Was it hers, or had it come from one of those farmers, lying out there on the yard?

Her hands were shaking with anger, with the blade-itch and hunter's rush, but she had lost her spears, and the dead-faced man was tearing through her men like the plague.

She scanned the yard for a dropped weapon.

It was the growling that brought her back. It was coming from the wrong direction, from near the wall. She looked up and saw the gheist, its hunched back of rough bark and stone quivering. It was staring at her with eyes that looked like shards of frozen sky. Its teeth were nothing more than broken rocks, a mouth full of grinding, splintered stone.

She scrambled in the hay for a fallen spear, fingers digging through cold mud, finding nothing. All she could do was watch as the beast crept toward her, stony claws sinking into the mud, a low, rolling growl vibrating from the creature's throat.

Her attention shifted as the priest's old nag stumbled into the pigsty, mud smeared across its chest. Frair Lucas slid easily from the saddle, landing smoothly between Gwen and the beast. He held up his staff, and Gwen saw that it was splintered like a tree struck by lightning. Then she noticed blood and cuts all along the frair's arms and face.

He had fought his way through.

How had he known where she was? And what sort of priest drew blood as easily as prayers?

Lucas raised what remained of the staff and started a blessing. A skein of whispering shadow gathered around his shoulders, drawn like moths to a flame, the energy slowly coalescing into a web of power. With a shout, he swung the staff toward the gheist like a fisherman throwing his line. The web of darkness settled over the beast's shoulders, dragging it to the earth.

An inquisitor. The priest was sworn to hunt pagans. Gods damn him!

"This isn't your fight, my lady," Lucas said. He kicked at the hay, and her spear hopped into the air and found its way to her hand. "Get your men out of here."

"The gheist…"

"Mine to handle," he said. "Gather your men, before you start another war."

Abruptly the web broke, snapping like taffy. The gheist loped slowly forward. Straight for Gwen. She tried to stand, but her legs wouldn't support her. She braced herself against the farm building, spear at the ready. Lucas stepped forward, putting himself between Gwen and the demon, holding the shattered staff in front of him like a dueling rod. Lucas started chanting, drawing the shadows from the sky.

The creature didn't even look at him. A stony shoulder barreled into his hip and the priest was over on his side, fighting to regain his feet as he slipped in the mud. The gheist pushed his rough snout into Gwen's face, shoving her to the ground.

She lay there, looking up at that mouth of grinding teeth, waiting for the bite. Waiting to die. She couldn't even summon the breath to scream.

The creature stared at her, eyes of frozen sky hovering inches from her face. Its breath smelled like burning moss.

Then it snuffled at her, a heavy, earthy breath equal parts growl and sigh. It raised its bark-encrusted snout and trotted off, leaping the low wall easily. It disappeared into the woods without looking back.

Lucas helped her to her feet with a skeptical eye.

"You're lucky it lost interest," he said.

"Strife be good," Gwen answered.

"Indeed." He pulled her to his horse. They had to lean on each other to keep from falling. They mounted quickly and looked around.

Gwen's men were rushing toward the gate. Many of the knights in Halverdt's colors were down, but the dead-faced man stood at their middle, blood on his sword and his face. He spotted Gwen and gave her a slow nod.

The priest whipped his mare around and barreled out of the village and over the bridge. The last of Gwen's hounds joined them, their confused barking mingling with the sounds of the river and the moans of the dead behind them. The air was thick with burning wood and the stink of slaughter.

Gwen gripped the priest tightly, squeezing her eyes shut as they hammered their way toward home.

14

MALCOLM FOLDED HIS helmet back into its box, securing the laces and padding the visor to keep the delicate scrollwork from becoming damaged. The previous day's Allfire celebration had left him feeling unsettled.

Not half as unsettled as the tempestuous environment of the tournament, the rising tide of bad feelings that were growing between Tenerrans and Suhdrins. Gabriel Halverdt was continuing to put him off, leaving him waiting in the doma, the throne room... a never-ending parade of empty chambers and offended pride. So that morning Malcolm had withdrawn his name from those who would enter the lists, though several of his knights were still planning to ride. He wasn't willing to risk it.

Something had changed in the bearing of the Suhdrin knights. Many of them whispered about the Tenerrans, even in their presence, about the gheist's pagan followers and what the demon might have been seeking. It was an ugly shift in the tournament grounds, like the heavy air that preceded a storm, or the silence of a forest when the predator was hunting.

"Are we leaving already?" Sir Dugan asked. He was standing at the tent's entrance, helmet in hand.

"Not yet." Malcolm knelt beside his trunk and began fastening the hinges. "But I would rather be ready, should we need to do so in a hurry."

"Things are getting rough out there."

"Things are always rough at the Allfire tournament. Half a city full of drunk knights, sword in one hand and cock in the other. Even the women are murderous. It's a damn miracle anyone walks out of these things with their skin intact." Malcolm stood, wincing as his knees protested. "Much less their honor," he added.

"Still, it's rougher than usual," Dugan said. "Round of the melee got called when a Tenerran boy got his skull cracked open by a gang of Suhdrin lads. His brother's looking for blood."

"Doubtless his brother will find it," Malcolm said. "His own or someone else's. Gordon, my friend, there's nothing we can hope to do about that. As long as it doesn't become anything more than back alley fights and the settling of scores."

"Big fights start in a small way," Dugan said.

"And we must do the best we can to keep things from getting out of hand. Let the boy have his revenge. If we pen him in, he'll grumble into his cup and complain to his comrades, and eventually they'll do something worse. Something organized." Malcolm ran his hands through the basin of cold water beside his bed, then rubbed the sweat out of his eyes. "Keep it small, get through the Allfire, and go home. It's the best we can hope for."

"Ian has said he will enter the lists."

Malcolm paused, his palms cupped over his eyes, cold water running down his cheeks and into his beard. He sighed as he dried his hands.

"Yes, I know. Once he faced the gheist, there

was little chance he would stand aside while others gathered glory to their names." Malcolm tossed the rag onto his bed. "The city is buzzing with his story. It couldn't be prevented."

"But you forbade it."

"Let's not pretend that was going to stop him," Malcolm said, smiling. "If anyone asks, I gave the boy my blessing."

"And if your son asks?"

Malcolm didn't answer, but the silence was enough. He finished with the basin and put on a loose tunic, the breast and sleeves of houndstooth, then buckled a blade onto his belt.

Sir Dugan shrugged to himself. "I have guards at the entrance to the tents, and more wandering the lanes. If there's trouble, we'll see it coming," he said.

"Good," Malcolm answered. "Have the men prepare to leave should things get out of hand. If Halverdt's hospitality turns sour I don't want to wait around while the lads pack their breeches."

"Yes, my lord," Dugan said. He looked as if he meant to say something more, then slipped through the tent flap and walked away.

Ian's head was still pounding. It had been several days since the gheist's attack, and he hadn't stopped drinking in that time. Regardless, on the morning of the final melee he stood on the sidelines with a mug of ale in one hand and a poultice on his head, cheering as Martin Roard was drubbed by a heavy man in a leather apron, wielding a hammer clad in wood. He wouldn't have missed Martin's humbling for anything.

When it was over and the young Roard heir had been prized out of the mud, Ian met his friend by the exit. Martin smiled shakily, but took the mug of wine he was offered, gripping it in both hands as he drank. Half his body was covered in a cold, thick smear of grime.

"That went well, my friend," Ian said.

"I felt there were good moments," Martin answered gingerly, "but I'm not fond of the ending. Could have done with less hammer."

"So have you lived the moment thoroughly enough? Did you learn something valuable from our peasant farmer with the hammer?" Ian asked.

"Yes," Martin said, wincing as he raised the mug to his lips, coughing around the bitter wine. "Don't fight a man with a hammer. I'm sure there's a bigger lesson there. Something about archers, or not getting off your horse." He grimaced at his friend. "You know, you don't have to be so damn jovial about this."

"As I recall, I was the one who said you shouldn't be in this melee to begin with, so yes, I will be as jovial as I please." Ian put an arm around Martin's shoulders, flinching back when his fingers touched cold muck. "Your current condition is the inevitable result of your poor decisions, Martin."

"Shove it in your mouth, Ian Blakley. And choke."

Ian laughed, and after a quiet moment of pained indecision, Martin joined him in a fragile chuckle. They were walking down a street already crowded with the traffic of people just arriving for the day's tournament, and those who had never bothered to find a bed the night before. The event was scheduled to start that afternoon. Most of these people would maintain a rolling drunkenness through the rest of the week, but for men like Ian and Martin—knights who intended to enter the lists—the previous night had been the final chance for celebration.

They found their way to the ladies' field, picking up a carry-breakfast of belly and eggs at a butcher's block, and trading their mugs of wine for some hot coffee. The coffee cut through the fog of their hangovers like a knife, and they took places on the benches as they ate, watching the ladies of the court going through their morning sword forms as they prepared for the gentle tournament.

"How is little Nessie?" Martin asked. "It's a pity she wasn't able to make the tournament."

"My father forbade it."

"Your father is in the habit of forbidding things," Martin observed. "What will he do when Nessie is no longer at the age where she will bend the knee so easily?"

"I believe she's at that age right now. It was Mother who convinced her to stay behind." Ian sighed. "And the tournament doesn't hold much interest for her... not yet."

"Not even the gentle tournament? She seems like she'd be good with the blade."

Ian shook his head.

"Father won't allow it," he said. Martin snorted. "Or at least he discourages it."

"Why so? It's safe enough."

"It's not a proper Tenerran practice, Martin," Ian said, rolling his eyes. "'Women of the tribes do nothing gentle.' Those were his words when Mother brought the subject up last Allfire."

"So she'll be taking up the bastard sword, then?" Martin asked. "Very good. She certainly has the figure for it."

"I don't know how to take that, Martin, so I will ignore it. It's just that Father wants us to do the proper Tenerran things. He has her studying medicines, hunting, training to the bow. He wants to promote the peace, but not at the cost of having his son learn poetry, or his daughter wearing a dress while she pretends to hunt."

"And what of Hannah Thaen, hm?" Martin sat forward and gestured to the field. The oldest daughter of Duke Ewan Thaen was just entering the field. She was dressed in her family's blue and gray, the strange padded armor of the gentle art looking more like tapestry than protection. The girls were pairing off, the metal of their target discs flashing in the sun as they began the spear stage of the competition. "She's a fine Tenerran lass, isn't she?"

"Aye, and Thyber, too, and MaeHerron and Finnen, as well. You don't have an argument from me. Besides, it's not like the men of the tribes bound themselves in metal and rode at each other with lances." Ian slumped back on the bleacher, resting his back on the step behind. "Nessie doesn't seem to mind, and it's none of my business."

"Her husband might mind," Martin noted.

"Enough of this," Ian said. "You ask too many questions about my sister. I have the right to be uncomfortable."

Martin snorted, slapping Ian on the knee.

"We'll all have to take wives eventually, Ian—even you." When Ian frowned, he quickly changed the subject. "I hear your father has ordered his men to pack. Are you leaving early?"

"I'm here for the joust," Ian said. "Father worries. That's his right, but he listens too closely to Sir Dugan. The gheist should have reminded us of our common enemy, and our common faith. Instead Dugan is jumping at shadows and fingering his knife every time a Suhdrin knight walks past."

"Some of Halverdt's men do the same when they see a Tenerran," Martin answered. "More than one idle conversation has ended with blades in bellies."

"It's the Allfire."

"It's more than that," Martin said. "Have you seen the Deadface?"

"The monster of Greenhall? No, neither hide nor hair."

"That's because he isn't here." Martin leaned forward, lowering his voice to a rough whisper. "Halverdt sent him out, the night after the gheist attack. There was too much confusion for anyone to notice. Took a full column of knights with him."

"To hunt the gheist?" Ian asked, and Martin shook his head.

"I don't think so," he answered. "That vow knight, Sir LaFey—the one who drove the demon off—did not accompany them."

"So why, then?"

Martin shrugged. "No one knows, but if it's Volent, it's dangerous business."

"Well, at least we won't have to face him in the tilting." Ian leaned back to watch the gentle tournament. "That's all I care about today." Despite his words, however, he felt his stomach twist in anticipation—though he wasn't about to let it show.

Before Martin could reply the first round of the gentle tournament began. The lines of girls danced forward, jabbing, countering with the hafts of their spears and yelling as their points struck home. One contestant was on the ground, her opponent cringing in front of a judge. Ian couldn't imagine Nessie out there, her rosy eyes watering from a spear to the belly.

"Hannah does well enough," Martin noted, drawing Ian's eye to where the girl from Frosthold was sparring with a bigger opponent who had better reach and faster feet, but less form.

"She makes better use of the length of the spear," Ian agreed, "but falls back too quickly. She must press her advantage if she's to reach the next round."

"That's probably going through her opponent's mind, as well," Martin agreed.

There were several more passes between the girls, Hannah Thaen pushing forward, blocking the counterstrike and then falling quickly back. After a couple rounds of this, her opponent began to follow up on Hannah's retreat, challenging the smaller girl with a system of rapid jabs that put Hannah on her heels.

The third time, however, Hannah didn't fall back at all. After the counterstrike, she took one step back and then set her spear. Her opponent charged forward, expecting the retreat. Hannah's spear took the girl in the chin. The judge stepped in as the girl fell.

"A rough penalty, that one," Ian said. The head was off limits.

"Perhaps, but Hannah will take the round. Her opponent will be off her game after a blow like that one." Martin leaned back and smiled. "Especially if Hannah continues to press."

"You know this because you've studied the players?"

"I know this because I've played the spear with Lady Thaen," Martin said. "A hundred times, if twice—and get your mind out of the gutter. Hannah's a proper woman."

"You've practiced the gentle art?" Ian laughed. "I imagine your father was thrilled."

"Father doesn't know. I asked too many questions of the girl after the last equinox, and she offered to show me. I have more bruises from those lessons than from years with my father's man-at-arms."

"And what's the point of that? Practice in case you're called upon to fight a legion of women?"

"Ian, you make fun of our delicate Suhdrin ways, but there's a purpose to the things we do." Martin gestured toward the field. "These women are practicing for a war that may never come, but if it *does* come, they'll be ready. That's our history. Sometimes the men all die, or are sick, or are off at war when the raiders arrive, and someone has to hold the walls."

"Those raiders were usually Tenerran tribesmen," Ian noted, "and the war more likely a crusade, with soldiers putting steel in the bellies of pagan children."

"Aye," Marcus said with a sigh. "Let us be glad that those days are behind us."

"For now," Ian agreed as lightly as he could. Then a cheer went up from the crowd. Hannah had won her match, so the judge was holding up the blue and gray of House Thaen. Martin nodded to the girl on the field and smiled, then huddled back over his mug of coffee.

"It's as I said. Know your opponent, know the fight. Win a thousand times."

"Then I'm glad you and I will never have to compete," Ian said.

"The names for the lists haven't been drawn yet, dear boy," Martin replied. "We may cross blades yet."

They both laughed.

15

THE ROOM WAS quiet. The gathered host, men and women of Adair, including Gwen and her chosen blades, remained tense in their chairs. The priest, silent since their return to the castle, sat to one side, hunched over the table at the room's center. Colm Adair sat on the Sedgewind throne, his finger tapping lightly against its arm.

"Did they see you?" he asked after a long moment.

"We put steel into their bellies," Gwen said. "So yes, I think they saw us."

There was a brief smattering of laughter around the room. The baron rose suddenly to his feet.

"Don't be a fool," Colm snapped. "You know what I mean! Did Sir Volent see your face? Does he know who rode against them? Will he be able to lay those bodies at our gate?"

"I don't..."

"Because if this ends in blood, Gwendolyn Adair, it will be the last hunt you ride. Do you understand me?"

"You can't mean to withdraw my title," Gwen hissed. "I did nothing wrong. Unless you consider it wrong to stop the slaughter of innocent peasants at the hands of a madman?"

"I consider it wrong to provoke a neighbor whose

business we barely know. The peace that stands is a fragile thing, daughter. If the cost of that peace is turning a blind eye to the Deadface's blight, then that is a price I will pay."

"I do not care for that kind of a peace," Gwen said, bristling.

"Yet you are my heir, and it's about time someone reminded you of your duty to this family, as well as to the fallen gods."

Gwen seethed at her father. Sir Hogue cleared his throat and addressed the room at large.

"Perhaps the priest can speak to this. Was Sir Volent at fault? You were there, after all."

"There's nothing I can say that will help," Frair Lucas offered quietly.

"As always, the church is silent on Halverdt's depredations. What a surprise," Hogue said sharply. Colm Adair gestured the man to silence.

"Brother priest, we appreciate your help in hunting the gheist, and your warning us of the creature from Gardengerry," the baron said, "but I'm not certain this is the business of the church."

"All business belongs to the church, in some way," Lucas said. He stood slowly, pausing to rest his hand on the table before straightening. "This business more than most. Heartsbridge would not see war between Tener and Suhdra. Not over this."

"Do you speak for the celestriarch? Can you level his condemnation against Sir Volent?" Hogue asked with a sneer.

"No, that is not my business, nor my place. I can only advise. But you have no interest in such things, so I must go."

"Wait," Colm Adair said quickly. He shot a look at

his daughter, who was sitting quietly at the corner of the table, as far from attention as she could manage. "If asked, what advice would you give?"

"Simply this," Lucas replied. "Apologize to the duke. Seek your damages through the courts of Cinder. Keep your swords in your belts."

"And stand aside when Halverdt comes north to break us, I suppose," Sir Doone said.

"If the duke marches north, you will of course have the right to defend yourself, but if the word we've had from Greenhall is true, Malcolm Blakley is there now, seeking to settle matters before they get out of hand."

"That dog likes to be petted too much," Doone complained. "How convenient that he traveled south before Volent came reaving."

"It does seem fortunate timing," Colm Adair said. "I would never accuse the church of such trickery, but Blakley finds himself in a ripe spot to settle this."

"And that troubles you?" Lucas asked.

"He may make concessions to which we would never agree, simply to keep the peace. The Reaverbane has a taste for compromise."

"You think the church planned this, then put him in place to surrender your rights, and then manufactured a situation that would force him to negotiate," Lucas suggested. He shook his head. "Halverdt and Adair have been at each other's throats for decades. There would be no need to manufacture that kind of trouble. Indeed, if Blakley steps in, you should count yourself lucky. He has the faith of the south, and the trust of the north. No man is better equipped to speak for you."

"He has never spoken for me," Adair said quietly. "Blakley has always seemed more interested in appeasing the church—and Gabriel Halverdt."

"Ah, I see," Lucas responded. "Fine. Clearly you have arrived at your own conclusions, and have no interest in what I have to say. That being the case, I will leave."

"Where will you go?" Gwen asked.

"Greenhall. My vow knight is there. I must confer with her before we decide how to proceed."

"Proceed?" Gwen asked.

"We've had three gheists within a breath of the Allfire, a time that is never troubled by such manifestations. Does that not trouble you, Huntress?"

"I find it... odd," she allowed.

"As do I," Lucas said. "My calling is to investigate odd things, so my search must continue. Be careful, Huntress. If Sir LaFey can not defeat this gheist from Gardengerry, it may find its way into your territories."

"Where it will meet its death," she answered.

"I pray you are right," he replied. "And now, gentlemen, bladewomen, I bid you good day."

Before they could respond, Frair Lucas stepped briskly away from the table and out into the hall. He was nearly at the stables when footsteps caught up with him. He turned to find a knight approaching him, a man of later years and with Suhdrin features. Sir Merret—the man who had ridden with them against the gheist.

"I was expecting Gwen Adair," Lucas said.

"You will have to make do with me," he said. "She has asked me to accompany you."

"Are you coming to protect me, or to spy on me?"

"Neither. We are merely going to the same place."

"Oh? And what business do you have in Greenhall?" Lucas asked.

"My lord thought it wise to tell the duke of

Houndhallow and the other Tenerran knights what has occurred," Merret said. "In case there's trouble."

"Oh, there will be trouble," Lucas muttered. "Very well, we ride quickly, Sir Merret, and we leave immediately."

"I would have it no other way."

Concerned as he was with Elsa's safety, Frair Lucas was determined to reach Greenhall as quickly as possible. Faced with Sir Merret's age, the priest fortified the knight as they traveled south, enabling them to steal hours from the night and keeping fatigue from man's mind. As a result, less than a week found them at the verge of their destination, staring down at its walls.

Lucas brought them to a halt.

"This is as far as we go together," he said.

"Afraid to be seen in the company of a knight of Tener?" Merret asked. The man's voice was dreamy, reflecting the effects of Lucas's magics.

"I think you have more to fear in being seen with me," Lucas answered. "No, I would rather enter the city without the duke's knowledge of where I've been. Gabriel Halverdt is a suspicious man, and will not trust any rider from the north."

"Even a priest?"

"Well, this priest at least," Lucas said. "And your business is too urgent for that. Continue on, but if asked by Halverdt's men, make no mention of me."

"What should I say to the duke of Houndhallow?"

"My opinion on that matters little," Lucas said. "You're only stirring trouble, but go, do what you must."

Merret watched him for a moment, then spurred his horse down the road. As soon as he disappeared from sight Lucas turned, riding wide and fast around the castle. Entering the forest he saw evidence of the gheist and a great battle, but could not tell who had won. Yet the castle appeared to be secure, and the city was full of merriment and life.

He reached the southern road when his ears caught an unexpected sound. He ducked among the trees and drew the shadows tight, silencing his horse and cloaking his presence.

An armed host marched down the road toward Greenhall. Lucas couldn't see as well as he hoped, but a column of soldiers, knights, and mounted men-at-arms came into sight. To his surprise they continued to pass him by for nearly an hour. They might have been traveling to join the competition, except the tournament had already begun, and from the noise coming from the city, most of the revelers already seemed to be in the pavilion ground.

When most of the host was past, a carriage rolled into view. Strong sides and arrow-slits marked it as belonging to a merchant or a lesser noble, but there were no markings on its sides, and no tabards on the guards who ringed it—men in heavy steel riding in perfect formation, their eyes keenly on the tree line, their hands couching long spears and shields, freshly scrubbed of any paint.

There were other men, too—four of them, riding in a loose circle around the wagon. They wore fine clothes, but appeared unarmed and without armor. One of them drifted close to where Lucas was hiding. As he got near, the man paused and tilted his head in the frair's direction.

Lucas slid deeper into the naether, shivering as his flesh disappeared from the realm of blood. As soon as he did this, he recognized his own mistake.

These men wore naetheric armor.

The nearest man began to scan the forest, lines of naetheric force dancing through the trees. He was searching for a gheist, and not a brother of Cinder, so Lucas remained undetected.

The wagon and its guard came to a halt. After a moment, the door opened, and a man leaned out. He was simply dressed, wearing nothing fine, nothing sacred. He called out in a voice that demanded service.

"What's the matter?" he called. "We can't fall much further behind without drawing attention."

"Nothing, my holy," the closest man said. "Thought I sensed a gheist, yet the forests seem clean."

"There are no gods in these woods," the man answered. "At least, none we don't hold." He chuckled and reentered the cabin, then shut the door. After a moment the caravan continued on its way.

After they were gone, Lucas released his bindings. He would have to circle around the city and find another way in. Lucas had no interest in following in the wake of that man or his hidden army.

Lucas knew the voice of Tomas Sacombre, high inquisitor of Cinder when he heard it.

16

MALCOLM COULD SEE Ian watching the gentle tourney, his head bent in conversation with Lorien Roard's oldest son. Martin, that was the boy's name. Malcolm couldn't help but wonder what would become of their friendship, should Suhdra and Tener fall to warring. He had faced one-time friends on the battlefield, had even put the blade through their bellies when they wouldn't yield.

He hoped to spare Ian the same pain.

"Your son?" asked a voice behind him. He stood and turned.

The vow knight, Sir Elsa LaFey, who with him had ridden out against the gheist nearly a week ago, stood in the shade of a nearby tent. Her hair was growing back, the sides and back still rough stubble, the top unkempt where she had trimmed away the charred curls. Her cheekbones were pockmarked and raw. She was wearing informal robes in the red and gold of her order, hands resting loosely on the pommel of her sword.

"Yes, it is," Malcolm answered. "He's more comfortable in the south than I will ever be, I'm afraid. Hard to convince a child of the value of winter when he's just reaching the heart of his own spring."

"He'll come around," LaFey said. "It's natural for

children to covet what they don't have. I went through a northern phase, myself."

"Yes?"

LaFey nodded, a twist of a smile on her lips. "I spent a year as ward to a baron in the far north, Allfire to Allfire. Swanston. Do you know him?"

"Yes, of course, and I'd imagine you had a rough year. Lord Swanston's domain is mostly rocks and iron trees. Fogdeep, isn't that the name of his little castle? Quite a change from Suhdra."

LaFey shrugged.

"I found it invigorating. My family is from the Spear. I wouldn't call it a soft life, but," she shrugged again, "I didn't have a difficult childhood. You're right, though. Fogdeep was carved from a harsh realm, held together by the people and their bonds. Family. Honor." She nodded at the memory. "It was a good year."

"How did a daughter of Suhdra end up as ward to a backwater barony in Tener?" Malcolm asked. "It takes some effort to imagine you, a frail Suhdrin lass, wrapped in furs and howling at the moon."

LaFey chuckled, clasping Malcolm by the shoulder and turning him down the street. They walked together.

"I had my oldest sister to thank. She fell in love with one of Swanston's iron-hard sons. They married, and his father expected them to live in Fogdeep and raise iron-hard sons of their own, but Millie wouldn't have it. So I went in her stead, as an act of good faith between the families."

"You were there only a year?" Malcolm asked.

LaFey's face grew still. "Yes. Millicent died— in childbirth. An iron-hard son, after all. Too hard for Suhdrin flesh. Her husband was heartbroken.

Couldn't face the south without his wife, so he came home. Then he couldn't face the sight of me in his halls. Too much like my sister." She clapped her hands. "But I found a love for winter. It was in Fogdeep that I decided to swear to the order of the winter sun."

"Well, I'm glad you did," he replied, "and I'm glad to see you again. I wanted to thank you for helping me the other day. Ian gets in over his head too often, and too quickly for anything to be done about it. Without your help he might well be dead."

"It was an honor to ride into battle with the Reaverbane," she said with a smile. Malcolm made a dismissive gesture, moving the conversation hurriedly on.

"You came to Greenhall with a warning about the gheist," he said. "How did you know?"

"My frair and I were drawn to Gardengerry by a scryer's warning. When we found the town mostly destroyed, he sent me on to warn the duke of Greenhall, while he tracked the demon through the woods."

"Yet the gheist arrived before you. And your frair?"

"Elsewhere. He sent a messenger, saying that he's tracking another gheist north as we speak. From what I've seen of the aftermath of your son's heroism, our gheist is moving in that direction, as well. Hopefully nothing will come of that, but it's troubling." LaFey paused at an intersection, staring down toward the tournament grounds. "Whatever drew that creature to Gardengerry, it was no natural manifestation. Someone had to summon it."

"And now it travels north," Malcolm said.

"Yes, into Tener. Into pagan lands."

"You've lived among us," Malcolm said. "You know we're faithful to the church. Even in Fogdeep, as far from Heartsbridge as you can imagine, I'm sure

Swanston sang the evensong and bent his knee at the doma's altar."

"Yes," LaFey agreed, "but there was always something more. Something beyond the walls, among the trees. Something lurking in the night."

"The old gods remain, as well you know. Your life is dedicated to controlling them. Just because they live, however, it doesn't mean the forests are filled with witches and shamans." Malcolm took the vow knight by the elbow, turning her toward him. "There's enough mistrust between our countries, Sir LaFey. We can't let these suspicions persist."

"No, you're right," LaFey agreed. "Even so, someone drew that gheist toward the city, and someone is drawing it north, like a lodestone to iron."

"Drawing it north, or driving it there," he said. "There are pagan hearts in Suhdra, as well."

"Few enough, though—the inquisition sees to that. Perhaps if the church of Cinder had free rein in the north…"

"You and I both know what would come of that," Malcolm said tightly. "Witch hunts and chaos."

"Yet those are appropriate, Duke, when you are hunting witches," she said.

"You would be finding witches everywhere you looked, I'm afraid," he countered, "no matter how faithful your victims might be."

"Now who's letting suspicion cloud his mind?" LaFey asked, her smile sharp and cold.

The tournament horn sounded below. Malcolm and Elsa stood silently, measuring each other, waiting.

"My son is riding in the lists," he said. "I'm afraid I must—"

He stopped at the sound of running feet, as Sir

Dugan hurried up to the duke, his face flushed from the exertion. He pulled Malcolm away from Sir LaFey.

"What's gotten into you, Gordon?" Malcolm asked. "My apologies, my lady," he said over his shoulder. "Some Tenerrans can't seem to learn even the most basic of courtly manners."

"Never you mind manners," Dugan hissed. "We need to speak... *alone*."

"Oh?" Malcolm said, turning to his master of guard. "What of?"

"There's been a problem."

"With Ian?"

"Not yet. No, it's..." Dugan looked over Malcolm's shoulder, but LaFey was already marching away, her sword and cloak swinging through the lane. "It's something with the Deadface, my lord. Sir Volent and the young Adair huntress have tangled."

"Meaning..."

The horn sounded again, and the crowd gave out a cheer. Sir Dugan looked nervously down the road toward the arena.

"Never mind. We have to hurry, my lord, before something dangerous happens. I will explain on the way."

17

IAN MADE HIS way to the tourney entrance, where a crowd was gathered to examine the matchups. Nervousness dancing in his stomach, he scanned the board to find his banner, the Blakley hound, black on white, with the crest of spring leaves that indicated his rank in the family. First son, last son, only son.

Sir Baird was waiting for him. The tall knight, his curly hair laced with braids heavy with fetishes that reached down to the middle of his back, smiled broadly as Ian approached.

"There you are, lad," Sir Baird said, pointing at the board. Ian's name and heraldry were posted near the bottom. Across from him was the black spear and red rose of House Marchand, a garter of vines around it to indicate the youngest son.

"Young Andre Marchand," Ian said. "He's old enough to joust?"

"He's your age, m'lord. He's just... small. Looks like they're matching up the heroes of the gheist fight."

"Andre didn't ride against the demon," Ian said. "It was his father, and old Gair turned tail as soon as the beast showed its teeth."

Baird glanced around nervously, but no one seemed to have heard.

"The people don't know the difference," he said, his voice low. "Andre will wear some favor on his spear, blessed by the church. The crowd will roar with holy vigor." Baird shrugged. "A good show, if not entirely true."

"As long as the crowd stays for the joust, and we give them the good show they expect," Ian said, "Andre can claim any blessing he likes."

"Aye, well, let's get you prepared. Won't do for the true hero of the gheist to fall to some coward's youngest whelp."

They made their way to the stable yard where the Blakley mounts were kept. The nerves in Ian's belly were getting worse. He tried to focus on the simple tasks of putting on his armor, securing his saddle, checking each strap and buckle and harness until he was sure everything was in place. Then he went over them all again.

He was so engrossed in his preparations that he didn't notice the growing tension in the crowds that passed by the stables. When he looked up, small groups of Tenerrans gathered here and there, carrying weapons and wearing armor. The Celestial guards had organized into larger groups, abandoning some of their posts to muster in greater numbers elsewhere. The majority of Suhdrin in the streets walked with grim expressions. Whispers filled the air.

Sir Baird pulled one of the attendants aside and sent him to find out what was going on. When the stable boy returned, his face was pale.

"Sir Volent has returned to Greenhall," the boy said.

"What of it? Does he mean to join the joust?" Baird asked.

Ian listened for the reply. It was several heartbeats in coming.

"No, my lord, but there has been a fight. The men he rode out with… there are a great deal fewer of them."

"Was there another gheist?"

"No, well, I mean, yes. A gheist was seen, but it didn't attack the column."

"Then what? Gods, boy, speak on! It's enough to make a man insane."

"Word is that it was Gwendolyn Adair who attacked them, while Volent and his men were questioning some pagans. Adair's men ambushed them, disguised as pagan rebels. Volent lost over half his number."

This drew Ian's attention. He knew Gwen well, though she was a few years older than him, and rarely gave time to the social pleasantries that occurred between young men and women of noble standing.

"Gwen attacked the Deadface?" he asked. "You're sure of that?"

"That's the word going around the tourney, my lord," the boy said. "They say there were gheists in her hunting pack. The demons led her to Volent's men, and drank the blood of those what fell."

"Well, that's a load of horse shit," Ian said. "Gwen is their huntress. She wouldn't be riding with gheists."

"Again, my lord, the people will care little for the details," Sir Baird said. He paused, and looked around. "No wonder everyone is on edge. There will be blood in the street before nightfall, if even half of it is true."

"None of it has to be true," a voice said from nearby—it was a knight. Ian recognized him as one of Lord MaeHerron's men, though he couldn't conjure his name. "The story will be enough to spill blood. The church guards are making plans to sweep the streets at the first sign of trouble."

"That will solve everything," Baird said. "Tener and Suhdra are putting swords into each other, and then the church starts drawing steel, as well." He spat angrily. "One thing's for certain." He turned to Ian. "You can't ride the joust, my lord."

"What?" Ian asked. "Why not?"

"Tempers are too high. Every joust between Tenerran and Suhdrin has the potential for riot. We'll have to concede the pennant." Baird started disassembling the trappings on the caparison on Ian's horse.

Ian stopped him.

"Like hell we will," he growled. "The Marchands aren't suddenly going to put steel tips on their lances, are they?"

"No, my lord, but…"

"Then I will not shrink from the lists." He climbed slowly up the mounting block. After a second's hesitation, his attendants hurried to help him.

"Your father has already ordered the men to pack, in preparation for a quick departure," Baird said. "He will want us to leave. Immediately."

"If that is his will, he can tell me himself."

"My lord—" Baird started again, as Ian settled into his saddle and put on his helmet.

"Enough, sir. I mean to ride."

With Sir Baird sputtering behind him, Ian guided his horse out of the stable ground and toward the jousting yard. The nervous fire in his belly was little calmed by the hordes of spectators and the loose knots of Suhdrin men-at-arms glaring at him suspiciously.

The air around the jousting arena smelled like hot

metal and horse shit, the breath he sucked through the narrow slit in his helmet hardly enough to fill his lungs. Ian tried to relax into the saddle, to center himself on the horse, but he kept swaying back and forth dangerously as he cantered into the yard. The tip of his lance caught against one of the overhanging banners, startling him, and he almost dropped it.

Sweat drenched the padded undercloth of his chest. The low murmur of the crowd was muted through the steel of his helm. A hand clasped his leg, and Ian flinched away, nearly toppling out of the saddle.

"Settle, lad. Just settle," Sir Baird said. Ian twisted around in his saddle to try to see him, but the constraint of the jousting kit wouldn't allow it. "There's nothing to this, but it won't help if you fall into the sand. Keep an eye on your target, another on his lance, and both eyes on your horse. And watch the crowd."

"That's more eyes than I have, Sir Baird." Ian's vision began to swim in the heat of the tight helm. Sweat stung his eyes, and the blood pounding through his head was beginning to make him dizzy. "I think I'll just focus on not falling off the horse."

"Gods hope you can, boy. I'll be serving as your second." Sir Baird gave his horse a pat. "Wouldn't want to explain to your father why his son got beaten to a pulp in a tournament he wasn't supposed to ride."

Ian nodded, and Baird slapped him once on the leg and pushed him toward the lists. The crowd gave an appreciative roar as he appeared out of the stable ground, and he raised his lance in salute. Even through the helm, their cry sounded like the grinding tide of the ocean, beating against the black cliffs of Frosthold. Ian twisted back and forth in the saddle, trying to see the people, the pageantry... hell, even the nobles' booth, so he knew where to salute when the time came. A ripple of laughter went up, and he realized how ridiculous he must look.

How did his father manage it? How did *any* of the knights manage, when all they had was this tiny little slit of air? If only...

Ian paused, cursing himself for a fool. Balancing his lance on his stirrup and resting it against his shoulder, he reached up and torqued the clasp on his helm, then threw his visor open and breathed in a healthy lungful of fresh air. Ringlets of sweat-drenched hair tumbled down his cheeks. His face was red with embarrassment and the stifling heat.

The crowd rose to their feet in laughter and applause. Ian gave another good-natured salute, trying to stay calm under the gaze of so many people. Oddly, there was no one in the opposite list. Andre Marchand was either still struggling with his horse, or had decided against showing up at all. The grass of the field was already torn from the first few matches, and there was a spray of blood on the wooden boards of the tilt gate.

A horn drew his attention back to the crowd. The herald of the tourney came out from beneath the Celestial box, the tournament scroll in hand. He addressed the crowd, bowed in the direction of the distant Celestial dome in Heartsbridge to acknowledge the holiday, and finally to Ian himself, commending the results of the tournament to Strife's good blessings, and Cinder's just eye. One of the priests in the box said something Ian couldn't hear, and the herald nodded.

He addressed the crowd, but his words were lost in the din of Ian's close helm. The spectators seemed enthused—

their cheering made Ian's head hurt even more.

When the cheering faded away, the herald continued.

"I have read the histories and blessed the match!" he said. "Is the young Marchand not present to defend his honor?"

The crowd waited anxiously, a murmur rising up. Ian chewed his lip nervously. Then there was some movement from the stables opposite. The crowd rippled in anticipation.

A knight rode into the stadium.

He was wearing Marchand's colors, but where Andre was slight and supple, this man was nearly the size of the horse he rode. His armor was well dented, his tabard faded with wear, and the horse bore scars across his nose and flanks. Ian whistled, low and long.

"Andre went through a bit of a growth spurt, eh?" he murmured. There was frantic whispering behind him, and he twisted in his saddle to see Sir Baird, joined by Sir Dugan. They were gesturing for him to return to the stable yard.

Ian shook his head and turned to face his opponent.

The knight lowered his helm and gave Ian the slightest nod. Then he turned to the herald and spoke.

"Graceful Andre Marchand must forfeit his place in the tournament, as his good and godly duties have called him back to Highhope," the knight said, "but I shall serve in his stead."

"Chev Bourdais, your name is already entered for another battle," the herald said.

"Then strike it. For the honor of my master, the Marchand name must advance."

Ian frowned. Chev Bourdais was Marchand's master of guard, and a familiar figure at the joust.

He had ridden beside Sir Grandieu in many battles, ridden beside Ian's father in many more.

It wasn't going to be a fair fight.

For a long moment no one spoke. The herald was the first to recover. He made the annotations in his scroll and signaled to the attendants, who gathered the Bourdais banner and removed it from the standings. Then the crowd was on their feet, arguing among themselves, and in the box above the priests appeared to be in a hot discussion with a group of new arrivals, these in the colors of the church guard.

Finally, a priest came forward—the one with whom the herald had consulted.

"Lord Ian Blakley of Houndhallow, son of Malcolm, will you accept the challenge that has been presented?" he asked.

Sir Bourdais rode across the lists. Two servants ran out to his side, offering him assistance. Ian knew he had the right to refuse such a change in opponent.

"I accept," he said weakly. When no one reacted, he cleared his throat and said it again, this time at the top of his lungs. "I accept the challenge!"

"Then so be it. Gentlemen, ride for glory. May the bright lady watch you, and the gray lord judge your worth!"

A cheer went up through the crowd, and Ian felt a great warmth fill his blood. Chev Bourdais lowered his helm and surged down the tiltyard, his horse hammering forward, his lance held high and straight. Shocked into action, Ian slammed his spurs into his horse's flank, then nearly fell out of the saddle when the destrier jumped forward. It took a stride or two to right himself, his lance bouncing high in the air.

He quickly settled into his saddle and couched the lance more steadily against his side, lining it up with the oncoming knight. Bourdais was already dipping his lance, timing the descent of the tip to intersect with Ian's charge at just the perfect moment.

The wild gallop of Ian's charger made control difficult, but he brought his tip down—perhaps too quickly, perhaps too slow. It went low and danced off the gate, crossing Ian's body. He pulled it tight and re-centered it on Bourdais' shield, but the moment was past.

Thunder burst across his face and a force like a hammer's fall jerked his head around, throwing him skull-first out of the saddle. Bourdais' lance had struck home, a blow to Ian's head. Whether his opponent's target was intentional or just bad luck didn't matter. The pain was the same.

Ian landed on stone-hard sand, bouncing once and then rolling over. The air left him, and blood and sweat filled his mouth and clouded his eyes. He lay there, gasping for air that wouldn't come, his skull ringing like a bell, blood in his eyes.

Someone took him by the shoulder and pulled him up. Ian's gasps for breath were replaced by wrenching pain and he vomited hot bile against the grill of his helm. The stink was overwhelming as it slithered down his chin, and he pulled free and went to his knees, heaving. Finally, spew-tainted air tore into his mouth. Numbly, he tried to undo his visor to clear the vomit from his face.

"No, lad," Baird yelled, and it was the first sound Ian heard, full of fear and anger. The man slapped Ian's weak hand away from his head. The force of the blow dumped Ian onto his butt, sending jolting pain through his back and neck. "Keep that damn thing on!"

Ian squinted through his visor. There was sand in his eyes, smeared with blood. He couldn't make the shapes around him assemble into a coherent world. His first clear thought was that he was probably badly hurt, and he wondered if his skull was split. There was certainly enough blood for that. He raised his hands to see if they still worked, since he couldn't really feel them, and was surprised to see that they, too, were covered in blood and grit.

His blood? Probably.

Sir Baird grabbed him by the shoulder and hauled him to his feet. Dizziness swept over him, and the tide of bile in his throat came up and spattered against the inside of his helmet once again, but he didn't fall. Instead, Ian staggered against the fence and held it in both arms. There were other sounds now creeping through the bell in his skull. The crowd, perhaps, or the herald. And drums. Ian could hear drums.

Or something else. Hoofbeats?

He looked up.

Chev Bourdais was charging at him again. He had abandoned his lance, which was probably in splinters anyway, and bore down with an iron mace in hand. The rest of the world was a blur of color and sound. Sir Baird stood between them, a heavy wooden shield grasped in both hands. It was the size of a door, and just as thick. Bourdais rode around it smartly and wheeled in place. The iron-shod hooves of the horse cut the air around Ian's head.

He tucked and rolled behind Baird's shield, just as the horse landed and Bourdais struck.

The mace went wide, beginning a game of dodge that Ian was barely fit to play. Bourdais wheeled and struck, wheeled and struck, the heavy iron head of the mace shattering splinters off the shield each time it came down. Ian kept moving to stay behind the shield, and, under its massive weight, Sir Baird was straining to keep them both safe. It wasn't long before he was dragging the bottom of the shield in the sand.

A cry arose from the crowd, and Bourdais glanced up. He yelled out, took one last strike at the shield, and then whirled away from the pair.

Ian fell to one knee, and Sir Baird collapsed to the ground, the remnants of the shield sliding over him as he fell. Ian watched as Marchand's master of guard retreated to his end of the tiltyard. Several men-at-arms waited there, with the black spear and red rose of Marchand on their chests, wearing chain and armed with long spears. They looked terrified as the knight slipped between them and disappeared.

Bourdais had just tried to kill him.

Why are they afraid?

A sound beat that thought from his head—the sound of horns and terrified cries from the crowd. Some of the spectators bolted, creating chaos and confusion. Ian turned.

Malcolm Blakley stood at the center of a group of soldiers, men and women dressed in a motley of colors from the various lords of the north. Finnen and MaeHerron, Thaen and Lann and Dougal, even a knight from the Fen Gate. Sir Dugan flanked the lord of Houndhallow. They marched onto the jousting field with swords drawn.

"Did you draw blood?" Malcolm asked. Ian blinked up at him unbelieving, trying to understand the question. "Are you listening, boy? Did you draw his blood?"

"I imagine not, unless he tore a blister on his palm from beating me."

"Gods be good," Malcolm said. He looked at those who stood around him. "Disperse to your masters.

Gather your knights and your ladies, and flee the city. Engage no one. Fight only to defend yourselves."

"There's Adair blood in the dirt," the man from the Fen Gate spat. "They've killed good knights." His clothes were dusty from the road, and sweat streaked his face. "We must form a council of war, and…"

"We must do no such thing," Malcolm snapped. "Not today. Not here on the tournament ground, with the fire of the bright lady still in our veins. Half of our men are too drunk to count the months, much less declare war." He spun back to his son. "Count yourself lucky that you didn't kill that fool."

"Kill? Father, I barely escaped with my life." Ian struggled to his feet. "If not for Sir Baird…"

"If Sir Baird had done his proper duty, you wouldn't have been on this field at all." Malcolm shot the knight a sharp look, then turned to the soldiers, who were still lingering in the duke's shadow. "You have your orders. Go. Get out of the city. The truth of this will be found soon enough."

"My lord, we mean to escort you back to your pavilion." One of the soldiers gestured with his sword. "To ensure that the Suhdrin dogs…"

"Go!" Malcolm bellowed. He drew his own blade, the song of its edge ringing out above the arguing crowd, the dark feyiron blade as black as night. "Before it's your own blood I'm spilling!"

The men hesitated, but slowly moved into the stands.

The crowd was up in arms. Friends of those who had been trampled in the initial panic drew steel, which caused others to follow suit. Yet no one moved, the spectators looking at one another drunkenly, wondering who would strike first without wondering as to why.

As the line of Tenerran soldiers marched toward

them, some took it as a military advance. Drunken Suhdrin merchants hurled themselves at the Tenerrans; others ran for their lives, howling about rebellion and armed pagans in the tournament grounds. The Tenerrans didn't hold back, cutting their way free of the press. It wasn't long before the screams were radiating out from the arena, spreading like wildfire through the tourney grounds.

"Gods *damn* them," Malcolm growled. Sir Baird and Sir Dugan stood warily at his side, watching the chaos unfold. "Halverdt won't even have to excuse his monster's actions. They'll have a war by dawn."

"They already have it," the man from the Fen Gate said, lurking in Malcolm's shadow. They turned to him. "The Deadface declared it, with or without his master's word."

"What's this I hear about Gwendolyn Adair ambushing Volent's men by the Tallow?" Malcolm asked.

The man shrugged. "She did what she felt was best, to save the lives of the innocent."

"The lives of the innocent?" Malcolm loomed over the man, veins standing out on his neck and forehead. "Do you know how many innocent lives will be lost if there's war? The harvest is nearly upon us! What happens to the crops if we pluck the farmers from their fields? If Halverdt's armies burn their way through our wheat and slaughter the cows to feed their fighters? How many children will starve under Cinder's judgment this winter?"

"A tragedy," the knight said, "but their blood will be on Halverdt's head, not Adair's."

Malcolm peered silently at the man for a long moment, fist clenched, and it appeared as if he might strike him.

"Get out of my sight!" he yelled. "Return to the Fen Gate, and pray that we can make peace before the season turns."

"My lord, sending this man out into the tournament grounds will be his death," Sir Dugan said. "He has ridden day and night to reach us, his horse is spent. He doesn't have the luxury of flight. His face is known to Halverdt's men. They will kill him before night falls."

Malcolm paused, glaring.

"What is your name?"

"Sir Alliet Merret," the man said.

"A Suhdrin name."

"I am sworn to Colm Adair. I rode with his daughter into the fight at the Tallow."

"Then we have you to thank for this mess," Malcolm said.

"He was slaughtering them like pigs... women and children! Would you have done less?"

"We will discuss that later," Malcolm said. "Take off your tabard and cover your head. You will ride north with us."

"I will not hide my colors," Merret said.

"Then die here, for no reason," Malcolm replied. He strode off, marching straight for the stables. "Baird, Dugan, with me." The two knights hesitated, then rushed after their master. Ian was left alone on the field with Sir Merret.

"Your father is a hard man," Merret said.

"Did you expect something less from the Reaverbane?"

"No, I suppose not," Merret said. He looked out at the roiling crowd. The paths cut by the Tenerran soldiers closed and were replaced with Suhdrin blades and Suhdrin faces. "This is not how I planned to die."

"Then come with us," Ian said. "You can't serve Gwen Adair with your blood feeding this field."

"Aye," Merret said sadly. "I suppose."

He pulled his tabard free and dropped it to the ground, then the two of them hurried after the duke. Malcolm huffed at his son.

"Gathered enough glory?" he snapped.

"There was nothing glorious about that," Ian said.

"No, there wasn't," Malcolm said. Then he hurried on, blade in hand, loyal knights on either side and the ring of battle in the air.

The city fell into madness around them.

2

BLOOD AND IRON

AGAINST THE NIGHT

18

THE GHEIST WAS perched among the ruins of the village, its stony head alert to any sound. It stood like a statue in the square. All around, the many bodies of the dead were cloaked with flies and decay. The fires had long since burned out. Of the buildings and walls, only ashes remained. Here and there portions of the wall remained standing.

"So this is what remains of Tallownere," Elsa murmured grimly. She stood shielded by a tree several feet behind Frair Lucas, only her head peeking out. The frair crouched much closer to the river's bank. The shadows of the forest clung to him like spider webs, bending and stretching to cloak his physical form. If Elsa hadn't known where the older man was, she could easily have looked past him.

"That is what she called it, our huntress of Adair." She heard Lucas's knees creak as he stood. "Let's have a closer look."

"What of the gheist?"

"We'll have a look at it, too."

Some portion of the bridge remained. Lucas ghosted across it, his body tucked securely into the naetherealm from which the faithful of Cinder drew their power. His toes raised puffs of dust each time they touched the charred wood of the bridge. The dappled light of the road passed through him like sunbeams in a dusty church.

The gheist saw him approach. When his heels settled into the mud beyond the bridge, the demon let out a growl and moved to the entrance to the village.

"So much for the silent approach," Lucas said. "You may find your way across, Sir LaFey."

Elsa stepped from the tree and walked down the road. Her divine armor clanked and rattled, her sword slapping against the meat of her thigh. She stopped at the edge of the broken bridge, staring down the gheist.

"Glad to have that done," she said. "Not sure I could have managed quiet, anyway." Elsa lifted her sword and drew a line in front of her. A beam of light as bright and golden as the sun split the air at her feet. She stepped into it and, with a flicker, blinked over the slowly rolling Tallow. Her form stretched thin, snapping forward like a whip, leaving a dazzle of sparks in her wake. When she landed next to Lucas it was with a crack as the air cooked off. A wave of heat and the smell of burning dust rolled off her sizzling armor.

"Why isn't it running?" she asked. The gheist awaited them, pacing back and forth, hackles of bark and stone bristling as the priests and the vow knight approached.

"That is one of many questions, Sir LaFey." With the butt of his staff Lucas dug a divot in the hard soil of the road. "There's no hint of pagan sanctity here: nothing to draw a gheist of this size, and certainly nothing that would keep it around. So why has it remained, rather than dissipating once the residents were gone? If they were pagans, as this duke, Halverdt, would have us believe, then their deaths would end their worship. Thus, no gheist."

"Then rather than being summoned," Elsa said, "it came to be here naturally."

"As do most gheists," Lucas said, nodding his head. "Drawn to ancient sites by the memory of worship, or following the patterns of nature that led to their birth." He drew his staff along the ground. "Ley lines, the scryers call them. The original pagans built their altars where the gods already were, after all. Yet there's nothing particularly holy about this place."

Elsa sniffed, twisting her hand around the grip of her sword.

"So what, then?" she asked.

"Perhaps this is a new god, or an ancient one that even the pagans never knew." He frowned.

Elsa grunted.

"Why are we wasting time talking about this?" she asked. "Our duty is to the church. To kill this demon and free the land from its murderous blight."

"Because there is more happening here, sir, than is apparent," Lucas answered. "This gheist could have killed Gwen Adair, but did not strike the blow." He gestured around them. "And the destruction you see here was not delivered by its hand." Bones and broken wood stuck through the grim layer of ash. He turned his attention back to the demon. "Why did you bring us here, young hound? What drew you? What birthed you?"

The gheist's pacing took it back to the scorched stone ring of the village well. It kept one stone-dark eye on Lucas and Elsa. Its back rippled muscularly with each step, the jagged claws of its feet tearing up the ground. The stone and bark that made up its skin flexed like scales.

"This is not the gheist from Gardengerry," Elsa said.

"No," the frair agreed. "Which is disturbing. The god I was tracking crossed paths with this one, but did not spawn it. Yet even one gheist on the Allfire is unprecedented. Two is unthinkable." Lucas drew a silver chain from his robes, the links hung with icons of the winter faith, and started the slow invocation of discernment. "How many more might be waiting in the forests of the north?"

"Why did the huntress of Adair fail to kill this one?" LaFey said.

"She was otherwise occupied," Lucas offered, then he pointed. "Someone else has been here, don't you think?" He gestured to the borders of the village. "There are fresh invocations around the wreckage."

"Pagan?"

He hesitated. The taste of the lines of power was unusual. Familiar, but twisted. They had the taint of pagan power—the organic, musty funk of earthen forces—but their construction was different. Clearer. He thought of the corruption that erupted from the bear spirit.

"I don't know," he said. "Perhaps."

"Then let's make the kill, and move on," Elsa said.

"No," Lucas said. "Engage it, but don't destroy." He finished his invocation and conjured a circular rune of naetheric energy into the air. It hung before him like a reflection in clear water, the twisting shadows of its power barely visible. "In conflict, let's see what we can learn of it."

"With joy in my heart," Elsa said. She stepped forward, drawing the invocation of Strife in the air before her with the bloodwrought tip of her sword. Each line of the invocation drifted away, shimmering with sparks of lumairien power before

222

dissipating as it reached the ground.

The light in the ashen village changed, spots of sun becoming amber-thick and bright. Elsa drew it toward her. Lines of light and power stretched like tar to tangle in her sword, the runes of her armor, and the glowing veins in her face and arms. A crackling pattern of golden lightning formed across her cheeks, growing from her eyes in jagged barbs of copper light.

"The lady will rise!" she yelled as she charged into combat. The gheist's reaction was sharp and fierce. It stopped pacing and planted its massive paws in the ground, facing its attacker with its broad shoulders. The rumble of its growl died.

Elsa's assault burned a furrow into the earth. She barely touched the ground as she plowed forward, the heat and fury of Strife glowing off her, like a drop of sun visiting earth—a furnace bright with will and power and hatred. The air tore behind her, the heat of her passage ripping the oxygen into thunder.

When the gheist struck, Lucas never saw it move.

It reached out and batted her aside. Its movement was so fast as to be invisible, the strike of claw, the swiftness of shoulder and leg and paw. Sir LaFey crumpled as though struck by a siege stone. She rolled through the ash and back onto her feet, straight into an easy guard position.

"It's fast," she said breathlessly.

"Observed," Lucas said. "Be careful."

"Yes," Elsa said. She circled the gheist warily. It held its ground beside the well, turning slowly to face the vow knight. "It looks like it's guarding something."

"Maybe it is," Lucas said. "If you can get on the other side, I might be able to hit it from behind."

"Stay out of this, frair. This isn't a battle of wits."

"Thank the gods," Lucas said lightly. "If it were, I wouldn't like your chances against a dog."

"Later, old man," she replied with a grimace. "You'll pay for that later." She took another half-step around her opponent, then lunged forward, launching a feint that turned into a guard when the gheist lashed out. A quick series of claw strikes batted Elsa's blade aside and scythed across her chest. The metal of her armor sang with the attack, long gashes left behind revealing bright metal under the crimson enamel.

Elsa wheeled and struck again, this time gathering the heat of the sun into her blade. She had no hope of landing a strike, but with each stroke the gheist was forced to edge away. It skittered back, heavy paws dragging through the ash. Soon she stood nearly at the side of the well.

"Is there anything in there?" Lucas asked. He began to gesture again.

"I'd love to tell you," Elsa said, "but I've got better things to do with my eyes at the moment. Have you discovered anything?"

"Not yet... not just yet," Lucas said. His hands danced around a naetheric construct hanging in the air. The shadow-tinged runes whirled and focused.

"Well—" Elsa started, but the gheist interrupted. It lunged forward, pouncing off the tiny stone wall of the well and leaping over her. She swung at it, the air whining as the forge-hot blade passed by, but the beast was too high. Landing nimbly, it ran to the far side of the tiny village and started to do a circuit, loping along the perimeter of ash that marked the boundary of the devastation.

"Coming your way," Elsa said.

"Yes, yes," Lucas answered. He clutched the

shimmering ghost of divination to his chest, twisting it small between his hands, then knelt on the ground. He watched the gheist come, loping slowly in his direction, fangs bared. "Come on, pretty one," he said. "Come closer."

At the last moment the demon charged, splitting the air with a sound like thunder, its jaws and claws flashing in the weirdly attenuated light. Even though he had watched Elsa fight the beast, it moved faster than Lucas expected.

As the gheist pounced, Frair Lucas dipped his heart into the naether. With a flicker of shadowy light he dissipated, his form falling into ribbons of twisting, purple light that broke apart as the creature passed through him.

Lucas fell into the naetherealm. Ice gripped his chest, his lungs, the pure fury of winter scouring the thin bones of his face like sleet. He took one startled breath and pushed back into the mortal world.

Where he reappeared, an icy blossom of frost burst out across the ground, lightning as white as snow and just as cold dancing through the ash—a brief, brilliant flower of cold that immediately began to melt in the summer heat. The air around his body shivered with the vacuum, his clothes were stiff with rime, and his breath was sharp with fog.

Continuing its momentum, the beast ran smoothly across the summoned ice, then turned sharply back toward Elsa.

"Are you all right?" she yelled, her eyes on the demon. The sword in her hand still shimmered with heat, the blade the color of molten iron.

"Yes, I'm fine," Lucas answered weakly. The air in his lungs was still cold, his words barbed with frost, and he shivered. "Gods, but I hate that place."

"Your god, not mine," Elsa yelled as the gheist launched a new attack. While she and the creature continued their circling dance of feint and strike and guard, Lucas summoned an icon that irised open, then flexed and bent, turning Cinder's discerning eye to the whole village. There had to be a reason the gheist had been drawn to this place.

His search found something strange. All around the village, he could see huddled forms, but these weren't the bodies of the dead. They shimmered with the purplish light of naether, their forms little more than grim outlines of human beings, head and arms and legs sketched in scribbled lines of light. They flickered like torches caught in a harsh wind as they stood around the village, moving slowly from place to place.

"Souls," Lucas whispered to himself. "The dead villagers, unless I miss my mark." Then his investigation was interrupted by a piercing scream. He was so startled by it that he banished the icon in his hands, its form dissipating like fog.

Elsa stood beside the well, one hand on the wall, the other holding the sword at an awkward angle. The gheist was on the other side, resting on its haunches. The sword looked strange, as though the tip had melted into a pulsing blob of metal. In several places around them the ash was spattered with small pools of bright light, steam hissing upward.

"What happened?" Lucas asked, rushing forward, drawing on his limited array of battle summonings. As he ran, shadowy armor appeared across his shoulders like a cowl. "Are you hurt?"

"Molten iron," Elsa gasped. She shook her sword and the strange blob spattered to the ground. The ash puffed and disintegrated at its touch. "The damn thing bleeds *iron*."

Lucas looked at the gheist. It was wounded, a broad gash across its shoulder that glowed with forge-light. The blood that leaked to the ground was, indeed, molten iron. As the frair watched a scab of throbbing red metal formed around the wound, its crust brittle and hot.

"That complicates things," Lucas said. "How do we kill it, when its very blood could kill *us*?"

"It's my mistake," Elsa said. "Trying to ease my way into the lady's graces. I should have burned bright, right from the start. Put an end to that thing."

"But you're still recovering from the attack on Greenhall."

"Aye," she acknowledged. "You'll have to carry me, when this is through." She waved him back, and began the summoning. "Get clear. Run."

"Elsa, wait," he said quickly. "It's holding the souls of the dead in the village…"

"I said RUN!" Elsa shouted.

There was no stopping her.

Lucas ran, moving as quickly as he could across the village, skidding past the bridge and down the river's shallow bank. Above him, a ring of fiery light washed over everything. When it had passed, he crept up the bank to watch.

Elsa was a splinter of the goddess in the center of the village. If the ground hadn't already been ash, if the trees around the village weren't charred and the buildings destroyed by Sir Volent two weeks past, then all of those things would have been devastated. Forge-bright and swinging a sword that looked like a shard of the sun, she threw herself into the fight. The lightning-red scars on her face were the brightest of all, pulsing with each blow, each attack, each ground-shuddering strike of that terrible blade.

The gheist fell into a strategy of survival. Wounded, it limped away from the vow knight's assault. It fought back only to put Elsa off her stride, battering her with claws forged of earth, then jumping away when she tried to return the attack. With every movement Elsa gouged great ruts in the earth, throwing up plumes of ash and gravel that clattered away into the forest. The sun waned beneath the cloud until it was nothing but an angry red wound in the sky.

Still Elsa attacked, and still the gheist fell back, circling around, unwilling to leave the confines of the village.

Lucas drew a quick icon across his eye, opening the unseen world. The ghosts of the dead were following the gheist around, dragged behind it like fish in a net. They clumped together in its wake, shivering and howling in that unseen wind.

"Is he feeding off of them?" Lucas muttered to himself. "Binding them?" The souls shouldn't be here at all. The faithful dead were drawn out of the world and into the quiet house, a shrine at Cinderfell where the lord of winter ruled over the souls of those who had died. There the priests of Cinder looked after them, stilling their troubles and easing their journey into the nothing that lay beyond death. A soul that wasn't successfully severed from its body might end up haunting the place of its death, sometimes even becoming a gheist itself. It was part of the duty of the church of Cinder to perform this final rite for the dead, to ease their passage.

Either these souls had never been severed from their bodies, or the gheist had found some way to draw them back from the quiet. Perhaps the gheist was a manifestation of the tragedy of their death. Yet it had appeared before Volent had put the village to the sword.

Something else, then...

While Lucas speculated, Elsa found her rhythm. The gheist pounced at her and she blocked, drew back and struck before the demon could limp away—a quick crossing blow that scythed into the gheist's belly, then its chest, biting deeply into the muscle of its back. The demon howled and fell, rolling nearly to the other side of the village before it stopped.

This appeared to be as far away from the pack of souls as the gheist could be without leaving the village. It also was as close to the souls as Lucas could possibly get. He saw his chance, and took it.

Rising quickly, he ran into the village. He didn't spare any attention or power on summoning naetheric armor. Instead, the frair held his staff in front of him and recited the rites of severance.

"To Cinder's wound, I send you. To winter's rest, I send you. From Strife's love, I cut you," he yelled, scattering blessings and benediction around the barely seen souls of the dead. "From summer's warmth, I cast you away. To the spirit you return. From the flesh, be severed!"

The effect was immediate. The sketchy images of the dead, their bodies as insubstantial as a candle's afterglow, squealed and fell away. Even with his kinship to the naetherealm, Lucas could sense nothing of their passage. One breath they were, and the next they were not.

The gheist barreled into Lucas, delivering a hammer blow that threw him to the ground and sent his staff skittering away. The beast loomed over him, legs as solid as stone pillars, rapidly cooling iron scabbing over its skin, the heat of its blood washing over the priest, taking his breath away. Droplets of molten iron fell alarmingly near, landing with a hiss. The growl that rolled out of its chest was as deep as thunder, and full of fury.

He reached for the naetherealm, bracing himself for the plunge into winter's heart, racing for the invocation before the demon decided to finish him off.

He never got there.

With a bound and a leap, the gheist ran away. It abandoned the village and disappeared into the forest, spattering the ground with tears of molten iron that started tiny fires and singed the bark of each tree it passed. Lucas eased himself to his knees. Elsa's hand found his shoulder. Her skin was still hot, her armor pinging with the residue of her summoning.

"Do we chase it?" she asked. She sounded weak, and he looked up. The scars on her cheeks and jaw were as red as fire, weeping ash. By the pallor of her skin and the heat washing off her bones, the vow knight was broken.

"No," Lucas said. "Not today. We get you back to Greenhall, and we rest."

That Sir LaFey didn't protest said a lot about her condition. That Lucas had to carry her back to their horses, his skin blistering at her touch, said a great deal more.

19

A SCATTERING OF DARK riders went north. At first they went in groups of two and three, traveling with whomever was at their side when they fled the city, carrying their lives on their backs. Their armor was an odd mixture of tournament finery and rough-spun wool. They had little in the way of supplies. Halverdt's men had blocked access to the visitors' camp as soon as the troubles began. Malcolm's preparations were useless. His men were forced to abandon their belongings in their haste to be free of the city. As the days passed their numbers grew, small groups pooling together, trading support and protection, until they were a column of knights and spear-attendants, servants and lords, all making do with what they could manage.

Their way had been slow and dangerous. Avoiding all the roads that led north and sticking to the untrammeled woods had taken time, made worse by the need to hide every time one of the outriders spotted a patrol. Still, they were finally approaching the Tenerran border, and hopefully safety beyond.

At the fore rode Malcolm Blakley, duke of Houndhallow and hero of the Reaver War. He was still wearing the formal tunic he had worn to watch his son's joust, with his plate-and-half buckled over. He had donned the armor so quickly that he didn't have a padded tunic beneath, and after a short time in the saddle the metal chafed his skin. Even after a week, he bore this pain quietly.

His son was less graceful.

"Gods, my back," Ian mumbled. He squirmed beneath his cloak, trying to stretch muscles that hadn't moved since he mounted that morning. "I feel like my spine's been replaced with a tanner's hook."

"Better your back than your feet," Sir Dugan answered. "You could be walking back to Houndhallow."

"Not in this gear," Ian said. He was still in the tournament rig, the stiff greaves and intractable shoulder plating, designed to take a hard blow but unforgiving to movement. His partly crushed helmet was stowed in a burlap sack on the saddle's side.

"You should have dumped that clatter back at Greenhall," Malcolm said. "You're wearing out our horses faster than we can rest them. We'll never cross the Tallow at this rate."

"And face Halverdt's arrows in thin cloth?" Ian replied irritably.

"If we keep moving, we won't have to face them at all," Malcolm answered. The other men drew away from the argument between lord and heir, though Sir Dugan stayed close enough to intervene, if necessary. "You are letting your stubborn fear hold you back from the best course of action. Fleeing is a hard choice, but the necessary one." He adjusted his reins irritably. "Hold fast to Cinder's words, and you will be able to make the hard decision."

"Cinder's words? Gods around, Father, do you forget who just drove us from Greenhall? That it was the church who closed the gates? Their guards who harried us north, until the walls of that cursed city were out of sight? How can you invoke the gray lord's name in this situation?"

"The same way you can blaspheme it, boy," Malcolm said. "They closed the gates to keep the riot from spreading to the city, and to protect what little peace remained in the tourney ground. If they hadn't stood between us and Halverdt's court, gods know what tragedy would have followed. And as for harrying us—" he pulled his horse in front of his son's, forcing the boy to stop "—that was an escort, sent to make certain some hotheaded knight didn't try his luck on our blood. Without that assistance, we might not even be alive."

"How thoughtless of me," Ian answered, his anger turning him red around the tight collar of his breastplate. "Perhaps one day I can return the honor."

The two stared awkwardly at one another for a long minute as the rest of the column flowed around them. Eventually, Malcolm snorted and rode his way back to the fore. Ian was about to follow when Sir Dugan pulled him to the side.

"Give him his time, boy," the older knight hissed. "This has been a low season for your father."

"He doesn't have to take it out on me."

"He does, actually."

"Why? Because he blames me for riding the lists? Because I risked my life against that gheist, and gathered more glory than the old man has seen in the last decade? Or is it just that I'm his son, and he expects more of me than I can give?"

"It's because you're wearing that ridiculous armor," Dugan answered as he rode off. "Lose it.

233

Before you kill one of the horses, and my goodwill with it."

Malcolm's column sighted the Tallow from the edge of a scrub forest at the top of a rolling hill, late the next day. This far east the river was broad and slow, bounded by limestone bluffs that occasionally dipped to allow a ford or tumbling waterfall that led to flat brown lakes that baked in the midsummer sun. There was still a day's ride ahead of them. Grassy, rolling plains stretched ahead of them, with folds that hid much of the ground, and soft peaks topped by scattered stones and the few sparse, wind-wrenched trees that could survive.

"No cover," Dugan muttered. "We'll be mice to the hawks out there."

"We should go east. Cross at the Reaveholt and ride to Houndhallow," Ian said.

"And add days to our journey, if not another week," Malcolm answered. "We haven't the food or luxury. The church won't be able to keep Halverdt's men off the road forever. The sooner we have Tenerran dirt beneath our feet, the better off we'll be."

"I can't imagine Colm Adair will be happy to find us at his gate," Dugan said. He glanced over at Sir Merret, standing some distance down the hill with Sir Doone. "Or the fact that we bring Halverdt's attention with us."

"Colm Adair won't mind the fight," Malcolm said. "Gods know he's earned the attention."

"You think he sent Gwen out on purpose? You think he was looking for this trouble?" Ian asked.

"I think he'd be a fool to draw Volent's attention," Malcolm said, "and Colm Adair is no fool. Yet I know nothing of his daughter, and this story about gheists has me worried."

"Superstition and fear," Dugan muttered.

"Aye, and both are powerful enough to see us to trouble," Malcolm replied. He stood up in his stirrups and called to Doone and Merret, who were making their way up the hill. "What news? Is there any other way forward?"

"Ways enough," Doone answered. She had taken control of the loose column of knights and spear-attendants, while Dugan tended to the needs of the duke and his son. "None of them good. There's an old crossing well west of here, but it would mean weeks in the Fen, and those paths are dark. No godsroad leads that way."

"I would scoff at the worry of meeting gheists this close to the Allfire, but the last few weeks have proven the threat real enough," Malcolm said. "Still, that is too far to travel. We must make directly for the Fen Gate, and disperse from there to alert the north."

"Or gather banners," Sir Merret answered. "I'm sorry, my lord, but it may have come to that."

"It may," Malcolm agreed. "Let us take this one treasonous act at a time. Sir Doone, what are your thoughts?"

"I don't like crossing here. I don't like crossing to the west," she said, squinting into the setting sun. She turned back to Malcolm and his attendant knights. "And I don't like delaying to go east, either. Frankly, I like nothing about this situation."

"Then how are we to please you, sir?" Dugan asked.

"By taking the least terrible choice and driving it hard," she said. "Let us cross here, and proceed as quickly as the gods will take us."

"I will settle for the speed of our horses," Malcolm said. "Sir Doone, gather the troops. We rest here tonight, and take to the fields tomorrow."

"Why not go now?" Ian asked.

"We will have to ride hard and fast, and these horses have had no relief since we put Greenhall behind us," Malcolm answered. He barely looked at his son as he spoke. "Also, if we cross now, we will be forced to spend the night on an open field, whereas here we can camp in the cover of the forest. No, we must risk discovery tonight to increase our chances of success tomorrow. Settle the horses and eat whatever food you can manage. We don't want to carry a single pound more than is necessary."

A sound reached Ian as he lay in his bedroll—a soft murmuring from the night. He rolled to his feet and stared into the darkness. Beyond the perimeter of the camp, he could see shadows pooling. He crept closer.

A single rider waited at the edge of the forest. The man held a spear across his lap and stared between the trees, shifting in his saddle to peer into the murk. The man's horse cropped the grass at the tree line. The sound of the beast's teeth clapping together was what had drawn Ian's attention.

The man could be one of the Tenerran knights, driven from Greenhall and making his way north to the safety of the Fen, independent of the Blakley column. He could be a scout of House Adair, or Halverdt, or the outrider for a larger force. Or he might be a lordless knight, unfortunate enough to get caught along the border in difficult times.

Ian looked back to the camp, and saw Sir Doone crouching twenty feet further down the tree line, staring at him. She signaled him back, then crept into the shadows. Ian followed. They met among the sleeping knights of their company.

"Thinking of saying hello?" she hissed at him.

"No, of course not. We don't know who it is."

"Not yet, but he's none of ours."

"He could be a scout from House Adair."

"No rider from the Fen Gate would be caught south of the Tallow, not since Gwen Adair stirred the pot." Doone felt along the ground by her bedroll, coming up with a pair of spears. She pushed one into Ian's hands. "He doesn't seem to have noticed our presence. So we watch, and if he sees more than he should, we stop him."

Ian nodded. Together they snuck back to where the rider sat, then split up, finding his flank and waiting. The man had moved farther into the forest, perhaps just following his horse's appetite, perhaps because he thought he saw something among the trees.

The rider wore armor, perhaps brigandine, perhaps simple hunter's leather, but his spear was too long for boar-hunting. Ian tried to get closer, to see if there was a tabard across his chest, or barding on the horse.

His heel came down in mud, his leg slid forward, his back crunched against the dry bark of a tree. He held his tongue, but the sound of his fall carried through the forest.

The rider straightened but didn't turn his head. Instead, he started to ride slowly out of the forest, approaching the crest of the hill where Ian and Malcolm had observed the Tallow earlier that day. He moved without panic or speed.

Maybe he didn't hear...

Sir Doone stepped out of the trees and let fly. Her spear arced silently through the air and thumped into the rider's shoulder. The man twisted but didn't fall. A second later he spurred the horse forward. In moments he would be over the crest and out of range of their spears.

"Idiot, throw!" Doone yelled. Ian snapped out of his horror and stood, running out of the tree line and hauling back with the spear. It would be a long throw, and hard to make, but it felt good as he released. He watched as the spear reached the top of its flight, hung there for a moment, then dipped and raced back to the ground.

It landed quietly in the ground, the shaft humming. The rider thundered past it, up the hill, and then disappeared over the ridge.

"Godsfuck," Doone spat. "Wake your father, and the rest as well—we need to set out immediately. With luck he'll bleed to death before he reaches help. They'll know we're out here, but hopefully..."

She drifted to silence as another sound rolled over the plains. There was a shout, and then a pair of flames crested the hill: a pair of spearmen, torches held high, the tri-acorn and cross of House Halverdt on their chests. They yelled down the hill, and then a new thunder rose from the grass.

A column of riders came over the hill. They followed the scouts' waving torches, the sound of their passing like clattering metal and falling stones.

Doone was already running. Ian turned and followed, shouting for his father to wake, for the knights of Tener to gather arms and prepare to fight. The first torches winked to life among the trees, and the sound of sleep-addled knights and their attendants mingled with the gathering of steel.

The war had found them.

It would not wait till morning.

* * *

Malcolm woke to strange lights among the trees and the taste of blood in his mouth. He was standing, naked, with blade in hand. A man was dying at his feet.

"My lord!" a voice called from his left. Malcolm turned and saw a knight rushing in his direction. The man faltered at the sight of the lord of Houndhallow naked and soaked in blood, but only for a second. "We are found, my lord."

"I am awake," Malcolm muttered. The knight blinked, nodded, and stepped close.

"A Suhdrin scout stumbled on us. Your son and Sir Doone thought to ambush the rider, but he was not alone. We don't know their number or bearing, but they are upon us." The knight glanced around, looking for something to cover Malcolm's body. Malcolm recognized the man, but couldn't put a name to his face. One of MaeHeart's bannermen, he thought, but without tabard or the light of Strife, Malcolm couldn't be sure.

The knight retrieved a cloak and placed it on Malcolm's shoulders.

"It's fine," Malcolm said, brushing the cloak aside. He looked down at himself. His body, ridged in scars and gray with hair and rippled fat, shivered in the night air. The hulking musculature that had been his youthful pride was turned to crust and crumb, old bones sticking through skin as weary and worn as parchment. He straightened his back, threw back his shoulders, and scanned the battlefield. "I thought it was a dream."

"No, my lord."

"Then let us fight. Gather the knights to the center and leave the spears among the trees. Get rid of those lights, in case they have archers on the ridge. We don't want to give away our numbers or position, if possible."

"Yes, my lord," the knight said, then hurried away. Malcolm called after him.

"Where is my son?"

"None know, my lord!" the man yelled as he disappeared into the shadows. Malcolm sighed and blinked into the darkness. There was a steady stream of torches pouring down from the ridgeline and into the forest, moving fast and bounding, as though on horses. There were voices all around, and the clash of steel. He looked down at the dead man at his feet, put a toe to the corpse's shoulder and turned it over. Suhdrin colors on his chest, and fair hair on his scalp. Good. He hadn't mistakenly killed one of his own in a waking delirium.

This moment of peace was interrupted by a push in the darkness. The trees around Malcolm were suddenly crowded with knights and men-at-arms, all in various states of undress, trying to escape the onslaught. Horses appeared among them, the riders striking down at the defenders, spraying blood and fear. Malcolm was moved back, stumbling as the fleeing Tenerrans pushed away from their attackers.

"Enough!" Malcolm yelled over the fray. "Men of Houndhallow, to me! Rally! Rally!"

The footmen around Malcolm paused, surprised to find themselves in the presence of their lord. He shouldered them aside and rushed the closest rider. The man was hewing blindly through the press with a horseman's axe, heedless of how far ahead of his fellows he had gotten. Malcolm slid to the man's side, avoiding the dashing hooves of his mount, waiting until the rider turned toward him.

The man looked down at the naked, scarred, wild-eyed attacker at his boot, and sneered.

He raised his axe.

Malcolm swung twice, fast and long, the bare tip of his blade dancing across the long muscles of the rider's chest, just beneath the armpit. The Suhdrin's right arm went limp, and the axe with it, the weight too much and the fury of battle too great. The axe cartwheeled to the ground. The rider drew a short blade with his other hand and tried to stab Malcolm in the face, but he danced back, forward, and back again, hammering the forte of his sword into the man's gut. The rider fell, and then the horse turned back the way it had come, galloping a path through the attackers.

The retreating men of Tener rallied, rushing around Malcolm to take the battle forward. Malcolm followed, screaming and naked and blade-hungry, disappearing into the night with his sword held high and the blood of his foes in his mouth.

The battle continued until morning, and by the time Strife's warmth found the shadows of the forest, there were many dead among the trees. Half of Malcolm's host lay silent, most cut down before they could don armor or defend themselves, lost in those first few chaotic moments of the attack.

Three times their number of Suhdrin had fallen, half of them the riders who had charged into the woods, the rest archers and spearmen who had followed their brothers into battle, only to be trampled during the rout. The last moments of the fight had been grim, exhausted men and women battling until the breath left their lungs and the strength was gone from their bodies. It reminded Ian of the lesser melee at Greenhall, when he had watched Martin Roard fight in mud and dishonor, seeking some glimpse of what true battle would feel like.

The column had been a scouting patrol, riding as quietly as they were able among the foothills south of the Tallow, fortunate enough to stumble on the Tenerran campsite in the darkness, and unfortunate enough to find battle. Those who had not died in the darkness were fleeing east, to find the godsroad and reinforcements.

Malcolm stood on the ridge, watching the survivors beat hooves through the whirling grass. Ian came to stand beside him.

"Father," Ian said, "I've brought your robes."

"Robes?" Malcolm asked. He looked down. He was still naked, the scraggly hair on his chest and loins flaked with blood, his limbs smeared with mud and sweat. He was shivering in the first light of dawn. "Yes, thank you."

Ian helped his father cover himself, then stared down at the retreating column.

"A good fight," the younger Blakley said.

Malcolm snorted with contempt.

"A bloody mess. Half of those who are dead never woke up, and none of them had time to prepare for the fight to come." He shrugged deeper into the robes, clenching them to his chest, hugging the dented sword to his ribs. "And those riders will tell tales of mad, naked, bloody pagans howling through the woods."

"Do you think any of them knew they faced the lord of Houndhallow?" Ian asked with a smirk.

"Gods grant that they don't," Malcolm snapped. "Gather the men. Get them on their horses. Array the dead and bless them to Cinder, then give them to the forest. We have no time for burial rites."

"Father…"

"I will mourn their names at the Fen Gate, and raise tribute to them in Houndhallow," Malcolm said irritably. "The gods will see them to the quiet. But we must ride!"

"We may not have the opportunity," Ian said. He pointed down the narrow defile between rolling hillocks. A host was riding toward them from the east. Three abreast and winding over the hills like a river, the riders sounded horns as they approached.

"Well, gods be good." Malcolm squinted in their direction, letting the robe fall from his shoulder. "At least we have friends to guide us."

Ian peered at the column of riders. At their fore, a banner slipped free of its silk, and then caught its colors in the wind. It was the red and black of the Fen Gate.

The iron fist of Adair.

20

GWEN RODE SWIFTLY down the hill, gathering the view. A tangle of men on foot paced along a ridge just north of the woods. To the west, there was a column of riders in full retreat, their line ragged and panicked. They flew no colors, but Gwen knew Suhdrin scouts when she saw them, with their high saddles and meaningless horns. They thought of themselves as junior knights, and often raced into battles that would be better harried, charging shield walls when their training and equipment suited a softer approach.

The men on the ridge were another matter. They looked a loose group, in varying uniform and, though armed, seemed to lack the cohesion of a military force.

When her scouts had brought word of torches and war along the border, Gwen expected to find a Tenerran column in full regalia, perhaps marching west from Dunneswerry, or returning from action deeper in Suhdra. Now she worried that she had roused her banners and ridden south in support of a band of mercenaries, or worse.

"Form a round and fly the banners," Gwen called over her shoulder. "I will speak to their leader. Don't hesitate to strike if you see trouble."

"I see trouble enough from here," Sir Brennan said.

"They look too ragged to be much threat," Gwen answered.

"Mayhap, but Acorn's men found threat enough."

"Aye, well, who's to account for Suhdrin fear?" Gwen laughed. "Stay your hand. If they saw fit to thrash some of Halverdt's men, then I'll see fit to speak with them."

"They have colors, my lady," Sir Baxter said from her flank.

"Oh?"

"There. The tall one on the hill. I'll swear he's wearing the hound."

Gwen narrowed her vision. Sure enough, a few of the men milling about the ridge were wearing black and white, with the Blakley hound on their chests or emblazoned on their shields.

"Perhaps they'll have word of their lord," Gwen said. "I'm sure the duchess of Houndhallow would be happy of that."

"Long as the news is good," Brennan answered. "If they come from Greenhall, perhaps Sir Merret is among them."

"Gods grant it," Gwen said. She hadn't liked sending Sir Merret to Halverdt's court, but her father insisted that the duke of Houndhallow and the other Tenerran knights celebrating the Allfire should be warned of what trouble might be coming their way.

In silence they covered the short distance between hills. Her men rounded behind her, forming a circle of swirling cavalry lines, bright with spear and banner. Gwen took Sir Brennan with her, and rode up the ridge to meet the loose crowd of swordsmen who waited. They looked rough, blood spattered and tired to a man. There were women among their number, as well, all looking as if they had spent the night slaughtering cattle. They watched her indifferently.

"Who among you can speak for this host?" she asked as she rode up.

"I'm as good as any, and better than most," said a gaunt man in Blakley colors. He was dressed in loose linen, worn and sweaty, though the tabard belted to his chest looked fresh. He had a patchy beard, though it was still soft and thin. Gwen smiled.

"A squire?" she said. "Surely there is a knight among your number who would be better able." She looked at the dozen or so swordsmen standing in the young man's wake. A few of them wore bits of armor, and at least one—a woman—was dressed for war.

"The mud hides my honor, but such is the way with war. I am Lord Ian Blakley, son of Malcolm, heir to the Hunter's throne and the hallow of the hound." Ian stood straight. "And you?"

"Gwendolyn Adair. I wouldn't have recognized you, Ian. Last we met, you were still putting arrows into haystacks. Have you trained to the lance, now?"

"He's done more than that," the woman said. She came to stand beside Ian. "Faced a gheist at Greenhall, and entered the lists against Chev Bourdais."

"And lived? Well, that's something to report. You lead this host?"

Another came up the hill, this one without color or armor or fear. Gwen almost didn't recognize him, until he smiled.

"My lady," Sir Merret said. "You should be kind to the boy. I would be dead without his help."

"Everyone can stop calling me 'the boy,' please," Ian said tightly.

"Yes, yes…" Merret waved him aside and went to stand beside Gwen's horse. "I have a lot to report, but you've probably guessed at the worst of it."

"This is all that remains of the Tenerran host from Greenhall?" she asked.

"This, and an equal number dead in the trees below."

"And the duke is not with you?"

"My father is alive and well, and spent this night in better service to his land than you, I suspect," Ian said. "He is below, seeing to the wounded and preparing to ride."

"Then you have horses. Excellent, because we have few to spare. Those scouts of Greenhall will find support long before we reach the Fen." She nudged her horse closer to Ian. "I was hoping that you would be able to ride in strength from Greenhall. We are few along the border."

"Halverdt took most of our gear and an equal measure of our strength before we were free of his walls," Ian said. He wavered on his feet, looking for a moment as though he would fall from fatigue, then put a hand on Gwen's boot to steady himself. She ignored it. "It has been a difficult ride. My father will be thankful you have come."

"We came to help, and to get help. There is much to discuss. Come." She offered him a hand. He took it, and Gwen pulled him up to the saddle, to sit in front of her. He stank of the road and battle, but it wasn't a terrible stink. "Let's find your father. We must reach the Tallow before night. Sooner, if we can."

"He's below. Hopefully dressed by now."

"Dressed? Surely…"

"They came at us in the night. Father was killing

them before he found his boots, much less his dignity."

"Well, then," Gwen said with a smirk, "we will ride slowly, and hope the duke has found at least one of those before we arrive."

They crossed the Tallow in strength, the ragged remnants of Malcolm's force happy to be on Tenerran ground once again, despite the loss and tragedy that had brought them here. Malcolm Blakley paused at the river's shore to bathe, joined by a dozen men and women from his train, all of them lame from fatigue. They turned the churning water to rust.

When he emerged, though, it was as though Malcolm had left a great weight of worry in the river's current. The war had come, and there was nothing he could do to avoid it. So he would be ready.

"You say my wife has ridden to the Fen Gate?" Malcolm asked as he donned fresh robes.

"Aye, with some number of riders. When she heard of the troubles in Greenhall, she sent word to the northern lords and their bannermen," Gwen said. "Your wife is preparing for war."

"She should not have come to the Fen Gate," he muttered. "She should be guarding Houndhallow." He mounted without armor and signaled the advance. They crossed the river in column.

"Will you leave us to guard the border alone, then, and return to Houndhallow?" Gwen asked. She had to yell as they splashed across the water.

"We have a border with Halverdt, as well, you know," Ian said. "If he decides to cross the Tallow, there's nothing to keep him from riding there instead of here."

"We will not abandon our alliance with you,"

Malcolm said crossly. "Blakley and Adair have stood against Suhdrin aggression since shadows first stretched over Tenumbra. This time will be no different. It just would have eased my mind to have the duchess behind our walls. That is all."

"The defense of Houndhallow will be seen to," Gwen said. "If we defeat Halverdt here, however, there will be no need."

"You speak of defeating him here, and making a stand on the border," Malcolm said, "but where will we stand? A skirmish with scouts does not make or break a war, my lady. I know you are huntress of your house, but battle is not joined in the hunter's way, by creeping through the woods until you find your prey. There must be open ground, and a meeting of armies. We may have no army to meet: for all we know, Halverdt has contented himself with throwing us out of his keep, and will not stir from his walls."

"Oh, I assure you he has stirred," Gwen said. "As you shall see, if you follow me."

She refused to say anything more. Malcolm frowned, but he followed.

They proceeded east, until in time they reached the edge of a narrow lake, called White Lake. There was a ford at the point where the river entered the lake, and another on the other side, where the river Tallow again flowed out of the lake. A Tenerran army had made camp in Suhdrin land along the lake's southern shore, and now spread out in a crescent. Their banners hung lazily in the air, but tents and wagons and temporary forges crowded the shores of the lake, and rank after rank of armed men waited. Gwen led them across the nearest ford to join the army.

The plain to the south rose slowly to a gentle ridge anchored by a wooded hillock. Along the ridge and down the slope bristled the gathered armies of Suhdra. Among the bright banners of the houses of Suhdra, fully half of the spears arrayed against them flew the black and gray of the inquisition.

The south had marched against them. The war was joined.

"You've already crossed?" Malcolm asked in disbelief. "The armies of House Adair cannot decide to invade Suhdra on a whim! We'll have a war, certainly, but if we'd stayed on Tenerran soil we would at least have had the advantage of land and heart. Any negotiation we undertake—"

"Two things," she replied, cutting him off, "before you get in over your head. First, any negotiation that we undertake will be from the victor's chair, and not while begging for Suhdrin mercy." She sat straight in the saddle and waved her hand to indicate the encampment. "And, perhaps most importantly, that is not an army of House Adair."

Malcolm turned again to view the army. A smaller congregation of Tenerran lords was gathered on the near bank, and there the banners rested. To his surprise, he saw the gray and black of the Feltower, the multi-green of Drownhal, both of them from Tener. But there was also a Suhdrin banner: the blue and white of House Jaerdin. Castian Jaerdin, duke of Redgarden, had ridden with him during the Reaver War, and often opposed Halverdt in the Suhdrin Circle of Lords. He was the only Suhdrin in the host. Malcolm was pleased to see him.

"You would take commands from a Suhdrin lord?" Malcolm asked. "I grant you, Castian is as fine a general as the south has raised, and a true friend, but it would suit better if Tenerran nobles asked for Tenerran blood."

"I agree," she replied. "Which is why the central banner flies."

The banner at the center of the commander's encampment was lazy, large and heavy, its edges frayed with golden tassel and the seals of a dozen campaigns. Then the wind rose, and the banner stirred. The Blakley hound, a black shadow against its white field, lifted into the air. Soon it was cracking like thunder in the breeze.

Malcolm spurred his horse and charged down to the banner-hold. A line of spearmen formed to meet his charge, until someone recognized the riders and blew a horn, and they parted. He hammered toward the commander's dais, from where the council would watch the coming battle. When he got close, Malcolm slid from his saddle and stumbled forward. There was a murmuring from the gathered lords. He ran toward the stairs.

Standing at the front of the commander's dais, sword at her hip and chain over her dress, was his wife, Sorcha Blakley. She looked down at the stumbling madman who had just appeared at the flank of her army and, when she recognized her husband, gave a little start. Then she rushed down the stairs and into his arms. The rings of her mail gave a *shing*ing sound, like a handful of coins let slip to the floor.

"It's good to see you, husband," she said when she had finally pulled away. With one hand she brushed a tear from his eye, putting it to her lips.

"And you, my love," Malcolm answered very quietly. "What brings you to the Fen?"

"I came looking for my husband—and see? I found him." She smiled sheepishly, an odd look on her face. "I brought you an army, dear."

"It's good that you did," Malcolm said, shaking his head. He couldn't believe this woman sometimes. He hoped he never finished with being surprised at her. "We're going to need it."

21

THE AIR IN the tent was close and hot. The white linen panels of the walls were dazzlingly bright from the sun's radiance. Malcolm and the other lords of Tener were crowded around a narrow table at the center, squinting down at a ragged parchment map that showed a rough approximation of the battlefield outside. The sound of drums and horns and the slow, rolling clamor of hundreds of soldiers echoed over the lake.

Malcolm was losing his temper.

"This battle, yes," he said, "*this* battle we can win, but the border is broad and loosely held. If we commit our full strength here, there will be Suhdrin banners hanging over the Feltower by winter."

"Your only worry is Houndhallow," Duncan Rudaine said. The duke of Drownhal was an uncommonly quiet man, given to sour moods and swift anger. He stood at the verge of the council's circle, hands folded into his belt, thumb resting on his ever-present hand axe. "We all have a stake in keeping this fight off of Tenerran land. Which is why we must commit here."

"Is it wrong for my father to defend his home?" Ian asked. He stood opposite Malcolm, dressed for war, but also carrying the spear he had used to face the gheist. It kept banging into camp chairs and generally getting in the way. "We are here to protect Tener, are we not? Is Houndhallow less worthy of that protection than the Fen Gate?"

"It is not a question of worthiness, but reality," Gwen said. "The Suhdrin army is here." She pointed to the map, then to another location nearby. "The Tenerran army is here. We are where the fight will take place."

"Unless it occurs to Halverdt that there's more to be gained in taking the halls of your allies, and drawing us away from the defense," Lord MaeHerron grumbled.

"The Suhdrin lords are more worried about running afoul of gheists in the savage north than we are of getting lost in the south," Rudaine answered. "But we should keep in mind that we are in Suhdra, even if Tener is just across the river. I'm sure the Circle of Lords finds that an aggressive stance."

"The presence of this army on Suhdrin soil has rallied southern banners," Castian Jaerdin agreed. The only Suhdrin in their number, his silk and silver looked painfully out of place in the crowd of leather and steel, but his voice was even and calm. Malcolm was glad the man was there among them, to remind his fellow lords that the enemy wasn't all Suhdra— that Halverdt's actions were not universally approved of in his own land.

"Outrage at the trouble at Greenhall has drawn the closest of Halverdt's allies," Jaerdin continued, "but those farther south are taking the time to think things through. If this is to be a defensive battle, the lords along the Burning Coast will not be drawn into the fight."

"May aye, or may nay," Rudaine said sharply. "If we sit here and wait, it's possible Halverdt will draw even more forces to his banner, until they have enough to crush us. And so we'll fight."

"As I've said time and again, this is not the fight we need to have," Malcolm said. "We should secure the border, make sure Halverdt's men stay on this side of the Tallow, and wait for the fire of his anger to burn off. To hold the Tallow, we will need reinforcements, and not just Tenerrans. Castian has sent riders south already. We should count on help from Roard, from DuFallion, from Marcy and Bealth."

"No offence to the duke, but I'd rather have a pack of dogs at my back than Suhdrin knights by my side," Rudaine grumbled. "We've steel enough to win this fight. Why are we waiting?"

"Because we will spend our strength against this force, and have nothing left for his reserve. If we…"

"If we break him here, his reserve can squat!" Rudaine said sharply. "We must strike while the opportunity presents itself. There is no value in waiting."

"There is great value in not overreaching ourselves," Malcolm insisted. "Yes, this is a fine opportunity, but blood may be spared and steel kept sharp if we fall back today, only to face him with greater strength tomorrow. Perhaps with allies enough to avoid the fight altogether. If more Suhdrin lords join the duke of Redgarden in opposing this action, Halverdt will be forced to stand down."

"Halverdt's committed, in mind and body," Rudaine pressed. "He and the high inquisitor have been spoiling for this fight for quite a while. Right now I'm of a mind to give it to them."

"I came at the duchess's call, to stand by her husband," MaeHerron answered, "and here stands the duke of Houndhallow. Seems to me the seed of this fight rests with Adair, and the Fen Gate. If Halverdt was spoiling for blood, then it was Gwendolyn Adair who gave it to them."

"Steady, now," Gwen Adair said, stepping in. "Halverdt's crimes against Tener reach far beyond our border. Don't think he would settle for the Fen Gate, if the whole north sits open to him."

"You have put us in a difficult place, Miss Adair," MaeHerron said. "The church has raised its banner beside Halverdt's, and given its weight to this fight. We are all faithful Celestials, each to his own doma, but my tower rests in the shadow of the winter shrine. Half my sons are sworn to the priesthood, and half my daughters train at the Lightfort." He shifted uncomfortably. "If this becomes a fight against Heartsbridge, then my strength will have to fall away. I can not raise my banner against the gods."

"The high inquisitor is looking for an excuse," Gwen said angrily. "He seeks to put the north under his banner, to raise a pogrom the like of which we haven't seen since the crusades. Aye, we're all faithful Celestials. The gods know this. It's the high inquisitor who doesn't seem convinced."

"Fighting him is poor proof," MaeHerron mumbled.

"Tolerating Halverdt's crime is no more proof of our faith," said Sorcha. "And remember, it was the high elector of Strife who sent my husband to Greenhall, to 'make peace' between Tener and Suhdra." She leaned into the table, resting her knuckles against the map. "It is not the Celestial church that we fight, but Gabriel Halverdt, and if High Inquisitor Sacombre stands beside him, then it is he who defies Heartsbridge. Not us."

"That will get you hanged," MaeHerron said as lightly as he could manage.

"Hanged for speaking the truth," Malcolm said.

"I don't like it, but I can't deny it, either. Whatever Halverdt's goal, he doesn't stand with the church on this. Heartsbridge seeks peace, and if we must fight for that peace, then we will fight."

"So we march?" Rudaine asked.

"So we stand," Malcolm answered. "We must hold the border."

"The battle lines are already drawn," Sorcha said. "If we try to retreat across the fords, our men will be butchered."

"There will be a battle," MaeHerron said. "Today."

"Yes," Malcolm agreed, "and once it is won, we must restrain our lines. We can't pursue them deeper into their lands. We must not give them more reason to draw their banners. We must give the southern houses time to find the nerve to oppose the inquisitor's army."

"Which cannot be done if we march south," Jaerdin said. "Win today. Secure the Tallow, and then we can think about tomorrow."

"Gwen," Malcolm said. "The land we passed through after you rescued us: do you know it well?"

"I was born to it," she said. "The Redoubt, it is called. I've hunted those cliffs since I was a child."

"Very good. I would ask you guard that land, if you're able."

"And by whose will do you order me?" Gwen asked sharply.

"This army was gathered to rescue Blakley, by his lady wife," MaeHerron said. "It is now his to lead."

"But it is our land that was first attacked," Gwen said. "Adair lands that lay beyond this river. The iron fist of Adair should lead us. I should…"

"Child," Sorcha whispered. "That is not how this will happen."

There was awkward silence around the tent. Finally, Gwen nodded.

"Very well. If that is how it is to be, then I wish to ride with you, my lord," she argued. "To protect my father's borders from the Suhdrins."

"Unfortunately, your presence on the battle line will only spur Halverdt's men to greater violence. I would rather the banner of Adair not fly over this host today, if possible."

"Do you level this insult against my house because you wish to splinter the north?" Gwen asked sharply.

"Not at all, but because I wish to bind the north and south together. Whatever the facts around the events at Tallownere…"

"Halverdt's monster was murdering my people like pigs!"

"Whatever the facts—" Malcolm held out a hand to still her protest "—we need to remove the insult from the Suhdrin mind. Riding beside you will only remind them of the slight, and give weight to Halverdt's argument."

"By hiding my banner, you give in to their fears," Gwen countered. "If you mean to unite Tener, you can't do it by dividing us first."

"I'm not dividing us. I'm just playing the wise game. There is no insult in this," Malcolm said.

"You know better than that, Father," Ian said. "You're bending to the church first, and your blood last."

Malcolm clenched his jaw, then rested his hand on the table and turned stiffly toward his son.

"We must consider the church before our blood. It is the church that ties our lands together, Suhdra and Tener. If there is to be peace between us, it will be through the church."

Gwen and Ian both replied together, their voices

a babble of offended honor and sharp criticism. Malcolm waited until their rage had burned out.

"You have your orders," he said to Gwen. "Go."

There was silence around the table. The gathered lords of Tener stared down at the map, weighing their chances and keeping the peace.

Gwen stood stiffly, then sighed and marched out of the tent.

"Battle today," Rudaine whispered. "Leave tomorrow to the priests."

"Agreed," MaeHerron said.

"Then it's settled," Sorcha said. "Form your lines, gentlemen." She plucked a dagger from the map's corner, letting the dry parchment roll up on itself. "There will be no more plans made today."

The councilors slowly filed out of the tent, each to his or her pavilion. Ian made to depart when Malcolm took him by the shoulder.

"Where will you ride?" he asked.

"At your shoulder," Ian answered. "As is fitting for a son."

"No," Malcolm said. "You tested my authority and my patience, and you've been carrying that damn spear around like it's a trophy."

"How many men can say they stood against a gheist?" Ian asked.

"As many as have been saved by someone else, and survived despite their foolishness."

"Foolishness? You yourself set the bloodwrought spear in my hand at birth. Is it my fault that I followed through on that promise?"

"I ride with priests at my side, and knights of the vow at my fore. You are no hunter, Ian Blakley, and no warrior, to be risking your life in the charge. You will rule Houndhallow one day. Your blood and your name are more important to this demesne than your glory." Malcolm closed his hand on Ian's shoulder, gripping so tightly that the boy cringed. "If you haven't the sense to protect that name, then I must do it for you."

"What worth is my name without glory?" Ian asked, his voice turning shrill. "Who is the Reaverbane to tell me that I must sit back and watch other men gather fame?"

"A man who knows better than you. Before I hand command to your mother, I am assigning you to the flank. Our army is bounded by two fords. The main body of the army holds the eastern ford, but the western ford is beyond our battle line."

"What difference does that make?" Ian asked.

"This," he said, then opened the map once again. "The Sudhrin side of the western ford has already been claimed by Halverdt's men. The river bends in such a way that we cannot reclaim it easily. If they have a mind, they could cross the river and cut off our retreat or wreak havoc among the caravan."

"Gwen is responsible for those crossings," Ian said.

"No, Gwen is holding the fords farther west, along the Redoubt. I want you to hold the western ford, to act as a buffer between our forces and those of Adair, as well as protecting our route of escape, should things go badly."

"A milkmaid's duty! An old man could hold the ford!"

"Not if our lines collapse," Sorcha said, stepping in and giving her son's cheek a disconcerting smudge with her thumb. "You may be called upon to oversee the rout, and that's a bloody business."

"Don't patronize me," Ian snarled. He spun and pushed out of the tent, snapping the flap closed as angrily as he could. When he was gone, Sorcha sighed and gave her husband a look.

"He only wants to be like you, you know," she said. "He only wants to live up to your name. Why do you treat him thus?"

"I only want him to be better than me," Malcolm said. Then he went to the hammock in the corner, laid his creaking bones in the canvas, and fell promptly and fitfully to sleep.

Hours later, Malcolm stood at the head of the inlet ford, the eastern crossing that led across the lake from the Tenerran command to the battle lines. The sky was gray, a low fog creeping through the trees and rising from the lake. The other lords had already crossed with their forces. He had waited behind to speak to his wife.

"You didn't have to give me command," she said.

"I didn't give it," Malcolm said. "It was yours all along."

"The men will still bow to your will. If we stand together on the dais and things begin to go wrong, they will turn to you for advice. For command."

"No," Malcolm shook his head. "I won't be at your side today."

"No? Then what will you do with yourself, husband? Where will you be?"

"I will be where I belong. Where I should have been all this time." He signaled to his squire. "Prepare my horse and my sword, and see that my armor is bright. I want Halverdt to know where I am. I want the men to see me, and the Suhdrin to fear me."

"You mean to fight?" Sorcha asked.

"I mean to fight," Malcolm said. "I mean to kill."

Sorcha sat quietly for a minute before reaching up to her husband's shoulder.

"I will move the commander's platform to the other side of the lake, then," she said.

"Why? If the line breaks, you will be exposed to a charge. Don't be foolish."

"If I'm to lead, then I must be there. Communication across the fords is too slow. Besides, if my husband falls, I would fall beside him."

"Much too poetic," Malcolm said. "I would feel better, *fight* better, if I knew you were safe."

"Perhaps you will fight better if you know I am not safe," she said. "It's not your job to protect me. I'm the commander here. I've given my orders."

"Yes, my lady," Malcolm said with a grin.

"Very good. Now, go put on your pretty armor. There's a battle to win."

There was already smoke on the battlefield, hovering over the grass in cotton wisps. The Suhdrin had wheeled several wagons of hay into the middle field and set them alight. Even after the wagons were consumed, the smell clung to the air, the sting of hay and old wood.

The spear lines shifted nervously. Horns sounded sporadically over the low murmur of thousands of men and women preparing to kill each other. The Tenerran cavalry rode back and forth in front of their lines, silent but for the hammering of their spears against shields and the tattoo of hooves. Arrows arced lazily from the Suhdrin side of the valley to fall harmlessly in the trampled mud.

Scores of the Tenerran faithful stooped to the old ways, saying a final prayer to the river, offering silently to the gods that murmured beneath the water. Priests of Cinder and Strife stood in the lake, wet to their knees, sprinkling benedictions and water on the crowds that had been gathering on the shore all morning. Now that the battle was ready to begin, however, the priests had packed up their icons and retreated across the lake, to wait with the supply wagons, taking their silent gods with them.

Only the commander's dais remained on the shoreline.

Malcolm said a final prayer, then walked over to the dais. He adjusted the clasps on his armor, struggling to get the shield to sit comfortably against his chest, testing the range of his sword arm, trying to ignore the creeping pain in his back. Sorcha had brought his battle rig, as sure of finding her husband as she was of the need to exact vengeance for the attack upon her family once they were reunited.

A thoughtful woman, he mused.

His squire descended on him to make final adjustments that hampered his sword and pinched the increasingly angry nerves in his back. Another led a barded horse to his side and bent to help Malcolm into the saddle. He waved the boy off.

"Where's Gray Mourning?" he asked. "I can't ride just any horse into battle."

"She's spent, my lord. Weeks on the road without rest, and rough handling at that…"

"I handled her more than well!" Malcolm snapped.

"Blessings, Mal," Sorcha called from the stairs, "but horses were never your gift. Leave the poor girl alone for a day, and ride another. This one is from the duke of Drownhal's personal stable. A child could ride him through hell and never burn a toe. Stop being a fool."

"I'm used to her," Malcolm growled. "It's a battle. I don't want to try a new horse during a battle."

"You pout like a child, Malcolm. Now get on the horse and get to your place. All of these nice people are waiting for you."

Malcolm sulked, but he allowed the squires to hoist him into the saddle and secure him, then he took his lance and shield. His sword was secured, as was a quiver of throwing spears, plus enough knives to supply a kitchen.

"Drownhal likes knives, I take it," Malcolm said.

"Never without a blade, that one." On the stairs, Sorcha was now eye-level with her husband. Malcolm nudged the horse closer to her. The mount really was very responsive. That somehow only made it worse.

"The men will expect much of you, love," Malcolm said. "Don't be afraid to take their advice. Try to not overextend the line, but also don't…"

"Hush," Sorcha said. "I've read some very interesting books about this sort of thing. I'm looking forward to plunging you into some treacherous situations… letting you fight your way out."

"So I guess I don't need to insist that you not worry about me."

"Worry about you? Malcolm, I've done nothing but worry about you for the last several months. I raised a damned army to ease that worry, and now that I've found you, the first thing you do is decline to sit at the back and sip tea, as is fitting for your position. You demand to ride to the front.

"You know you have nothing to prove," she added.

"Don't I? I'm the man the church trusted with securing the peace between Adair and Halverdt. We all know how that worked out. I've done everything I can to prevent this war, and it's won me no allies. If there's no avoiding a war, then I might as well do what I can to win it."

"You can't do that from the ease of the commander's dais? Is that not an appropriate place for you?"

"It has nothing to do with appropriate."

"That's good. I'd hate to think that you relegated me to command because it was beneath you."

"Sorcha! I meant to honor you with command, not insult you." He stared at her earnestly. "You've earned your place at the head of this army. These are your men, your banners, and your honor. Not mine. All I did was ride back from Greenhall." Malcolm brought his horse even closer and leaned in. "My manner of diplomacy has failed. It's time for someone else to hold sway in the north, and I'd rather it be you than that lout Rudaine."

Sorcha glared at him for a handful of heartbeats, then her expression softened. She put a hand on his shoulder.

"Be safe. Fight well. Remember the hallow," she said softly.

"The hound. The hallow," he answered. "Sorcha? If things go wrong, please gods have the sense to make a clean escape."

"Husband," she said with some amusement, "do you honestly think I would run?"

"No, I suppose I don't—but I had to ask." He trotted away, then took his helmet from a squire and started toward the front. Yards away, his wife called to him one more time.

"Win this fight, Malcolm. Bring me the peace you promised."

"There will be more to this peace than one fight," he answered, "but I will win it, one way or another."

"Gods grant that you're right," Sorcha said. Then she turned and ascended the dais, to lay aside her place as wife and mother, and take up the mantle of command.

Malcolm snaked his way down to the Blakley line, greeting the men and women of his levy as he went. They were enthusiastic, excited to see their lord among them, singing praises to Cinder and Strife and other gods. Sorcha had brought nearly five hundred spears and several dozen mounted men-at-arms, along with a good core of knights at their center.

Unlike many of the Tenerran troops, Blakley men dressed and fought in the southern manner, with the foot supporting and positioning the mounted force, setting up a devastating charge that could shatter even the strongest shield-wall—as long as they stayed away from the massed ranks of pikes, or the withering fire of crossbows that shielded the flanks. Or unless the charge balked, or a countercharge met them before they could reform. Or...

Malcolm looked up and down at the other Tenerran forces. MaeHerron's lines were drawn up to fight in the same manner as the Blakleys, with priests among them, and dirges rising from their signal corps. Rudaine, green-clad and vicious, followed the wilder order of the tribes, light cavalry and throwing spears, ranks of hard men with axes, even a loose scattering of houndsmen with their armored packs riling along the flanks.

Malcolm remembered stories of the old days,

when House Blakley would bring more hounds than men to a fight. Legends held that the first of his line, Black Colm and his ilk, actually *rode* giant hounds into battle. A story, of course, but a sturdy one. He wondered at the change that had overcome his army in those years. His lines resembled those across the valley more than those of his brothers beside him.

As Malcolm mused, the battle started. There was no grand horn or call to fight. The Suhdrin left flank had been creeping toward the lake, a unit of spear acting as protection for another force of crossbowmen. They were trying to establish themselves on a hillock that overlooked one of the fords, an offshoot of the bluffs that dominated the Tallow for most of its length. It would offer a commanding view of the Tenerran forces.

Gray shadows darted among the trees that clothed the Tenerran side of the hill. Suddenly the baying of hounds was joined by the bellowing of men, and then a loose formation of axemen followed the hounds in, a scrum that turned into a skirmish.

Before either side realized it, the fight was truly engaged. Cries arose as the crossbow wielders were cut down before they could mount a defense. As the Suhdrin spearmen fell back, a unit of light cavalry rode out to support their retreat. These strayed too close to the center of the field and met a countercharge from the riders who had been cycling in front of the Tenerran lines. The bloody exchange of steel and hoof drew yet more forces from both sides, and then the space between the armies collapsed.

Finally the call to battle sounded, first from the dais above, and then on down the line as heralds took up the song. The men to either side of Malcolm looked to their commander. The ground before them was clear, but without the usual preparation, the seeding of arrows and sowing of spears. It was the worst possible situation for heavy horse. Malcolm stood in his saddle, raised his lance, then pointed it down the valley.

"You heard the horn," he yelled. "For the hound! The hallow!" He dropped his lance and hammered down the field like thunder, like lightning, like an avalanche of steel and breaking iron.

22

THE HORSES MOVED like a river broken free from the lake, a flood bursting from the dammed discipline of the battle line, their barding bright in the sun, shields and lances dancing over them like leaves on the water. Banners snapped in the wind, men screamed and arrows fell, the terror of battle lost in the exultation. Malcolm gritted his teeth and committed to the tumble, nothing in his head but the flow of his horse, the weight of his spear. Nothing in his heart but violence.

The green expanse of the field closed around him. The fog mingled with the last smoke from the burned haystacks. He couldn't hear anything but the rattle of his armor and the hammerfall of his horse's charge. He knew he was shouting because his throat was raw, but it was lost in the cacophony of a thousand voices, each one screaming and swearing and making promises to the gods.

The distance closed, and there was only violence.

The twin waves of heavy horse crashed into each other, swords and shields and skulls crashing together with a din like heaven's bell breaking under a god's hammer. A spear glanced off his shield, its bearer struck from his saddle by one of Malcolm's companions, and then another, this one snagging on the exposed plate of Malcolm's pauldron. The metal crumpled around his shoulder, striking him numb, and the force of the blow twisted him sharply in his saddle, squeezing the breath from his lungs and dizzying him.

Malcolm bounced forward on his mount, reeling from the strike, the battle flowing around him while he collected his head. The spear pass was over, and they were thick among the Suhdrins, the fight coming to sword and mace. Everything around him was a fog of banners and steel and screaming men and dying horses. He blocked an attack from one side, sword bouncing off shield once, twice, then the attacker was past and Malcolm never saw his face. The crushed shell of his pauldron pinched into Malcolm's shoulder. The familiar, warm trickle of blood crawled down his arm. He wheeled his horse, snagging his spear in the ground as he turned, quickly dropping the now useless weapon and drawing his blade.

A swirling mass of armored men surged around him, beating swords against shields, crushing helmets, drawing blood, killing horses, dying with steel in their guts and mud in their teeth. When they fell, it was to disappear between terrified mounts, screams cut off before they reached the ground. There was no telling who was winning, even in this small part of the killing.

His thoughts were cut down by a hard press of Suhdrin knights to his side. Peering through his visor, Malcolm wasn't sure which direction he was facing, whether he had pushed beyond the enemy line and was caught now by their reserves, or if his own lines had collapsed, but there were suddenly many more Suhdrin than soldiers of the hound. They came at him with double-hand maces, swinging wide arcs of iron flecked with blood. Their horses were terrified, eyes rolling, jaws speckled with foam.

The knights were in a wedge as blunt as an axe, cutting through a line of Tenerran faithful. Malcolm's first instinct was to dive aside before they rode him down, but his knees were crushed so tightly against his fellow knights that his horse could have been dead and not fallen. So instead he turned to face the wedge. There was just a moment before they struck, a heartbeat stretched into a dozen, and still they came straight for him.

They were Fabron's men. The black anvil and red sun on their tabards were surreally clean in the middle of battle, unstained by blood or sweat or the field of mud—as though they had been delivered from the Black Mountain of their master's domain whole and untouched by the hand of god, placed in the midst of this chaos before the filth of war could reach them. Malcolm had broken bread with Emil Fabron at last Frostnight, swearing a whiskey-oath as though their mothers were sisters, and their children kin.

Emil was at their fore, the open face of his helm revealing teeth white and wild as he screamed toward Malcolm, the black iron of his mace clenched in fists the size of bread loaves. Leading from the front.

Good man, Malcolm thought. *Leading as the gods meant lords to lead.* He wondered if a flash of recognition crossed Emil's face in the breaths between blows, if the man knew who he was about to ride down, or if he was lost in the battle's song.

Fabron struck down the nearest Tenerran knight, his mace punching through the skull like wind through wheat, trampling man and horse under iron hooves, then he surged forward and was at Malcolm's side.

He muscled the mace over his shoulder, keeping the momentum of the swing, raising it over his head like a woodman's axe and turning his attention to the next target, the next skull to be crushed and heart pulped, the next knight in this endless harvest of heretics and rebels.

In the tiny space cleared by the fallen knight, Malcolm bucked forward, his horse straining through mud and broken bodies. He lay flat against his horse's neck as Emil's mace whistled overhead, and then the iron duke was twisting again, drawing the heavy weapon back and over. Malcolm punched with his shield, clapping Emil's screaming mouth shut and breaking his jaw, then stood in his saddle and struck down, down, down again with his sword. The metal of Emil's helm bit and broke, spilling blood across his face.

The mace came around, the haft of it crashing into Malcolm's ribs. Sharp pain popped through his chest, blood dragging through his breath, but the momentum of Emil's attack was gone. Still, Fabron's horse pushed forward, along with the rest of the wedge, crowding into Malcolm, sliding him along the edge of their formation. Emil slipped past, but before he left Malcolm's range, the lord of Houndhallow swung again, dropping shield and safety to grasp his sword in both hands.

He crashed the forte of the blade into the back of Emil's head and felt metal and bone give way. The man's head flopped forward, blood vomiting from the ruin of his face. Malcolm drew the length of his sword through the breached neck of Emil's armor, slicing clean through. The head fell into his lap, the bright white nub of his neck bubbling like a fountain, and then he was past, horse charging forward, limp body bouncing lifelessly in the saddle, and the next Suhdrin knight was in Malcolm's face.

The battle moved on.

Malcolm was caught in the tide of the Suhdrin charge. There was a moment of wrath among the men of the Black Mountain in the wake of their lord's violent death, their battle cry mingling with tears of rage, and their attack was full of vengeance. It took all of Malcolm's strength and sword-sworn skill to batter them away, the impetus of their charge taking them swiftly past as he slid away, and then the wedge was past and the Tenerran mass swallowed them.

Fabron's charge had been premature, and his men were paying in their blood the price of his poor decision. Alone and surrounded they were cut down, one by one, then in groups, and soon Malcolm sat on his horse in the middle of a moment of peace on the battlefield. He stood in his stirrups, craning his neck to see the rest of the lakeside field.

The banner of the hound fluttered at the center of the battlefield, though the man holding it was not the same knight who had carried it at the start of their charge. The rest of Malcolm's force swirled around him in a tight knot. A third of their number had gone into the mud, part of the crawling, writhing carpet of fallen knights that covered the ground all around. Riderless horses galloped madly behind the lines.

To either side the battle raged. The Tenerran cavalry carried the center, Suhdrin spear- and bowmen held the right, and the head of the field in the nape of the tiny hillock, where the fight had started, was a swirling mass of hounds and banners and screaming men, the battle lines as murky as whirlpools in a crashing stream, forming and swirling away with each breath. He could not see who held the day among the trees. Malcolm and his men were dangerously far forward in the center of the field. On the opposite side, the Suhdrin lines shifted and massed, preparing a countercharge. The fallen banner of Fabron lay nearby. Malcolm hooked it up and raised it, then struck it in the ground.

"My lord, you'll give them a rallying point," one of his men said, and made to push the banner down. Malcolm stopped him.

"He was a good man, and a good friend," he said. "Sound the withdrawal. Let his kin collect the colors, and his body. If they can find all the pieces."

"But the field is ours," the man complained.

"As long as they let us have it. MaeHerron held back and we won't be able to hold without his pikes. Come on, before they take it from us."

With a fury of horns, Malcolm formed up his men and did a circling pass around Fabron's banner before thundering back toward the lake. The Suhdrin bowmen along the right gave a half-hearted cheer and a volley, but the flights fell short. The promised countercharge came, though the riders only traveled far enough to surround Fabron's grim banner and reclaim it. The duke of the Black Mountain was still on his horse, headless corpse slouched forward, blood streaking through the destrier's mane so thick the beast looked fey.

"We'll gather the lines and try again," Malcolm said to the men who rode beside him. They were watching the Suhdrin countercharge with sullen anger, no doubt counting their dead and what little ground their blood had gained. "Let them crash around us. Taking the field is well and good, but we need footmen to hold it. If we can get MaeHerron…"

A great shattering noise rolled down the valley. Malcolm stopped and twisted in his saddle. The fog along the right flank split open, spilling knights of the line down the field's length. The swirling confusion of that flank resolved into an armored cavalry charge that threatened to wipe Malcolm and his men off the earth.

"Their reserves!" he cried. "They must have circled behind the foot, formed a new flank in the confusion." It was impossible to tell their numbers, but it hardly mattered. The ranked spearmen on the left had reformed into an arc that presented shields both to Malcolm and the broader Tenerran line. Malcolm's men would be crushed between the spearmen and this new charge. He looked back at the Tenerran forces. There was no movement, and they were too far away to run to safety.

"Form on me! Form on the charge!"

"We'll never make it, my lord!" his sergeant yelled. There was a murmur in the ranks as the men realized their plight.

"Not back, lads." Malcolm circled his horse a few times, drawing the Blakley knights to his side and settling their lines. The hammering descent of the Suhdrin forces filled the air and shook the ground. When the wedge of knights was to his liking, Malcolm took the place at the head of the formation. Spear and shield gone, Malcolm waved his sword over his head and pointed forward. He started the charge.

They rode down the field to its center, to the ground they had just surrendered. He thundered past the ruin of Fabron's charge, sheering away from the Suhdrin attack, ignoring the threatening flank of spearmen to his left, abandoning the safety of his own line. Charging toward the opposite side of the field and the gathered banners of Halverdt and LeGaere, Marchand and Bassion, and above them all the coldly flickering colors of the high inquisitor.

The men hesitated only a heartbeat, then threw themselves into the charge with the wild abandon of the mad and the doomed. They vaulted the bodies at the battle's center and started up, up, into the jaws of the Suhdrin defenses. The banner of the hound snapped loudly over their heads, rippling in the wind of their passage. A loud, bellowing cheer went up from the Tenerrans far behind them as this small pocket of knights raced toward their deaths and glory.

Malcolm was deaf to it all. He felt suspended in time, with only the horse, the banner, and his men.

The colorful lines of the Suhdrin defenses wavered. They were not prepared for the charge, expecting to watch as Malcolm was run down, shocked to be suddenly setting spears and steadying nerves as this hundred-count of horse and knight barreled toward them. Drums signaled up and down the line, horns and the screaming commands of sergeants and lords, but in the ranks there was doubt. The campaign had been built on stories of fear, stories about the dangers posed by the pagans and their mad gods.

Fear was natural. Fear was Malcolm's best hope.

As the line approached, Malcolm's men tightened their wedge. It took only one man on the spear line to fail, one soul to tremble at their approach, one shield to dip and pike to drop, and then his brother beside him, and then the charge would find its heart. But as they charged forward, the spears held. He was down to heartbeats now, a breath and a half before impact. He was screaming.

Then they were among the thicket of spears. The

man beside Malcolm fell without a sound, a barbed tip through his throat and then he pitched up and away, the horse tumbling like a boulder. A spear skittered over the barding by Malcolm's leg, clipping his knee as it passed, and then another dipped toward his head but broke before it reached him, its wielder lost beneath hooves and mud. There was the tremendous, rib-breaking crash of horse into shield, body into steel, flesh and bone and blade thundering as they met.

Malcolm was among the lines. One second he was charging through wavering spears, and the next he and his horse and what remained of his men were surrounded by the levy. He was weaving back and forth, striking hard to left and right with his sword, his horse trampling any foolish enough to get close. There were hundreds around them, and more beyond, but for a brief, bright moment Malcolm was reaping blood and reaving fear.

Soon the footmen beneath him were falling back. In the respite, Malcolm's men swirled around him, their hundred down to dozens, but the banner still flew. Behind them, the cavalry that had threatened to crush them was having trouble of their own. Their mad charge had followed Malcolm for a while, until the Tenerran lines had seen their flank and formed into their own charge. The center of the valley was a mad melee, axes and archers mixing in the ruin of mud.

Some number of the Suhdrin knights had fought their way to the arc of spearmen on the left and were reforming in the shelter of the shields. Close by, the enemy line was breaking. Malcolm's charge had taken them by surprise, and the ranks of spear and shield were peeling away like dying flesh. Their reserve had been spent in the battle at the valley's head, and that force was now wasted, trying to recover on the left. In the gap, MaeHerron had finally roused his forces and come pouring down the field.

The Suhdrin forces wavered. They could break at any second.

And then they did. Malcolm raised his sword to strike the next skull, but there was no one around him. He looked around, squinting through the visor of his helm, and saw that the line had broken. He and his men stood alone at the edge of the forest. Between the trees he could see glimpses of men and horses in full retreat, their banners cast aside, their shields littering the floor like autumn leaves.

Malcolm stood in his stirrups and screamed at their backs. His men took up the call, and their voices reached the sky and shook the trees and lifted the hearts of the soldiers behind.

Then he collapsed into his saddle and let the pain and ache and fatigue overwhelm him. He sheathed his sword before he dropped it, then slouched against his horse's neck and waited for someone to lead him home.

23

THERE WERE A lot of priests in the Suhdrin army.
Fully half of the soldiers who milled about the
camp that settled along the southern bank of the
Tallow wore the church's colors, and there was a
troupe of inquisitors and naethermancers at the core
of the force who kept to themselves. Elsa was the only
vow knight in the camp, and none of the other priests
seemed interested in talking to her. None but Lucas.

The pair walked through the camp in silence,
surrounded by ranks of knights and their attendant
men-at-arms. The army was in shock, still recovering
from the defeat at the battle of the Tallow. Their
numbers grew day by day. There were a lot of sharp
blades in camp, getting sharper each night.

"This does not feel like an army defeated," Elsa
whispered while they walked. As soon as she had
recovered from her fight at Tallownere, she and Lucas
had come north to see what had occurred.

"Because they are not. Those who were at the
Tallow are angry at having been defeated, but these
legions that have joined them..." Lucas shrugged.
"They're confident, they're arrogant, sure that things
will be put right now that they've arrived. Sure they
would have won that fight."

"Seems like trouble."

"Aye. The veterans will hate the newcomers for their arrogance; the newcomers will hate the veterans for their failure. Both sides are shamed by their brethren."

"And both are furious at the northern lords, for putting Suhdrin pride to the sword," Elsa said. She watched a group of young knights gathered around a keg, drinking and swearing and making claims of prowess. Their armor was too bright and their voices too loud. It would be a miracle if any of them survived. "There will be no peace."

"Not until there's a great deal more shame, at least."

"What of the southern lords who have joined Adair? The duke of Redgarden stands with them, I know, and there's talk of Roard," Elsa asked.

"Roard will stay with their blood as long as they can, but they're not eager for the fight. Jaerdin's loyalty is to Blakley, not the north."

"There's a difference?"

"Not today, there isn't," Lucas said. They came to a stop at the top of a small hill that overlooked much of the river valley. The fields bristled with pikes and banners. They stood in silence for a while, looking at the host of war, measuring its size, its intent. Lucas sighed. "Where do you think they'll cross?"

"With this many banners?" Elsa asked. "Wherever they damned well please."

Lucas snorted, then started down the hill.

"Come on," he said. "We have a council to attend."

The duke of Greenhall's tent squatted at the center of his army, flanked by a canvas doma on one side and a bonfire on the other. The scent of frairwood reached their noses long before they got to the tent.

The guards at the entrance scowled at Sir LaFey, but at Lucas's insistence they let her inside. They seemed accustomed to taking orders from priests of Cinder.

Inside there were more priests than lords. Gabriel Halverdt sat glumly at the center of the tent, slumped forward in a field throne. High Inquisitor Sacombre stood at his side, hand draped casually over the back of the throne, the staff of his office leaning against his chest. A trio of lesser priests waited in Sacombre's shadow, hands folded in meditation. To Lucas's surprise, one of them had the tribal tattoos of Tener on his face and neck.

The only other person in the tent was Sir Volent. The Deadface lurked in the corner of the tent, as far from the priests as he could manage. Volent turned his head and looked hard at them when Sir LaFey closed the tent flap behind her.

The air was thick with frairwood and sweat. Whatever conversation had been going on before Lucas's arrival settled into an uncomfortable silence. He took the time to look each man in the eye before speaking.

"I was told this was a council of war," he said. "I came to advise, in hopes of peace."

"What do you know of war, priest?" Halverdt grumbled without looking up.

"What do I know of anything?" Lucas answered. "Where are the other lords?"

"This is a private audience," Sacombre said, "and a private matter. You were invited to give your insight into certain things, and then you will be free to leave."

"Free, or required?"

"Do you always speak to your master in this way?" the tattooed priest hissed. Lucas looked him over again. Clearly Tenerran, and maybe a little mad. Fresh converts were always the most zealous. Lucas laughed.

"My master is Cinder, god of winter and reason and death," he said, then gestured to the high inquisitor. "This is a man. Do not confuse the two."

Sacombre chuckled, a low, rolling laughter that carried as much joy as threat. He stood up, casually setting his staff of office against the throne and strolling to the center of the tent, where a low brazier burned. He rubbed his hands together and held them out to the smoky fire.

"Always the rogue, Lucas. Always the wise blade. We've missed your wit in Heartsbridge."

"I truly doubt that you have."

"Some of us have. Some of us mark your absence, at least."

Frair Lucas nodded sharply. The two had disagreed in the past, usually over matters of atrocity and justice. The high inquisitor had a keen theological mind, Lucas knew, but his approach to the north was too absolute. That, and he always seemed to be leering, even as he prayed.

"Tell your tale, priest, and be gone," Halverdt said. He readjusted the thick cloak around his knees, in spite of the heat. "I've had enough of the clever words of holy men today."

"Which tale would you hear?" Lucas asked.

"You were at the court of the Fen Gate prior to this travesty," Sacombre said. "We would know the mind of Lord Adair."

"You know it well enough," Lucas said, not taking his eyes off the duke. "You have provoked him often enough. Little surprise that he has bitten back."

"I hardly consider raiding one of my villages a *little* surprise," Halverdt said. "Nor interfering with the justice of my rulings. Nor is the summoning of a gheist—"

"We know little enough about that," Lucas said. "Let's not make accusations we can't prove."

"The pagan bitch followed that gheist to my men," Sir Volent said. "A huntress and her hound. What more proof do you need?"

"I find it difficult to believe that the woman charged with killing the old gods would somehow be their servant, as well," Lucas answered. "Not unless she is doing a truly terrible job of it."

"Let us stay to the facts we know, and the result of those facts," Sacombre said. "There has been an unprecedented surge in gheists, wouldn't you say?"

Lucas paused, feeling his way around what Sacombre was saying.

"This is true," he allowed.

"And this surge corresponds uncomfortably with our recent troubles."

"It's more reasonable to say that the surge may be the cause of our recent troubles," Lucas said. "After all, it was the events at Gardengerry that led to your men riding out to Tallownere. The violence that occurred there may have drawn the gheist, which then drew the huntress who was tracking it."

"Enough!" Halverdt bellowed. He stirred beneath his embroidered cloak, standing from the throne. He was a larger man than Lucas remembered, as though swollen with anger. "Tener has raised its banners at my border, and I will defend myself. All of Suhdra stands with me. The church stands with me! I will not sit here and listen to reasonable men argue the details of my offense!"

"My lord, it was not our intention—" Sacombre began. Halverdt cut him off.

"I thank you for your support, priest, and your blessing, but this is a matter of blades, not prayer. I accept the banners you brought north, and those of your priests who are willing to fight at our side, but do not stand here and debate the justification for this war. House Adair has offended me." Halverdt gathered his robes and settled once again onto the throne. "They have killed my men and were behind the murders at Gardengerry. I will take my justice from their bones."

Sacombre bowed slightly, just enough to be respectful but not far enough to be kind. The trio of priests followed suit.

Lucas and Elsa didn't move.

"As you wish, my lord," the high inquisitor said. "That is why we have come to you. My favored servant—" he gestured to the tattooed priest "—Frair Allaister Finney has learned of a hidden road through the Fen that will allow you to fall on Adair's castle without warning. You will be able to cut the heart from this rebellion before the north can fully rise against you."

"Through the Fen?" Halverdt snorted. "Yes, a brilliant thought. Why feed my knights to the gheists one at a time, when I could lose them all at once? The Fen is thick with pagan danger. No army can march through it."

"Your men will be safe in the company of my priests," Sacombre purred. "Whatever danger the Fen presents, the strength of Cinder will protect you. And Frair Allaister will lead the company personally. No other man is more capable of seeing you safely through."

"What makes him so capable?" Halverdt asked. "He looks more pagan than the huntress bitch."

"Indeed I was. Born to the shaman's way, but I have seen the cold heart of reason," Allaister said. "As to my knowledge of the Fen, I must admit, I have never walked those paths."

"You would have the blind lead the foolish, Sacombre?"

"Not blind," Allaister said. "I have in recent days been tracking a certain gheist. It was summoned by pagans in Gardengerry, and has traveled north ever since."

"Wait a damned minute," Lucas said. "I've been hunting this same gheist. Sir LaFey and I have followed it from Gardengerry, and she did battle with it outside your walls, my lord."

"And still it roams?" Halverdt asked.

Elsa bristled and stepped out from behind Lucas.

"You ask what the frair knows of battle, but I ask what you know of killing gods?"

The room grew tense, and the light changed. Lucas turned to see that Elsa had flared her goddess, the subtle lines of sun-bright energy pooling in the runes of her dented armor. He smiled.

"My lord, my brothers," he said. "I'm afraid that if this hunt is to travel north, I must insist on coming along."

"So you can warn the Tenerrans?" Volent asked. "No, I think not."

"I have no side in this war, if war this is to be. My only service is to the faithful of all Tenumbra, and to their protection." Lucas settled his eyes on Halverdt. "This is a dangerous gheist, my lord. The town of Gardengerry lies in ruins. Disaster in Greenhall was only averted by the presence of Sir LaFey, and the brave action of Malcolm Blakley's son. If Frair Allaister and his company are to be busy protecting your men and easing their passage, then someone else will have to see to the gheist. Sir LaFey and I will serve that duty."

Halverdt grunted, but made no move to deny Lucas his request. The duke looked to Sacombre.

"Very well, Frair Lucas," the high inquisitor said. "Your talents will be welcome."

"What of the other lords?" Halverdt said. "I can't withdraw from the border without weakening their position, or drawing the attention of the Tenerran dogs. Will they be consulted?"

"That is the gift of this plan, my lord," Sacombre said. "You need take only a small force: several dozen, say, drawn from Greenhall, rather than from the border outposts. Gather men who have not yet been sent forward, and the other lords will never know what we do."

"Why am I keeping such a secret from my fellow lords of Suhdra?" Halverdt asked.

"Blakley has spies among us. He must," Sacombre whispered. "Redgarden has already betrayed his blood, and whispers speak of treachery in Roard, and DuFallion. Who else might abandon his brothers and stand with the pagans? We can't afford to take any chances."

"A small force," Halverdt said. "Fair enough, but the scraps I have at Greenhall will not make much of a threat. Recruits and codgers, the lot of them. I have trouble believing they can take the Fen Gate."

"Lord Cinder has foretold it," Allaister said. He bent his knee before the duke. "Your victory is assured."

"Assured, yes, but still," Sacombre gestured to Sir Volent. "They must be led, and who better to lead them than your knight-marshal?"

Volent looked startled, as much as his numb

features could show surprise. He shook his head.

"I will not go into the Fen, my lord. Not for gods or glory."

"Do you fear the gheists, Sir Volent?" Sacombre asked.

"I fear nothing," he said, "but my place is at the border, leading my lord's men to victory."

"And so you shall. Final victory." Sacombre drifted to where Volent was huddled against the canvas wall. "It is your blade that will end this war."

"He's right, Henri," Halverdt said. "They will need a true leader: a warrior to drive them, and a blade to inspire them. You are both."

"My lord, I should not..."

"Silence. You will do this." Halverdt turned back to Allaister. "This gheist that you track. How will it help me?"

"After the battle at Greenhall, I was able to find an artifact of its summoning. Something you should have discovered, Frair Lucas," Allaister said sharply. "It will let me track it through the wilds, no matter where it goes."

"How will that get you to the Fen Gate?" Frair Lucas asked. Allaister ignored him, keeping his eyes on Halverdt. He treated the question as if the duke had asked it.

"Because it is going home, my lord," Allaister said. He drew something from his robes and held it up in his palms. It was an iron gauntlet, scarred and pitted as though by acid. The shadows of the glove slithered in the flickering light of the tent. Lucas was reminded of the corruption he had seen in the bear spirit, and the shimmering blackness that Elsa had described to him as the gheist's main form. The gauntlet itself looked like the crest of House Adair, and could easily have come from that family's collection of tribal icons.

"It is seeking its master," Allaister said, "and we will follow."

24

THEY PUSHED THE boat into the middle of the western ford, its flat bottom grinding against the smooth stones of the river as it beached, then hung a white flag from the prow and started pouring the wine. Ian settled into the makeshift bench and table that dominated the vessel. He waited. Martin Roard splashed across the ford on his charger and swung from his saddle directly into the opposite bench. Ian smiled.

"This is hardly dignified," Martin complained. He took his flagon of wine and squinted into it, then drained it and poured another.

"Last we spoke, you were still recovering from the peasants' melee," Ian said. "You have little cause to complain about dignity."

"That was a tournament. This is war. War will always be violent, unforgiving, horrifying and messy. All in all, undignified. Which is why it is incumbent on us to maintain whatever dignity we can manage."

"Which is why we're sipping wine in a raft under a flag of truce, rather than rattling our swords and gnashing our teeth across a field of battle," Ian said. "Appreciate what you get, Martin."

"If this is what passes for wine in the north," Martin muttered.

"You are an odd man, Sir Roard."

"Odd enough. So." Martin set his flagon aside and rested his hands on the table. "How's the rebellion?"

"Rebellion?"

"That's what they're calling it," Martin said. "The high inquisitor and his happy little band. They're saying all manner of things. That Tener is withdrawing from the Celestial church. That you've appointed your own electors, and your own celestriarch. That MaeHerron is turning Suhdrin pilgrims away from the winter shrine, or holding them hostage, or planning on destroying Cinderfell."

"All ridiculous," Ian said. "Halverdt's just trying to stir trouble in the south. Convince you to join your banners to this ridiculous crusade."

"Why do you think I'm here?" Martin asked. He glanced over his shoulder at the ranks of spears, the rows of tents and pillared campfires spread out on the hills behind him. The banner of House Roard stirred lazily among the tents, alongside Marchand and LeGaere. "My father pressed to hold this flank alone. The high inquisitor doesn't trust us, Ian."

"And if Marchand and LeGaere march across this ford, will you march with them?" Ian asked. Martin drank slowly from his flagon, pausing to refill it and stare sightlessly down the river before he answered.

"Nothing is known today," he said. "Sacombre is making a difficult case. House Adair's actions cannot be denied, and they are deeply suspicious."

"Suspicious in what way? That Gwen decided to stand up to Henri Volent, rather than stand aside and let him commit slaughter?"

"The gheist, the summoning, even the priest that rode with her. Apparently this Frair Lucas is something of a rogue in the inquisition. Not got the best reputation. It was his attendant vow knight who rescued you in Greenhall."

"What in gods' names has that got to do with any of this?" Ian sat up straight, forgetting the wine half-raised to his lips. "Martin, there was a riot in Greenhall. Not because of anything that we did, but because that monster Volent spread his lies and got Marchand to overstep the bounds of the tournament. That man tried to kill me."

"It's a tournament," Martin mumbled. "People get hurt."

"Gods, listen to you. I thought we were friends."

"We are, and not just you and I. Our houses. Which is why I'm here." Martin fiddled with his wine for a minute more, then set it aside and leaned urgently forward. "You need to promise me something."

"I don't like the way this is going."

"Just listen for a minute. Sacombre has more than convinced the majority of the Suhdrin lords that this is the beginning of a war. Not against Suhdra, or the church, or even against Halverdt. People are starting to believe that this is a war against the gods themselves."

"Martin, you can't believe that," Ian said. "You know my heart as well as any man. I'm faithful to the church, if not all of its priests. Especially not to the inquisition. But that doesn't make a heretic of me."

"Yet you have the tribal ink, and that pagan dog in your tombs..."

"That is a matter of tradition," Ian snapped. "Not faith. I'm Tenerran, as you are Suhdrin. We're not going to tear down our houses and put up white marble villas, just because our walls remind you of the old ways."

"It makes things difficult. You must know that," Martin said with a sigh. "There are murals of the Spirit Wars—"

"Call them what they are. The crusades," Ian interrupted. "The pogrom."

"Names, hundreds of years old," Martin said dismissively. "There are murals of battles in the halls of my home. I have seen these murals since I was a child, of Suhdrin knights and godly priests fighting the hordes of the mad spirit warriors from your history. Abominations of man and god tearing through holy men, their blood painting the trees of the forest, and rank after rank of tribesmen, each face scrawled with the pagan script. It's a difficult image to forget."

"Men like Sacombre make sure no one forgets," Ian said tightly. "Especially those in the north."

"Ian, don't take it personally. I have knelt with you at the Frostnight, drunk your health on the high days and seen your ashes on the low. I know you're a man of the gods." Martin paused and leaned back. He couldn't bring his eyes to meet his friend's gaze. "What I don't know is the faith of your fellows."

Ian was silent for a long time. The river flowed around them, the skip creaking roughly against the riverbed, the distant sounds of two war camps drifting over the water.

"You believe him," he said finally.

"No, not... not entirely. Sacombre has an agenda, and there's something else going on. I don't know what. There were many priests, all traveling with him and his little army..."

"And I am supposed to surrender, simply because Sacombre has a couple dozen guards among your banners?"

"Half our number, maybe—but that's not the point.

Most of his priests are gone. Disappeared in the night, like bad dreams. No one's seen Sir Volent, either."

"Gone back to Greenhall?"

"Ian, you're not listening to me. I think House Adair is manipulating you. All of you. I think they want a war with the south."

"Was it House Adair that drove us out of Greenhall? House Adair that nearly killed me on the tourney ground, or hunted our host through the forests of Suhdra and chased us to the banks of the Tallow, killing our people as we ran?"

"No, but Gwendolyn Adair tossed the stone that created that avalanche," Martin said. "And Gwendolyn Adair was waiting for you at the Tallow, ready to join your strength to hers. I think you know less of her than you should."

"I know enough. I know her name, and I know her blood." Ian stood, shifting the balance of the raft ever so slightly. The prow began to nose into the current. "We are Tenerran, and we will stand together."

"There is more to faith than culture, Ian. Don't forget that."

"You asked for a promise," Ian said. "What is it?"

"If we come across this ford… *when* we do," Martin answered, "find me. I can offer you sanctuary. I'm not sure the other Suhdrin knights can make that promise."

"When you come across this ford, Martin, you should find me." Ian vaulted over the raft's side and landed with a splash in the water. "But all I can offer you is my blade, and I'm sure the other Tenerran knights will be eager to make the same promise."

25

A NEW FOREST WAS gathering at the border. It was a forest of banners, pavilion hills, and fields of spears massing along the Tallow, with another closer to the Fen, much larger. The survivors of the disastrous battle of the Tallow had reformed, reinforced by new columns from the south. An army of Suhdrin lords and their loyal men.

Gwen watched them from the limestone bluffs, an area of sheer cliffs and rough water known as the Redoubt. Her men were camped along the flat tops of the bluffs, all taken from the force alongside which Malcolm Blakley had refused to ride during the previous week's battle. She counted five dozen good spears under her banners, most of them men-at-arms, with half that many archers and half again knights. All told, she had just over a hundred men to hold a border so long it would take five days to march from one end to the other. It wasn't enough.

"I don't think Houndhallow understands the task he has given us," Gwen muttered.

"He knows it well enough," Merret said. "Just as he knows only an Adair can hope to hold this land."

"Perhaps, but the Suhdrin numbers grow by the day. It doesn't seem as though Castian Jaerdin's letters found many receptive ears."

"True," Sir Merret agreed. "Even spread across the whole border, there are too many." He stood beside his lady on the bluff, supporting his weight on the banner that flew her colors. "More than enough to see us finished."

"If met in the open field, yes," Gwen agreed. "Happily, the Fen is short on open fields." Their view extended from the field of the battle of the Tallow to the east, all the way to where the Fen's rolling forests crossed the river and spilled into Suhdrin lands. The Redoubt split this distance, and this section of the Tallow ran fast and deep. If Greenhall meant to cross into Adair land at any of the dozens of fords that covered this distance, Gwen's knights would be ready.

"I count six of the great houses of Sudhra," Merret said.

"I didn't think to find Roard among them. They are close to the Blakleys, I'm told."

"We are close to the Blakleys," Merret answered, "but he had no interest in riding with us in battle. Their friendship may mean less than we thought."

"As much as I hate to admit it, Houndhallow was right," Gwen said. "Our place is on this side of the river. In defense." She adjusted the buckling on her shoulder plates, squirming under the heavy metal. She wasn't used to this much armor—it had taken her father's direst warnings to get the huntress into plate-and-half. "We have much to protect," she muttered, thinking of the witches' hallow, tucked away in the forests near her ancestral castle, bounded by pagan wards.

"Still, to miss out on that first battle..." Merret said. "The Blakley victory seems only to have strengthened the Suhdrin resolve. We must hold them on that side of the river. If they make it beyond the Tallow, their numbers will bear against us. They can fill the forests with their banners, and drive to the Fen Gate in less than a month."

"A bloody month," Gwen said.

"Aye."

"Once beyond the Tallow their horses will mire in the swamps," she said, "and those shiny spears will get tangled in the Fen."

"Houndhallow's army holds at White Lake. His son defends the flank. All we must do is wait, and hope the armies arrayed against us strike elsewhere."

"I'd rather not wait," Gwen said. She pulled her banner from the ground and marched down the hill toward their campsite. "It is not in my nature."

"Houndhallow tasked us with holding the Tallow," Merret said.

"He did, and we shall," she replied with a grim grin. "Just not this side of it."

There were other ways across the river. Gwendolyn left Sir Merret in charge of the Redoubt, then took a handful of knights and forty men-at-arms—nearly half her complement—and marched west. They left their banners behind, so that any eyes that watched the Adair camps might not notice the deficit in their ranks.

Each man brought two horses and enough food to last a week. If they needed more than that, her plan had already failed, and food would be the least of their concerns. Gwen's pack of hunting dogs followed at their flanks, sliding smoothly through the forest like gray fog.

Two days and they came to the ford at Highbeck, a dead place in the distant woods, once a village for shamans and the witching wives who used to attend some lost pagan site, abandoned after the crusade. A gnarled tree grew out of the village well, its limbs twisted and gray with moss. Still in the saddle, Gwen drew her men around her in its sparse shadow.

"We'll camp here," she said. "Camp and hunt. Brennan, Hogue, each of you take half the men and establish barracks here in the village. One of you will hunt while the other rests and guards the village. I want spears in the forest at all times."

"There's boar enough in these woods to keep us going for an age, m'lady, but why did we come all this way to hunt?"

"We're not hunting boar, though we'll need food soon enough. No, we're here to hunt Acorns. The hunting party will cross the ford and find the Suhdrin flank. Harry their scouts, nip at their heels."

"Halverdt will just turn his face to us, and we haven't the men to resist him," Brennan said.

"The bulk of Halverdt's force remains at White Lake, and the rest are watching the Redoubt. He may send a lance or two in our direction, but nothing we can't handle. Especially in this terrain." Gwen stood in her stirrups and looked out over the gathered men. "There is nothing of value in these woods, nothing but the old, mad gods and broken villages. No army could pass along these trails. None would dare. If nothing else, fear of the gheists will keep them at bay."

"These woods are haunted, my lady. Their fear is just," one of her men said. He was one of the younger ones in her party. "We should not be traveling here."

"You have your huntress with you, sir. Why should you fear?"

"What if our trouble is more mortal than godly?"

another asked. "If Halverdt stirs and turns toward us? If he sends Volent to come at us with strength?"

"We fall back across the river," Gwen said. "We run for our lives."

There was grumbling at that, but the men knew that if they were to hunt, they must also be ready to retreat. The war had to be waged at advantage, or not at all.

"Listen to me," she said, her voice rising. "We will not be gathering glory or ransom. We will not be capturing banners or freeing the land from the tyrant's boot. Greenhall will not fall by our efforts, but if we are fast, and cruel, and committed to the blade, we may disturb the Acorn's sleep. The duke of Greenhall will not rest easy while we hunt, nor Sir Volent reave without cost. Because wherever he walks, the ground will be soaked in the blood of his men. That is our prey, good sirs. That is our ransom." She drew her blade and held it aloft, anger twisting her words. "The blood of lesser men! Their blood and their fear!"

The men stirred from their saddles, raising in their stirrups and cheering. Then Gwen divided them according to their ranks and handed command over to Brennan and Hogue. They established a camp in a ruined beer hall, building hidden guard posts to overlook the ford and the paths that approached the village. After a short rest, Sir Brennan drew his men together and led them across the ford.

Gwendolyn rode with them, her hounds eager at her flank, diving into the woods, the scent of blood in their noses.

They twisted their way through the Fen and brought their spears to the broad plains beyond. Their first prey was a hunting party of Suhdrin rangers, gathering meat for the war party to the east. Gwen's men fell on their camp just as dusk reached the sky, coming out of the setting sun on horses as fast as the wind.

The rangers thought themselves far from the battle lines and their watches were lazy. Gwen led the charge, yelling her heart's rage as she scythed into the camp. A few of the enemy reached their bows and sent arrows into the charge, but they were tipped with broad arrowheads meant for tearing flesh and bleeding deer. Their shafts rattled off Gwen's men, whose armor was more than a match for the volley, and then it was down to the chase, horses overrunning soft huntsmen, hooves shattering bones and spears piercing bellies. The gore of their first kill was still steaming when Gwen's men finished with the slaughter.

They found the only landed man among the dead, a lesser knight whose signet of a deer's head and spear was unfamiliar to Gwen, and splayed his body on the long spit over the ranger's fire. Then they burned the fatty corpses of the boar that the hunters had already gathered, denying the meat to Halverdt's army.

"Let them eat their dead," Gwen muttered as she led her men back. Brennan plundered the deer-banner from the hunting party, and they flew it whenever horses appeared on the horizon.

She took them farther east on the return trip, hoping to gather a few more dead from Halverdt's army before she took her rest in Highbeck. In her head she kept hearing the animal screams of those peasants as Volent slaughtered them. The sound drove her on.

There was a thick orbit of scouting parties closer to the main body of Halverdt's army, attentive men on swift horses who from a distance saluted Gwen's party as though they were expected. That trick wouldn't last long, she mused, once the bodies were found.

Two days out and three back, and they found themselves once again in the Fen. Gwen's pack ran down a brace of deer to keep them fed. She ordered Brennan to burn the banner and cover their tracks. Any party they stumbled across in the near hills and tight paths would be too close to trick.

She ambled at the head of the column, their ranks tight on the narrow path, spears stowed to keep them from getting tangled in the low-hanging branches of wirewood that clogged the horizon. She and Sir Brennan discussed their next turning, and whether it was time to head back to Highbeck to give Hogue's men a turn at murdering Suhdrin bastards.

"They'll be after us as soon as they find Sir Deer," Brennan said, referring to the dead ranger left turning on a spit. "Best to be clear before Volent gets a sniff of our trail."

"And let Sir Hogue face them in all their strength? As much as I'm sure he would appreciate the glory, it hardly seems fair to sneak away without leaving a few more bloody bones in our wake."

"I'm okay with fewer bloody bones if it means getting home with all the men. There will be no proper burials on this trail, no priest to cut them into the quiet house, no cairns to pile. These are honorable men. They deserve a good death."

"A good death," Gwen said with a smile. "By which you mean a death on a field, under the sun, in the charge, and not skulking around the Fen, cutting down rangers, and burning wagons full of grain."

Brennan shrugged. He wore the Adair colors, but his shield was blazoned with his family crest. The blue axe and fist were spattered with mud, as were his face, his hair, and the bright tackle of his horse's kit. All the men looked the same, their faces grim and tired. Their voices mingled with the birdsong to raise a low murmur among the trees. The sound of it was mesmerizing. Gwen found herself swaying in her saddle listening to jangling bridles, the thwack of spear shaft on tree, the *shing* of chain mail, and grumbling voices and laughter.

The ford came into view, and the sound of the Tallow's waters drifted through the trees. Gwen rode to the head of the column. One of the men who had been sent forward to scout was waiting for them. Sir Brennan spurred forward to get a report. He and the scout talked briefly, then he motioned Gwen forward.

"Nae good," he said briefly. The scout who sat behind him looked grim. "Wellem believes we should find another route."

"Squire Wellem is out of luck," Gwen said sharply, studying the scout. "We left Sir Hogue at Highbeck, and we're going to relieve him, regardless of what has happened up ahead."

"The path is cursed, my lady," Wellem said. "There's nothing but death there."

"Death can be anywhere. More men have died in their beds than will ever bleed out on a battlefield, and yet you lay your head down each night without a whimper. Come, show me this place of death."

Wellem balked, but he and Sir Brennan flanked Gwen as they rode to the ford. The smell reached them before they caught sight of the river.

Something lay burst and bloody in the center of the ford. Gwen figured it for a horse at one time, but nothing but rags of meat and the wretched smile of freshly exposed ribs remained. Other bodies lay in the river, just beneath the surface, their armor resisting the current, folding the river over them like a clear, smooth blanket. The water swirled around their bulk, dimpling the face of the ford with swirling eddies and dammed pools, gathered in place by stacked knights and their mounts.

The river ran clean, the blood long since drained.

"How many?" Gwen whispered.

"No saying."

"Any sign from the village? Smoke or signal?"

"Nothing," Brennan said, shaking his head. "If any of our men survived, they're making themselves scarce."

"Wise enough. If Halverdt's men got this far, there's no telling how many of them are ranging through the Fen. Hogue is simply preparing for another assault."

"Or his force was killed to a man," Wellem whispered, "and now it's the blades of Greenhall that are lying in wait beyond the river."

"Yes—or that," Gwen conceded. "Have the men loose their spears and prepare. Gods know what we'll find ahead."

The remaining men of Gwen's column gathered at the ford and picked their way carefully through the wreckage of battle. They stared down uncomfortably at the water-softened faces of the dead, stepping over blade-ruined corpses. The horses whickered nervously as they advanced. Many of the dead were familiar, though changed awfully by their time in the river.

"Sir MaeBrun and young squire Hance," Brennan noted. "And Steffen. There are many ghosts in this river, my lady."

"Many dead," she agreed. "What I don't understand is why they are here, and not beyond."

"You ordered them to hold the ford. Perhaps they were encircled, and decided to fight their way out."

"That would require treachery, sir, or incredible luck." Gwen twisted in her saddle, judging the lay of the dead. "Maybe Halverdt's men established a shield wall of some sort, and Hogue thought to break it with a charge."

"If so, it didn't go well," Brennan said.

"No," Gwen answered quietly. "It did not."

They had yet to find evidence of enemy dead, though the identity of many in the river could not be determined. Gwen ordered her men into a wide crescent as they approached Highbeck.

26

T HE RUINS OF the village were silent.

"Go slowly, building to building," Gwen ordered. "Expect an ambush."

There was no ambush. The dead lay in bed or gathered around a cold campfire. A pot of stew congealed over the charred logs of the fire. Some of the bodies showed signs of rapidly donned armor, or held swords or the remains of torches in their lifeless fingers. Their wounds were horrendous, the edges blistered or crushed, as though the flesh had crumbled like ceramic.

Of the enemy there was no sign.

"Demons," Wellem insisted.

"Gheist," Brennan said. "Sir Hogue would never have fallen so completely to a mortal enemy."

"What difference?" the younger knight whined. "We need to get out of here."

"Patience, Wellem," Gwen said. She knelt beside one of the bodies that had been next to a fire. The man's arm had been severed, the edges so clean that even the rings of his mail were cut. Usually such a wound would drive the chain into the flesh, tearing through the skin like a saw, but the sleeve of the dead man's armor just lay over the wound. No blade was that sharp. "Strange that a gheist would strike here, of all places."

"It's a place of the old gods," Wellem said. He made the sign of sun and moon, carving their horns and crescents in the air with his thumb. "All know that! We should never have camped in such a cursed place."

"Aye, well…" Gwen stood and did a quick count. She turned to Sir Brennan. "I have eight in the village and surrounds. What do you want to bet that if we took the time to dredge the ford we would find twelve good men?"

"Sir Hogue among them," Brennan agreed. "Whatever attacked them, they tried to cross the Tallow to escape."

"And died in its waters," Wellem said sharply. "A gheist of the river, then, one of the drowned gods! My lady, we must…"

"Be silent," she said sharply. "Sir Brennan, gather the men. There will be no rest tonight, not until this place is well behind us. I don't think the likes of Wellem here could sleep near these bodies anyway."

"What of the dead? We should shrive the bodies, and send them on to the quiet house."

"The dead will remain dead. Once this madness is over we will send a priest and build a pyre, or whatever the church requires of us."

"Yes, my lady," he said. "We can have word to the Redoubt in a few days, if we ride hard. Sir Merret and Houndhallow need to know that this flank is lost."

"It is not lost yet. Not while we remain." Gwen circled the ruined village, scouring the woods, looking for signs of passage. She paused to the north and dismounted. "Here. Branches dragged across the trail, and this copse has been rebuilt. A force of some number has passed this way."

She plunged into the forest, pulling down branches and trudging through undergrowth until she reached a small hill. Many of the trees had been cut and moved, and were beginning to brown. The ground beneath was trampled. Once she reached the rise, Gwen stopped and pointed. A path north had been cleared by the trample of hooves and boots.

"See, Wellem? If a gheist was involved, it walked on a hundred feet," she said.

"And carried the Halverdt flag," Brennan said. He stooped and tore a scrap of cloth from the undergrowth. Green, with a stitch of gold across the top.

"Send a rider to the Redoubt. Our quarry travels north and east, toward the Fen Gate. Father will need reinforcements."

"And what are we to do?" Brennan asked.

"We hunt, Sir Brennan," Gwen said. She stood and remounted smoothly, turning her horse north. "Gabriel Halverdt has raised his banner in our land. I would see it burn."

The sun was still high when the soft jingle of armor carried down the trail. Gwen hushed her riders, then ordered them forward at a trot. With luck the sound of their riding would be masked by whatever was ahead.

Another column sauntered lazily in the same direction down the trail, two horses wide and winding away around the curve, their banners struck and colors covered. Gwen didn't need banners or colors to recognize Suhdrin knights. The riders at the rear were tired, slumped in their saddles, shoulders bent forward from weeks in armor and little rest.

The two Suhdrin knights at the back of the column

turned slowly, their eyes registering confusion, then surprise, and finally alarm as they recognized the colors on Gwen's tabard. They opened their mouths to shout a warning.

"Iron in the blood!" Gwen yelled, her family's war cry going back to the tribes. "Iron!" The path was too narrow to make effective use of the spear, so she drew her sword and spurred her horse into a sudden gallop. Brennan was right behind her, shouting the charge, and within heartbeats the rest of her column was a thunder of armor and drawn blades, the sharp song of swords and hoofbeats and fury.

The Suhdrin riders who had seen them tried to turn their horses, but the path was too narrow and they both wheeled, snarling their bridles together and starting a fight between their mounts. Gwen went between them, bowling the mounts aside and striking at the rider on her right. Her sword bounced off his shield, but she took the momentum and back-swung into the other knight, striking him on the bridge of his helm and cracking metal and bone.

Leaving them in her wake, she twisted to wrench her shield into her fist, struggling to get it to her shoulder before she reached the next pair of riders. These two held spears, letting the butts drag in the dirt to keep the heads out of the overhanging trees. The man on the left dropped his spear and tried for his sword, but the other executed a clever reversal on the shaft, taking it in both hands and presenting the tip to Gwen's hammering charge. The iron point skittered off her shield, catching a loop of her hair and tearing it free, jerking Gwen's head to the side. She battered the spear aside, striking with the forte of her blade and then thrusting the tip into the man's throat. His blood spilled out of the ragged wound in a gush.

Gwen whirled the gory blade over her head, taking a swing at the dead man's companion. He had gotten enough of his sword free to parry the attack, but the huntress merely whirled the sword again and drew it across his shoulder. It bit deep, driving the rings of his armor into the wound and slicing into muscle. He screamed, but she was already past.

Beyond that, the path became a maelstrom of startled horses and screaming knights and the bright, bloody scything of swords. Gwen lost herself in the rush, barreling past riders and laying about with her sword, howling the charge and trusting her men to cut down anyone she didn't kill. Someone landed a blow to her arm, and another to her leg, but the pain was washed away in the thrill of combat. Life was a blur of raised shields, wide, white eyes, horses and men—a face that split as she cut it and a man's innards emptying through the wound opened by the tip of her sword.

And then she was through. The trail ahead was empty. Behind her she could hear screaming and the rattling crash of shattered wirewood trees as horses were driven from the path and tumbled into the undergrowth. Gwen whirled around, ready to run down any Suhdrin knights who might have survived the charge, but her men were through, as well, their swords hacking up and down at the fallen column.

Sir Brennan rode up next to her. A gash across his cheek was leaking blood down his jaw, and his eyes were wild. The axe in his hand was bright red, and his armor was sprayed in blood. The knight took one look at his lady and let out a hearty laugh.

"Well, that was something of a surprise," he said.

"More for them than us," Gwen said. "Any lost?"

"Gods know. I saw Doucey fall into the trees, and Sir Jance took a spear to the belly, but we'll have to count the cost later." He paused, wiping blood from his blade and wrapping a bandage around his knuckles. "Strange to find such a number in column, this deep into the Fen."

"Aye. Where in gods' names were they headed?" Gwen asked.

"This was no patrol. They rode too heavy for that." Sir Brennan trotted over to the nearest corpse. "Plate-and-half. Sword, shield, mercy-blade, axe. These are front-line riders."

"Days from the front line," Gwen muttered.

"Unless the front line has moved," Brennan mused.

"There aren't enough here to have overwhelmed Sir Hogue," Gwen said. "I don't like it. Send two riders ahead, whoever has the freshest horses. I want to make sure no one escaped the column."

Sir Brennan nodded and peeled two men away from the melee. He pointed them down the trail. The rest dismounted and went among the dead, offering mercy to the wounded and gathering whatever loot was worth carrying. A few knights asked for ransom, but Gwen shook her head.

"No prisoners, no ransom," she said. The men grumbled, but they buried their blades in the rich and the poor alike. They rolled the dead into the forest and caught the horses that had survived, to lead them back to Highbeck. They were just preparing to move on when Brennan's men returned.

"Any runners?" Gwen asked. They shook their heads, but their faces were as white as snow.

"No, my lady," one of the men replied. "We found something more."

The Fen was an ancient place. Mounds of earth—rocky and topped with iron-hard trees as withered and tough as bones—dimpled the landscape in all directions. The low trenches between these mounds were soft loam, sodden with run-off and groundwater, more swamp than land. The paths that wound through the land were narrow and rocky, hard to travel by foot or horse, overhung with unyielding branches. Limestone bluffs sprouted from the ground like broken teeth.

Every trail gave a hundred chances for ambush. The sight lines were always close, the air humid and cold, the nights dark and bristling with insect life. It was no place to drive an army. Despite the broken ground, two dozen knights and their attendant men-at-arms were camped at the intersection of three of the old roads, tents thrown across the rocky ground and clinging to root-gnarled hillocks, small, smoky fires palling the air.

Gwen and her men watched from the thick tree line of a broader plateau, the ground under their feet more stone than earth, the trees twisted from trying to suck nutrients out of the cracks between limestone shelves. Their horses waited two hillocks back, penned like sheep.

"So we know where that column was headed," Brennan whispered in Gwen's ear. "Do you think he's moved away from the Redoubt?"

"No," she said. "We are fewer and traveled faster. The ones we rode down were exhausted. They must have been on the road for weeks." She scanned the sad banners hanging around the camp, their canvas limp in the humid air. "All of these men are vassals to

Halverdt himself. None of the other Suhdrin lords are represented here."

"I wonder if Roard and Bassion know about this force?"

"May yes. May no." Gwen did a quick count. "They have three times our number, and this is no ground for heroic charges."

"We should have brought archers."

"Merret needed them to hold the fords." Gwen slid behind the rise of the hill, resting her head against the mossy ground. "We must warn the Redoubt, and my father, but we have to get around them first." She nodded toward the encampment.

"We could ride west. Circle around. There are many trails."

"Ride west and we're too far from the Redoubt to give warning in time," Gwen said. "Besides, these men are riding north and east. They ride for the Fen Gate."

"What happened to hunting?"

"There are too many," Gwen said.

Brennan sighed and rubbed his eyes.

"So what do you propose?" he asked.

"We wait until night. Send men back to those bodies. Gather the tabards and their banners. Those men were clearly expected."

"You can't think to just ride up at a canter and through?"

"Not at a canter, no," Gwen said. "Not at all."

Night fell quickly. When the stars came out and Cinder peeked between the thin branches of the wirewood, Gwen cut her hounds loose to find their own way home, then ordered her men to mount up. They were wearing the colors of the dead. Gwen tucked her hair into a dented and bloody helm, then gave Sir Brennan the banner they had plundered. She brought a torch and gave him his lines.

"A bit dramatic, don't you think?" he asked.

"I want them to see the colors," Gwen said. "Besides, fire always brings out the best in soldiers."

They started yelling several curves down the road, spurring to a hard gallop and beating their swords against their shields. They dropped torches into the underbrush, the wirewood taking the flame as quick as dry grass, filling the sky with plumes of black smoke. As they approached the final bend, Gwen leaned over and put the banner in Brennan's hands to the torch. Fire danced along its trailing edge, illuminating the tri-acorn and cross of House Halverdt.

The sentries heard their approach, along with the rest of the camp, and had their spears at the ready. As Gwen and Sir Brennan came into view, the camp guards shouted for the riders to halt.

"Ambush!" Brennan yelled. "Fire arrows and pitch! Clear the way!"

The sentries hesitated, and Gwen's mount faltered, slowing briefly. She kicked it again into a gallop. The banner in Brennan's hands whipped in the wind of their passage, trailing sparks through the air. By its light, the guards could see that their armor was dented and bloody, their horses flecked in foam. Another moment of hesitation, during which Gwen and Brennan hammered closer, still screaming, and then the sentries gave way.

Gwen was forced to vault a makeshift barricade before the guards could drag it aside, and then she was in the camp and charging forward. She passed dozens of shocked faces, men and women peering out of tents and stumbling aside to clear the trail. She ran through a campfire, scattering embers into the night.

"How many?" one of the guards yelled as they passed.

"Half an army! Gods, maybe the whole of the north is at our heels!"

"Gheists?" came the reply.

"Gods be good!" was all that Brennan could manage, and then they were past and bulling their way through.

Gwen and her men, fifteen strong, slowed once they were past the first round of guards, but kept to a fast pace as they wound their way between campfires and tents. They were forced to ride single file, and she hoped her battered helm proved disguise enough. Not many knew her face, but recognition at this point would mean disaster for them all. More than one knight saw the flaming banner and saluted, muttering curses and the Halverdt words, "Against the night" as Brennan passed. It wasn't until Gwen could see the sentries at the far end of the camp that she gave the signal and her men picked up the pace.

"Foray! The pagan dogs have been sighted north of camp!" Brennan yelled at the sentries. The men, confused, pulled the barricade aside and watched in awe as Gwen and her column rumbled past.

"Your flag's on fire," one of the guards pointed out.

"So it is. I'll get another," Brennan said, then threw the banner into the hard ground like a spear, just ten yards beyond the sentry line. It stuck, the flames flickering up the pennant, consuming the green and gold like a candle. Once they were around the corner, Gwen gave another signal.

Her men fell into two columns.

"Hard canter. They'll figure out what happened before long. Best we're far down the road when they do, and better that we keep the horses as fresh as we can." She gave Sir Brennan a bright smile. "In case there's a fight."

"Gods be good," Brennan said, shaking his head wearily. Then he laughed. "Gods be damned good."

27

Henri Volent stood at the mouth of his tent, watching the column pass through his camp. He counted fewer than twenty Suhdrin men, with a burning banner at their fore. They cantered out the northern sentry line, leaving the banner behind, then disappeared into the forest.

He heard hounds baying in the distance.

"Who the hell was that?" he muttered to himself. The camp was in disarray, with several tents set ablaze by scattered campfires, and a cadre of troops by the southern entrance mustering as though they meant to make a foray. He headed in that direction, buckling his longsword to his belt as he walked.

An infantry captain by the sentry line was organizing his troop into a shield wall, and three knights-errant were buckling themselves into plate and calling for horses. Volent stood in the middle of the activity, his gaze going from the empty southern road to the fallen banner in the north. There was a distant fire to the south, its dim flames flickering between the wirewood trees. He took the captain by the shoulder and spun him around.

"Make your report, captain."

"Riders, my lord," the man stuttered. "A full

column to our south, with archers among them. I've sounded the alarm…"

"You haven't, actually," Volent said, "and I would advise against it. On whose report do you know of these pagan riders?"

"The reinforcements, my lord. The men from Stoneturn what we were expecting. They were ambushed, and…"

"Those riders?" Volent asked, pointing north. The captain squinted in the direction Volent was pointing.

"I suppose, my lord."

"You suppose. Because the riders who just entered this camp, who rode past your post, they have just exited the camp to the north."

"My lord? Why would they do that?"

"Why indeed?" Volent spat. "And if there was an ambush, why would it be set up to our south? On the road over which we just passed this morning? Within earshot of our sentries, and bow shot of our ranks?"

"I don't know, my lord."

"No, you do not. Sir Havreau." Volent shouted to one of the knights who clattered nearby, preparing his mount. "Get down the road, and tell me what you see!"

"Yes, my lord. As soon as my plate is affixed and my sword blessed by the inquisitor."

"To hell with your plate," Volent snapped. He grabbed the knight's horse from its attendant and swung into the saddle. "Send word to Inquisitor Finney. Have the man waiting for me when I get back."

He dodged around the barricade that was only now being dragged back across the road, then galloped south down the darkling path. The wirewood trees bent down over him like the crest of a silent wave, frozen in flinty silence. The darkness passed quickly.

Once around the first curve, Volent was bathed in firelight. Torches lay at the base of a dozen trees, their pitch-wrapped heads guttering in the char. Riding on, Volent found the site of the attack. Bodies lined the trail, stripped of their valuables and their colors. Dead men. His men.

Swearing, Volent whipped his horse back to the camp. The inquisitor waited at the sentry line, his eyes flickering in the flames. Volent dismounted smoothly beside him.

"I was at my prayers, Sir Volent, and had a vision. I heard hounds baying in the forest. Demons in the pagan night," the inquisitor said.

"Demons, hell. Those were Tenerrans. It smacks of that huntress bitch."

"Your men decided not to stop her?"

"Greenhall has not blessed me with the finest minds in his service. Despite your assurances, I think the duke suspects this is a fool's errand. What of your lot, frair? Why didn't your priests of Cinder warn us of her presence? If she makes it back to the Fen Gate, we'll have lost our element of surprise. This whole expedition may already be lost!"

"Lost? When such an opportunity has presented itself?" Finney asked. His voice was as smooth as moonlight, and just as clear. "Even if we win this war, the Tenerran lords would have sued for peace eventually, and they would never have handed Gwen over to the inquisition. But now that she is within our reach, we don't have to ask for her surrender. We can simply take her."

"Poor luck for her," Volent muttered.

"Cinder's justice is always done," Allaister said.

"Priests have a funny way of saying that they've

gotten lucky. But luck or providence, she has already passed us by," Volent said. "She has riders with her, and knows these paths like the veins of her body. The only way we could catch her is by breaking my force apart and spreading out."

The vow knight, Elsa LaFey, strolled up out of the darkness. Even at night, her eyes seemed to glow with a glint of copper sun.

"Hardly wise," she said. "One of two things will come of that. Either the huntress will lie in wait and pick your rangers apart piece by piece, or she will outdistance them as they beat the underbrush."

"Neither is an acceptable solution," Volent answered. He would rather not have the vow knight and her companion on this ride, but there was nothing he could do to prevent them from coming along. "What would you do, Sir LaFey? You have hunted these woods before, have you not?"

"For gods," she said, "not little girls—and this business with the House Adair has nothing to do with me. I am here to find the gheist."

"Then go find it, why don't you?" Volent snapped. He turned back to Allaister. The shadow priest had fallen strangely silent when LaFey arrived. "Can your priests be of any help, Inquisitor? Do you have any scryers among you?"

"We are here to guard your troop from the pagan night," Allaister said. "Nothing more."

"Then this is hopeless. Gwen Adair will make for the Fen Gate, summon reinforcements to its walls, and burn us out of the Fen," Volent said. "We might as well withdraw immediately."

"I will not leave the north until I have that gheist," LaFey said.

318

"Then you're on your own," Volent answered. "Inquisitor, prepare your priests. We march south in the morning."

"And I will continue north," Elsa answered. "The gheist is near. I can smell its corruption in the air. I will go speak to Frair Lucas."

Allaister remained silent while the vow knight marched away, waiting until she had disappeared before he spoke.

"There is another way, Sir Volent," he whispered.

"Yes?"

"We are inquisitors, after all. Frair Lucas may spend all of his energy on hunting gheists, but it is also our duty to root out the pagan savage. Without the witches and their shaman drones, the old gods would have no hold on this world. We have rid the south of the old henges, and Suhdra is now safe from the gheists."

"The old gods still stir in the south, Frair," Volent answered quietly. "I know that better than most."

"Perhaps you do. The point is that my men have turned their arts to sifting the hearts of mortals, to find the truth of their faith, and to searching the villages for hidden enemies. We have certain necessary skills."

"You can hunt for Gwen Adair?"

"I can," Allaister answered. "As Sir LaFey can taste the corruption of the gheist in the air, I can sense the paths of pagan hearts."

"Why didn't you say so earlier? We will decamp immediately." Volent turned to call one of his attendants, but Allaister held his arm.

"There are considerations. We cannot work our power in the company of your men."

"Why not?"

"My sect must hold its secrets tight," Allaister answered. "Knowledge of our rites is a crime punishable by death. Or madness. None may be permitted to exploit them for personal gain."

Volent stared the man down for a heartbeat, wondering what sort of shadow Allaister could cast that would be so fatal to witness. Then he shrugged.

"What would you have us do?"

"My priests and I will keep the huntress occupied. Even if we don't catch her, I can guarantee that she won't make it to the Fen Gate."

"How are we to navigate the Fen without you?"

Allaister answered by producing a map from his robes. It was very old, and very fragile. The priest gingerly laid it on the ground and crouched over it. He motioned Volent closer.

"We are here, or close enough," Allaister said, stabbing at the map. The geography depicted was strange, with several sites, marked in fading ink, that didn't correspond to anything he knew. Nevertheless, he was able to find the Fen Gate, and the Tallow.

"Farther north than I expected," Volent said.

"Yes. This land shifts beneath our feet, to confound as much as to protect."

"Then won't we be just as lost marching south as north or east?" Volent asked.

"The magics of this place are meant to protect the castle—" the priest's eyes flickered to the map "—and its environs. The wards will not hinder your exit. It is only if you try to travel north that you will be confounded."

Volent looked again at the map, and the unnamed sites dotted throughout the Fen. He wondered what secrets lay in the forests around House Adair, and why the church was willing to risk so much to find them.

"What of the huntress? What if she has warned the commanders at the Redoubt? We will be marching into a trap."

"I assure you," Allaister said with a leer, "her attention will be elsewhere."

The tents of the camp were cold and dark when Allaister and his fellow priests slipped out into the night. They passed by the sentries without being seen, their bodies bound to shadow and the shifting silence of the moon. When the flickering lights of the Suhdrin camp were out of sight, they gathered in the pit of a small grove, surrounded by gnarled trees and the smell of fallen leaves.

They lit a fire among the mosses, and fed it with their blood.

Allaister stood at the heart of the circle. Flames lit the narrow planes of his face, the coiled ink of his tattoos crawling between the shadows like snakes in a forest. He took from his robes the gauntlet that he had bound to the gheist in distant Gardengerry and laid it in the blood-fed fire. The flames shunned the metal, snapping away from it as though a stiff wind blew from its surface.

The blood of the priests leached out of the fire to crawl across the blackened steel of the glove, magically drawn from the flames to settle in the runes etched across the metal's skin. As the fire grew, the runes began to pulse.

In time with a heart.

A sound came from the darkness of the forest. The circle of priests turned to face that direction, forming a half-moon with Allaister at the center. The shadows grew and thickened, winding through the trees until a shape loomed black at the edge of the fire's light.

A god stepped into the light.

The gheist was a chaotic mass of shadow and fog, a rough huddle of squirming lines that shifted under the gaze, never staying true to one form or another. The other priests bowed their heads, either from fear or awe, but Allaister stood straight and true in front of it. The mass was anchored to the darkness of the forest, and as he looked around he could see more of it among the trees, flowing around their firelight, slithering through the branches and blocking out Cinder's silvery light.

The priest smiled.

"You've grown," he whispered.

"I am becoming," the gheist replied, and the mass shivered and solidified into something like a human form, only taller, thicker, like a man wrapped in thick cords. "Becoming what I was. I was so much more than this."

"No longer," Allaister said sternly. "Whatever you were when the pagans put you in that tomb, I have made you something else."

The gheist didn't answer. It shivered, and waited.

"I have a new task for you," Allaister said. "There is a girl in this forest. A girl of pagan blood."

"One of the wives?"

"I think not," Allaister said. "Though perhaps. She is the huntress of her tribe. Her name is Gwendolyn Adair."

"Adair, Adair," the gheist murmured, its voice a hollow echo. "Gwendolyn Adair. There is iron in her blood."

"Yes," Allaister nodded.

"And the other god—has its hiding place been found? Am I no longer to hunt the hallow among the Fens?"

"She will lead us there, if we pursue her."

The gheist remained still for a long time. Its attention seemed to be elsewhere.

"Can you do it?" Allaister asked.

"I have found her," it said. "She is fast, and warded, but she is no witching wife."

"Then we hunt. We are leaving the demon-bound one behind, so there is no need to hide yourself any longer."

"This one is sick," the gheist rumbled. The humanoid form slouched closer, pushed forward by the tendrils that anchored it to the darkness in the forest. "We will need another."

"Sick?" Allaister asked.

Without warning the wrapped form of the gheist cracked open, breaching like an egg, and a body slumped out. It was dressed in priestly clothes, a look of horror on its face. Oily blood leaked from its mouth. The circle of priests flinched back.

Allaister knelt by the body, cradling the man's head in one hand. He stared into the dead, slick eyes.

"Ah, Frair Montandon, I am sorry for your loss— but we all make sacrifices." He raised his free hand to the tip of the crescent of priests. "You may have this one."

The priest who stood there stared at Allaister, then dropped his staff and stumbled into a run. The frayed clump of shadow that had held Frair Montandon didn't move, but as he approached the edge of the fire's light, a pillar of squirming darkness spilled out of the shadows and swallowed him in a cascade of writhing night. A brief, sharp scream was cut off as the gheist filled his flesh.

Then there was silence—none of the remaining priests seemed to breathe. As quickly as it had arrived, the hunter god disappeared among the trees. The pale light of Cinder's face filled the clearing once again. The fire hissed and spit.

Allaister stood and, with his hidden court, followed the god into the night.

"What do you think of this?" Elsa asked. She and Lucas stood hidden in the groves that overlooked the previous night's camp. Sir Volent and his men had struck camp and were winding south with haste, their banners struck and their mood grim.

"I think their mission has changed," Lucas answered. "Frair Allaister and his men are gone from their ranks, and they have turned their backs to the Fen Gate."

"Perhaps they return to Greenhall," Elsa agreed. "They may have split with the priests, and are determined to head home."

"That may be, but it's more likely that they seek an easier prey," Lucas said. "Last report had Blakley's forces stretched thin along the Redoubt. A sufficient attack upon their rear could break the defenses along the Tallow."

"It's been a month since that report," Elsa replied. "Things could have changed. The war may be over."

"This is the sort of war that is never over," Lucas said. He twitched his reins, and his horse turned north. "But that is none of our concern. Not yet, at least."

Elsa followed suit, peering around with a troubled look. "I can feel the strangeness of this place closing in," she whispered. "The land has found us, and it does not approve."

"I am a shadow, Sir LaFey, and you are the sun." Lucas shrugged. "We will stand together, and the land will not confound us."

"Still, this is a haunted place. A place of great power," Elsa said.

"Yes, and something else," Lucas said. "Do you feel it?"

"I do," Elsa said. "The scent of corruption is gone. Our gheist is missing."

"We will find the trail again, I'm sure," he replied. "I can sense something just north of the camp. We will start there. Perhaps we will find where Frair Allaister has gone, as well."

"What good will tracking the frair do us?"

"An interesting question," Lucas said. "I'm sure there will be an interesting answer, as well."

28

THE WATERS OF the Tallow flowed peacefully over the smooth stones of the ford. They started as snowmelt in the high Suhdrin mountains that surrounded Heartsbridge, then washed down into a hundred lesser streams that eventually became the Wyl. At Dunneswerry that river split, half into the Tallow, half into the Silverlyn. When it entered the Fen, the Tallow cut its way through limestone bluffs and narrow gorges, sometimes rushing white and fast, other times as slow and gentle as summer, until it reached the Felling Bay and emptied into the sea. It served as the natural border between Tener and Suhdra, a line drawn by the gods.

This river had seen a lot of blood, and still it ran clean and cold.

Ian stood at its northern bank and washed the dust from his feet. He waded slowly out into the depth of the river, feeling the tug of the current and the flickering touch of curious fish, then dropped beneath the surface. The cold arced into his bones, yet Ian felt relaxed in a way he hadn't since Chev Bourdais had tried to kill him on the fields of Greenhall.

He sunk his feet into the mud and let the current drag across him. He gave his mind to it, reciting the rites of Cinder that settled his thoughts and invited cold reason. Ian was angry with his father for shuffling him to the flank, keeping him from the glory of the battle. All these weeks later and he was still angry with Martin for implying that Tener was at fault in this struggle, and he was furious with himself for letting these things keep him awake at night. So he let the anger go with the water.

The light above him was crystal green. Lady Strife's golden face shimmered through. The end of summer was approaching, and already the mornings had taken on the bite of autumn. Soon it would be the equinox.

Floating in the Tallow, Ian turned his mind to the increase in gheists, and the dangers of lesser holidays that marked the ebb of the powers of Cinder and Strife. There would be more vow knights on the roads, and more gheists in the forests. The war might affect that. If the vow knights could not safely travel, they might stay in the Lightfort and leave Tener to its feral gods. He would need to take precautions, to protect his men from the marauding gheists. He wondered what Martin would be doing to keep his Suhdrin knights safe. Perhaps their fear could be turned to his advantage. Dress his raiders in woad and strike at their flanks. Give *them* some sleepless nights. He smiled at the thought, and started to float back toward the surface.

An arrow dimpled the water over his head. Ian stared at it for a second, wondering how someone's target practice had gone so badly astray, then another bolt landed beside the first, to be joined by an entire flight that fell like rain.

Gasping, he stood and looked at the southern bank. The tents of Marchand and Roard remained where they had been. There were soldiers among them, and quite a few on the bank, but none of them had bows or stood in the concentrated ranks necessary to launch such a flight. The men and women Ian could see were all staring at Ian's camp, shock on their faces. Which meant the attack wasn't coming from the south.

A horn went up behind him, then another. Ian whirled to find that several tents were on fire. Another flight of arrows came from the forest to the north, this one trailing streamers of smoke and burning pitch. Rally horns called shrilly from the length of the camp, joined by clarions from the Suhdrin side of the bank.

Ian splashed to shore and started pulling on his clothes. A knight ran up to him, a woman he didn't recognize. She wore the colors of House Dougal, the hart and harrier, and was carrying a collection of armor that Ian recognized as his own.

"My lord," the woman said matter-of-factly, then she bent to help Ian prepare.

"What's happening?" he snapped.

"Arrows from the trees. Seems like most of the sentries are already dead, for them to be so close. Raise your arms."

Ian did so, then ducked as a quarrel hissed over his head. The woman slapped his arms back up, then tossed a chain shirt over his head and fastened it to his belt.

"Will have to do," she said. "Don't get shot in the leg." Then she marched back to the tents. Dark-cloaked soldiers were boiling out of the forest, pouring through the camp and cutting the men down before they were properly armed or armored.

"Wait! We must rally the banners! Sound the horns..."

"Already done," she yelled over her shoulder. "Your sword is there. Draw it, and earn your name." Then she drew her own weapon and waded into the chaos of the camp, the swirl of combat, screaming the words of her house.

On the opposite bank, the Suhdrin horns were sounding, mustering their forces. Lines of spear and bow were forming at the ford, and Ian could see a swirl of horsemen donning armor and preparing for the charge. They would be coming across the river in just a few minutes. The Tenerran guards at the ford had all turned to face the threat from the forest. They were pressed from both sides, though how this force had gotten into the forests to the north was beyond him. If Ian didn't rally the defenses, the whole camp would be swept from the field.

Gwen Adair has failed us.

He pulled on his boots and drew his sword, tossing the scabbard aside. The attackers from the north had fought through the pickets and were among the tents, cutting free the harnessed mounts and driving them from their pens. Whoever these soldiers were, they were nearly silent in their attack, but didn't seem terribly effective. Most of the arrows had flown over the camp, and even in the state of disarray, it seemed as though Ian's banners had rallied and were giving a good showing.

A column of Suhdrin attackers stumbled onto the riverbank. Their shield line was broken and their spears bristled in all directions, rather than moving in concert. A party of Tenerrans crashed into them, brushing aside their spears and hammering the shields.

"The hound! The hallow!" Ian screamed as he joined the fight.

* * *

The battle was closely fought and quickly over. The Tenerrans broke the Suhdrin shield wall like a baby's spine, grinding them apart and spitting out the refuse. Ian stood on the far side of the carnage with his ears ringing and his hand numb from striking sword to bone.

Suhdrin forces massed on the southern bank of the Tallow, but had not made a move to cross. He looked around and saw the knight who had helped him with his shirt.

"Sir..." he said.

"MaeWulf," she answered. Her eyes were on the dead at her feet. "These are children."

"Dead ones, aye—and old men, the infirm... not much of a fighting force," Ian said. "If they hadn't taken us by surprise, there wouldn't have been a threat at all."

"How in hells did they get behind us?" MaeWulf muttered. "We've got eyes from here to Dunneswerry, and Gwen Adair was holding the fords to the west."

"A question for Gwen Adair," Ian said.

Without warning, another flight of arrows dropped on the camp, this one drawing blood, though it fell on Suhdrin and Tenerran alike. There was a rumbling confusion, then the nearest line of tents collapsed. In the cloud of dust that rose, his own warriors appeared, fighting a retreat, their faces turned to the distant forest.

The battle line moved to the banks of the river, sweeping Ian, Sir MaeWulf and their attendant knights along with them. It was pressed by an organized spear line, soldiers fighting like madmen and anchored by a core of mounted knights. At their center was a banner, and the knights clustered around it.

At their fore was Sir Henri Volent, the Deadface, fighting like a demon, killing like a butcher.

Across the Tallow, a horn sounded, and the enemy began to move.

"Defend! Defend!" Ian shouted over the clamor. He waved his sword in the air, but the men and women around him did not see it. "Hold the line!"

"There is no line, my lord," MaeWulf growled between gritted teeth. She'd sustained numerous wounds, blood leaking through her chain mail, but she fought on. Ian tried again to rally the fight, but only drew the attention of the Suhdrin attackers.

They pressed closer to him.

A spear snagged his shoulder, gathering up the links of his mail and tearing the coat, leaving rings to spill down his chest like coins. The weight of the unsettled armor dragged down his sword arm. Without a shield, Ian had to depend on his blade for protection, and it was slowing him down. He stumbled back and splashed into the river. The water that had flowed so clean a few minutes before was now murky with blood.

A face broke through the shield wall and he struck at it, breaking bones and teeth. That man disappeared, and another threw himself forward, hacking madly at Ian's blade. The men-at-arms around Volent fought with rabid strength and a complete disregard for their own flesh. It was as though demons drove their blades. A shield bashed into Ian's chest, and when he fell backward it was into deep water.

He dropped his sword, and struggled against the weight of his armor until he got his feet against the muddy riverbed, pushing his head above water. Volent's mounted knights were splashing through the river, struggling to keep their horses calm in the current.

With water up to his chest and his sword missing, Ian was caught in the retreat of his men. Herded like sheep, the Tenerrans beached themselves on the slick stones of the ford. They crowded into the shallow water, milling about like spawning trout. Ian found himself pressed tight on all sides. Even if he hadn't lost his sword, he wasn't sure he would have been able to fight. The air was full of the screaming of horses and men, the crash of arms, and the sound of distant horns.

Then there was a near horn, followed by hoofbeats.

The screaming got louder.

A wide lance of knights-errant—in full armor and flying the banners of Roard, Marchand, and LeGaere—crashed through the ford. They crushed the dismounted Tenerran rabble like eggs.

Something struck Ian's shoulder. He wheeled away from the blow, seeing a spray of crimson that he only distantly recognized as his own blood. Then he was in the river, this time falling on the far side of the ford, and the cold drove the air from his lungs. He sank, mud between his fingers and in his face. Bodies piled on his back and his lungs burned for air. He squirmed free, but his armor kept him under the surface. His left arm wouldn't move, but with the numb, aching fingers of his right he found the hem of his ruined shirt of mail.

He shrugged free of it, the links snagging in his open wounds like fishhooks, tearing flesh from fat and spilling blood into the water. Then the shirt slipped free of his body, and he floated with the current. The light above his head was clear and green. The air left his lungs, and darkness filled his head.

Ian drifted, the current taking him westward,

away from his father, farther from the Tenerran lines and safety. The river bore him on.

The first horn came from the western picket. The oxbow crescent of Malcolm's army was anchored at either flank by the two fords they had used to cross the Tallow, with each defended by heavy lines of spear, backed by the majority of the Tenerran archers.

To the east, there were no more crossing points until the Reaveholt, the walled city that managed most traffic between Greenhall and the Fen Gate, while to the west the river was punctuated by various fords and lesser bridges. Gwen Adair held the fords farther to the west, while Malcolm's son was charged with the nearest major ford, just beyond the river's bend.

There had been no word from Ian.

Yet the perimeter guards were signaling an attack. Malcolm shifted on his campstool, turning away from Rudaine, and stared in that direction. Like most of his men, he had taken to wearing his armor day and night. It was beginning to wear on him, but the immediate fear of attack washed his discomfort away.

"Are they probing the flank?" Rudaine asked. He and Malcolm had been discussing their options, whether they would fall back across the Tallow or press on to Greenhall.

"No, I think it's more than that," Malcolm said. He stood and called for his horse, then began buckling on his scabbard. "I see no movement along the Suhdrin line."

"Neither do I," Rudaine answered. The bulk of the Suhdrin army was spread out before them. "They stir, but I think it's as much curiosity as preparation." A few riders tracked along the Suhdrin line, but most of the forces were still clustered around their fires.

He glanced up at the sky.

"An hour to dusk. A terrible time to mount an attack."

"And yet, the horns."

Malcolm grunted. Someone brought his horse and shield, then several men helped the lord of Houndhallow into his saddle. Rudaine still stood on the ground. From his perch, Malcolm could see the whole Suhdrin line, as well as the western pickets, where the horns were still sounding. Ian's position was still out of sight on the northern side of the river, and the forces arrayed against him were equally hidden.

"No, there's nothing. If there's an attack on the western ford, it's led by ghosts. Sir Bray, get a rider to that picket and find out what the hell they're on about." Malcolm waited until the knight was on his way, then leaned down to Rudaine. "Those are your men, Duke. Are they prone to fright?"

"No man who marches out of Drownhal is prone to fright."

"Well, I don't know what to tell you. There's no movement on the southern line. Either your scouts have decided to call the hunt, or..." Malcolm turned to receive a report and his eyes drifted across the Tallow, to the supply camp that lined the northern bank. "Gods be damned," he muttered.

A silent line of riders was scything through the camps, cutting down the few guards and securing the northern mouth of the western ford. Rudaine looked in the direction of Malcolm's gaze, then swore and took off at a run.

"Mount a charge on that ford, Drownhal!" Malcolm shouted after the retreating figure. "We can't afford to be cut off!"

Rudaine didn't answer, but kept running. Malcolm whirled his horse and rode to the river's bank. Men and horses were stirring as their commanders slowly realized what was occurring. A call drifted over the river valley, this time from the Suhdrin camps. Halverdt must have received word.

That's madness, Malcolm thought. *Why wouldn't he have known of a flanking attack on the Tenerran position?* Still, there was no denying that the Suhdrin lines were only now shifting themselves.

"My lord," Sir Bray called, "they fly Marchand and Roard banners! Scouts spotted them riding down the embankment from the direction of your son's position at the ford, but only called the alarm when they realized the number. They thought it a ruse." The knight stumbled up to Malcolm's flank.

"There was no warning from my son?"

"No, my lord. We must assume that his position has been overrun."

"And my wife?"

"She is on the northern bank, my lord. There were messengers from several uncommitted Tenerran lords. They were dining among the wagons, for safety."

"Well, they're involved now," Malcolm spat. He looked up as a shout came from the western ford. Rudaine was leading an assault, a small fist of mounted knights that crashed into the water under a hail of arrows. "They have archers in the woods. This'll be a bloody business."

"What should our men do?" Bray asked.

"See that the eastern ford is secure. It's unlikely that they would have circled all the way around, but gods know what's possible. Keep an eye on the south. If the Tenerrans..."

"Riders south, my lord!" a messenger called, riding hard and fast from the front lines. "There seems little plan to it, my lord, but the Suhdrin knights are mounting."

"We're in for it, then. Get the pikes set. Make sure MaeHerron gets his shields to the center of the line, and don't let them engage until the Suhdrin force is committed." The messenger nodded to each command, edging his horse away in his eagerness to relay the orders. Malcolm reached out and took the man's reins. "Listen carefully. Whatever is happening, Halverdt is as surprised as us. Have the commanders calm their men. Have them take time for prayers. Show no fear in the face of this. Do you understand?"

"Yes, my lord, but…"

"Enough," Malcolm spat. "We hold this line or we fall." He released the man's horse and gave it a slap. "We fall all the way back to Houndhallow, and gods help us."

"What of your wife, my lord?"

"What of her?" he asked. "She knows the blade."

The Marchand banner fluttered and fell, the black spear and red rose spotted with blood. The air was heavy with smoke and the screams of dying men. The only light was the flickering fire of the Tenerran supply wagons, and the sweet stink of charred meat mingled with sweat and spilled guts.

Lord Daeven cradled the broken head of his son, his hands sticky with blood. Sorcha Blakley stared into the night, watching the last riders of the failed flanking attack disappear among the trees. She ground the shaft of her long spear into the mud and looked down at the fallen child.

"Now will you join us, Lord Daeven?"

Daeven shook, his shoulders heaving, his cheeks slick with tears and his dead son's crimson. The Earl of Blackvaen glared up at her.

"Do not think you can twist a child's death into another hundred spears for your heresy, Duchess."

"His blood is on Suhdrin blades, Daeven. You will not see that avenged?"

"I will not see my other sons killed," he said. He stood, cradling the body. The boy's head rolled back on what remained of his neck, a fresh gout of blood freed as the flesh tore and bones ground together. "Nor my daughters raped, nor my wife widowed."

"You came to talk banners," Sorcha said tightly. "Perhaps to talk peace, and they brought the blade to our table."

"You," he said. "You brought the blade. They have only answered in kind."

"Lord Daeven, there are thousands of Suhdrin spears clustered on our border. Even now…"

"Enough. I must bury my boy as far from this slaughterhouse you've built as I can manage," Daeven said. He wrapped the child's face in his cloak, gathering the broken pieces back into the whole, wincing as his son's blood-streaked face disappeared behind the cloth. Without another word, he turned and disappeared into the night.

Sorcha sighed and put her spear aside. She was still dressed in her dinner finery, hastily crushed beneath a breastplate and chain skirts, the whole outfit ruined with blood and sweat. The riders had fallen on them so quickly, there hadn't been time to find shelter for her guests. Even Earl Daeven had taken up his sword, to defend his son as much as his own life.

It hadn't been enough.

One of her maidens ran up, bow in hand. The girl was naked beneath her armor, except for a loose shift of wool. She had taken a quicker and less modest approach to the ambush, cutting her silks away when the assault had come. Sorcha almost regretted not following her lead.

The girl saluted, then bent the knee.

"Get up, child. What is happening?"

"The last of the riders have fallen back. We're rooting the archers out of the forest now. They were children, my lady. Boys and old men."

"They fought well, for boys and old men," Sorcha said. "And the other guests?"

"Lord MaeFell has already sworn his numbers to us, though he hasn't called his banners. It will be weeks before they reach us. The rest of your guests are safe enough."

"Not all of them," Sorcha said, looking down at the drying blood at her feet. "See that Earl Daeven receives an escort home. What of the southern side of the river?"

"Darkness and the songs of war," the maiden said.

"I would rather not wait until dawn," Sorcha answered. "Gather what blades you can. Are the fords open?"

"The Suhdrins hold the western ford. They were able to hold out against Rudaine's assaults until joined by Halverdt's spears from the south. They have built a new bridge with the dead of Drownhal, my lady."

"You have a horrific way with words, girl." She turned. "We go east, then, and pray that Ian has gotten away or been ransomed."

The maiden bowed and ran away, her bare feet thumping in the grass. Sorcha freed her hair from its impractical braid and started binding it together into something her helmet could accommodate. She walked as she worked. As she approached the eastern ford, her ears were met by a cataclysm of crashing metal and shouting men.

"The fight has shifted?" she asked one of the guards who were watching the ford in horror. She didn't recognize the man, and when he didn't answer she took him by the shoulders and twisted him around.

There was a slash across his forehead, and blood dripped down his chest. His eyes were wide and empty. He stumbled back from her, then dropped his sword and started stumbling north.

"Home," he muttered. "Going home."

Sorcha snatched up his blade and looked around. Most of the men milling around this end of the ford showed some sign of combat. A steady stream of soldiers was crossing on foot, some of them carried between two or three of their fellows. Many wore the black and white of Houndhallow, but there were also soldiers in Rudaine's green and Jaerdin's bright yellow and blue.

The opposite bank was absolute darkness.

"Bring me torches," Sorcha yelled, "and a shield wall! Men of the hound, rally to me!"

Those coming across the river ignored her, but several dozen men who had already reached the north side stirred from their stupor and came to her side. Her maiden joined them, with a handful of her attendants. They began to shuffle into a defensive position, their spears pointed in the direction of the ford. The battle moved, like a storm of clamoring shields and swords.

Then the storm broke. The darkness swirled, and a great company of horses thundered across the ford.

They bowled through the injured and the lame. At their rear, a smaller force of knights fought a retreat. Behind them came a tide of Suhdrin blades.

Malcolm Blakley fought at the center of the Tenerran retreat. He had lost his horse, his helm, and his banner, but he was alive. When he reached dry ground, Sorcha signaled the charge. She and her spears closed the gap, sealing the ford. In the darkness, the enemy assault faltered. Quickly they fell back across the river, content at having driven Blakley's men out of Suhdra.

Sorcha turned to her husband. He was smeared in ashes. Malcolm collapsed heavily to the ground, barely staying seated in the mud.

"Is there anyone else?" she asked.

"Rudaine sought to fight across the western ford," he gasped.

"No one crossed in the west."

"Then they are lost. We are all lost," Malcolm murmured. He slid onto his back and stared up at the night sky. "Sound the retreat."

"I am commander of this army," Sorcha said to him. She knelt at his side, making certain he still breathed, that there was no blood seeping from his armor or broken bones in his skull. Then she stood and signaled to her maiden.

"Sound the rally," she said, "and then the retreat. We march for the Fen Gate."

29

GWEN CLUNG TO the mists, her group of a scant seven men snaking behind her like a river of metal, every hoof fall hushed, every word a whisper. Though this was her home, these woods her birthright, the land felt alien. Something stalked through the night. Something waited for Gwen and her men in their dreams. It was killing them. Little by little, terror by terror, heartbeat by heartbeat, and there was nowhere they could run to escape it.

A week had passed since they had rushed through Volent's camp. At first, they had ridden hard and fast through the forests, putting as much of the Fen as possible between them and Halverdt's pet monster. A day or two of that, Gwen had thought, and there was no way Volent would find them. She thought they would be safe.

Whatever was pursuing them, it was not Sir Henri Volent. Their hunter was not bound to flesh and blood.

They came to a river. Trees continued a few yards into the water, their roots clinging to the slick mud of the banks, moss creeping up their trunks and dripping from their branches like curtains. A blanket of fog hung silent and thick over the river, the current beneath stirring the air above.

Gwen pulled the column to a halt.

"There's nothing to like about this," Sir Brennan murmured. He leaned forward in his saddle like a sick man. The first few deaths had come as a shock. The subsequent disappearances, madnesses and hauntings had worn their spirits to the nub. They were following Gwen out of numb determination, and nothing else.

"Not much to like, no," Gwen agreed. "This is the Castey? Maybe somewhere near the headwaters?"

"Gods know. I haven't seen a familiar plot of land since…" He paused. Wellem had been the first, his silent body submerged in slick mud that bubbled from his mouth when they hauled him out. "It's like the earth has turned beneath our feet."

"This is Adair land," Gwen said stubbornly. "Adair land, and Adair blood. I will not be driven to fear my birthright."

"The land, aye," Brennan allowed, "but the night belongs to something else."

Gwen didn't answer that. Truthfully, she had begun to doubt her hold over the spirits of her home. With the Allfire well past, the days were slipping closer to the equinox. Her family's faith in the old ways was no guard against the gheist, especially when Gwen rode as the huntress. Yet she had trouble believing that the old gods would turn on her so bitterly.

Besides, the spirit hunting them didn't feel like the old gods. Yes, the feral spirits that haunted Tenumbra were mad. Yes, they were unpredictable, and in some ways utterly incomprehensible to the mortal mind, but they rarely hunted. They were rarely so persistent. The god that followed them was clear of mind and purpose. It was driven.

It hungered.

Hungered for Gwen's blood. She could feel it at night, stalking the edges of her dreams. Each morning she woke up to find more of her men dead, and less of her own mind in place.

"I would rather not test the horses in unknown depths. We'll follow the bank until the fog clears, and hope we can find a ford. If this is the Castey, then we can't be that far from the river road."

"Then we're farther north than I expected."

"Which is why we're going south. Give the men a minute to rest their mounts, then start them along the bank. We can't be that far from midday."

Brennan nodded and went back to the column. The men slid from their saddles and jangled through the underbrush, relieving their bladders and their fears. Food was growing short. If they didn't find a settlement soon, Gwen would have to devote time to hunting. She might do that anyway, just to give the men something to think about, something to focus on besides running— which didn't seem to be working, anyway.

Gwen knew exactly how far north they were. She must have been subconsciously driving them closer and closer to the witches' hallow, hoping to slip into the wives' protective wards, and to serve as another line of defense should Volent be pushing for the hallow. She couldn't imagine that the knight-marshal of Greenhall had uncovered their secret after so many generations. Then again, *something* was pursuing them.

She worried that her flight north had put the Redoubt in danger. Gwen knew that she should have sent riders east the minute she discovered Volent's force. Her duty to Tener, however, was outweighed by her sworn allegiance to the hidden god of the Fen. She prayed Houndhallow would understand. She prayed the old gods would reward her faith. Mostly she prayed to see the light of day.

The men began forming up into a column. Sir Brennan claimed the lead, then began the slow process of picking his way along the river. Gwen followed at the rear, letting the fog drift over her as she rode. The tree line was close to the bank, and where it blocked their path by the water, Brennan led them into the forest.

On one occasion they lost sight of the river, stumbling through darker woods until, suddenly, the Castey appeared in front of Sir Brennan's mount, masked by mist so thick that none of them saw it until his horse was up to its chest in water. Several minutes of backtracking got them back to the bank, but the mud and cold were taking their toll. The horses were exhausted. The men were faltering in mind and spirit.

The fog frequently betrayed them. Swirling streamers of gray cloud rose slowly from the water, immersing the men in a thickness that turned the sky into glowing pewter, and hid one rider from the next. As soon as the darkness rose, Gwen stood in her stirrups and called forward.

"Close ranks," she instructed. "Don't lose sight of the man in front of you."

The column tightened, but even with their horses nearly on top of one another, it was easy to feel alone. Thick bands of mist twisted between the men of Adair, and then it stirred. The swirling eddies sped up, faster and faster, until they were riding through a silent storm.

The mist became a knife. The wind tightened into blades, and their blood joined the air.

The fog muffled the screams of man and horse, and then shapes loomed in the murk, tall, thin figures formed of shadow, their bodies barely etched in ribbons of darkness. Gwen watched as the man in front of her was torn to pieces, his armor worthless against the shadowman's scything blades.

She drew her bloodwrought spears and charged the demons. Her horse shied away from the terrified screams of its mates, but Gwen lashed forward, spurring the beast into the fog. They vaulted through the remains of the closest rider, ignoring the grinning bones and slick blood, the tree roots that writhed in the mud like snakes. The path widened, and another rider stood crosswise on it, staring blindly into the fog. Gwen rode past him.

There was something seeping down the man's face—blood from a wound that crossed his eyes, or perhaps something darker.

One of the demons drifted toward her, and she struck. The red-flecked blade of her spear passed through it, turning shadow into ash. It flickered back into the mists with a shriek, though not before raking icy claws down Gwen's leg. She felt blood spring up from the wound, though the leather and steel of her armor was unblemished. She was staring down when her horse balked and stopped short, nearly throwing her from the saddle.

They were alone in the fog. The trail was gone, and the trees. There was no sound. Shapes shifted in the gloom, far then near then gone, in silence.

"Hyah, then," she whispered to the horse. "Hyah, get on."

Her mount broke into a slow trot. The ground beneath his hooves hardened, the sound of his steps sharper and clearer with each yard. Black pillars resolved into trees, and then the mist began to thin.

The pewter sky split open, and the sun came rolling out. Gwen spurred her mount forward, and then they were riding through high grasses, and the trees were gone. They were alone in a clearing.

Gwen looked back. The bank of fog churned behind them, a solid wall with a thin prickle of treetops poking through the top. Of the rest of her riders, there was no sign.

"Hello!" she called. "Sir Brennan! Riders of Adair!" She stood in her stirrups, a quiver of spears clutched in her fist. "Iron in the blood!" Her words fell empty into the forest. She settled back into her saddle. What price had she asked of her men? What price had they paid?

A tangle of darkness moved in the fog bank. Shadowy tendrils lashed out from the murk, snaking through the grasses, slithering toward Gwen and her mount. She caught her breath and prepared to fight, and then the whole, monstrous god roiled out, a coiling mass of dark ribbons, form without form, sharp and fast as thought.

Gwen turned her horse and prepared to run.

A semicircle of robed forms stepped out of the forest at the other end of the clearing, cutting off her escape. They wore the black and gray of Cinder, and carried the darkwood staffs of the inquisition. The man at their center threw back his hood. His face crawled with pagan ink and hatred.

"Gwendolyn Adair," he hissed. "So good to finally meet you."

Clenching her jaw, she couched her spears and spurred her horse. At a canter, then a gallop, the wind and grass rushing past her, the deaths of her men on her heart and hatred in her blood, Gwen bore down on the broken men of god.

30

T HE ROPE THAT bound her hands was hung with icons of the inquisition, and the wounds across her face and shoulders bore the brand of Frair Allaister's staff. The shadow priests had thrashed her within an inch of her sanity, their attacks taking their toll more on her mind than her body.

Such was the way of Cinder's faithful.

That first night had been awful. The priests had dragged bodies into the clearing, shriving their souls and burning their flesh. Gwen counted only five, and of Sir Brennan there was no sign. That meant two of her riders had escaped, or perhaps they had been destroyed by the gheist and their remains lost to the everealm. The priests seemed to hold no animosity to the dead, and afforded them the full rites of the Celestial faith, even adding their names to the evensong dirge.

It was Gwen they shunned.

Allaister had asked his questions. She had told her lies, and when morning came, another of the priests had dressed her wounds and bound her to the saddle of a broken-down nag, having taken her destrier for themselves. They rode slowly through the trackless Fen, making little progress for their efforts and jostling her injuries mercilessly. Every once in a while, Frair Allaister would ride back to the middle of the column where Gwen was kept and perform some kind of ritual with her blood. He never said why he was doing this, but Gwen knew.

He was looking for the witches' hallow. The inquisition knew of the heresy of House Adair, and rather than bring charges before the celestriarch, the frair was hunting for the hallow on his own. Which meant he either had no idea what he was looking for, or he knew all too well, and had his own ambitions. Neither possibility comforted her.

They were on the trail for days, camping in absolute darkness, with neither campfire nor torch and the wild insect life of the forest roaring all around them. Gwen could feel the pull of the wards trying to steer them away from the hallow, and every time the vertigo of paths soared into a fever pitch, Allaister would come back for a visit and some blood.

"It's no wonder your people never settled out here," Allaister said after finishing one of his painful rituals. "Nowhere to plant or build, the roads forever decaying, the valleys as damp as lakes and the hilltops scoured by this damnable wind. Though I think that was not always the case, was it, my lady?"

"The Fen is as it has always been," she answered. He had been like this since her capture, casually friendly and yet always threatening. His questions of the previous night had seemed nonsensical at times. Gwen truly wondered if he was mad.

"Yes, yes, but I've seen more than a few ruins during my travels here." He gestured broadly to a limestone ridge that framed their path. "Unless I'm mistaken, that was once a wall, or perhaps a tower... and here, the remnants of a well. But they are long abandoned."

"Life can be difficult. Perhaps the people moved on to easier climes."

"That is hardly the Adair way, though, is it? What is it you're so fond of saying? 'Iron in the blood'?" Allaister slid a wedge of apple into his mouth and crunched loudly, chuckling to himself. "Doesn't leave a lot of room for comfort."

"These are more civilized times," Gwen said. "We have cities now, just like your fancy Suhdrin masters."

"Oh, I would hardly call a place like Beckwright or Fenton a city, my lady," he said. "But you're a faithful Celestial. Surely you've made the pilgrim's walk to Heartsbridge." He looked at her out of the corner of his eye, that crooked smirk on his mouth. "You know what a real city looks like."

Gwen folded herself into her saddle, refusing to engage the priest any further. Allaister had been feeling out the edges of her heresy since they began the trip. The less she said, the better, especially in her current foul mood. The frair continued on, however, opining at length about the fate of the ruins they passed, the pagan henges they saw in the distance. Eventually he lapsed into silence.

That night they made camp in a narrow gorge that led into a field of grass and streams, rare in the Fen. She knew exactly where they were. These streams would twine together a short distance north to form the Glimmerglen, the river that bounded the hallow's southern border. The hidden and deceptive trails, revealed by the ritual of Gwen's blood, were coming together to show the true path.

Only a few days on horseback separated them from

Allaister's goal. The wards were failing, and there was nothing she could do about it. The hallow recognized her blood, her history, the oaths that bound her to the old ways. The slumbering god was welcoming Gwen home, and the inquisition with her.

She eased herself onto her bedroll and tried to relax. Hours in the saddle left her grim and sore, made worse by the bonds at her wrists. At night the priests loosened them but hobbled her ankles, and four priests stood in a loose circle around her tent. They gave her privacy, at least, but there was no question as to her captivity.

Had it been Frair Lucas who had seen evidence of her heresy and sent this Allaister on her trail? If it was revealed that House Adair was true to the old ways, that the inquisition and Halverdt were justified in their accusations, what would that mean? They were already at war with the Suhdrin. Would the faithful Tenerran houses turn on them as well?

Ever since the Celestial church had dissolved the reign of kings in Suhdra, the priests of Cinder and Strife had freely used the noble houses of the south to wage war on the pagan tribes. It was only Tener's conversion to the faith that had spared them total war, generations ago. Would any of the Tenerran houses risk that sort of war again, just to stand beside one house that had never foresworn their beliefs and had betrayed their trust?

Her father had always intimated that there were other houses faithful to the shamans, that counted witching wives among their ladies and claimed gheists as their totem gods. But in all her years at court and in service to her father's house, Gwen had never seen evidence of this.

She suspected they were alone.

The flap of her tent rustled, and light filled the narrow space, followed by heat. Gwen hauled herself to a sitting position. To her surprise, a vow knight marched inside, a lantern in one hand and sword in the other. She hung the lantern from the central pole of the tent, dragged a campstool closer to Gwen's bed, and sat down. The woman rested the tip of her blade in the dry grass, so that the yellowed edges of vegetation crisped and turned to smoke.

"Who are you? I saw no vow knight in our company," Gwen said. "The guards aren't supposed to let anyone in. Inquisitor's orders."

"I am Sir Elsa LaFey, and the frair is seeing to the guards," Elsa said. "He has taken an interest in you, Gwendolyn Adair. Meanwhile, I'm trying to figure out if you're worth it."

"Worth what?"

"Heresy," the vow knight answered.

Gwen squirmed on her bedding, trying to look dignified even though her ankles were tied. Sir LaFey glared down at her.

"I'm not going to deny it," Gwen said after a time.

"That's usually best," LaFey said. "The frair finds these things out eventually. Apparently he knew about you before we met."

Lucas. It has to be him, Gwen realized suddenly. "And you didn't?" she asked.

Elsa shook her head.

"Frair Lucas doesn't always tell me everything. Right annoying." Elsa scratched at the grass with her sword, looking more like a petulant child than an awe-inspiring weapon of righteousness. "The frair's talking about getting you away from this lot. About letting you go."

"The inquisitor would have you both declared apostate, if he didn't kill you outright."

"I'd piss my name in the snow if this Allaister fool would lick it up," Elsa said. "Sacombre's pet. Never been a hero of mine, but it's not like we're going to stick around to ask Finney's opinion on the matter."

"Why would you let me go?"

"Why not? Why anything? I do what the frair says, and the frair thinks you're worth more than a trial and a heretic's death." The vow knight leaned forward, gesturing with the flat of her blade. "I hope you are—for his sake, if not your own."

"I'm sure she is," Frair Lucas said, stepping into the tent. His frosty head pressed against the canvas of the ceiling. Before the flap closed, Gwen could see that at least one of her guards was gone. "We had better be about this business," he added.

"How did you find me?" Gwen asked.

"Well, we didn't, not really," Lucas said. "But that gheist that spooked your riders, and nearly killed you, we've been hunting it since Gardengerry."

"Damned interesting to find it in the company of a frair," Elsa muttered.

"An interest that I intend to take up with the celestriarch," the older frair said, "but not tonight." He leaned over Gwen, peering at her wounds with mist-shrouded eyes. "They seem to have left your important parts intact. Flesh and spirit, at least. How do you feel?"

"Like I could run forever, given the proper motivation," Gwen said. "And Allaister has given me motivation enough."

"Glad to hear. So let's get you up and moving."

"Not that I'm ungrateful," Gwen said. "Not at all, but why would you let me go?"

"Let you go?" Lucas took a small knife with a silver crescent blade out from his robes and bent down beside Gwen. He took her ankle in hand and drew the blade across flesh and bond alike. "That's an interesting idea."

Gwen pulled back from the cut, but the frair's hand held her ankle in place. It was all she could do to keep from screaming. The only thing that kept her quiet was the fear that her guards might be near.

Lucas took a carefully folded piece of linen from his sleeve and pressed it against the wound. As the blood spread, turning the white cloth into crimson, Gwen saw that it was covered in arcane script. Then the runes disappeared.

"What the hell are you doing?" she hissed.

"Opening a bond between us." He mopped up the last of the blood, then handed the cloth to Sir LaFey. The vow knight took it with a rueful smile. The wound had already closed, forged shut by some arcane trickery. "Well, opening a bond between you and Sir LaFey, to be precise."

"I don't need dogs to hunt," Elsa said, tucking the cloth into the armor at her shoulder. "Though pagans rarely offer their blood beforehand."

"You haven't answered my question," Gwen said stubbornly.

"There isn't much time," Lucas answered. "We'd best make use of what we have."

"I'm not going until I have some idea what you're doing, and why. I don't like being fucked around with."

Lucas chuckled drily as he struggled to his feet. Elsa hopped up from her seat and helped the old priest sit on the stool, then went to stand by the door of the tent.

"Fine, fine. Have you spent much time near Heartsbridge?"

"Never had much cause. The pilgrimage, five years ago. Not since."

"Yes. There is little need for your type down there. Hunters of gheists, that is. Not Tenerrans," he added quickly. "Between the inquisition, the knights of the winter sun, and the vigilance of the Suhdrin lords, most of the gheists are gone."

"No true vow knights," Elsa muttered quietly.

"Yes. My friend Elsa thinks little of the knights who swear their oaths at their father's shrines and spend their service walking from the tavern to their lover's bed. Many of the southern knights of the vow are second sons of famous lords, committed to protecting the realm only so far as their father's money goes. A different life than the one that Elsa has led, to be sure."

"You should be happy they can be lazy," Gwen said. "If ending the gheists' existence is what you mean to do, then it sounds like the vow knights of the south have fulfilled that goal. Haven't they?"

"Yes, and now the south is dying," Lucas answered. "The fields around Heartsbridge are dust, the rivers thick with silt, and the fisheries catch more kelp than salmon. While you can eat kelp, I don't recommend it. That is part of what's driving this push north. Resources."

"If they want a war, why not just declare one?" Gwen asked.

"Because the church will not allow it, and without a king to lead them, the dukes of Suhdra could never agree on a plan of action. Or that such a plan would even be necessary."

"What does this have to do with me? Why would

you risk your place in the church to release a heretic? Is it to stop a war you don't believe in?"

"No, to save a world. The gheists have been around a lot longer than you, or me, or this collection of men and spirits we call the Celestial church." He leaned against the central pole, setting the lantern rocking back and forth. "I think they have something to do with the health of the land. That's the story the pagans tell, isn't it? That's the story your father tells you."

Gwen hesitated. It was one thing to be known as a heretic. It was another to trade theology with a priest of the inquisition.

"He says the gheists must be held close, if we want to survive," she admitted. "If we want to thrive. He says that without them, the earth will crumble…"

"…into dust," Lucas finished for her. "Those are the words I have heard, as well, so for now we must keep your secret safe. Your family's secret, too, though I do hope to visit this hallow of yours someday. For now, however, it's more important that we keep people like Frair Allaister away from it, I think."

"What's to keep him from finding it on his own?" Gwen asked. "I can't allow that to happen."

"With you gone and the wards still in place, Frair Allaister will have no trail to follow. It will take more than luck to find the witches' hallow," Lucas said. "Besides, I think that once we're past the shadow patrols…"

"The witching wives will not welcome you into the Fen," Gwen said.

"Hopefully you'll be able to change their mind, Huntress," he said with a smile.

"If we're going, I need my things. My spears, my clothes…" Gwen didn't say anything about the hidden icons in her cloak, or the secret blessings bound to her weapons. She was sure the inquisitors would have found those things, but she hoped their purpose remained secret, and she couldn't risk Allaister taking them back to Heartsbridge, to discover it on his own.

Lucas nodded to the vow knight. Elsa snorted, then tossed a package onto the ground at Gwen's feet.

"If that satisfies, we should be on our way," Lucas said with a smile, then he gestured for Gwen to stand. He snuffed the lantern and led her outside. Her guards were nowhere to be seen. The rest of the camp was quiet.

Frair Lucas closed his eyes and lifted his face to the moon. He raised his arms and curled his fingers tight. The night came loose in his hands, dark bands filling his palms and coalescing in the air. He started to weave an orb around the three of them, Elsa wincing as the shadow-stuff pressed tight to her head. Its touch was as cold as the tomb, and just as welcoming. When he was done, the frair placed his arms on Gwen's shoulders and turned her toward the grassy field. Elsa huddled close behind him, so they formed a loose chain.

"Across the field," he whispered into Gwen's ear. "Stay close."

She stumbled forward, the blood slowly working back into her numb feet, her tired legs. A dozen steps and she was in the grasses, yet their tall heads barely moved at their passing. The ground beneath her felt as soft as fog, and with a startled breath Gwen realized that her body had faded into shadow. Lucas pressed her forward. The three of them walked over mud and water as if it were solid ground.

At the edge of the field they came across a swirling presence in the darkness. She recognized the corrupt touch of naether as she passed, and barely glimpsed a shadow priest standing guard among the trees, a spear and the twisting energies his only weapons. For a second his eyes passed over them, and Gwen could hardly breathe for fear of being seen, but nothing happened. The priest didn't move or shout.

The forest folded around them.

Then the shadows fell away. Lucas laughed quietly to himself, and Elsa hissed him quiet, but Gwen paid them no mind because she was running, staying quiet, quiet, and she was away. The field was behind her.

31

T HERE WERE GIFTS of moments.

Ian felt nothing, but there was a heaviness in his chest, and his limbs dragged like lead through the water. He caught glimpses of light above the water, and then a dream of the moon and a sky brittle with stars. Thoughts of the quiet house came to him. He worried that there was no priest in the river. No one to shrive his soul, and Ian Blakley would walk the generations in the Tallow, haunting the muddy banks until his spirit unraveled.

Perhaps then the everealm would accept him.

Other moments found him. Stones and a cold pool, and the incredible weight of his lungs. Something ran along the bank. Between the trees, a wall of dark flesh, loping, eyes bright, a mouth of teeth so sharp and wicked that he could feel their bite from across the river. The beast trailed him. Its breath wrapped through his head and filled his lungs with air forge-hot and fetid.

Ian blinked and was alone. He was kneeling in a pool of water cold as ice. The bank was a ruin of gritty sand. His sluggish mind traced a paw print as big as a shield, and then he dragged himself from the water. His lips were blue, and his skin was as pale as snow. He had lost the feeling in his hands and feet, and it was with numb fingers that he clawed through the muddy bank. He beached himself against a smooth black rock that jutted out of the mud like a tower, and started to shiver.

The memory of the hound cartwheeled out of his mind, and he let it go.

Ian turned on his side and spat river water. His clothes were soaked and his sword was gone, along with his chain shirt. His father had gifted him that sword, on the tourney day, in Greenhall, and now it was gone—sold to the river.

None of that mattered. All he felt was the cold, and the damp, and the mud squishing through his clothes.

After a few minutes of mourning and worry, Ian pulled himself to his feet. He looked up at the moon. It was after midnight. He tottered numbly up the bank and into the narrow forest, quickly finding a path up the bluffs. He had to be near the Redoubt by now. If he could get topside, he might run into one of Adair's patrols, or at least be in the clear when the sun rose.

That was his greatest priority. Sunlight, and the warmth it brought.

Scrambling up the rough scree of the hillside left Ian exhausted. Blood leaked from his palms and ragged knees. Despite the soaking cold of his time in the river, Ian was sweating. When he reached the flat heights of the bluff, he peeled off his shirt, discarding it along with his boots. They would all have to be replaced anyway. And he was so warm! At least there was grass here. The feeling came back to his extremities, the soft, crisp embrace of the grass cradling his feet as he strolled through the field. It was a beautiful night. The stars above and the soft ground below, and Cinder's silver face watching all of it.

Then his foot struck something sharp and he stumbled. He rolled to a stop, his limbs flopping like a ragdoll, his head thumping into the ground. The ground was as soft as rose petals. His foot hurt badly, though. He lay there for a moment while his foot throbbed and his head burned with fever. Finally he curled into a ball and ran a finger over his foot.

There was a long gash by his heel, a soft flap of skin hanging loose and swollen with blood. Ian examined his fingers. A *lot* of blood. He squinted into the darkness, trying to figure out what sort of grass cut that deeply, feeling on the ground. He found a sword, discarded in the dirt, and laughed to himself.

"Gods give," he muttered to himself. "Maybe if I stumble around a bit more I can find some armor, or even a horse. Though I think…"

He looked again. The sword was lying next to a shield, and then a helmet, though when Ian fumbled the helmet around in his tingling palms he saw that the head was still in it.

He stood and, ignoring the pain in his foot, saw so much more. Swords and broken spears tangled in the darkness, bodies mounding the night, fallen from horses or trapped beneath. Here was a trumpet, and there a banner, and then he noticed that the grass was so soft because it was churned into mud—blood instead of water, bones instead of grit.

Ian went to his knees and pulled the ruined wad of a banner out of the mud. He spread it out on the ground. A black gauntlet on a field of red, the fist clenched in simple defiance, or in strength, or pain. Below it the runes of an old language. Iron in the blood. The sigil of House Adair.

Ian dropped the banner and lay down among the

Tenerran dead. Cinder, the lord in gray and ash, bent his head to the horizon, and surrendered to the dawn.

That he woke at all was a miracle. Ian dreamt of earth's tight embrace and the sun laid low. Lady Strife but not the lady, some lesser sun rising out of the water to spread her warmth over his skin, the fire passing through his flesh to stitch itself into his bones.

He dreamt of the hound. In the dream Ian lay limp across the gheist's broad back, his fingers twined into the thick mass of its fur, his mouth and nose full of the smell of torn earth and mulched leaves, the silent promise of autumn, the first frost of a dying summer.

He woke in stones. Ian tried to sit up, but the weight of rock on his chest held him down. There was some other constraint, something that pinned his arms against his side. It was soft and warm. A shadow passed over him, and then someone was peering into his face. A woman. There was the weight of age in her eyes, but her face was young. The sharp planes of her cheeks were knotted in ink, the Tenerran runes scrolling up her face and into a crown of arcane symbols.

"You were dead," she said quietly.

Ian craned his neck and saw that he was lying in a cairn. The small rocks of his burial were dark and smooth. A fire smoldered just behind the woman, a broad wedge of ashen timbers that shimmered with heat.

"Is that why you buried me?" he asked. His voice was dry and sore. The woman snorted and disappeared, returning with a tin ladle. She poured water over his mouth, a good portion of it going down his throat, the rest wetting his hair.

"Warm rocks and soft skin," she said, nodding to the fire. Ian saw that a pile of the smooth black stones nestled among the ashes. "You were dead of the river. Cold as mud. Which is interesting. It takes a determined man to drown so far from the river's bank."

"I was looking for... I thought I could find..." He looked around the field, and recognized it as the Redoubt, now that he could see it in the light. The ranks of dead were drawn into battle lines and fields of retreat. His mind traced the progress of the battle. "They're dead."

"Yes. Not dead like you. Dead of steel and stone," the woman answered. "I can't help them, but old river is a friend of mine, so I know the way to your death."

"Okay," Ian said. He rested his head. "I'm going to sleep for a while."

"No," she said. "No time. People are looking, and I don't think you want them finding." She started plucking the stones from Ian's cairn, using a square of sooty deerskin to throw the stones back into the fire. Showers of ash and cinder plumed into the air with each stone. "Sleep later."

"I feel like sleeping now," Ian said.

"Sleep and they will find you, and then you'll die the iron death." The woman finished with the cairn and did something around Ian's chest. The constriction of his arms disappeared, then the woman lifted a large animal skin and tossed it over her shoulders like a cloak. "Iron is no friend of mine. Come... stand. We are going."

With the woman's urging and the support of a gnarled staff, Ian got to his feet. He was wearing boots again, mismatched and obviously scrounged from the dead. He couldn't help but stare at the ruined battlefield. Murders of crows fluttered through the air, landing and swirling from one corpse to the next, their dark wings as glossy as black mirrors against the grass.

"This is the Redoubt," he mumbled. "How have I traveled so far?"

"A good question. The river was with you perhaps, or something else." She brushed a hand against his cheek. "There is something mystical about you. That you're alive at all. It's best to not question. Just be thankful you live, unlike these fools and their iron skins."

"What happened here?" Ian asked.

"Dying. Killing," the woman answered. "Come. The others will not wait. They wanted me to leave you, but I know you. I wouldn't leave you, but they wouldn't wait, so we have to hurry."

"Who? Who wouldn't wait?"

The woman smiled at him, wrinkling the runes of her ink. She took his hand.

"You know who we are. You have seen our gods." The woman walked firmly down the hill toward the distant tree line. "The hound led us to you, and now I will lead you to the hound."

Together they stumbled to the edge of the field. In the forest their pace quickened, the ground passing beneath them more and more quickly, each step sliding over the ground as if the leaves were ice, and the earth a shifting plane. The sun hesitated in the sky, and the forest was a blur, trees whipping past like the lances of a cavalry charge. Ian's fever grew and changed until he felt as if he was flying, and then he was, and the woman's hand was a claw, and feathers, and the trees dipped their heads and let them pass into the sky.

The Redoubt and the bordering thin line of the river disappeared, swallowed by the humped and twisting hills of the Fen, veins of stone choked with wirewood and swamp grass. The sun hovered motionless in the sky while they traveled. After a time that felt like nothing but could have been hours, the woman guided them toward a clearing among the trees. Ian became aware of his body again. They landed in a plume of leaves that puffed up into the air, as though he and the woman had burst from the ground.

At first Ian thought they were alone. The clearing was on the top of a hill, one of the rare gentle slopes that dotted the Fen, rather than the sharp elevations of bluff and limestone that were so common. It was crowned with wirewood, a few larger aspens, and a single oak on the southern slope. Ian did a single spin, scanning the tree line. When he turned back to the woman she was on her knees, palms pressed firmly to the ground.

"Are you all right?" he asked. He started to kneel next to her when a hand grabbed him firmly by the shoulder and pulled him back. A man, dressed in leathers and a cloak that looked as if it was made entirely of leaves, hustled past him.

"What did you do to her?" the man asked. He rested a staff across the woman's shoulders. "Fianna? Are you well?"

"Tired," Fianna said. "The river had claimed much of him, and Dun'Abhain was feeling stubborn this morning." She waved a hand at the man. "You traveled farther than I expected. Already dipping into the hayways, and the birds were stubborn. It is nothing, Cahl. See to him."

Cahl seemed disinterested in Ian's well-being and continued to focus on Fianna. Something was passing between them, a spider-thin web of greenish light that draped from the staff to Fianna's ribs like puppet strings. She brushed them away.

"If you must help," she said, "I could use wine and bread. In that order."

Ian looked around the clearing again. Faces peered out from the shadow of the oak, and several men and women crept up the slope with spears in their hands and shadows dripping from their cloaks. He took a step back, bumping into Cahl.

He was a large man, dark hair woven into a knot of braids pulled back and held in place with leather straps. He had a nose like a battleax, broken and scarred, and the ink on his face was interrupted by a pair of scars that ran from his forehead to his left ear. The eye on that side of his face had an iris the color of thin milk, the pupil floating in the middle, wide and black. Cahl smelled like an angry bear.

Ian took a step back.

"What have you done to her?" Cahl asked again.

"Nothing," Ian insisted. "She woke me up. I think she saved my life."

Cahl snorted and continued to loom in a manner that seemed to be his primary form of communication. A trio of women, one young, one old, one middling, passed around the pair of men to kneel by Fianna.

The men formed a rough circle around Ian, spears loose in their hands. There were more than Ian had thought at first, at least a dozen, with others coming out of the trees all the time. They all wore similar cloaks, which Ian could now see were a motley of stained leather in the shape of leaves, stitched together like a jigsaw, each piece dyed in autumn colors.

"This is the hound?" Cahl asked no one in particular. Fianna didn't seem too anxious to answer, so Ian straightened his back and let his hands rest on his belt. The palm of one hand slid unconsciously over the hilt of his knife, the only blade the river had left him.

"My name's Lord Ian Blakley, son of Malcolm, duke of Houndhallow." He squared his shoulders and leaned in to the man. "Who are you?"

Cahl answered with another snort, shook his head, and trotted down the slope toward the tree.

"Get her moving," he said. "The hallow has called us, and we must answer. The demon is closer with every breath we waste talking to this fool. There's nothing more we can do here. We must go."

"You have had word from the hallow? Are the wardens safe?" Fianna asked, stirring from the attentive care of the other women.

"Nothing is safe. Shadows stir in the Fen." Cahl hesitated a moment, as though uncomfortable. "Our eyes are clouded."

"You cannot see the paths?" Fianna asked.

"I can see nothing. The sun and moon rise between us." Cahl grimaced at Ian, then turned away. "We've wasted our time on this one. He is the sun and moon. The hound led wrong." With that he stalked down the hill, surrounded by the other men of his pack. The women clucked disapprovingly, but Fianna watched him go with pity in her eyes.

"What the fuck is going on?" Ian asked.

"We are far from our henge," Fianna said quietly, "and the dreams are failing us." She sat quietly for a handful of heartbeats, then smiled and looked up at him. "Our home is far to the east, across the Wyl, near the coast. Our spirits belong there, but the wardens of the Fen dreamt us a warning and a plea. Shadows were stalking their spirits, and so we came west. To help."

"You..." Ian looked around nervously, the reality

of his situation slowly settling on him. "This is a coven. You're a witch."

"And a wife," Fianna agreed. "To the spirits, but never to flesh. Do you think any old crone could pull you from death?"

"I can't be here. You can't..." Ian sputtered. "You must return me to my father. Immediately. If I am caught in the company of pagans..."

"What will you say? If the inquisition questions you, will you tell of the hound that breathed its life into your lungs? Of the gheist that carried you through the night?" Fianna waved off the increasingly nervous ministrations of the other wives. The women fled down the hill, to disappear among the trees. "Would you rather be dead than grateful, Ian Blakley?"

"Of course I'm grateful, but..." He collapsed to his knees on the hill. "You have to understand how dangerous this is for me. For my family."

"More dangerous than drawing your sword against the high inquisitor? More dangerous than raising a banner and marching on Greenhall?" Fianna leaned back, resting on her palms, stretching her legs in the grass. Ian had no idea how old she was, but fatigue had softened her face and added weight to her years. "We are fighting a similar war, Ian Blakley. We may not be on the same side, but we are battling the same monsters."

"No," Ian said. "I have killed your gheists. You worship gods that haunt my nightmares."

"You cannot kill a god, Ian. You may undo its body, and unknit the soul that binds it to our blood, but it remains, to rise again." She stood, brushing off her skirt. Dry grass fluttered down from her legs, and Ian saw that the ground where Fianna had been sitting was charred and dead. There was a glow to her skin, as though her age had been scrubbed away with an iron comb. She held out a hand to him. "Come. Cahl is impatient, and our path is unclear."

Ian took her hand and stood. They strolled down the hill, apparently to meet with the other pagans, though Ian could see no one among the trees.

"Will you take me to my father?" Ian asked.

"Not yet. Wherever our path goes, it is not yet to the Fen Gate. Cahl will want us to answer the wardens, but the hallow is far, and greater troubles may have grown between here and there. I have never seen the Fen in such turmoil."

"This hallow. Is it like the one at Houndhallow?" Ian asked. "I had no idea House Adair had their own. I thought ours was the last in Tener."

"Everywhere is hallowed, Ian Blakley. It takes a Suhdrin mind to think otherwise," Fianna answered. "Some places are more holy than others. But now is not the time for such things. Here," she raised a hand, and the rest of the pagans appeared from the trees. "We have much to discuss."

"No, we don't," Cahl said. "The wardens call. We answer."

"When the wardens' call was the only song, we sang along," Fianna answered. "But there is more sickness in the Fen than we thought."

"Nothing is more important than the hallow," Cahl hissed.

"What good is the..." Fianna paused, and it seemed to Ian she was purposely not looking at him. "What good is that, if a Suhdrin flag flies over the Fen Gate?"

"The bond was made with the tribe of iron," Cahl countered. "Their stone house is no matter to me."

"The house, no, but the land belongs in Tenerran hands—and that is in doubt."

"My father is helping defend the border," Ian interjected. "House Adair will not fall."

"Your father runs north, leaving blood in his wake," Cahl said angrily. "Yet we delay to rescue his pup."

"If my father has lost the border, then it's more important than ever that I join him. He will need every blade he can muster."

"Every blade?" Fianna asked. "Would he accept our strength at his side?"

Ian hesitated, drawing another derisive snort from Cahl.

"We save his life, and yet he is afraid to be seen in our company." The pagan spat. "Leave him here to limp his way home. The hallow needs us."

"The tribes need us. We must consider where our spears might be of the most use," Fianna said. "The army that marches north will grind the tribes from this land. Who will guard the hallow then?"

Cahl was silent. He shook his head.

"None of this matters if the hallow falls."

"None of this matters," Fianna agreed, "but nothing matters more than our choice. So what will we do?"

The pagans looked among themselves. No one spoke. They were waiting on Cahl. Finally, the shaman stirred.

"You are the wife of the gods," he said. "What do they ask of us?"

Fianna nodded, then drew herself up and gave Ian a smile.

"We walk with the hound," she said. "We stand with the Fen."

"Then we fight," Cahl said. He grimaced at Ian. "Whether these Celestials want us or not."

32

T HEY FLED THROUGH wirewood and darkness, coming eventually to a small valley that was surprisingly dry and thick with brush. Exhausted, both from their flight and her days under Allaister's care, Gwen collapsed against a boulder and watched listlessly while Elsa and Lucas prepared the camp.

The shadow priest spent half an hour marking the perimeter of their camp and weaving the night into some kind of ward. Elsa cleared brush and started making a fire.

"You shouldn't light that," Gwen said. "It won't be long before they come looking for us."

"Thanks to the frair's ward, no one will see this light, nor smell the smoke," the vow knight said in a low voice. She looked to Lucas, who finished his preparations and gave a quick nod. "Besides, you can't expect a knight of the winter vow to sleep without a little bit of light to give her comfort."

"And I like my soup warm," Lucas added as he swung a pot down from his saddle and rested it over the embers of the fire.

Gwen watched quietly while the two went about the business of camp. They hardly spoke, clearly accustomed to long silences and the comfort of working together. When Lucas handed Gwen her own cup of soup, she thanked him, then asked the question that had been bothering her since Elsa had first stepped into her tent.

"How did you find me? The last I saw you, you were heading to Greenhall."

"Journeys have a funny way of going in circles," Lucas answered. He explained how Frair Allaister had convinced the duke to give him a small force of soldiers, and how Halverdt insisted on putting Volent in charge. "Sir LaFey and I attached ourselves out of curiosity and, ostensibly, to finish our hunt for the gheist of Gardengerry."

"Look where that hunt has brought us," Elsa muttered into her cup.

"Yes, some unusual circumstances, I'll grant," Lucas said. "Truthfully, there was something about Frair Allaister that discomfited me. The gheist, as well. Something in its essence that didn't seem right. Now I know what was bothering me—on both counts."

"What's that?" Gwen asked.

"Frair Allaister has leashed that gheist, and is commanding it, though for what purpose, I cannot imagine. The high inquisitor will have to deal with the matter." Lucas slurped down the rest of his soup, banged the cup against a rock, then leaned back. "A difficult thing, accusing one of your brethren, but Cinder's justice knows no affection for family or creed."

"What will be done with me?" Gwen asked.

"That remains to be judged," Frair Lucas said. He arranged a blanket around his legs and nestled into the ground, pulling his hood over his eyes. "However, as I have told you, I am beginning to think that our way of doing things has served us poorly. There is something holy in the gheists, those few who escape corruption." His voice began to drift as sleep approached. "There are a few. Which is why I'm interested in your hallow, my lady." Moments stretched, the silence growing. Lucas stirred.

"And its god."

Elsa sighed and collected the frair's cup, cleaning it with a wad of grass. She gave Gwen an uncertain look.

"That's heresy," she said very matter-of-factly. "I will take first watch. Sleep, and I will wake you for the second." Then she disappeared out into the night, leaving behind the spark of sun that stirred among the embers of the fire. Gwen couldn't help but feel that the flames watched her.

She settled into her blankets, whispering the forgotten names of the Fen, and wondering what the frair's words could mean.

It wasn't Elsa who woke her, but a dream. Gwen was floating in darkness, wrapped tight in arms of air and earth, when a light rose from her chest and pulled her ribs into the sky. She was following it, shrugging free of the flesh that held her, drifting through a city of dark towers and gray rain when she woke up and realized she was standing in the middle of the forest, alone.

She looked behind her and saw, some forty yards away, the strange circle of light that marked their camp. Elsa was still sitting on the stump, just barely visible, facing away from Gwen. She could see nothing of the frair. A twig snapped in front of her.

A witching wife stood just an arm's length away, holding a broken twig in her outstretched hand. Gwen stumbled back.

"Thought you'd walk all the way to the Fen Gate

if I didn't wake you," the woman said. Her voice was as quiet as a snake's whisper, passing the distance between her mouth and Gwen's ear and no farther. "You have strange friends, Huntress."

The wife said that last word with stiff contempt. Gwen's place in the world of the Celestial church had always troubled the guardians of the witches' hallow, though her father insisted that they understood the necessity.

"Not friends," Gwen said as quietly as she could. "They rescued me. There are others in these woods, a frair with the old ink. I think he's looking for the hallow."

"A score, almost, and twice that many shadows," the wife answered. "They bring the stink of the south with them."

"Have they found it yet?"

"No, but we can't hold them for long. They hound the little god."

"Little god?" Gwen asked. "You mean the gheist?"

"A tangle of shadow stitched into the shape of men and horse. Quick through the woods. I know it. It was sealed away generations ago, a god that had gained a taste for mortal blood, and had to be imprisoned. The fools must have let it out. It's a hunter, Gwendolyn Adair. Like you."

"The gheist from Gardengerry," Gwen said with a nod. "Frair Allaister seems to have tamed it."

"A priest of the moon god, riding a gheist? What is this world becoming, Huntress?" The witching wife settled against a tree, and Gwen caught sight of a glimmer of slick blood on her side. Gwen took a worried step forward. The wife waved her off. "We have been bending the inquisitor's path, but his shadows harry us. They bite. Anything hunted will bite, eventually."

"You're hurt," Gwen said.

"More than that, child. I am dead. How else do you think I could find you?" The woman laughed, and Gwen realized the sound rustled only through her head. "Many of us have moved on to the everealm, but I remained behind, to warn you, and prepare you."

"For what?"

"Tomorrow. Those few who remain will bend the gheist's path. It will take all that they have. You must take the chance."

"Where will you bend it? I should leave the priest and the vow knight here if I'm to keep them from discovering it," Gwen said.

"You will need them, Huntress. You will not be able to kill this demon on your own. We have tried to tame it, to feed it, to return it to its cycle—but they have broken this god, Gwen. Broken it beyond hope. So you and your friends must kill it."

"Then where?" she asked. The witching wife was fading, her form slipping into the tree at her side. The wives could shift through the forest this way, wrapping tree bark around their skin and sliding from sacred grove to holy branch, covering great distances in the space of a thought. The wife's body was losing definition, her face melting into the bark. "Where will you drive the gheist?"

"Here, child. We will bring the god to you, and you must kill it before the corruption spreads."

"How…" Gwen started, but the woman was gone. The tree where she had been standing creaked and shifted, raining leaves. They shuffled off her shoulders, velvet and soft, to gather at her feet.

She returned to camp. Sir LaFey never moved, and when Gwen settled back into her tent, the vow knight shook herself and then came to wake the huntress for her turn at the watch.

Gwen considered warning LaFey about the coming threat, but to do so she would need to reveal the presence of the witching wife—something she dared not do. No life—not even her own—could be worth the risk to the hallow. It was her life's work to keep its secret safe. So she spent the rest of the night watching the trees, and wondering when the little god would find them.

33

THE SHADOWS OF an unnatural night followed
them north. The darkness between trees loomed
deeper, and each sunset brought shivering terror to
Malcolm's bones. He stopped sleeping. The men and
women around him followed suit, the whole ragged
mob shambling forward without thought to formation
or discipline. They were running. They were in a rout,
easy pickings if the Suhdrin bothered to follow. It was
Strife's blessing that they didn't do so immediately.

Sorcha was among them, though her eyes were
hollow and her fire broken. She rode beside Malcolm
during their long retreat. He didn't ask where the
others were. In the sharp madness of the attack, each
had looked to his own. He cursed himself for leaving
her side. At least she had survived. Her death would
have sealed his own madness.

They didn't speak for days, but even her silent
presence was enough to give Malcolm hope. They
held hands at night, though neither of them slept.
There were dreams waiting for them in the darkness
that neither wanted to face.

The one thing they didn't discuss was their son.
Both knew that Ian had been with the forces that fell
at the western ford, knew by the presence of knights

of Marchand and Roard in their flank that his position had been overrun. Few of the men assigned to that post counted among the survivors, and none had news of the heir of Houndhallow. Malcolm continued asking, each night, searching the camps of stragglers for some sign of his son.

Sorcha stayed quiet, and a faint spark of anger began.

A week on the road, gathering survivors as they fled and giving them some direction, pulling broken men from the forest and goading them north. This had given Malcolm some purpose of his own. North had been the natural direction, the way the horses had run, the direction soldiers and knights and attendants had taken when their lines broke, and the way they kept walking when the rout had ended. It was the path home.

After the initial flight ended, and the days continued with no sign of Suhdrin pursuit, Malcolm began to form a plan. It took time for it to settle in his mind, and more to work up the courage to speak of it.

"We must hold at the Fen Gate," he said finally. Sorcha gave no hint of having heard him, so he repeated himself. She looked over. Those hollow eyes. They would spark again, he promised himself. They would be bright again. "We don't have a choice," he added.

"The men are scattered," she replied. "The shields are crushed and the spears broken. You can't make them whole, Malcolm."

"If I don't, the winter will break them. Most of these men are weeks from their homes. Months, in their current condition. The storms will come before they reach any destination. They'll die on the roads."

"So you would have them die at the Fen Gate,

instead," she said. "What's the difference?"

"They'll die fighting, and maybe we'll hold. We have to," he said. "If we run, there will be nothing to stop Halverdt. If these men freeze along the road, the strength of the north dies with them."

"They will find friendly hearths along the way. Thyber. Runninred. Dunneswerry. There will be shelter from the storms."

"Those, yes, and Houndhallow, as well. If the Fen Gate falls, do you think Halverdt will stop there? You brought the armies of the north to oppose him. Will he rest while those armies still exist?"

"I came to find you," Sorcha muttered angrily. "He was merely in the way."

Malcolm smiled, glad to see a little of his wife's fire still smoldering. He laid a hand on her knee. She slid her fingers into his, and they rode in silence.

"So," she said at last. "The Fen Gate?"

"If we mean to fight, rather than crawl home and hide until the high inquisitor comes for us."

She nodded, squeezed his hand, then split off from the road to start gathering the men. Malcolm watched until she disappeared into the trees, then turned and went the other way. The army was spread thin and wide. They had to be formed up. They had to be given a direction.

They found most of the banners. Thaen's crown of frost and splintered sun, white against the blue and gray of his field, was tattered but proud, flapping beside the flaming crescent moon of MaeHerron and the hart and harrier of Dougal, each stained with blood and the filth of a week-long rout. Even a few battered knights in Drownhal's multi-green filtered in from the forests, trailing slowly behind the rest of the column.

At the column's head stood the hound of Blakley, the white now the dirty color of sleet, the beast's snarling jaws torn and tired. Sorcha rode beneath the banner, with Malcolm beside her and the remaining strength of their force behind. What remained of the army was moving again—marching, rather than fleeing. It was enough to bring a smile to her face.

The one presence that discomforted them was that of Lord Daeven. The mourning earl of Blackvaen marched with the ruins of the army, carrying the blanket-bound corpse of his young son in his arms. Malcolm wasn't sure how the man managed, though madness could bring strength. Daeven talked to no one, acknowledged no one. It was as if he traveled the mourning road alone.

The Fen Gate lay slightly west of the main road that cut through Adair's territory, the same road that led to Houndhallow, splitting to find Dunneswerry to the east and the river Wyl. A good part of their army had fled into the Fen, never to return, and many more likely were making for Houndhallow and points north. Nevertheless, the Blakleys had managed to gather enough spears and knights to present a respectable force to Lord Adair for the defense of his walls and his name.

To the west lay the Fen. There were stories about Suhdrin forces in its murky depths, but so far the scouts had seen nothing. Other stories told of gheists, many more than should be expected, even this close to the equinox. None of them attacked. Somehow that worried Malcolm more than if the old gods had been ravaging the landscape. There was a stillness in the air that promised great snow and greater cold.

The season was turning against them.

Sentries patrolled the borders of orderly camps, scouts ranged into the lightening forests, rangers brought game to the spit and reported troop movements at the duchess of Houndhallow's nightly council. Big Grant MaeHerron, having taken command of his father's forces when the baron disappeared in the rout, showed up each night and silently honed the edge on his axe while Lord Dougal and Sorcha Blakley talked about the coming defense of the Fen. The soldiers seemed alive for the first time since 'they had been forced across the Tallow in the dead of that bloody night.

A week brought them to the Fen Gate. No fires burned in the village that huddled at its foot. The surrounding fields hung heavy with unharvested grain, but there were no farmers in sight. At the castle, the famous black gate was sealed, and the walls bristled with archers. Two banners flew from the keep, one from each of the black towers of the castle: the crimson flag of House Adair, and a black banner of mourning.

"Not the reception I was expecting," Sorcha said.

"They look ready for war," Malcolm answered. He rode beside Castian Jaerdin, whose men of Redgarden had broken free of the rout and ridden hard to reinforce his allies of Blakley. The Suhdrins spent the nights grimly discussing whether they would be welcome back in the south when this was all over.

"Such readiness is fortunate, given the circumstances," Castian answered. "Look, the sally gate has opened."

Malcolm squinted, but couldn't make out what was happening at the gates. A few moments later a rider came into view, galloping from the castle under a white flag. Malcolm smiled when he recognized a familiar face.

"Sir Merret!" Malcolm called when the rider came into range. "I'm glad to discover that you weren't lost at the Redoubt!"

"One of few who survived, I'm afraid," Merret said. He reined in his mount beside Malcolm and Sorcha, keeping the Blakleys between himself and Jaerdin. "We depended on the river for our defense, but they came at us from the woods. Gwen had thinned our ranks to pursue her own glory, and when Volent fell on us from the east we were ill equipped to defend."

"Volent? I thought he rode with Halverdt's army. How did he get behind you?"

"Gods know," Merret responded. "Is Gwen Adair among your ranks?"

"The huntress is missing?" Sorcha asked.

"Aye, she went reaving to the south, thinking to take the fight to Halverdt's flank. A few survivors stumbled back to the Fen Gate three nights ago. They ran into a Suhdrin force deep in the Fen, led by Sir Volent and accompanied by a host of inquisitors. They tell incredible stories." Merret paused, his eyes flickering to Jaerdin. "Unbelievable stories. And we must believe that Gwen has fallen into Suhdrin hands."

"Better that she died, rather than find herself in the Deadface's care," Sorcha said. "That explains the banner of mourning flying from your walls."

"What I don't understand is how any of this happened. Gwendolyn Adair was to hold the western fords. She should never have ridden south of the Tallow. And failing that, if she discovered a Suhdrin force within the Fen, her first priority should have been to send warning to our flank."

"My understanding is that the huntress had other priorities," Merret said.

"Other priorities? What in gods' names is that supposed to mean?"

"I know not, and can answer no further," Merret said. "Before you get too indignant, however, I would remind you that her choice cost me my command, and many of my friends."

"As well, I would remind you that her choice may have cost me my son," Sorcha said evenly. Merret paused, struggling between anger and regret. Finally he bowed his head.

"This is a time of much loss, my lady. You have my sympathy, and my prayers for the boy's safe return."

"It's a pity Gwen Adair isn't here to answer for herself," Sorcha answered. "I would have *her* explanation... as well as her regret."

"We pray that she is well, of course," Malcolm said quickly. "Perhaps any further discussion should wait until we've had a chance to speak with Colm Adair. We have a defense to plan."

"We see that your gate is already secured, and your peasants gathered," Castian broke in. "Were you expecting an immediate assault?"

"The peasants saw your approach and assumed you were the vanguard of Halverdt's army. They don't know banners from words, I'm afraid."

"Well, raise the gate and summon your lord," Malcolm said. "We've ridden long, and have much to discuss."

Sir Merret bowed, then turned his horse and started down the road. Malcolm signaled the advance and was about to follow when Sorcha pulled him aside.

"I will not forget the girl's betrayal," she hissed. "Whatever her reason, her decision lost us that battle."

"Be as that may, the mistake is made and the battle gone," Malcolm said quietly. "We must prepare for the next fight. As long as House Adair is our ally, it might be best to not blame their dead child for the loss of our son."

"Pray that she is dead," Sorcha answered. "Pray that she never has to answer to me for her failure."

The Sedgewind throne was not ornate. Carved from a petrified trunk of gnarled ironwood, the ancestral seat of House Adair was bent and twisted, with spiny branches hanging over the throne room, swept all in one direction by generations of harsh wind. The conquered banners of the enemies of House Adair hung in tatters from those branches, intermingled with leather-bound icons of the old tribes. The trunk itself was rooted as though the entire structure had erupted from the floor of the castle. Legend had it that the Fen Gate had been built around the throne, slowly accreting over generations of tribesmen and lesser lords, until it became the seat of Colm Adair.

The baron sat, attended by a dozen knights of court, all dressed for war, and a single priest. Malcolm led his bedraggled entourage into the room. Every mile he had spent on the road weighed on his shoulders.

"Houndhallow," Colm Adair said quietly. His black armor was plain, though he draped it in crimson silk and ebon chain. His eyes flicked to Castian Jaerdin. "I did not expect a Suhdrin lord in your army."

"The duke of Redgarden has stood with me since the Reaver War, and will stand with the faithful sons of the Celestial church, regardless of their blood," Malcolm said.

"Doesn't he know that it is the church marching against us?" Colm asked.

"The inquisition is not the church, my lord," Castian answered. "While the difference may count for little in Heartsbridge, on the field of battle and in my heart, they are not the same."

"No, they are not," Colm allowed. "The inquisition is far more dangerous."

"As we have seen," Malcolm said. "I have it from Sir Merret that a host of shadow priests aided Sir Volent in his assault upon the Fen. What more can you tell us?"

"Nothing much. They moved through the night, defended against the humbled gods of the Fen and, when the time came, they haunted the souls and hunted the hearts of my men."

"We were wondering," Malcolm said, his voice brittle with care, "why your daughter did not ride to warn our flank of their peril. I understand that you lost a great many men on the Redoubt."

"As you lost many at the Tallow," Colm said stiffly. "Both our houses have paid a great price for Gwen's foolishness. If what Sir Brennan reports is true, then we may never know what my daughter had in her heart. Personally, I think she was riding home to warn the castle."

"The castle's walls were safe as long as we held the Tallow," Castian said.

"You could not have held the Tallow if Sir Volent had led his force here, and taken this stronghold. From here he could have harassed your rear and cut off all supply from the north."

"He chose instead to fall on our flank, and rout us utterly," Malcolm said, "as any wise tactician would have done in his position. Perhaps Gwen was not up to the task of command. She is, after all, simply a hunter."

"You will not question my daughter's right to lead," Colm said sharply. "Especially not while her mourning banner still flies over my head."

"I *will* question it," Sorcha said. "To the end of my days, I will regret giving command to that huntress."

"I will remind you that I have lost a daughter," Colm hissed.

"And I have lost a son," Sorcha replied. "Not in glory, not in honor, but for the foolish mistake of a girl. So do not speak to me of her right to lead. Do not speak to me of mourning, nor of death!"

The chamber was quiet for a minute. The dozen knights of House Adair shifted on either side of the throne, tension traveling through their hands to the hilts of the swords. It was the priest who broke the silence.

"You are right, of course, Duchess, but we must not let our common tragedy lead to our common downfall." The man fiddled with the icons at his neck, and drew out a crescent moon, the sign of Lord Cinder. "The winter god is harsh. His judgment is sharp, and his season unforgiving. This is his war. A war meant to separate the faithful from the fallen. Let us not falter in his gaze."

"I am afraid, gentle frair, that all I can do is live through winter, and pray for spring," Sorcha said bitterly.

"That is all that is left for any of us, my lady," the priest answered.

Sorcha had nothing more to say. The anger had burned through her.

"Whatever has come between us," Malcolm said, stepping slightly forward, his hands well away from his blade, "we must not let it divide us. Halverdt rides north with an army of some thousands. We have our hundreds, and you have your walls. Together we may stand against him."

Colm Adair leaned back in his chair, resting an arm on the sword by his side. The room waited in silence. When he leaned forward, the banners that hung over the Sedgewind throne stirred quietly, but there was no other movement.

"Well we might," Colm said with a nod. "And we must."

34

THE FIRST SOUND was a slithering crackle that stretched out beneath a morning sky the color of tarnished pewter. Gwen stood and drew her sword, staring out into the bare dawn light, able to see little more than tree trunks and shadows. Her heart was hammering through her ribs.

"Sir LaFey!" she hissed.

The vow knight was beside her in an instant, the veiny scars on her cheeks thrumming like molten gold. The woman pulsed with heat, and the air around her smelled like boiling sweat and hot leather. The shadows in the forest shrank from her.

"Should we wake the frair?" Gwen asked.

"He's already out there, somewhere," Elsa answered. Confused, Gwen looked back at the priest's tent. The old man sat in the mouth of it, legs folded under him, chin resting on his chest. "The line between dreaming and searching can be strange with him," the woman said. "Not that he doesn't trust you. I think he's more comfortable like this."

The sound grew closer and faster. The hill at the crest of the next valley shivered, its carpet of trees swaying and then buckling as something massive moved beneath their boughs. A trench opened in the distant tree line. Gwen caught a glimpse of the gheist rolling languidly forward like a boiling fist of tar.

"It got bigger," she said.

"Aye," Elsa agreed. "We need some space."

Suddenly Frair Lucas stood up like a dead man summoned to life by some dark god, his lips quivering as he drew frenzied breath.

"We need to get higher," he said.

"I just…" Elsa started, but Lucas cut her off.

"There's a ridgeline south of here. Some boulders. We need to get among those," he said, then started off in that direction. Sir LaFey pushed Gwen after the priest.

"Your armor?" Gwen asked. The vow knight had shrugged it aside before she went to sleep. Gwen had considered warning her of the gheist's imminent approach so that the vow knight might prepare, but couldn't see a way to do so and still keep the secret of the witching wives.

"I have my faith," Elsa answered, but there was worry in her eyes. "Or my sword, at least."

Gwen took quick stock of her own supplies. She had her blade and wore her plate-and-half. Now that she was running through the woods, though, she wished she had pared down to the leather armor she usually used to hunt. A quiver of three bloodwrought spears banged against her back.

"Do not stop," Elsa said from behind. Gwen turned to answer, but in so doing again saw the gheist as it topped the hillock. The night was still hanging on to the sky, and the sun was well below the horizon, but Gwen had all the light she needed. The thing was enormous, its rolling bulk clutching dozens of bodies in the shadow-black ribbons of its form—men and women, horses, bears, the wretched and the dead.

Gwen stumbled to a halt. She was beginning to regret not warning her companions. Then Elsa grabbed her roughly by the cloak and pushed her on.

Ahead of them, upon the ridge, was a jagged line of boulders, some twice the height of a man, with mossy channels cut between them by years of rain and the patient work of roots. A bristling crown of trees topped the largest boulder, roots and trunks spilling down its sides like melted wax running down a bottle. Frair Lucas stood in the gap between that rock and the next, peering past them at the gheist.

A shriek reached their ears.

"We're going to need new horses," he said as Gwen pushed past him. Her heart ached at the thought of the beasts, tethered and unable to run. She only hoped neither she nor her companions would share their fate.

They ground to a halt just beyond the frair. The gap he had chosen offered just enough space for them to move around and swing a sword. A great place to hold against a charge, or to wait in ambush. Not so good against a gheist. Gwen went to the far side of the gap and looked down. The ground tumbled away in a shallow decline dotted with rocks and jagged roots—difficult to retreat across. The gheist was close enough now that running was out of the question anyway.

She went back to stand beside Lucas.

"What dò we do?" Gwen asked.

"Fight, I suppose," Lucas said. "Elsa?"

"It's the same gheist," LaFey answered, "but it's been adding to its hosts."

"Could it have split?"

"That's a miserable thought," Elsa said. "And it's best left for later. Can we just kill the god that's here, please?"

"Hopefully," Lucas said, and he turned sharply. "Gwendolyn, keep them away from us, and try to not get killed."

All this time the gheist had been rolling up the hill toward them. It seemed confused, casting back and forth through the trees, like a hound that had lost the scent. Gwen wondered if the witching wives had done as they hoped, if the gheist was still under their influence. She had a momentary panic that it might slip its leash and dart away. With their horses gone, there was no way they would be able to catch up with it.

She calmed her nerves and focused as it came closer, grew larger, sticky ribbons of shadow lashing forward to pull it up the hill. The wreckage of their horses stuck to the outside of the roiling ball of umbral energy, slowly dissolving into the demon's flesh.

"Here we go," Elsa whispered as it got close. Standing beside the vow knight, Gwen suddenly realized that Lucas had disappeared. She glanced around and found the priest behind her, sitting cross-legged on the ground, the short staff resting on his knees, hands folded over it as if he were in prayer. Elsa grabbed Gwen's shoulder and pointed.

"He's helpless when he's like that," she barked. "Keep them away from his body."

"Then what—" Gwen began to ask, then a twisting helix of dark power swirled up from the ground, a lightning strike in reverse, static energy dancing across the priest's skin and lifting the loose folds of his robe in a tearing wind. Leaves and loose gravel clattered into a whirlwind, scouring the boulders and forcing her to squint.

The storm settled down, and a ghost of the frair hung in the air above his unconscious head. The edges of his shadow form were frayed and wavering, lines of force that trailed in the air like tattered banners. The priest's shadow held its staff like a mast.

"And now we fight, perhaps to die," Lucas said. "The will of the gods be done." His words echoed through both forms, the voice of the shadow all gravel and doom, his mortal voice little more than a whisper, spoken as though in a dream. The shadow form flickered over Gwen's head.

He flowed like a swallow through the air, darting and striking at the gheist, harassing the much larger demon among the trees. The demon seemed startled by this, at first, and for the briefest moment it stopped and huddled in on itself, the lesser entities of its body circling tight to protect the core.

Frair Lucas scythed past the demon, cutting with shadows as sharp as knives. The flickering specter dancing through the trees was a far cry from the timid man sitting on the ground beside her. She looked from one to the other, wonder etched on her face.

"The speed of the mind," Elsa said with a smirk. "Those bones have gotten frail, but he's as sharp as an arrow in that skull of his—and just as fast."

"I had no idea," Gwen whispered. "I've never seen a naethermancer's art."

"Few have." Then Sir LaFey started to move. "It looks like my step in the dance has arrived." She marched out of the gap between boulders, sword and shield at the ready. The gheist was so occupied with the frair's sharp orbit that at first it paid her no mind. That changed as she began to invoke the bright lady's many blessings.

With the sun still below the horizon, Elsa was forced to draw what power she could from the gloaming. The strange magics of the Celestial church were always weakest during the transitions, dawn and dusk, spring and autumn, and with the equinox looming, her powers were reduced by the time of day to a fraction of their glory.

Still, she drew from the pewter glimmer of sun reflected off the sky, calling out Strife's power, heat stored in the earth and the air. She pulled that power into the bloodwrought runes of her armor and the etched blessings on her weapons. The metal flashed like lightning, and the plants closest to the vow knight curled into ash. Gwen felt a wave of heat wash over her.

"This way, demon!" Elsa yelled, throwing her shield wide to draw the gheist's attention. "Step into the light and be seared!"

The creature howled with its dozen voices, the braying of horses and terrified mouths of dead peasants and soldiers joining together to vent the rogue god's frustration. It rolled forward in a mass, tendril-wrapped bodies leaping ahead to stop and draw the bulk after it. A farmer slithered forward with shadow-choked arms to grip a tree on one side, the corrupted body of a knight surged toward Elsa on the other. Between them came the twisting, sickening tumor of the gheist.

The two met, mad deity and vow knight, Elsa standing like a lighthouse against a shadowy tide. It broke over her, arms scrambling to get closer, ribbons of inky night darting out to test her defenses, the puppet bodies of those who had fallen pressing around her perimeter. They screamed with their gaping mouths, grabbing for Elsa's shield, her arms, snatching bits of cloth from her cloak like fish striking bait. Still she stood, blocking and striking, swinging the sun-bright blade of her sword in shimmering arcs that cut through flesh and bone, clipping the inky ribbons that manipulated the dead soldiers.

The gheist wrapped around her, its enormous mass stretching beyond her flanks, staying just out of range of that hated sword. It flowed like a river around a rock, and on the other side it found Gwen.

She was forced back. The boulders on either side directed the demon's attack, with only a couple of the dead able to squeeze between the rocks and shamble toward the huntress. She drew her spear back and let fly, taking the first puppet in the throat. The tendrils that gripped the dead man skittered back, abandoning the body like ice melting away from a lightning strike. The peasant, bloodwrought spear dangling from his throat, tumbled to the ground and was still.

The gheist kept coming. The fallen body was replaced by another, and then another, and then the creature was climbing up the boulders and slithering along the sides of the tiny depression in which they stood, scrabbling with broken fingers over stone and moss until its many forms loomed into the sky. Gwen stumbled back, and bumped into the frair's still form, resting in the center of the clearing.

"Watch the body, girl," Frair Lucas whispered.

Abruptly the shadow of the priest—the flickering, scything specter of the naethermancer—swooped into the gap and started cutting through bodies. He quickly cleared the forms off one of the boulders, only to have a wave of the monsters sweep down the other, bodies trailing ribbons of dark power. Gwen tripped, her legs tangled in the biting tendrils, falling to the mossy ground beside the priest. She stabbed down at the loops of black force that were slithering around her ankles—cut through her own boot and drew blood, swore and spat and stabbed again.

The gheist retreated, only to bring another limb to bear against her. A knight, his armor broken and his face crushed beneath the constricting threads of the demon, clattered down the boulder and landed with bone-breaking force. One of his legs was shattered, so the possessed knight held himself upright with one arm on the rock. With the other, he raised his sword.

Gwen parried the first blow, but when the second nicked her shoulder and sent her sprawling, she no longer regretted wearing her plate-and-half. The huntress had never seen an opponent like this— had never faced a demon so capable of attacking so many opponents. Gheists were usually half-mad with isolation, berserk forces of nature unleashed on the world. This one moved with precision, bypassing Elsa's threat to attack Gwen.

No, she realized too late. *To attack the frair.*

The possessed knight twisted and struck Frair Lucas with the pommel of his blade. The shadow priest, his spectral form hovering at the top of the boulders and battling a different host of enemies, dissolved with a howl of pain that forced a shiver through Gwen's spine. The projected weapon of his mind—the shadowform—tangled into a knot of naetheric power, then spun back into Lucas's body.

The frair flopped to the ground, writhing with spasms as the naether flowed back into his mouth, his eyes. His scream of pain was choked by the ribbons of power as they reeled back into his soul.

He fell to the ground, and was still.

Without hesitation the bodies that the priest had opposed tumbled down the boulder's face, rushing to finish the frair's life. Gwen stood over him, blood leaking from foot and shoulder, her wounds sending bolts of pain through her with every parry and stroke. The bloodwrought tip of her spear dissolved the gheist's tendrils, robbing the bodies of unholy life wherever she struck, yet it was one blade against a tide of demonic force.

And then Elsa was in the fray.

The vow knight fought her way back through the tide of dead and dying, appearing at the head of the gap like a bonfire in the night. The storm of the gheist receded around her, shying away from her blade. Despite her own wounds, Gwen gasped. The woman was torn, blood thick on her face and chest, running down her arms, slick in her hair. The lightning scars on her face had burst and were glowing in the dim light of dawn, the blood that seeped from the wounds dancing with embers—a fire to match the madness in her eyes.

Gwen feared she would drink too deeply of the bright lady's blessings, and lose herself in the fervor. Strife was the goddess of war, yes, but also the goddess of madness, the blessed mistress of the insane. "My frair!" Elsa shouted. She brushed the huntress aside and straddled the priest. Gwen tucked herself against the boulder, shielding her face from the bright arcs of light sparking off Elsa's sword, the sun-bright runes of her armor. With only one clear opponent, the gheist pressed its bulk into the gap. The sky disappeared behind the stitched mass of broken bodies and broken weapons. A wall of darkness surged toward them, its face a nightmare of shadow-choked corpses.

They spoke.

"A needless death," the gheist said, its voice echoing from dead mouths. "But Cinder guides our hand. I will see you safely to the quiet, priest."

"The ashes you will!" Elsa screamed. "Any hell you open will be your own."

"Patience, patience," the wall of dead whispered. "Accept our blessing, and your death."

It grew as still as a pond. Something floated to the surface—a body, wrapped and fetal, thin limbs wasted as though by atrophy. He wore priestly robes and stepped gingerly free of the grasping ebon surface. The ribbons of darkness crossed lovingly over his chest and filled his mouth, but when his lips moved, only one voice filled the narrow space.

"As you can see, sir knight, Cinder has blessed this demon. The lord of night has strange tools. Winter can be harsh for those who fall." The priest raised his arms in benediction. "Go gently to your grave, faithful woman. Do not resist the will of your god."

"I know my god, demon," Elsa spat. "And I know my enemy just as well." The gheist-possessed priest just smiled, a strange parting of lips that tore skin and cracked the bones of his jaw.

"Well enough, then you shall die," he said.

Before Elsa could move, however, Gwen jumped to her feet, drew her spear back, and let the bloodwrought tip fly. It went straight and true, burying itself in the gheist-priest's chest with a meaty *thunk*.

Nothing happened.

"What in hell," Elsa whispered. The vow knight took a step back.

But Gwen was still moving. She had taken the measure of this gheist-priest, and knew the weapons of the church couldn't harm it. He had said it himself. Cinder had blessed this demon, and with that blessing came protection.

While the spear wobbled where it had struck, Gwen drew a second weapon from a hidden pocket in her belt. Something she kept hidden, especially around Celestial priests. It was a sharp blue splinter of crystal that glowed in the dim light. Tears of the earth, the witches called them, and to hold one was heresy. Gwen carried a matched set. It was a miracle that Allaister hadn't found them.

Its mate was buried in the shaft of her spear. Gwen raised the crystal so that the demon could see it, could know it for what it was. A look passed over its face, and then the calm surface of the walls that surrounded them burst with reaching arms.

"No," Gwen said simply, and she broke the crystal in her hand.

The light inside flashed, erupting from the crystal like a lightning bolt. It arced to meet its twin, hidden in the spear, shattering the shaft. Coruscating energy danced through the air, punching through the gheist-priest's body like a crossbow bolt. His ribs spread open like a flower, and the meat beneath seared into ash. The ribbons of the gheist's form fled from the priest. His body tipped backward, falling to the ground like a tower whose foundation had succumbed to the sapper's tunnel.

Tendrils whipped and slashed through the air, drawing into each of the bodies that the gheist had added to its form. Screaming in pain, in fear, and disbelief, it dissolved, limp bodies flopping out of it as the shadow ribbons fell away. The screaming diminished as it lost each mouth, until it stopped completely. The last of the tendrils flew up into the air, to dissolve in the early light of dawn.

Elsa stood still, staring at the dozens of corpses, the

weapons, the broken remnants of the gheist. Then she turned to face Gwen.

"Well," she said, slowly, dangerously. "I suppose there's no question as to your heresy, Huntress."

"There has never been," Frair Lucas said from his place on the ground. "Not in my heart, at least." His voice was quiet, his eyes closed, the pooled blood from his head wound smeared across his cheek. He opened one sticky eye and looked at Gwen. "She is as I suspected. As I hoped. Now let us pray it's not too late. The shadows of Cinder will have felt that loss. We have less time than I thought."

3

FIRE AND SHADOW

THE HOUND! THE HALLOW!

35

THE FOREST FELT heavy on his shoulders. Ian was wrapped in fog so thick that he couldn't see the man to his left, or the woman to his right. The valley below was as gray as a winter morning, and every sound was muffled. Even his heartbeat was a soft thud in his chest.

A shadow moved far to his left. Whether it was man, god, or pagan, Ian wasn't sure. In the time that had passed since his near death and new birth, he had become used to the divine presence of his new companions. They were as common as the mist, though no less strange.

He was drawn from his reverie by a new sound—a clatter of wood and creaking metal that drifted up from the valley. He tensed forward, straining his ears and peering into the murk, his breath tight in his chest. The man to his right leaned out just enough to catch Ian's eye.

They were perched on limestone bluffs that sat ragged above the valley floor. Ian gave the man a nod, then shifted his spear forward and waited for the sound to repeat. Creaking wood. The fog below them stirred and cleared, revealing a trail that wound through the valley, and a caravan that traveled it.

Three wagons crept among the trees, surrounded by nervous guards and fog.

Cahl had found them two days ago, just far enough from the rest of the Suhdrin supply train to fall victim to his tricks. He and the witching wives had teased this group away from the main roads north, baiting them west with nightmares and mist, drawing them into deeper forest. The guards whispered to one another about the bedeviled north. Their prayers at evensong focused on protection from the gheists and the pagan night.

It was not the night that would end them.

A call went up and down the line, barely heard but deeply felt in the blood. A cloud of spears fell from the tree line opposite Ian and his hidden companions, and mortal screams cut through the fog. The horses of the front wagon bolted, their driver impaled by a Tenerran spear. They clattered off out of sight, crashing through the woods and leaving the trail behind. The guards who remained closed tight to the remaining wagons, turning shields and spears to the forest, placing their backs to the bluffs—and their enemies.

Another wave of spears crashed down, finding flesh and wood. The master of guard raised a banner and rallied his men, sounding a weak horn. The drivers of the rear wagon left their charge and sought shelter under the one in front.

At another signal, Ian and his companions fell from the ragged stones behind their prey. Their descent was wrapped in fog, thick tendrils holding them close, giving a soft landing and silent approach. He didn't yet understand how this magic worked, other than to know that Fianna stood somewhere behind them, wrapping the mists around her like a cloak, drawing and guiding them, blinding the enemy and cloaking the attack.

They were a dozen strong, not even a third of the guardsmen's number, but they rushed forward without a sound, without warning. Ian's cloak fluttered behind him as he ran from the base of the cliff, rock as gray as rain and just as ragged. The semicircle of Suhdrin guards knelt beside the wagon, their spears bristling from a wall of shields scarred by spear fall. They looked ragged from lack of sleep and creeping fear. Their master paced behind them, leaning in to his men to steady their nerve and polish their formation.

He was an older man, bent and scarred, a brace of daggers on his belt, gripping a sword that was more bitten than straight. He was decades bald, his beard neatly trimmed and washed, even after weeks on the trail. The men around him were young, the stubble on their cheeks too soft and wispy to hide their skin. They wore new armor that didn't fit, clutched new spears that had never been thrown for blood. Recruits, and a grizzled master of guard meant to keep the children safe. Now they were here, in this trap, at the tip of Ian's spear.

The master of guard heard something, or sensed it, turning just as Ian reached him. His eyes changed, grim determination fading to relief, weeks of fear settling into a moment of regret and then violent hatred. The man swung his blade. Ian blocked it with the haft of his spear, brushed the old man's arm aside, then buried the petal-shaped tip into the master's chest. Ribs cracked and parted. The man's eyes went soft and he toppled back into the shield wall.

This was the first warning the soldiers had, and the last, and then it was reaving and the letting of blood.

Ian dropped his spear, letting the master of guard

twist to the ground, and drew his sword. There was a clatter of metal as the Suhdrin guards tried to turn, and ended up banging shields into spears, tripping over one another to meet the new threat. Ian sliced into the two closest, putting his sword through collarbones and necks before the men could get to their feet, while the rest of the pagans kept to their spears. They had a strange way of fighting, sweeping feet and hooking blades with the complicated barbs of their weapons, treating the spears more as staves. The Suhdrin had no counter, and within seconds the silence of the forest was restored. The horses fled into the fog.

"We should follow them," Ian gasped. He was out of breath from the fall and the fight, and the half-dozen heartbeats when he had held his breath as they ran forward. Cahl shook his head.

"The gods will take them," he said. This was followed by a distant baying of hounds. The fog began to clear.

"And the wagon that bolted?" Ian asked.

"Already done," Fianna said. She stepped out of the stones of the bluff as if they were shadows. Her face was flushed and her eyes tired, but her voice was strong. "The horses took a wrong turn."

"Gods be good," Cahl said.

"They usually are. Ian, take five and gather supplies from the wagons. Burn whatever you can't carry. Cahl, we need to get back to the train."

"How long are we going to do this?" Ian asked.

"As long as it takes to bleed them dry."

"There are a hundred wagons for each of these," Ian said, gesturing around them. The others were freeing the horses, soothing them and cutting their bridles before releasing them into the woods. "And a hundred spears for each wagon in Halverdt's army."

"Then we'll be at this for a while," Cahl said. "Best you get to your task."

"By the time we bleed them all, the north will have fallen."

"Your north," Cahl answered. "Mine fell generations ago, but we're still here. Perhaps you will learn to live among us."

"Do you really care so little for the houses? Does it mean nothing to you that the Blakleys, MaeHerrons, Rudaines... do you hold no love for the old names?"

"The old names call themselves duke, and baron, and lord." Cahl wiped his spear on one of the dead, then slid it home in the quiver at his side. "They wear Suhdrin clothes and Suhdrin titles. Why should they have my love?"

"Then why are we fighting at all? Let the high inquisitor wage his war and topple his enemies," Ian snapped. "If you don't care any more for Tenerran blood, why bring your spears to this war?"

Cahl snorted, then turned and walked away. A half-dozen or so of his men followed, leaving Ian alone with the witching wives. Fianna shrugged.

"He fights because I tell him to fight," she said, "and I fight because I hope for something more of you, and your family."

"So what are we doing here? You know this is useless. Halverdt has more spears than we'll ever be able to starve. Whatever we take from the supply train, he just steals from the countryside."

"Yes, but we are doing more than killing Suhdrin."

"Really? What, then? What are we doing?"

She folded her hands and stepped over the dead to stand at Ian's side. The effort of drawing the fog and muffling the ambush had taken much from her, but what remained seemed to burn brighter. Fianna was like a seething ember buried at the heart of the forge, her fire concentrated. Not a flame or wisp of smoke was wasted. Ian could almost feel the heat washing off of her. There was a strange beauty in this silence and fury—so unlike the wild, unkempt girls of the Tenerran court. Ian felt himself flushing as she drew close, and told himself it was the aftereffects of battle.

"What have you seen of me?" she asked quietly.

"I don't... I'm not sure what you mean, my lady."

"My lady, your honor, your grace," she said dismissively. "We don't carry those titles into these woods, Ian of Houndhallow." She came closer still. There was fatigue in her eyes, an exhaustion that couldn't be satisfied by sleep. "You know what I mean."

Ian hesitated. The business of disassembling the ambush went on all around them—dragging the men off the road and hacking through their supplies, the bloody labor of patching wounds and dispatching foes who had not gone gently to their graves. Ian felt suspended between those activities and something else. Something only he and Fianna shared. He shook his head.

"Fog. Beasts in the forest." He smiled. "An unnatural affinity for the river."

"Do you doubt the power of those things?"

"No, I never have. The inquisition doesn't chase ghost stories, after all. They have reason to fear what you can do. There is power in the forest. In your history."

"In our history," Fianna said. "And what of you? Do you fear the powers in the forest?"

Ian cleared his throat, and fidgeted.

"When I was eight years old and the equinox

approached, my father took my sisters and me, and he hid us in our rooms. Right in the middle of dinner. A man was at the gates, that's all he would say, a man who couldn't be trusted." Ian looked around the ambush site, his eye catching on Cahl, who was waiting on the periphery of the forest. The shaman was watching them. "A man of some power. I tried to get a view from my window, but I couldn't quite see. So I climbed out on the ledge..."

"You're going to tell me that this man was a pagan. Perhaps a shaman, perhaps just a vessel for one of the old gods," Fianna interrupted. "Your father barred the gate, summoned a priest, and killed him. Yes?"

"A vessel. An interesting way to put it. Yes, a vessel. A man from the village, the blacksmith, in fact. Frae Dunham, his name was. While traveling to a nearby town to make a delivery, Frae Dunham was attacked, killed, and his body possessed by a gheist. It was nearly the equinox, and not even the godsroad can protect against the old spirits all the time."

"A pity, but if our shamans were able to perform the rites..."

"A pity?" Ian said sharply. "A pity for his wife, for his sons, for Frae himself. Taken from the road and corrupted, and then sent by someone, some*thing*, to attack my house. So, yes, my father summoned a priest and his knights, and they killed Frae Dunham. In front of the whole village, and most of the castle, they filled him with arrows and prayers, and then they burned his body. I tried to get a view, but couldn't. I wanted to see the excitement.

"The next day I learned what had happened, that his wife had watched while he burned alive because bloodwrought steel couldn't bring her husband to his knees, so they dumped pitch from the ramparts and put flame to his body. I couldn't see, but gods, I could hear the screams."

Fianna stood silently, reading Ian's face, her eyes as bright as candles.

"I'm sorry," she said. "There are those among us who favor such tactics, and there are certain gods who are drawn to riding the flesh of their victims. In times past, a willing vessel would take the god and live through him until the time of sacrifice came, or until the god's festival had passed. They seek our worship, and follow the old ways. In their madness, the gods don't know what they do to us."

"That is little comfort for Frae Dunham's family… or for me."

Fianna nodded and stepped away. "Then that is why we are here, doing this, rather than riding to fight your duke of Greenhall." She sighed and walked carefully among the bodies. "You don't believe us yet. Nor will you."

She went and spoke to Cahl, who made a dismissive gesture before the pair of them disappeared into the forest. Ian felt as if he had failed something, disappointed them in some way. If they were expecting him to convert to their religion of twigs and mad gods, they were in for disappointment—but he couldn't stand waiting at the edge of the fight. The duke of Greenhall, with the high inquisitor at his side, was marching through Adair's territory in great force. Somewhere out there Ian's father was preparing, perhaps wondering where his son was. Wondering if Ian was still alive.

One of the pagans splashed oil on the wagons. When he was done, Cahl struck tinder and put the wagon and its remaining supplies to the flame. The sudden bonfire bathed the forest in heat and light, burning away the remaining tendrils of fog that Fianna had summoned.

Yet despite the heat, Ian shivered. The pagans looked wild in the sharp light of the fire, their clothes and inked faces picked out in flat contrast, bright and dark, fire and shadow, sun and moon. Despite the fact that Fianna had saved his life, Ian would never be comfortable around them. His place was by his father's side, fighting his father's war. Ian had to find a way to get to him.

His eyes cleared, and he saw that Cahl was staring at him. He looked like a wolf at the edge of a campfire, counting his meals, and then he was gone, whirling into the shadows, leaving the fire and the blood behind, disappearing into the forest.

In the distance the hounds bayed.

36

SCOUTS REPORTED THAT Halverdt had rested on the banks of the Tallow for five days, celebrating their victor and gathering their strength, before he struck camp and marched north, marching in greater strength than any expected. Those same scouts reported that he was approaching under the banners of all of the southern houses.

When he heard of this, Malcolm and Sorcha brought together the other lords who had joined them at the Fen Gate and rode out with them, along with a sizable guard. They received the blessings of the priests. Malcolm wanted to see this army for himself, to weigh its strength and prepare his mind for what lay ahead.

"They say that Halverdt marches with three columns of men-at-arms," Ewan Thaen said. He had arrived the previous evening with a force of pikemen and archers, to join the knights of his banner who had been at Greenhall for the Allfire and had fled with Malcolm when things turned sour. "Plus twice that many mounted spears—to say nothing of his legions of foot and arrow."

"I have trouble believing those reports," Colm Adair answered.

"As do I," Sorcha Blakley agreed. "There were

many banners at the Tallow, from many houses. If all of those lords brought their full strength to the field, they might reach those numbers, but that is unlikely."

"Thank you again, Thaen, for joining us at the Fen Gate," Malcolm said, turning to the duke of the Frostwell. "Your men have fought bravely. I can only imagine that their strength will redouble with their lord at the fore."

"What news from the north?" Castian Jaerdin asked. The Suhdrin duke was the only one of their host wearing heavy furs. The first touch of autumn had left a chill in his southern bones, more than his pride was willing to stand. "Can we expect more support from the other Tenerran lords?"

"That depends on the days to come," Ewan answered. "Many of the houses are waiting to see what comes of this battle. None like to defy the church."

"It is not the church they are defying," Colm said. "It's the duke of Greenhall."

"And yet the church rides against us," Ewan persisted. "With the high inquisitor at the fore, and while Tomas Sacombre has few friends north of the Tallow, there are many who fear him. Justly."

"MaeFell has sworn to us," Sorcha said. "He offered me his promise on the field of battle, after we had turned away the Suhdrin assault."

"That was immediately before you were routed from the field," Ewan reminded her. "I'm sure MaeFell means well, and his promise is good, but when I passed the Docent Tower on my way south, the farmers were in the fields and the harvest was heavy on the stalk. The duke may reach his walls in a few weeks, but once there he will need to call his banners and shift his people from their hearths on the eve of winter. This battle will be fought without his spears."

"Lord Daeven has continued on as well," Sorcha said. "I fear that whatever tale he tells in the northern marches, it is unlikely to draw more banners to our cause."

"That's as may be," Malcolm said. "We have the spears that the gods have given us. We must not pray for more."

"Hope is never worth much on the field of battle, anyway," Ewan muttered. "So easily lost, and so falsely given."

"I look forward to fighting at your side," Castian said grimly. "It will be an uplifting experience, I'm sure."

"Enough," Sorcha hissed before an argument could take wing. "There are riders ahead."

A crown of banners crested the next hill. There were few riders for the number of pennants that flew—no more than three dozen knights, with nearly a dozen colors aloft. When the riders sighted the Tenerran party, two of them trotted to the lead together and unfurled another flag. White, the banner of truce and parley.

"Perhaps your scouts only counted their banners, and not their spears," Grant MaeHerron rumbled. They were the first words he'd spoken since they had ridden out of the Fen Gate that morning. Ewan Thaen didn't answer.

"DuFallion, Marcy, even Bealth," Castian said, counting off the banners that flew over the small contingent. "I hoped they might join our cause."

"They seem to have decided otherwise," Ewan said.

"We hoped that Roard would treat peacefully with us as well," Sorcha said. "All know how that turned out. And their banner is before us as well."

"Yes," Malcolm craned his neck to see the riders

beneath the yellow of Roard. "It is the father, but not the son."

"Whatever that portends," Sorcha said.

"I see Marchand, LeGaere... gods, the colors of all Suhdra fly in that contingent!"

"Not all," Castian pointed out, but the others ignored him, for the sky was crowded with the banners of most of the great houses of Suhdra—the golden barque of Bassion, the peaks of Fabron, alongside Galleux, Thoussert, Maison... and the tri-acorn and cross of Halverdt rode above them all.

Malcolm let out a long and withering sigh.

"I don't like this," he said.

"You advised us to stand together," MaeHerron said. "Did you think the lords of Suhdra would do any differently?"

They rode in silence until the lead riders of the Suhdrin contingent were close enough to hail them. The pair drew to a halt, signaling back to the Suhdrin knights, who also stopped.

"Stay here," Malcolm said, then he turned to his wife. "If they draw steel, return to the Fen and prepare the walls. Do not wait for me."

"I came all this way to rescue you, husband," she replied firmly. "Do you think I will leave you to their care?"

Malcolm shook his head, then trotted forward. The rest of the lords and their guards joined him.

The man holding the banner of peace was a knight of the church, his house and name cast aside to serve the celestriarch, though he hadn't taken the winter vow. He was clearly Suhdrin, though. The rider beside him was Marcus Beaunair, high elector of Lady Strife.

"Houndhallow," the high elector called. He had lost some weight, and his smile was lacking the brilliance it had carried when Malcolm last saw the man. "We have come far, my brother. Farther than I wanted, I must admit."

"High elector," Malcolm greeted him. "Things in Greenhall did not go as we hoped."

"No, they did not, and they have only gotten worse."

"Why are you riding under Halverdt's banner?" Malcolm asked. "Has Heartsbridge finally given its blessing to this madman's war?"

"There is no madness in honor, sir," the Celestial knight hissed. Beaunair gestured to him dismissively.

"Ignore Sir Gissert. He is freshly sworn, and still has the zealot's fire in his belly. I ride with Greenhall because I wish to finish the task I set you to, Malcolm."

"You still seek peace?" Sorcha asked.

"Many of us do," Beaunair said. He nodded back to the riders on the hill. "You will not find allies among them, but you will find mercy."

"What if we are not seeking mercy, but justice?" Colm Adair hissed.

"Then you may lose both," Beaunair answered. "Come, speak to them. They will not harm you in my presence."

Malcolm looked among his fellow lords. Ewan Thaen shrugged, then spurred his horse forward. They signaled for their guards to wait, then rode together in a line with Beaunair slightly ahead, and Sir Gissert trailing behind. The Suhdrin lords awaited them at the crest of a sharp hill, their number spread across the road and onto the verge on either side, nearly to the trees. It was a subtle reminder of their number.

Such subtlety didn't last long, though. As the

Tenerrans reached the crest of the hill, the valley beyond came into view.

"Sweet and blessed gods." Malcolm whistled.

"Where have they... how..." Colm muttered.

"Now we know what kept Halverdt at the Tallow for most of a week, I suppose," Castian said. Beaunair twisted clumsily around in his saddle.

"Yes, my lords. You see, while you may find mercy in the south, if you reject that mercy, you will not like the justice they provide in its wake," he said.

The valley was full of spearmen, archers, hosts of knights and the endless streams of wagon trains and marching columns of pike and axe and sword. The land bristled with the weapons of war. A ceaseless drone drifted up from the valley, the clattering rush of thousands upon thousands of boots hammering the ground. It was the inexorable sound of war.

"They have brought peace," Malcolm said to himself, his voice distant and lost in the spectacle before him. "And the blades to force it."

It was agreed that a Suhdrin delegation would travel to the Fen Gate the following day. Then the Tenerran lords returned to House Adair as quickly as possible.

Colm spoke to his manservant, then saw to it that Blakley and Thaen were comfortable in their quarters. When an appropriate amount of time had passed, he slipped through the kitchens and descended the hidden stairs to the depths of the castle.

The witch was waiting. Only a single candle flickered in the darkness. She sat impatiently on the altar. Colm entered the room and knelt in the middle of the floor.

"I do not like the things I'm hearing, apostate," she said.

"I have no choice, my lady. The Suhdrins have arrived in such force that they will not be denied. I can't ask the other lords to die defending something they no longer hold holy."

"Most of them would turn you over to the inquisition, rather than say the rites in this place," the witch replied. "What of the hallow?"

"This castle may fall, and my name be burned from the peerage, but if we keep their attention here, they will never find the witches' hallow," Colm said. "Or at least that is my hope."

"The hallow does not stand without this castle, nor without this family." The witch crossed her arms and frowned. "We require your authority among the lords to ward against the church's influence, as well as your right to appoint the huntress of this march. A huntress who answered purely to the church would ruin the balance of the Fen."

"We live to serve, my lady."

"Of that there is no doubt." The witch stood and circled the room, trailing a hand over Colm's shoulders as she passed. "Who is coming? Who will be part of this delegation of peace?"

"The duke of Greenhall, as the offended voice, and his attendants. Lorien Roard and his son, representing the lords of Suhdra who seek peace beneath the church's banner, and a couple voices from Heartsbridge."

"Priests," the witch said with a frown. "That Frair Humble sleeps beneath this roof is bad enough. The spirits bless us that he's enough of a fool to ignore the heresy under his nose. Let's hope these representatives are as easily deceived. No inquisitors, I trust?"

"The high inquisitor, I'm afraid, along with the high elector of Strife."

"Well..." The witch slumped against the wall. "Fuck."

"Aye," Adair agreed. "We can only hope that they will be occupied enough with the negotiations to stay away from these chambers. You may want to leave the village while they're here."

"No, you may need me," she said. "Pray that you don't, but if matters become that dire, it's better that I am here than not."

"It will not come to that," Colm answered.

"Only the gods know for certain, and they have not seen fit to make things easy on us." She pulled him to his feet. "Listen closely, Colm of the tribe of iron. Your family has worked hard to preserve the hallow. Generations of witches and their shamans are in your debt, and now the weight of your debt may be lifted, but only if a final price is asked."

"Final price?"

"Yes. If the high inquisitor is in danger of discovering this place, or any evidence of the god that we all keep close, you must do anything you can to prevent that from happening."

"Of course," Colm said. "We have always—"

"Listen," she said. "*Anything*. You must be willing to die, and to kill, and to betray those who are closest to you. Even your family." The witch lifted the single candle from its nook in the wall and held it close to her face. "If the gods ask it, you will burn this castle to the ground and sow the earth with the blood of every man, woman and child within its walls."

Colm stood silently, staring at the flickering flame. The witch remained impassive.

"I have lived to serve," he said finally, "and will die to serve, as well."

"Yes," she answered. "You will."

Then she blew out the candle, plunging them into absolute darkness. He heard neither footfall nor rustle of clothing, but he knew he was alone in the shrine. He stood there a long time, listening to the quiet of the stone, breathing in the remnants of smoke.

37

THEIR CAMP WAS wrecked, but one of the mounts, Frair Lucas's stubborn and self-serving mule, had torn free of its bridle and watched the carnage from the next ridge. As soon as the gheist was dead, the mule trotted down the hill and resumed his morning meal among the rough grass of the Fen. Lucas laughed when he saw the beast.

"He's seen a lot," Lucas said. "Can't blame him for being alive."

Elsa had said little since the fight's end. She hovered over the frair and kept a sharp eye on Gwen. The vow knight had taken everything from her that resembled a weapon, from her spears to her table knife, along with the crystals hidden in her belt and the minimal jewelry on her arms. Anything that might be an icon of the old faith.

Between them they were able to get the frair down the hill and onto the mule. They gathered what little remained of their camp and started east. Lucas urged them to hurry, though he wouldn't say why. They went as fast as his injuries would allow.

The frair's face was gray and slack, and a swollen knot of blood and bruise squeezed one eye shut. He slouched forward in his saddle, both hands gripping the pommel tightly, swaying with each step. Even the mule seemed concerned for his rider, slowing on inclines more than was his habit. Elsa walked by the frair's stirrup, one hand on the mule's ribs, moving her gaze rapidly between Lucas's pale face and Gwen, who led them through the forest.

Gwen was surprised that they let her walk unbound, and was just as surprised that she didn't run the first chance they gave her. She wondered if there was some sort of mystical compulsion binding her to the priest and his knight. The ways of the inquisition were little known and mythically powerful. Nothing about Lucas's reaction to her attack made any sense, though.

They didn't speak through the afternoon, except for Elsa's occasional warning for Lucas to take care. Night found them closer to the hallow than Gwen preferred, but far enough away that the pagan wards had stopped blurring their path. Elsa chose a sheltered valley between two rocky hills. She and Gwen eased Lucas from his mount and set him on a log. The saddle was sticky with blood from some hidden wound, the sight of which sent Elsa into a furious tirade about his health. Lucas waved her off, leaned against a mossy tree, and dozed off.

"Stay with him," Elsa said tersely. "If anything further happens to him, I will take it out of your flesh."

Gwen nodded wearily. The vow knight disappeared into the gloomy trees, returning some time later with an armful of kindling.

"Should we be making a fire?" Gwen asked. Elsa didn't answer. Once the flames were going, she took a kettle from the frair's bags and began mixing an earthy tea that seemed more dirt than leaf. She brewed in silence, pouring a cup for the frair and putting it under his nose.

"Is there enough for everyone?" Gwen asked quietly.

"You wouldn't want it. Tastes like hoof."

"Never had hoof," Gwen said.

"There's a reason for that," Elsa said. Frair Lucas started as the smell reached him, then took the cup and forced the tea down.

"So I'm not dead," he said. His voice was rough, as frail as he looked. "That's nice."

"How do you feel?" Elsa asked.

"Not dead. I'm not sure I can commit to more than that."

"What are we doing?" Elsa asked.

Lucas didn't answer for a little while, swirling the dregs of his hoof tea in the cup and eyeing it maliciously. He sipped some more, held it in his mouth, then leaned forward and spat it into the fire.

"Running," he said.

"From what? The gheist is dead, and Frair Allaister is to our south. We have to do something with her," Elsa said, barely indicating Gwen.

"I'm not sure. Not exactly." Lucas closed his eyes and leaned back again, breathing deeply, as though he was tasting the air in his lungs. "As the gheist attacked, I could sense Allaister's presence. He drove that demon toward us."

"You said he held sway over the demon," Elsa said. "So why are we running? Why not face him?"

"They are strong enough to crush us, Sir LaFey. You may be fit for battle, but I'm not." He opened his eyes and peered at her. "In fact, I suspect you are less fit than you would allow."

Elsa didn't answer. She looked uncomfortable for a while, then went back to the fire and busied herself disassembling the kettle and stowing things back into the frair's bags. Gwen watched her for a minute, then turned back to Lucas. The frair was eyeing her closely.

"What will you do with me?" she asked eventually. "I'm the one Frair Allaister wants. If they catch us together, they will demand my head."

"That might not be in my hands. If given my choice, I would take you back to the Fen Gate, and then have a very long talk with your father."

Gwen didn't reply, and settled into herself. Though worried about traveling with a priest and a vow knight so close to the hallow, she had decided it was better to keep them close than let them wander the Fen on their own. Then the gheist attack had forced her hand. She had silently hoped that the witching wives would appear and take command, but her last contact with them left Gwen unsure of their ability to do anything, much less take down a healthy knight of the vow.

She was coming to realize that she wouldn't have the heart to kill the pair herself, and hoped it wouldn't come to that.

She looked at Lucas again. "He won't like that," Gwen said. "My father."

"I would imagine not," Lucas said. He made a groaning sound that might have been laughter. "I don't expect you to trust me—not yet." He set the cup down and rummaged through a pouch on his belt, drawing out a root that smelled like leather. He put it in his mouth and started to chew. "Dreadful stuff. Can I tell you a story?"

"About roots?"

"About gods. Your gods, specifically."

"I'm faithful to the Celestial church," Gwen said

stiffly. She wasn't about to admit to full-blown heresy.

"'Faithful' is such an interesting word," Lucas said. Whatever was in the tea, or the root he was chewing now, seemed to be doing its job. He looked better than he had all day. "I'm sure you say your prayers and sing your blessings. As huntress, you do a fair bit of reaving in the name of the Celestial gods. How do your witching friends feel about that?"

"We have an understanding."

"Yes. Understanding and faithful. Tricky words." Lucas spat a wad of chewed root into the woods. "So, your gods—all of our gods, really. They follow a calendar. This is obvious enough with the Celestial faith, the ascendance of Cinder in the winter, Strife in summer. The power Elsa draws during the day. My own strength at night." He gestured to the sky. Perhaps his health had more to do with the moon than the tea, Gwen realized. She would see in the morning. "Everything in between, and not just the calendar. The powers of the gods are dictated by geography."

"I haven't heard that," Gwen said. "How can the gods of sun and moon be affected by geography?"

"Not *our* geography," Lucas said. He jabbed a finger at the moon, which was just lifting its silver head over the trees. "The landscape of the sky. Where the gods live among the stars affects what we can do with their blessings. When Cinder draws a cloak across his face, hiding from our sight or shielding his light from the earth, it changes how my powers work. The same goes for Strife, though the movements of the bright lady are more subtle. Easier to hide."

"You shouldn't be telling these things to a pagan," Elsa said without looking up from the fire.

"She knows them, or knows their equivalent," he

423

replied, "because her gods are bound by geography, as well. Aren't they, Huntress?"

"The gheists commit to ley lines. They are bound to henges, or manifest in holy places. It's how the shamans were able to control them."

"Yes," Lucas said. "And no. The gheists are not bound to those sites. The old priests noticed the patterns of their gods and built henges to focus them. Those places were holy before mankind ever stepped foot in Tenumbra. We just gave each a building, and a ritual."

"What's the difference?"

Lucas shrugged. "Maybe nothing. The Allfire was holy before the first celestriarch built the first doma. The Frostnight is hallowed, with or without our observation. It's not our worship that sanctifies these things, but it's important to note that the gheists rise where they choose. Where it is natural for them to manifest. It's not the pagans who draw them. If you removed the witching wives entirely, the gods would still find form."

"That seems obvious, since the church has destroyed the old religion," Gwen replied, "and yet the gheists still trouble the land."

Lucas laughed. It dissolved into a wracking cough that left him curled against the tree. Elsa moved to his side, but the frair waved her off. When he had his voice again, he continued.

"They follow patterns," he said. "We know them. You know them—in your role as huntress."

"Within my own territory, yes," Gwen admitted. "I'd imagine your knowledge is broader. The church has kept secret what they know, however, out of fear that hidden pagans would use it to raise more gods."

"I suspect you know more about the spirits of the

Fen than even the high inquisitor," Lucas said with a knowing smile, a smile that made her very nervous. "Or at least I hope so. But yes, Elsa and I know much about the old gods. Some learned from the church, some from our years in the field. I have been at this business a very long time, and in that time I've learned something about the witching wives, and the shamans who work with them.

"People like your friend from last night."

Gwen went stiff.

"How did you know?" she asked.

"I dream in shadows," Lucas said, "and sometimes I don't sleep well."

"So you knew the gheist was coming?"

"I did," he replied, and there was no anger in his voice. "I was curious to see what you would tell us, if anything. Nevertheless, I took the time to scout the surrounding area, to find a place to make our stand. And I learned something more." His voice had grown rough. Lucas nodded to Elsa, who brought him a water skin.

"The priests who were following that gheist weren't just trying to catch us, though that is what happened. They are hunting something else. Some*place* else. It was leading them to something holy."

"Where?" Gwen asked.

"I don't know, yet. Perhaps you could tell me. Perhaps your father could."

Gwen shook her head.

"As you will. Secrets take time to unfold." Lucas made a dismissive gesture, even as Elsa tightened her jaw. The vow knight settled on a stump on the other side of the fire, glaring at Gwen and clenching her fists.

"In time, Gwen," he continued. "There are many

dangers. In time you may decide that I am the least of them." Lucas was tired. He looked unhappily around the campsite, as though judging where the least miserable place to sleep might be.

"I know what you are. I know who you serve. I've suspected it for quite some time. As soon as I noticed the broken patterns in the gheists, in their manifestations. The old rules stopped working, the old gods disappeared. New gods rose up. Surely you've noticed it," he said, then shook his head. "No, not here. Not in the Fen. You've maintained a balance here, a balance that is missing from the rest of Tenumbra.

"The breakdown of generations of godly pattern, the blight that has settled in the south, and through all of Suhdra… and yet the Fen was spared. I knew something had to be responsible for that." He raised his head, the slightest shake in his neck as fatigue claimed him. "And then I found you. The huntress of Adair. Faithful pagan and killer of gods, and I knew I had the cause."

Gwen was quiet. Elsa was hunched on the other side of the fire, one hand on her sword, the other resting lightly on her knee. Lucas rested his head against the tree and seemed to settle in for the night.

"Then why am I not in chains?" Gwen asked quietly. "Why have you let me live?"

"Because I think I can trust you," he replied. "I think that I *have* to trust you, in fact, if I'm to get to the truth." He shifted uncomfortably, not opening his eyes. "Trust you to do what is right for Tenumbra, and the church, and your old gods. In time I hope you will learn to trust me to do the same."

Gwen didn't answer. She shot Elsa a look. The vow knight's eyes were on the frair. When Lucas didn't say anything else, but seemed to be drifting off to sleep, she shrugged and stood up, preparing her bedroll.

"You will have first watch," Elsa said. "Prove yourself worthy of it."

"If I'm to guard, I will need a weapon."

"If there's trouble, wake me up. I will be all the weapon you need."

The vow knight settled into her bed. Gwen was about to douse the fire and find a good spot to set up her watch when a hound bayed in the distance.

Both Elsa and Lucas had their eyes open.

"They're following us," Elsa whispered. "They will find us. We should run, now, but he needs to rest. He needs the healing of a bloodwright."

"No," Gwen said, shaking her head. She made a decision. "I know a place. In the morning, I will lead you there. A place of healing, and of hiding. We will be safe."

38

T HE COURTYARD WAS quiet, the soldiers lining the walls and standing in ranks barely moving as the castle gates creaked open. Malcolm, Sorcha, and Colm Adair stood just inside the gates. A small group waited outside.

There were only six riders, three pairs. Gabriel Halverdt rode at the front, dressed in full plate, his pauldrons forged in the shape of oak trees swollen with acorns, the golden seeds encrusting his breastplate, gauntlets, and the buckles of his leg armor. The plate itself was enameled a green so dark that it swirled with oily shadows, and his chest was decorated in the gold cross and tri-acorn of his crest.

Halverdt's helmet rested on his saddle, and his hair, black shot with gray and silver, flowed long over his shoulders. He looked tired, though victory lit his face as he trotted into the courtyard. Seeing the collected ranks of Tenerran spearmen, he gave a dismissive sniff.

Behind Halverdt rode Sir Volent, still in his plain armor, though a new cloak of white and silver was draped over his shoulders. As always, his dead face betrayed no emotion as he entered the castle.

To Halverdt's left rode the high elector. Beaunair looked tired, as well—the fatigue of despair, a look that threatened to bring Malcolm's heart tumbling. If Beaunair had given up before negotiations began, what hope did they have? The priest wore the full vestments of his position, cloak and robe and mantle, though the gold-trimmed helmet that pressed into his forehead was more military than sacred. Beaunair rode in front of the high inquisitor. Malcolm wondered why Sacombre had chosen to follow Beaunair, rather than coming into the Fen Gate at Halverdt's side. He wore practical clothes, simple blacks edged in purple silk, with a darkwood staff couched in his stirrup like a lance.

The last two riders were of the House Roard. The duke of Stormwatch was in the lead, armed and armored for battle. His bearing held none of the contempt of Halverdt, nor his war dress the needless ornamentation. Martin followed in his wake. The younger Roard kept his eyes low, avoiding Malcolm and Sorcha.

"I have come to speak of your surrender, Blakley," Halverdt said without preamble.

"And I welcome you into this castle to speak of peace," Colm Adair answered. "Nothing more."

"Peace, then," Lorien Roard said quickly, before Halverdt could respond. "Peace beneath the banner of the Celestial church."

"Gods bless," Beaunair said.

"The gods may bless what they will," Halverdt answered, "but I am eager for the justice of Cinder. Let us be done with this as quickly as possible. I've only just arrived, and already I'm tired of your hovel."

"Brave words for a man surrounded by his enemy's blades," Sorcha snapped.

"Brave words for a woman," Halverdt responded with a smile. "Let's not pretend, Duchess. If any harm comes to me, the army at your gates will grind your bones into ash, and then burn your name from history. There will be no heir to Houndhallow. Though if what I've heard from Duke Roard is true, then that threat may be empty. I suppose someone would still need to murder your daughter. Nessie, isn't that her name?" he purred. "Yes, I think that can be arranged."

"Don't you dare—" Malcolm started.

"Let us find our rooms," Beaunair said, interrupting the exchange. "The sooner to feast, the sooner to begin negotiations."

"Agreed," Lorien said. "Let's leave the blood on the battlefield, where it belongs."

Malcolm bowed his head and kept his eyes down while Colm's men led Halverdt, Volent, and the priests. When he looked up, Lorien was still waiting, staring at him. Lorien looked back to his son.

"Martin?" the duke of Stormwatch prompted his son.

Looking embarrassed, the young man dismounted and came to stand in front of Malcolm and Sorcha. He carried a scabbard that Malcolm didn't recognize until he drew the blade. It was a fresh sheath, but it held Ian's sword.

"This was found among the stones of the ford, along with Ian's horse," Martin said, presenting it to Malcolm. He took the sword, then handed it to his wife. Sorcha turned it over in her hands. Her eyes were dry, but there was fear in her voice.

"And his body?" she asked.

"We found nothing, my lady. I am deeply sorry…"

"Enough," Sorcha said. "We are all deeply sorry, for different reasons." Then she turned and marched back to the keep. Malcolm watched her go, then turned his attention back to Martin.

"Ian always spoke well of you. I hope his friendship still means something to you, even in the quiet."

"It does," Martin answered. "More, actually. I have grown tired of regret."

"Then you have chosen the wrong war," Malcolm said. "It seems that we will have nothing of this but regret."

Martin nodded tearfully, then returned to the saddle and went with his father into the keep. Malcolm looked at the empty scabbard in his hands, newly formed, the leather not yet broken from drawing and seating its blade, the silver at its tip untarnished. He turned and handed it to Colm Adair.

"I have no need of this," he said. "Any of this."

The fire was low and the jug of wine empty. The lords of Tenumbra, plagued by fatigue and frustration, sat around a table littered with maps and ink-stained contracts, none of which brought them closer to peace.

Lorien Roard had gone to bed hours ago, frustration writ large on his face. Sir Henri Volent lurked in the corner of the room like the promise of violence. The incense that hung in the air had grown stale in Malcolm's throat. His mouth was coated in the stink of frairwood and frustration. Even the whiskey couldn't cut through the haze in his head as he shuffled the papers on the table like a dog rooting for food, sure that he's eaten every scrap yet stubbornly hopeful he'll find something new among the wreckage.

"What of Tallownere?" he said.

"There is nothing of value in Tallownere," Halverdt said. The duke of Greenhall sat frowning at the head of the table, staring into the remnants of the fire. Colm Adair stood at the opposite side of the room, near the door, his arms folded tight. "Nothing but mud and ash."

"Ash from the village your men burned," Adair hissed.

"A village that could be repopulated in time," Malcolm said quickly, before discussion disintegrated again.

"I will not have pagans settling on my border," Halverdt answered. "Better that the land remain fallow." He swirled the dregs in his mug, grimaced at the remnants, then tossed it down his throat. "The point of this exercise is to ensure the elimination of the Adair rebels. Elimination comes through obedience. Obedience comes from punishment. We should only discuss their concessions—not ours."

"As your proposal stands, you are requiring garrison rights at the Reaveholt, road taxes throughout the Fen, and wardship of Gwendolyn Adair," Malcolm said. "Whereas Colm has demanded the execution of Henri Volent, full reparations for the dead of Tener, and an apology from every lord and knight who has set foot in his land. Neither of these are valid proposals." He leaned back in his chair and rubbed his face. The late hour was wearing on his patience. "Neither of you is negotiating!

"Farming and settlement rights at Tallownere would be a good start, both financially and symbolically," he continued. "After all, Tallownere is where this whole mess began."

Halverdt stood, suddenly and violently. He threw his empty mug across the hall and struck the table with his fist, causing the maps and contracts to jump.

"This mess began long before the ambush at Tallownere!" he bellowed. "We have tolerated *generations* of disrespect and heresy from the tribe of Adair! That they have fooled their Tenerran brothers into thinking they were faithful is no concern of mine. It is the church in Heartsbridge that must judge them!"

"And yet you have appointed yourself to that role, my lord," High Elector Beaunair said. The priest had settled against the wall as far from the incense-wafting fire pit as possible. "Even Cinder expects balance in his justice. We cannot eat at the table of trust with judgment in both hands."

"To hell with the table of trust," Colm said. "You can't destroy this house with the stroke of a pen!"

"You can't, my dear baron," Halverdt said. "I have no such limitation. I have the strength of the south at your gate, and the blessing of Heartsbridge upon my actions. The reason you are at this table is because you're afraid of what will happen if I march upon the Fen Gate. You all know these walls will fall before me." He moved to Malcolm's side, grinning broadly. "And *you* have failed to stir the rest of Tener to your cause, Blakley. They want to keep their precious pagan lands free of the church's judgment."

"Gods and hell, Gabriel, you're worse than a drunk at his first joust." Malcolm folded his arms in exasperation. "The only reason you're here at this table is because half your army doesn't want this fight. We've kept the peace between Suhdra and Tener for years. Our countries have prospered, the peace of the church has spread, and the old gods have been kept in check. At dusk each night the evensong rises from thousands of throats from the Tallow to Far Watch, and the grace of Cinder and Strife is hallowed. Disrupt that, and you threaten more than just war."

"I think we're all tired, and most of us are drunk." Castian Jaerdin stood from his chair and went to the table. He gave Malcolm a thin smile as he gathered the night's paperwork into a single pile. "We may be better off burning all of this and starting afresh in the morning. Regardless, I'm certain we would all benefit from a night's sleep."

"Will Sacombre be joining us again in the morning?" Colm asked. "Every time we make progress, he adds in a pogrom, and we're back to the beginning."

"I don't know where the high inquisitor has gotten to tonight," Beaunair said. "Perhaps he and I could tour the castle tomorrow. You might do better without the church hanging over your shoulder."

"I'd rather have him where I can see him," Colm answered. Then he gave a wave of his hand. "I've had enough of this. Good night."

The baron of the Fen Gate stalked outside, slamming the door behind him.

"Then we are through," Malcolm snapped. "For tonight, at least... we have done enough. Let's all go to bed before someone's honor gets in the way and we're arranging a duel or a marriage or some such idiocy."

"I have all the time in the world," Gabriel Halverdt answered. He collected his sword belt from beside the table and buckled it tight. The scabbard was new wood and leather, and the hilt was wrapped in the blessings of the inquisition.

"New sword, my lord?" Malcolm asked.

"Indeed," Halverdt said smugly. "A gift from the high inquisitor. To protect me against the pagan night. Wrought in the blood of the choir eternal, and forged in Hollyhaute." He drew the sword with a song like a maiden's whisper and held it flat in his palms. The blade was etched in holy runes. "You will not see a more divine blade in all of Tenumbra."

"It's very odd," Beaunair said. He peered down at the sword and shook his head. "I don't recognize some of these."

"You are no inquisitor," Halverdt said with a sneer. "It's safe to assume that High Inquisitor Sacombre knows something more of the naether arts than you."

"No doubt," the high elector allowed. "After all, I am but a mortal instrument of the bright lady. The ways of naether and lumaire are closed to me. But still…"

There was a crash in the courtyard outside, and then the sounds of a brief struggle. Screams erupted in the courtyard beyond. Malcolm jumped to his feet, while Sir Volent flinched deeper into the shadows. Only Gabriel Halverdt seemed transfixed, staring at the door and smiling.

"He knew it would come to this. He knew I would be needed." Gabriel turned to Malcolm and smiled, a fevered, wicked look on his face. "He knew you would betray the divine, and so he armed me."

The door burst open.

39

SORCHA SPENT THE evening as far from the council chamber as she could manage. She couldn't abide the way Martin Roard looked at her, nor his words about faith and friendship. She ate in her rooms, then took a long walk on the walls.

The endless campfires of the Suhdrin army stretched out through the valley. She sat among the crenels and drank most of a bottle of wine. Malcolm insisted that they had friends among the Suhdrin host, that without the likes of DuFallion and Marcy, this host would have broken these walls and murdered any who dared oppose them. But she couldn't find any comfort in those fires. They twinkled like a bad omen among the stars, an ill sign, a promise of destruction.

When she was too drunk to care and too sober to find comfort, Sorcha took the shortest route from the curtain wall to her rooms. The sounds of the evensong echoed everywhere. The castle was full to bursting, but Sorcha was able to avoid everyone. Most people were either in the doma observing the evensong, or still at their dinners. The great lords were at their council. Even the guards posted along the wall were few and far between.

Something prickled at the back of Sorcha's neck.

The silence held an odd quality, a thickness in the air, that reminded her of heavy weather. She hurried up the stairs to her rooms, taking the steps two at a time.

Halfway up she heard the sound of wood breaking, and a tremendous *thud*, like a weight dropped from some great height. Heartbeats later there was screaming.

She started to run.

Her guards lay at the top of the flight, necks broken, limbs splayed out in the hallway. They were freshly dead.

Sorcha crouched next to one, drew his knife and stepped over the bodies. The door to their suite of rooms was closed but Sir Dugan's room, the closest to the stairs, stood open. It did not look as though it had been forced. Light flickered from the interior, as dim and inconstant as a candle. Sorcha crept forward, terrified of what she would find.

Dugan's room was wrecked, the bed and shelves broken and scattered about. There was blood, but not enough to fill a body, and the door was raked by great gouge marks. Sorcha had seen bears mark trees in the forest, but these were even larger, deeper. She wondered where the master of guard was, and who had done such a thing.

Screams began outside the window. The courtyard filled with the sound of clashing steel and panicked people.

She ventured farther into the room, her toe dragging through some kind of sand that was sprinkled along the doorway. The smell of incense filled her nose. There was something else in the middle of the room, a collection of wreckage that she had mistaken for broken furniture. She moved closer, and saw what it was.

Iron icons of the old faith lay in a circle, a bowl at

their center. The bowl was wood, carved with runes similar to the ones Sorcha had often seen on henge stones, and it was slick with blood. Most of the blood in the room seemed to have come from this bowl, scattered about like water from a censer. The stone floor within the circle of icons was scorched. Sorcha ran a trembling finger along the ground and came up smeared with ash and sand.

No. Too sharp for sand, too brittle.

Ground bones.

She looked up at the window. The shutters were broken, just like everything else in the room, but their wreckage wasn't inside. She went to the window and looked down.

Below her was chaos. Splinters of wood lay in the courtyard far below. A pile of dark mounds lay scattered beneath the window, splotches that resolved into bloodstained guards as Sorcha's eyes adjusted to the darkness. All around the courtyard she could see guardsmen rushing about, gathering spears and huddling in shadows. She couldn't see what had drawn their attention.

Something crashed on the other side of the courtyard, and sudden light spilled out from a door thrown open. A shape loomed in the darkness, briefly outlined by the light before disappearing inside. It had the shape of a man, wild hair, but was somehow broken in posture—like a scarecrow with its bones cracked open, shuffling forward on legs of straw and splintered wood.

Sorcha tried to figure what door it was that opened. It took her a moment to clear her drunken brain and orient herself to the courtyard, the front gate, the walls themselves. A scream broke out through the night, and the voices of the choir eternal, deep in the evensong, faltered in their praise and awe of Cinder. Steel clashed, and then the gheist alarm began to sound.

She knew where the beast was headed. That was the throne room. There was a god free and mad in the Fen Gate. A god wearing Sir Dugan's broken body.

The body of Gordon Dugan slouched into the room, arms and legs flopping with puppet-like life, taking numb steps, pushing aside the wreckage of the door. His head hung forward, neck broken, face loose on his skull. A web of bones sprouted from his back.

"Sir Dugan?" Malcolm whispered.

The rest of the men in the room exploded into action. Castian Jaerdin drew a silvered blade, dragging the map table to one side to give them room to maneuver. The high elector shied behind the table. Malcolm tore his eyes away from the ruin of his master of guard and looked at the duke of Greenhall.

The man was still smiling.

"What the hell is this, Gabriel?" Malcolm shouted.

The body of Sir Dugan shuffled into the room. Behind it, a line of guardsmen wearing the colors of House Adair moved in, spears leveled at the gheist, their faces flecked with blood and fear. There was a clatter in the choir loft. More helms appeared up there, men bristling with crossbows. Halverdt surveyed his audience, then raised his voice and pointed at the gheist.

"Do you not recognize your gods when you see them?" Halverdt answered. His voice boomed in the echoing heights of the great hall. He flipped the sword around in his hands, loosening the wrapped blessings from the hilt, keeping the point of the blade down. The strips of linen cloth slithered down the blade, twisting with strange, snake-like life. "A gheist in Houndhallow's company. The hound's treachery has shown itself!" Halverdt crowed. "Redgarden, your loyalty was given falsely. He warned me there would be treachery! Sound the alarm! Pray, fetch the high inquisitor. Sacombre will dispatch the demon, and then we can deal with these heretics!"

"This treachery is not mine!" Malcolm stood firm. Castian stood between them, looking hopelessly from Halverdt to the high elector. The priest was motionless, staring at the gheist. The crowd of guards shuffled nervously about, their number joined by soldiers of Blakley and Jaerdin. The Suhdrin faces turned to look at their lord, standing aghast in the court below. "What do you mean, he warned you?" Blakley demanded. "Who warned you?"

"The high inquisitor, of course," Halverdt replied. "Doubtless your lackeys have disposed of him, but that will not be enough. Sacombre warned me of such treachery, and prepared this blade. Get behind me, Castian, Beaunair. I can save you." Gabriel raised the sword, pointing it at Malcolm. "But I will not save your pet heretics."

"I will not stand by while you let them be killed," Castian said. He gripped the hilt of his sword with knuckles white and shaking, but he edged closer to Malcolm.

"Then kill the god yourself—or order your men to do it for you," Halverdt barked. He crossed to where Jaerdin stood and gave the man a shove in the back. Jaerdin stumbled forward, losing his balance and nearly falling at dead Dugan's feet. The gheist turned toward him, shoulders hunched and limp face lolling at the end of Dugan's broken neck. The webwork of bones that stretched from his shoulders tapped along the wall like a blind spider, scenting the stones. Jaerdin drew himself up and presented a dueling guard to the demon.

The bones stopped tapping and arched toward him.

"Defend your lord!" Castian yelled. There was a moment's hesitation, and then the gathered men of Redgarden loosed their bolts. Steel shafts thumped into the gheist, drawing blood and blackened bile, but otherwise causing the mad god no harm. Castian drew himself up and started marching toward the enemy, silvered blade raised high.

"Castian, no!" Malcolm yelled. He rushed forward, grabbing Jaerdin by the shoulders and dragging him back. The gheist rushed forward, oblivious to the thick frairwood smoke and the dozen wounds from the bolts in its flesh, scuttling insect-like to where his prey had been standing. Malcolm backed carefully away, pulling Castian with him. They bumped into the high elector.

"Watch yourself, priest!" Halverdt yelled. Hesitant now, he backed up to the Sedgewind throne that dominated the room, its foliage of banners and blessing swaying in the breeze from the open door. "That one bites!"

"Stop being such an imbecile, Halverdt," the priest hissed. "You have a godsblessed sword. Fucking use it!"

"Can't you banish it or something?" Castian whispered to the high elector. "Pray it away?"

"I was never that sort of priest," Beaunair answered. "My mistake."

"Give me the sword, Halverdt!" Malcolm yelled across the room. The gheist stalked between them, looking lost and languid. "If you haven't the balls to stand up to the demon, let me have a go!"

"As though I would put my life in your hands," Halverdt answered. "Very well." He took one step forward and raised the blessed sword over his head like a banner.

At the sight of the blessed sword, Sir Dugan changed. The rag-doll limpness in his limbs fell away. The bones of his arms split through the skin, hands wrenching open to form scythe-like fans, fingers crooking into talons, flesh hanging like a ragged sleeve around the new limb. His legs distended, the bones crackling as they split and split again. Splintered fragments of bloody white bone curled out of Dugan's body, creating a roiling stump that looked like the roots of a tree given seething, snake-like motion.

The possessed knight's ribs pierced his flesh, growing into a cage of bright white teeth. The bones that grew from his back unfolded into diaphanous wings, their webbing as insubstantial as fog. And from his mouth spilled a column of beetle-smooth teeth, prehensile and sharp. A gasp went up from the collected guardsmen. Someone in the loft began retching, a sound that spread throughout the room in seconds as more followed suit.

"Gods spare us," Beaunair muttered. The fat priest drew an icon from his robes and went to his knees. The gheist ignored him. Instead, it stalked toward Gabriel Halverdt.

Malcolm wished he had brought his quiver of bloodwrought spears to the council, but they rested among his things, back in the suite of rooms he and Sorcha occupied. His longtime friend's face hung loosely around the slithering mass of teeth that gnawed at the air. The sword in Halverdt's hand glowed, the linen strips that wrapped the blade wafting away from the gheist, as though a light wind blew from the demon's heart. The duke of Greenhall's face was calm as he faced the creature.

"I see your treachery now, Blakley," he yelled, still playing to the audience. "You hide a shaman in your retinue and think to strike me down. A pity the high inquisitor armed me with a blade blessed by the celestriarch himself. I'll make short work of your little god, and then I'll see to you."

"Are you mad? Dugan was a good man, faithful to the church and loyal to my house. He was no shaman!"

"We'll see what we find when we search his quarters," Halverdt said smugly.

Outside, the slow, deep horn of the gheist alarm continued to sound. Shouts filled the courtyard. More guards crowded into the doorway, only to shy back when they saw the abomination of Dugan's flesh.

"If we live that long," Castian said. He pushed Malcolm farther into the room, maneuvering around the kneeling form of the high elector. "On your feet, Beaunair. We have to keep moving."

The priest didn't respond. In fact, the round man doubled forward, the icon slipping from his grip. Their attention had been so thoroughly on the gheist that none of them noticed the high elector's distress. Malcolm glanced down. Beaunair's face was white, his mouth bubbling.

"The demon has killed the priest!" one of the guards yelled. The man, dressed in clean Blakley whites and only recently arrived in the doorway, threw down his spear and ran for the door. "This castle is cursed! The pagans have betrayed us all!"

A wave of fear went through the crowd. A half-dozen guards followed the first, and then a dozen.

The shouting in the courtyard was becoming a general terror that threatened the entire castle.

"What in hell?" Malcolm muttered. He went to one knee beside the priest. Beaunair turned to face him, his eyes wide with terror. Foam trickled down his fat cheek and, as Malcolm watched, his eyes rolled back into his head. He slumped against Malcolm, then fell to the floor and went into seizures.

"Gheists and poison!" Gabriel spat. "From your bottle, no doubt, Blakley. Do you believe me now, Jaerdin?"

"Stop making accusations and do something, you bastard," Castian snapped. He grabbed Malcolm by the shoulder and dragged him away from the twitching priest. The gheist loomed closer.

Halverdt laughed and took a step toward the creature. The strips of linen on his sword snapped tight, the invisible wind of the gheist's presence rising to hurricane force. The sword wavered and he faltered, gripping it with both hands, grimacing against the force.

"Now witness the power of the gods!" Halverdt yelled. "Now witness the justice of Lord Cinder!"

The gheist took him in the space of a thought. One second Gabriel Halverdt was grinning maniacally at the rogue god, and the next the demon's prehensile teeth had burrowed into his chest and torn out his ribs. The duke of Greenhall slumped to the ground, shock on his blood-spattered face. The sword slipped from his grasp and fell to the floor. When it struck, the blade shattered, as though made of glass. Splinters of it sprayed through the room, cutting the survivors with a sharp hail. The wounds burned like fire.

The room erupted in hysterical yelling. Spears clattered to the floor. The guards began pouring out of the doors, the loft, running for anywhere that was away from the gheist.

"Sweet Strife," Castian sputtered. "Bright lady save us."

"Oh, for fuck's sake," Malcolm spat. He pushed Castian behind the table and turned to face the gheist. His sword was worthless against this god, nothing but steel and the weight of his arm, but he couldn't stand aside. He whipped the weapon across the gheist's back. Pale shreds of skin fell away, exposing bony carapace beneath.

Dugan's broken face turned to his former master.

"Run!" Malcolm snapped. "Someone find the priests, the fucking inquisition if you can! Just run!"

Castian stumbled to his feet and made for the door. The gheist ignored him, drawing itself up to stand over the butchered body of the lord of Greenhall. Malcolm waved his blade again.

"Come on, Gordon. You always hated going to doma, but that's no reason to grow a new god in your heart," he muttered, tears streaming down his face. Dugan's face wavered at the end of that demonic neck. "You stupid, loyal, goddamned fool! They're going to kill you, so you better try to kill me first. Come on!"

The gheist lumbered forward. It broke the table, scattering papers, many of which fell into the fire pit where they flared briefly before rising as cinder and ash. The frairwood incense swirled around the razor-sharp talons in thick clouds. The high inquisitor had set the fire himself, assuring them the wood was properly blessed. He had promised Halverdt he was safe.

Sacombre had promised.

Malcolm spared a glance at Halverdt. The man seemed dead, but his mouth was still moving, opening and closing like a fish out of water. The shards of his godsblessed sword sprouted out his skin like spines. The blood that pooled beneath him was black in the dim light. Malcolm had spent his life opposing this man, but now he felt a touch of horror at his death.

He looked again to the gheist.

"What are we supposed to do, Gordon? How are we supposed to fight something that takes our friends and gives us common cause with our enemies?" The demon loped closer, talons scraping through blood, across stone, tapping. "How am I supposed to kill you?"

"You never could," Sorcha said from the door. His wife stepped into the room, double braces of bloodwrought spears crossing her chest. She let the first spear fly, catching the gheist in the wing, tearing bones and fog. As quick as the first spear was gone from her hand, Sorcha loosed two more. The spears bristled from the gheist's body. It stood still for a moment, shivering, Dugan's limp face looking from Malcolm to Sorcha, his eyes weeping blood.

Sir Dugan fell apart. The bony talons of his hands, the carapace that bristled through his skin, the wings and prehensile teeth, all of it became a puzzle, and came undone. The splintered bones slid away like shale, collapsing to the floor in ever-increasing piles. They clattered like dice on the stones. The rag of Dugan's body split like an overstuffed bag.

Malcolm stared—first at the corpse, then at his wife. He crossed the room and hugged her close. There was a loose crowd of guardsmen trickling back into the room, encircling their lord and his wife.

"Not much of a god," she whispered.

"No. But it was enough." Malcolm pulled away and looked down at the ruin of Dugan's body.

"Halverdt is dead, and it looks like the high elector, as well, though I don't know what that had to do with this. Castian will testify to that."

"Where is he?"

"Ran," Malcolm said. He crossed to Halverdt's body. He kicked through the remnants of the sword, brushing shards across the floor. "This blade was shit. Certainly not bloodwrought. I'm surprised the high inquisitor…" Malcolm paused, looked from Halverdt to Dugan, back again. "It was a trick. It was a trap. For Halverdt, as much as for us," he muttered.

They were startled by a sound from the corner of the room. Sir Volent leapt from the shadows, brushed Malcolm aside, and ran out the door. The knight had soiled himself. As he disappeared into the night, he was clutching his blade so tightly that his knuckles were bleeding.

"Where's Sacombre?" Malcolm barked. "We need to find the high inquisitor—preferably before that madman does."

40

"HIS DOESN'T FEEL like east," Elsa said. They were most of the way up a shale-littered slope, Gwen in the lead, with the vow knight helping Frair Lucas close behind.

"You should depend less on the sun," Gwen said. She scrambled to the top of the hill and sat down, sending an avalanche of small stones down the opposite bank. "We are going the way we're meant to go."

"That doesn't sound encouraging," Elsa muttered.

"Patience, Sir LaFey," Lucas said. "The huntress will get us where we are needed—wherever that might be." The pair of them reached Gwen's side and paused. The priest looked around, tutting and shaking his head. His injury was wearing on him. Despite Elsa's best efforts, the naethermancer was slowly dying in front of them.

"Where are we, exactly?" Elsa asked.

The land around them was swollen with color and light. Patchy copses of wirewood sprang clean and strong from pure rock outcrops; the streams were clear and bitingly cold, flowing lazily between smooth stones. Lady Strife was brighter than usual, the air itself taking on the sun's glow until everything pulsed with warm, golden light. It was a dreamscape.

"I have been dizzy for three mornings," Lucas announced out of the blue. "I thought it was my wounds, but that's not it, is it, Gwen?"

"Call me 'Huntress,'" Gwen answered. "Titles are important in this place."

"Where are we?" Elsa asked again tersely. "*Exactly.*"

Gwen shrugged to her feet. The hill descended in a smooth slope to a river as broad and smooth as the Tallow, though Lucas couldn't recall anything like it on his maps. Surely they hadn't traveled that far south? Beyond the river the forest closed ranks, the trees standing tight together like a shield wall. In the distance a hill of bald rock rose above the forest. Everything seemed more alive.

"You said you wanted to see my little pagan site," Gwen said quietly.

"You brought a frair of the Celestial church to..." Lucas paused. "Is it safe?"

"For whom?" Gwen asked. She started to scramble down the hill. Lucas watched her go, turning to Elsa once the huntress was nearly upon the bank of the strange river. The fever in his eyes held a twinkle of curious mischief.

"Be on your guard," he said. "Be holy, but keep that blade in its sheath, unless I say otherwise."

"That'll be something," Elsa said. "A vow knight raising her blade in the court of the pagan gods. Strife give us strength."

"And Cinder see us through," Lucas added. He reached out, grasped Elsa's shoulder, then started down the slope. "But go slowly."

This close to the hallow, the pagan wards that protected the shrine were sharp and thick. Elsa was focused on supporting the frair, and when she looked up the river had moved, the slope leveled, and the sky turned. It took her a few minutes of deeply considered panic before she could find her way forward. There were trees around them again, and they were closing in, their shadows as dark and wet as wounds.

Gwen tumbled out of the underbrush.

"This is more dangerous than I suspected," she said, dragging Elsa around to the true path. "You left the frair behind."

"I didn't!" Elsa insisted. "He's right…" She glanced to her shoulder to see that Lucas was not on her arm, nor anywhere to be seen. She was scrambling for her sword when Gwen slapped her hand away.

"No threats, not from a vow knight of Lady Strife. Even in my company, that would be fatal." Gwen pulled her forward until they stood beside the frair, who seemed to appear out of nowhere. Lucas was on all fours, staring at the ground and muttering to himself. "We need to keep moving," the huntress said. "The gheist is getting interested."

"Gheists?" Elsa asked. "I see no gheists."

"The forest itself." Gwen helped Lucas to his feet, then got between the two of them and started toward the magically shrouded river. "We're deep into the everealm here, my friends. Right at the source. The gheists are not forest spirits. The forest itself is the spirit. All gheist. Keep moving."

Elsa looked around nervously. The trees lurked closer.

"Right," she said. "Moving."

Together they made it to the river. Gwen called a halt, guiding Lucas to the ground and dusting off her hands against her pants.

"The people who protect this place... I don't really know what they're going to say about this. My bond to them is tricky. I kill more gheists than they like, but not enough to bring us to blows. It's a balance, but this I promise you." She stole a glance at the ailing frair. "They've never met an inquisitor that they like."

"Doesn't put us far off. I've only met one I can stand," Elsa said. "Know that if it comes to violence, I will defend the frair."

"As will I," Gwen said after a moment's consideration. "I owe you that much."

"You understand that when this is over, you'll probably still be facing a heretic's sentence."

"Of course, and I expect you to be at my side, pleading my case," Gwen said. "So I need to do everything I can to earn your trust."

Elsa grimaced. She thought seriously about leaving the huntress there and striking back toward civilization with the frair in tow. The trees behind her didn't look that threatening from here, as long as the sun was shining and the moon was bright. The river, on the other hand, was far too blue, far too luminous to be natural.

If she left, Elsa might never know what lay beyond those waters. And Lucas had risked too much to abandon this search now. She sighed.

"How do we get across?"

"We ask," Gwen said. Then she helped Lucas to his feet. "Are you well enough to go on, Frair?"

"Probably not, but I'm much too ill to stay here. So on we go." He made a grand gesture, lost in his frailty and their strange surroundings. "Lead on, Huntress."

Gwen stood the two of them shoulder to shoulder, facing the river. Then she placed herself in front of them. The tips of her boots touched the water, and a shiver went through her bones. She raised her hands.

"Glimmerglen, river of spirit, river of life. Guardian of the true hallow, the final god. Spirit of the river, the warden, the wife. Reveal yourself to us."

"Three of three," Lucas muttered to himself. "Interesting."

Gwen hushed him, then turned back to the river and repeated her invocation. And then again.

The river rose to meet her.

It was only a glimmer at first, beginning in a calm pool, a ripple in water that was still. Then the banks of the river swelled and freezing water surged over Gwen's feet. It lapped at the others, tasting them, dashing around the stones at their feet before drawing back. Something rose from the river's surface. A woman made of glass, but hardly a woman at all, no more a woman than a cloud was a storm or a stone an avalanche. Something remarkable drew itself out of the water and hovered in front of them, its skin clear as water and bright as lightning.

"You bring corruption," it said in a voice that crashed and soothed. "I will cleanse it."

"*No*," Gwen said too quickly, and the spirit tilted its head at her. "No…" she said again, holding her hands in front of her companions. "They're not… not what you think. A corruption follows us, maybe. We're here to hide from it. This one is dying. We seek healing from the wardens."

"Strife is fire, and Cinder is ash," the spirit of the river said. "They must be cleansed. Of their life, if not their souls."

"I don't like how this is going," Elsa murmured.

"Just be quiet for a minute," Gwen snapped

over her shoulder. "Glimmerglen, I need their help. Something is happening among the Celestials. Something terrible. I have worked with these two, protected them, fought with them. I owe them my life. I can not offer you theirs."

"Do they know the ground they are walking? Do they understand the hallow?"

"Does any child of flesh understand the hallow?" Gwen asked.

The spirit waited for a breath. The air stretched thin around them, the sun pinwheeled overhead in the long minutes that passed with each heartbeat. Then the spirit bent toward Gwen.

It swallowed all three of them.

The water was cold until it numbed, and then it burned. Elsa struggled against the bondage of flood, but there was nothing to push against, no current to fight. Nevertheless, she thrashed in the spirit's grip, her mind screaming out to Strife for guidance, for strength, but the sky didn't answer.

Then they were on the other shore. The world fell into place around them. The air cleared, and Strife settled into her usual position. Whatever strangeness had been in the world disappeared like a puff of smoke in the wind.

"What happened?" Elsa asked, startled and unnerved.

"We've passed the wards," Gwen answered. She breathed deeply, then motioned toward the stony hill just visible over the trees. "All that's left is to meet the wardens."

"And the god?" Lucas asked.

"Pray that it doesn't come to that. Though where your prayers will go from here, I'm honestly not sure."

She laughed and started into the woods. "Maybe best to just hope, and keep your mouth closed... for now."

The forest moved like a normal forest, its trees crisscrossed with paths that could have been cut by deer, the underbrush choked with fallen leaves. Strife's filtered light dappled the forest floor. They could have been among any trees in all of Tenumbra.

Gwen led the trio, with Frair Lucas shuffling frail and tired behind her, and Elsa at the rear. There was birdsong everywhere, and the air was cool and fresh, punctuated here and there by the smell of rotten branches and moss.

"Who are they, these wardens?" Elsa called ahead.

"Pagans," Gwen answered cheerfully. "They are precisely what you fear—a circle of witching wives and their attendant shamans, tending ancient places, keeping forgotten rituals. Keeping the old gods close."

"Or the old god," Lucas muttered. "That's where we are, isn't it?"

"Celestials," Gwen said dismissively. "Celestials and their discreet gods. What is a river without water, what is the breeze without air? We can name the river, call it Greenglove or Tallow, but in the end it's just water. Always different water, and the same."

"You should have been a priest," Elsa said. "You're just as unsatisfying to listen to, and twice as smug."

"I am," Gwen answered. "All of those things."

"If they are pagans, and if this is the source of their gods, what in hell makes you think they'll tolerate a Celestial priest and his vow knight in their presence?" Elsa asked. "For that matter, what in hell makes you think we'll tolerate being here? Do you understand our duty, child? Do you know what we must do with this place, given the power and the chance?"

"Do *you* understand?" Gwen countered. "Do you really understand what this place is? What destroying it would do? Not just to the north, but to all of Tenumbra." She pulled up, turning so quickly that Lucas stumbled into her. Gwen steadied him, then nailed Elsa in place with an angry stare. "I brought you here because of things the frair has said. Things I think he understands, or at least hopes to understand, and given the chance, I would answer his questions. But you, vow knight... you I have no reason to trust. So watch your way. This is an easy place to disappear."

"Listen, you brat—"

"Peace, Sir LaFey," Lucas said. He stood at Gwen's side, raising a hand to still Elsa's protest. "Peace. There is much we don't know, and I would truly like to understand some of it before I die. Which will happen soon enough if I don't find a place to rest. So, enough bickering. Let the huntress lead."

They stood awkwardly for a moment, until Elsa relented and nodded them forward. Gwen gestured Lucas down the road. She stopped Elsa before she could follow.

"I admire your zeal, Sir LaFey. I really do, and you should know that I share it. We serve different gods, but the same godhood. The sooner you get that through your scarred head, the better we'll all be."

Elsa frowned and didn't answer.

Gwen shrugged, then went to find the frair.

"The wardens will find us soon enough," Gwen called out. "The river will have informed them of our presence, if Elsa's shouting didn't give notice enough. We'll be able to negotiate some kind of peace."

"No, I don't think we will," Lucas said. He had

stopped at the edge of a clearing. The hill they had seen earlier, tall and bald, rose beyond the clearing. Elsa came to stand next to him.

The bodies of the wardens, woman and man and child, lay peacefully around a henge at the center of a bowl-shaped clearing. They were holding hands, their faces smeared in the ritual ink and daubed with blood, arcane tools at their feet. At the center of the henge was the circle's shaman. A copper blade had been plunged into his chest, his limp hand still on the handle.

They were all dead, their lives given in some final ritual, one last binding of the shields that protected the hallow. The wardens were gone, and only their wards remained.

41

THE SOUNDS OF screams and rending stone drifted through the courtyard like fine music. From the doma, the evensong stumbled to a halt. Voices raised, the guards along the walls all rushed to their stations, looking for forces along the castle's verge. An attack in the courtyard could mean only one thing.

Treachery.

Yet there was no attack. There was no plan among the Suhdrin lords to distract the castle's defenders in preparation of an assault. No one knew of the gheist that even now ravaged the throne room. No Suhdrin, no pagan of Tener. No one.

Except High Inquisitor Tomas Sacombre, who knelt among the shadows of the castle keep, watching as his scion crashed through the wooden door of the throne room, drawn by the cursed sword held by the duke of Greenhall. *Such an arrogant man, that one*, Sacombre thought. *Such an excellent martyr.*

The alarm horn rolled out of the huntress's watchtower. They would be searching for him soon. Looking for him to save them. Sacombre stood and crept away.

The summoning had taken so much from him. The blood of his heart had been necessary, drawn with naetherblade, the wound stitched closed with shadow. He was weakened. If any should challenge him now, mortal or godling, Sacombre could hardly resist—but he was not looking to fight. He sought knowledge. The secrets of the Fen Gate sang to him through the shadows, drew him deeper and down, so that all he had to do was follow their call.

The ink that scrolled across his chest and arms itched with vibrant power. The corrupted god that dwelt beneath his skin could taste the faith of the old ways seeping through the very stones of the pagan castle. How could Adair think that he could hide his loyalty? Had no one seen this corruption before?

They had not, and Sacombre knew why. It was because no one had taken the ink—the true ink, the pagan's ink. Not the nostalgic scrollwork of the fallen tribes, the barbaric and powerless runework passed from father to son, their meaning lost in ritual and tradition. A deeper knowledge was needed to bind the true ink to the skin and soul. Knowledge that Sacombre had paid dearly to acquire.

The high inquisitor had only discovered the practice by accident, the secrets buried in the inquisition's oldest tomes, dusty with neglect at the shrine at Cinderfell. The rites had taken time to master, and the process was imperfect. Even so, Sacombre was finally beginning to understand the power that tempted those who stayed true to the old ways. Only his determination to reforge those powers, to serve the true god of Tenumbra, kept Sacombre faithful.

With a step and a lurch, he nearly tumbled down a stair. He shook his head and looked around. He was standing at the top of a long stairwell, innocuous enough, hidden in the twisting pathways of the crypts beneath the castle. The air smelled of must and wet stone. Sacombre wondered how he had come to be down here, what guards and servants he must have passed to reach this place. He looked back the way he had come. There were bodies. Someone would notice that, and come looking.

Best that he be about winter's work, then.

Maeve felt the pull from her place in the stables. She and the rest of her family had sought shelter in the castle when the armies of Suhdra had crested the hill that overlooked the Fen Gate. She was kneeling by her daughter's bed, singing counterpoint to the eerie evensong, weaving a foundation of ancient faith in the child's mind, when the first dissonant note struck her heart.

Her voice caught in her throat. Little Ennie, her fat pink fingers plucking at the air, turned wide, wet eyes to her mother.

"Aye, child, the young are always closer to the everealm, h'ain't they?" she whispered, running a hand through the soft down of the babe's head. "There's something in the stones, yes? There's someone in the shrine."

"What's that?" Darrus asked. Her husband was standing at the door of the stable, hayfork in hand. The dear man had been standing guard ever since the Suhdrin party entered the castle. It was his place among the baron's stablemen that had won them this berth, and he was earnest to protect it.

"Nothing, love. Nothing is wrong at all," Maeve said, standing.

"Thought I heard you talking."

"I can talk to my daughter, can't I?" she replied, going to the small pack of instruments hidden in the hay, unpacking and then carefully hiding a few in the sleeves of her robe. "You should try to get some sleep."

"No, I think…" Darrus paused, straining his ears. "There. What's that?"

The first screams reached the couple. Darrus tensed.

"I knew't," he said. "I knew they were no good, coming in here. Southern bastards."

Maeve slipped behind her husband, pressing lips into his neck. His muscles relaxed.

"Sleep, I said," she whispered, catching him as he fell into her arms. With iron's strength and spirit's aid, she dragged him into one of the stalls. She would prefer the hayloft, but she hadn't the time or strength to spare. When Darrus was settled, she tucked young Ennie into his arms, then hushed her. A glamor and a prayer later, and the stable looked empty. Even if it burned, they would be safely nestled into the pocket of the everealm that Maeve had conjured.

With as much done for her family as she could, Maeve ducked under the hood of her robes and hurried toward the keep.

The gheist horn droned through the night.

There was no light in the shrine. Maeve breathed a sigh of relief as she passed bloodless through the stones. Her hand brushed the altar and found it unbroken. Whatever was happening up above, it had not yet reached the heart of the castle.

She found a candle among the niches and brought it forward, cupping it in her hand as she searched for the flint. Witches of fire had a much easier time with this, but Maeve had her own tricks. She held the flint next to the wick and, with a push of everam, teased the spark from the stone.

In the flickering light she saw two eyes, black and glinting, at the very edge of the candle's light. The shadows rushed in and, with a smothering hiss, extinguished the candle's flame. Startled, she dropped the wick and heard it splat dully onto the stones at her feet. The flint followed as she drew the twin blades from her sleeves and backed up against the wall.

"Do you greet all pilgrims thus?" a voice said from the darkness.

"You are no pilgrim," she hissed.

"A seeker, perhaps. A student." There was a shuffle of robes, a stir of air suddenly dry. The voice moved through the room like leaves on the wind. "Curious, like you—though you are not the person I was expecting."

"Then you've no idea where you are," Maeve said, backing along the wall. Something brushed her feet and scuttled away. The shadows scurried against her eyes. Oh, for the kinship of fire, but stone would have to do.

"I think I do," the voice said. "Or, at least, I think I have some idea. I've been to Houndhallow, you know. I recognize the darker shrines when I see them."

Without a word, Maeve slid toward the sound of the voice and slashed out with her blades. Air parted, and the shadows pulled at her robes, resistant as heavy curtains. The voice grunted at her side, then laughed sharply from behind her.

"Not for talking? I'd hoped to crack this shell without too much blood, at least at first—but we can do things your way."

The shadows around her coalesced, like ropes summoned out of smoke, and bound her arms. Her left hand pressed against her thigh, the blade pricking skin and drawing blood. With her right, trapped at the shoulder but free from the elbow down, Maeve tried to cut free of whatever held her. Something snaked around her leg, her neck, pressing into her eyes until she was sure her veins would burst.

She pushed everam into her free knife, drawing on the power of the hidden shrine and the closing equinox, but whatever her blade cut, the threads of shadow would reform in seconds. With a grunt, Maeve fell to the ground, squirming like a beached fish.

"A dangerous knife, that," the voice muttered. The speaker kicked the blade from Maeve's free hand, then leaned down and slowly peeled her fingers back to wrench the other weapon out. His touch was chill, as though his hands were made of clay. "Now then. Perhaps we can try this again. Where do I stand, and what words do I speak to unlock its path to the everealm, witch?"

"Fuck off," Maeve spat, then dropped through the stone floor like it was water.

The ropes of shadow didn't follow her, bound as they were to naether. Under the surface of the floor, Maeve's hearing was as muffled as if she were submerged, but her vision cleared. She could just make out the man, wrapped in shadows tinged the color of blood, stooped over the spot where she had just been.

A presence hovered in the man's shadow, a spirit that was wearing him like a mummer's puppet. It stretched from his back, arms tangled together, elongated head darting over his shoulder. This other consciousness tracked Maeve's fall. Its face split into a toothy grin, its mouth like a sundered corpse, gaping open after the executioner's blade has passed.

"God's own death," Maeve swore. The presence reached out for her.

Sacombre climbed the stairs as quickly as he could manage. The shadows drifting from his body carried something of his flesh with them, shadows tinged in blood and fed by his spirit.

The shrine was everything he had hoped, and nothing he could use. He alone now knew of the heresy of House Adair, of its generations of lies and duplicity. The family protected a secret, whispered about among the pagan tribes his trusted servants had infiltrated. Allaister had always believed it rested in the Fen itself, but Sacombre had never believed him, thinking that anything so precious would be kept close to the castle.

Allaister had been right.

Rising to the level of the crypts, Sacombre brushed from his robes the last of the dust of that profane place. Spots of blood grimed the hem. He would need to purge the vestments before he could speak rites in the doma, though it had been a long time since the high inquisitor had felt called to perform that duty.

Sighing, he looked around at the generations of Adair dead, their stony faces bland beneath their coats of grime. Sacombre smiled.

"No more lies, my friends. You've done well, and I promise that I will do more with your little secret than your gods could have imagined. Still…"

He paused as he heard a footfall, and peered up past the trail of bodies that he must have left. The nearest was a scullery maid whose crumpled face was dotted with specks of broken teeth and blood. Sacombre no longer feared the dead, at least not on this side of the quiet, but sometimes he was horrified at the state of the corpses he rendered.

Fighting had never been in his blood.

A man stepped from the shadows.

"Sir Volent!" Sacombre hailed. "The perfect man for tonight's proceedings. I have a task for you, good sir, a task that will bring your name to the lips of every pagan who dares defy the word of the Celestial church."

"I saw you give him that sword," Volent muttered.

"The sword? Oh. Oh, yes, and such a sword it is. Cinder-blessed and Strife-forged, hallowed in purpose and in heft. Why, foolish is the gheist who—"

"Shut up," Volent said. He came out of the shadows. The man was dressed for war, as always, and gripped his sword in a pale hand. "What have you done?"

"Done? I have done what I was anointed to do. What the gods require of me. What Cinder requires of me." Sacombre pressed forward, crowding into the newcomer's face. "You have followed me this far, Sir Volent. What sours your blood now, on the verge of victory, at the cusp—"

"You killed him," Volent said. He put one hand on the high inquisitor and pushed, casually, but with such strength that the priest went flying. "Gabriel Halverdt saved me. He found me, mad, quivering, a murderous bastard among murderous bastards, and he made a man of me."

"The duke of Greenhall is dead? Oh, gods, what tragedy!" Sacombre pulled himself to his knees, wincing as the gritty floor clogged the scratches on his shins, the palms of his hands. "We must flee to the army outside! Bring Cinder's justice down on these heathens. Gods, but I know it was a mistake to bargain for peace with pagans."

"A tragedy, yes," Volent agreed. "One which you

464

engineered—and that gheist? Don't you think that was a bit much?" Volent paced forward, swinging his sword back and forth, as if the edge ached to strike. "What black well have you dipped into, inquisitor, that you summon pagan gods to do your bidding?"

"Now listen, and listen closely, Volent. It is not your place to question the actions of the church. I will not stand here and be accused of witchcraft by the likes of you."

"You're kneeling," Volent pointed out. Then he rushed forward, sword drawn back, a glint of fury in his silent face. He was nearly upon the high inquisitor when Sacombre threw his arms out.

A band of shadow ripped across the dusty room. It snapped like a whip, and Volent stopped short. The black veins in his skin pulsed to the surface. He gave out a startled, terrified cry, and then was immobile. His sword clattered to the ground.

"Now then," Sacombre said, rising to his feet. He dusted off his knees and the palms of his hands. The demon song was singing in his head again, the streams of pagan power flashing through the air, clenching Volent tight. What had the witch called it? Everam? It was always good to know the proper name for things. He strolled up to Volent.

"That is enough of that, Sir Volent. I'm sorry for your master. I'm sorry that he had to die, but lessons must be learned, and sometimes, when the master dies, the dog goes mad." He placed a finger against the immobile forehead, quietly sketching an ancient rune in Volent's own blood, binding it in naether and flesh. He began to wonder what the limits were. Perhaps Strife's bright energy could be included, as well. He would have to visit the Lightfort one day, after all this was over. Initiate some of the girls into his order.

Volent's eyes shifted, clouding with ink. Sacombre smiled, then pressed his palm into the man's skull. Volent whimpered and then, stiff as a board, fell back to the floor.

"When a dog goes mad, sometimes you have to put him down," Sacombre whispered. "But even mad dogs have their uses."

Then he went up the stairs and into the night.

42

HENRI WOKE TO a green so dark it was nearly black. He was lying flat, his skin alive with motion, the tiny, burrowing grit of unseen life. Memories swam through his head—memories of travel, of distance, of battles fought and won, and comrades buried in the earth.

That's where I am, he thought. *Buried*. Yet there was light, and he saw leaves inches from his face. He stood, brushing past some undergrowth, the leaves scratching against his cheeks.

The trees were closer than he remembered. In fact, he didn't remember there being any trees at all. He stood shoulder to trunk with evergreens and oak, their limbs crisscrossing over his body as he took a step forward. Then they bowed aside, creaking as they moved out of his way. There was a path ahead of him.

He followed it, and it crossed another, and then another, joining and intersecting, becoming wider until the sheer number of trails became a clearing. A glen where the trees gathered above in a hatchwork of leaves and mossy branches, blocking out the sky. Despite that, there was no shortage of light in this clearing, pure as gold.

Gathered at the center of the clearing were figures,

tangled in shadow and light. Four men, standing in a circle, facing the center. He moved closer. They looked familiar.

"Who are you?" he asked quietly. The nearest two turned just a little, as though they had heard something, just over the shoulders. "Who are you?" Louder this time, more insistent.

It was a foolish question.

They were him.

"This has gone on long enough," the farthest figure said. He was more upright than the others, back straight, hands clasped in his belt, dressed as a knight at court might dress, fine velvet and silk, a sword hanging at his side. "We've marched under their banner long enough. It's time to draw our own colors."

"Your loyalties do not matter," the closest one replied. "Halverdt has served our purpose. Would Sacombre be any worse?" He stooped forward, as though his bones were too heavy, his head bent uncomfortably just to look forward. His skin was as white as snow and shot through with thick veins of purple and black. Henri came around to look into this face, but it was missing. A pit, deeper than the skull and creased with scars and blood, echoed with a demon's voice.

"It's foolish to even be talking about this," the demon said. "The priest is killing us, right now."

"Killing you," another of the figures answered. It was smaller than the others, more a boy than a man—a tall child, still soft in his joints, skin untouched by work or worry. A single crease wrinkled his brow. "Like you killed Papa," the child said.

"Be silent," the knight responded. "You have always been a visitor here—an unwelcome one at that."

"Leave Father out of this," the final shadow

snapped. He moved as if to lurch forward, but something held him in place. Henri pulled his gaze away from the strange pit-faced demon, then jerked and jumped back. This one was lined in blood, skin stained and teeth sharp, rotten, yellow and tinged in gore. His eyes were as wild as a madman's. His hands were cracked and dry. Each finger ended in a blade, steel erupting from the flesh like broken bones, and pus leaked constantly from the wounds.

The feral man looked at Henri, the first of the strange congregation to acknowledge his presence, and smiled wildly.

"This is no place for you."

"I don't know why I'm here," Henri said, holding his hands up and backing away from the feral man. He felt a hand on his shoulder and turned to look into the pit-faced demon's visage. Another voice rose up, shivering through his bones, whispering words that only he could hear.

His mother, screaming her husband's name as the gheist that consumed him drifted through the door. A memory, stirred from his nightmares, spoken in the heartbeats before he turned his back and ran out the door and into the rain.

"You killed them!" Henri yelled at the demon, the shard of the gheist that had lodged in his blood and stolen the life from his face. He whirled into the center of the circle of figures.

"It's gone on long enough," the knight repeated. "We must take our part."

"You're only here because I brought you here. You're only alive because I've kept you alive," the demon answered.

"You! You've kept *us* alive?" the feral howled

mockingly. "We've carried you all this way, like a burden strapped to our heart. I've carried you. All of you!"

"Please be quiet," the child said. "I don't like it when you're loud!" The others seemed to ignore him, but when they spoke again it was in hushed tones.

"If not for me, the duke would have discarded us," the demon said. "And as for you—" He turned to the feral man. "Without me you wouldn't even exist."

"Gods bless that were true, demon," the knight answered, "but you found a home in us *because* he existed, even then." He tossed his head toward the child, who quickly looked away. "In truth, I'm not sure either the duke or the high inquisitor has done us much good."

The feral man laughed, a sound both sharp and brittle. The bloody figure shook his head.

"Look at you," he said. "Silk and silver, talking about taking control. Do you think the duke would have raised us up so far, based on your skills? Father was a carpenter. We were never going to be anything more."

"You're one to talk," the knight snapped. "With you sneaking into the woods each night, to break bones and spill blood, we would have ended up in prison... or worse."

"Or we would have been free!" the feral man answered. "Living on the road, taking what we wanted, sleeping where we wanted, and sleeping well, I wager!" He pointed accusingly at the demon. "None of this gheist's godsdamned nightmares." He turned back to the knight. "But that's worse to you, isn't it? You never had a feel for freedom. You wanted power, and asses to kiss."

"You would have us living like a dog."

"Like a wolf—and wolves live well!"

"Enough," the demon hissed from the void. "I've given you both what you want, and more than you could hope for. You will not tear us apart."

"This is the priest's doing," the feral man whispered. "What did he do to you, demon? Why did you come to heel when he called?" The bloody figure inched forward, his fingers creeping out toward the pit-faced figure. "Whose side are you on?"

"Priests, priests, priests!" the knight said. "I tire of the machinations of priests. I will have no more to do with them."

"That isn't up to you," the demon answered, then he pointed toward Henri. "This is a matter for him."

"Who is he?" the child asked. The boy's presence made Volent uncomfortable—even more so than his feral aspect, or the demon.

"He is an older, less obnoxious you," the knight answered. "But he shouldn't make the decision—that should be my right."

"Why should you get a choice?" the demon asked. "You who followed orders your entire life?"

"That is the way of this world," the knight answered proudly. "I found my place in its order, and it has served me... served *us* well."

"To what end?" the demon said.

"To this end," the feral man answered. "To this moment." He snicked the knives of his fingers together, grinning madly.

"What moment?" Henri asked, but the ghosts ignored him. All but the child who stared at him with large, empty eyes. Angered by their disdain, Henri grabbed the feral man and spun him round. "*What are you talking about?*"

"I wouldn't..." the demon said, but he was too slow. The feral man took hold of Henri's shirt, and a good deal of skin with it.

"Opportunity!" the feral man howled. "The priest has given you to us, granting us the opportunity to make things as they ought to be." He shoved, and Henri stumbled into the center of the circle. "I'll be *damned* if I let you fuck it up for me!"

"It could be any one of us," the knight said. "It should be me."

"What do you mean?" Henri stood, brushing dirt from his face. With a start he felt his fingers on his skin. He looked down at his hand. The spider-growths were gone. He glanced up.

The demon nodded at him.

"Yes," the demon nodded. "While you are here, you are whole."

"And wholly *empty*," the feral man sneered. "Waiting to be plucked."

"That is for us to do," the knight agreed. "Go, and take the child with you." He waved Henri away. "Go play stones, or something."

"Stones," the feral man agreed. "Try to not get any blood in the water."

Henri began to protest, then stopped. He stood silently for a minute, looking from ghost to ghost. He wasn't getting answers from any of them—perhaps the child would be more... cooperative. As if reading his thoughts, the childlike figure walked over and took his hand, leading him away from the clearing.

The rest were arguing before they were out of earshot.

"Do you know what's occurring?" Henri asked.

"They argue a lot," the child said, "especially

the red one. We might as well have some fun." He walked loosely, swinging his arms in wide arcs, almost dancing. They came to a stream quite suddenly. The child bent, took a stone from the bank, and tossed it weakly into the water.

"That's not what I mean," Henri said, looking around. "Do you know why I am here?" The forest seemed closer. He peered across the stream. Among the whispering ferns there was a field of tiny banners in brown and gray, each one pinned to a small twig. The wind didn't move them. "Wherever this is."

"If you don't know that, they sure as hells won't tell you," the child said, then winced. "Pardon the cursing."

"Pardoned," Henri said automatically, echoing the words his father had said to him thoughtlessly, a hundred times. "The priest they're talking about—who is he? I remember something… bodies, and a tomb?"

"Mm-hm," the child responded. "Your master died. You're off the leash."

"The high inquisitor," Henri said, mostly to himself. "He tried to kill me."

"You were trying to kill him, and he needed someone to blame all of those bodies on. So he sent you here to go mad." The child tilted his head. "Madder, I suppose. No one's going to be surprised to find you at the end of a trail of bodies."

"I'll deny it," Henri said.

"Not if you're still in here."

"Then how do I get out?"

"Maybe you don't. Maybe one of the others will get to decide." The child lifted a stone from the water and held it up in both hands. It was sharp on one end, like a teardrop. "Maybe it'll be me."

"I don't understand," Henri said. The child's words

473

bothered him deeply, although he couldn't say why.

"That's never worried me, not understanding," the child said. "Can you help me with this?"

"Listen," Henri said, kneeling beside him. "Can you tell me something?"

The child paused, the heavy rock still in his hand, his eyes narrow.

"If I know the answer," he said, "and it isn't naughty."

"What do you remember of Father?" Henri asked.

The child hesitated, finally lowering the stone back into the stream. The water splashed loudly around his fingers. Finally he shrugged.

"He was big—bigger than me, and those other two. Bigger even than Sir Nasty-Face, and strong."

"That's all?"

"He smelled like wood, shaved wood, like from his shop. He made nice things—toys, and chairs, and… mostly toys. Least it's the toys that I remember best." The child pulled his hands out of the water and shook them. "Wish I had some of those toys now."

"To remember him by?"

"To play with," the child said. "I get bored." He glanced up and around the forest. "There aren't any more squirrels out here."

"Toys…" Henri said, the first hint of a smile on his lips. "I can't remember even that. Just his face, and his name, and what it sounded like when he died." The smile went away. "The dreams have taken the rest away." He paused. The child was looking up at him with sharp, angry eyes. "And Mother? What do you remember about her?"

"I didn't kill her," the child said, and there were tears in his eyes. "I *didn't*. It was the demon. I thought we had escaped him, but he followed. I ran, and ran, but he's in our skin. Do you know what it's like, living with that thing? Do you have any idea?"

"Hush, hush," Henri said. It was difficult, seeing himself like this. "It's all right." He didn't really know what to do.

"No," the child whimpered. "It's not all right. It never was." He spun.

The stone took Henri behind the ear, a weak blow driven by a child's hand, but enough to surprise him. He slipped and collapsed back into the stream, cold water splashing over his hips. The child rose from the bank, the heavy stone once again in his hands.

There was blood on it.

"When the master goes mad," the child whispered, "sometimes you have to put down the dog."

"What?" Henri sputtered.

"You shouldn't have left me in here," the child shrilled. "You shouldn't have left me with them!"

Henri crawled backwards, slipping on smooth stones as he struggled away from the murderous boy. The child came at him, the stone over his head, screaming. Henri turned away, and the stone bounced off his back. The boy fell against him, tiny arms battering his head, his shoulders, young teeth sinking into his neck. Henri could taste the blood and the fear.

He shoved the child away. His younger self fell into the stream, sputtering when his head went under. Henri pushed his head into the water. Young hands tore at his wrists, drawing blood. It was brief, the struggle, as the last moments of Henri's memories of his father washed into the river.

Try to not get any blood in the water.

Henri stood and returned to the clearing.

* * *

"Lose yourself?" the feral man asked.

"Shut up," Henri snapped.

"Oh, so now he has a backbone," the knight responded. "Too bad he can't keep track of a child."

"You, too," Henri said. "I've had enough of this—of your accusations, your assumptions." He drew his sword, which he wasn't carrying until he reached for it. "The duke may have shaped us, and the church may have guided us, but it's time I start making my own way."

"Yes, exactly!" the knight said. "Sense upon sense! All you have to do—" Henri thrust forward, sliding the blade smoothly through the silk and satin into flesh. The knight staggered, sputtered, and died.

"Ho, ho!" the feral man yipped. "I don't think he saw that coming!"

"I've had enough of fitting into someone else's sense of order," Henri said. "No more orders, and no more madness." He spun and brought the blade across the feral man's crimson neck, opening him up like a butcher's purse, sending him tumbling to the ground.

Then Henri wheeled on the demon. The pit-faced figure backed slowly away, feeble hands up.

"Be careful what you do here, Henri," the demon said, his voice slithering through the air. "There's no need…"

"It was you, wasn't it? You killed my parents!"

"I don't know…"

"I thought all of this—my face, my skin… the nightmares… I thought it was a scar in my soul, or a wound that would heal in time. It's not, is it?" Henri gritted. "It was all you!"

"You were fertile ground," the demon replied. "I have grown into more than I was."

"All these years, I've hunted the gheist, feared the pagan," Henri snarled. "You have been inside me since the beginning." He stepped forward. The demon stepped back.

"Son, wait," the demon said. He changed, his face swelling, eyes and nose and mouth welling up like water filling a hole. His features were like a dim memory.

Father.

"I am the god of memory, Henri Volent. I preserve the past that was lost." The demon stepped forward, hand outstretched. "I hold your father, and your mother, as well."

"The dead are gone," Henri growled. "Let them sleep."

"They're never gone. Not as long as you…"

"No," Henri said. Then he placed the tip of his sword against his father's face. The image of Jacque Volent whisked away like smoke. The blade passed through and into the pit of the demon's face. A thousand voices screamed, his mother's last of all, but then there was silence, and darkness, and weight.

He awoke lying among the tombs of the tribe of iron.

Something was burning, thick, black, inky smokey boiling up from the stairwell. That was the direction Sacombre had come from.

Henri stood, and felt tears on his face.

He wondered why that seemed unusual.

43

IAN KNELT ON the bare stone of a lonely hill. He sang the evensong to himself, bidding farewell to the sun, counting down the rites to the moon, binding the wounds in his heart. When he was done he held the silence of a long moment. His knees ached, but he didn't want to move.

Evening crawled on, and reluctantly he stood and started down the hill. There was a time in his life when he would have been nervous walking the deep forests of Tener, especially this close to the equinox. Fear of the gheists had dominated so much of his youth. With Fianna and her coven so close, however, and after a month of traveling in their company, in the host of their gods, he was no longer afraid.

So he had started observing the evensong again. Ian felt the need to put something between himself and these pagans. He needed to create a space, a sacred distance, and a time when he could feel the old gods again. When he could feel Cinder's judgment, and Strife's love.

He found it odd that he had started thinking of the bright lady and gray lord as the "old gods." Ian worried that he might not be remembering the forms of evensong. At first he had stumbled through them, gaining confidence with each night, but even now he wasn't certain he had it right. He might be committing heresy without knowing it.

He hoped the gods would understand, or perhaps not even notice.

About halfway down the hill, Ian realized that he was no longer alone. Off to his left, Cahl was walking parallel to him. The shaman slipped quietly between the trees, pointedly ignoring him. Ian slowed, then came to a halt. Cahl circled into the path Ian would have followed, turned, and faced the young Tenerran.

"You are learning to move through the forests, Ian of Houndhallow," Cahl said. "The time hasn't long passed that you would have stumbled through the darkness like an avalanche."

"I've had plenty of practice," Ian said.

"It's more than that," Cahl answered. He came closer, looking Ian up and down. "You are weaving the night into your bones. The silence of dreams cloaks you."

"I think I just got tired of falling on my face," Ian persisted. "Started looking where I was going."

"You started *seeing* where you were going," Cahl corrected. "There is a distinct difference."

"Are you here to harass me about my prayers?"

"Your prayers will not keep the spirits from your blood," Cahl said. "They will not keep you holy in this place."

"If you are trying to frighten me," Ian said, "it's not going to happen, and you're not going to cause me to change."

Cahl didn't answer. The big shaman just stood there, breathing slowly, as if he was tasting the air and the earth. Ian could sense the slight haze of everic power dancing around the man's skin, tangling with the trees and sky and quiet stones of the earth beneath their feet.

"No, you are not the type of man to take fright," Cahl said. "You are not the type of man to be leashed, either—or led."

"Fianna leads you," Ian said.

Cahl smiled, the first time Ian had ever seen. It was a broad smile, full of teeth, and not frightening at all.

"I do not understand her will for you," Cahl said, "but not knowing is part of this. There are many of my brothers who would have left you for dead. There are many more who would hunt you down without a second thought. But Fianna is moving something in you. Surely you can feel that."

"No," Ian answered. "Nothing about me is changing. I am of the Celestials, faithful to Cinder. Faithful to Strife. I am the heir of Houndhallow, and sworn to Heartsbridge. Nothing that has happened here will change that."

"So you say," Cahl said. "I have listened to your evensong, and I know those words, Ian of Houndhallow. They are older than your church." The shaman loomed closer still, his rocky face inches from Ian's nose. "I may never change you, but the gods are another matter."

Ian was about to answer when Cahl snorted and turned away. He loped down the hill, his broad back disappearing among the trees long before his footsteps faded.

"Such a load of bullshit," Ian hissed, shaking in frustration. "Gods, what's wrong with these people? We should be fighting. We should be at the Fen Gate. Damn it!"

Anger turned Ian's feet. He walked around the hill, avoiding the pagan camp and the sentries he knew were roaming the trees.

Word had filtered through the forest, from captured Suhdrin scouts foolish enough to wander far from the roads. They spoke about the size of the Suhdrin force, and the decimation of the Tenerran armies. It seemed unbelievable, but Ian had seen enough bodies, enough wreckage, had ambushed enough supply wagons to know that there was a seed of truth to what they said.

Your prayers will not keep the spirits from your blood. Fianna had said something similar, and now Cahl was taking up the chorus. Exposure to the pagan arts didn't make you a pagan. It made you *aware* of pagans. If anything, he felt more holy than he had before.

Frustration kept Ian walking. He wanted to be at his father's side. He wanted to settle the debt of blood he owed Martin Roard, and the whole damned Suhdrin army. They had taken his pride, and he meant to cut it from them, to take it back with iron. Yet until he convinced Fianna to move them north, they would be nipping at the edges of the conflict, taking pennies, when they should have been plundering a fortune.

He came to a creek, its water babbling happily through the night. Ian stared down into the current, trying to decide what he was meant to be doing. What he should be doing. What the gods expected of him.

Lost in thought, Ian did not at first hear the beast. Something came rushing through the forest, sliding through the trees. Before he knew it, the earth was shaking soundlessly. The night bent close, and his fears of the pagan night returned with a snap as sharp and fast as a crossbow loosing its bolt.

A fog crept out of the ground, gray tendrils snaking

between Ian's feet. He drew his sword.

A god came to a halt before him.

It was a hound, as big as a horse, bigger. Its tangled fur was twined through with twigs and leaves, its dirty coat cluttered with vines that seemed to grow through its body. It was black, black as night, and its bearded jaw hung open, exposing scores of star-white teeth, each as big and as sharp as a gardener's hook. Its eyes were fixed on Ian. He couldn't look away from them. They were the color of smoke from a fire whose timber is too wet, and wisps of inky darkness swirled down the creature's cheeks like tears of fog.

Ian placed his weight on his back foot, bringing the sword up to his chest, waiting for the charge. Waiting to die. The hound trotted closer, and he never took his eyes away from its horrible face. A cold fog swirled around his legs, and the sound of the creek ceased, as if the water had turned to frost at the gheist's approach.

The hound passed close to him, nearly brushing his trembling arm with its hulking shoulder. It smelled like freshly tilled earth and old, damp leaves left under the forest canopy for seasons without end.

And then it was gone. The night came back, the insects filling the world with their song, the creek returning to life. The forest peeled away from the gheist's path, leaving a road through the trees. Ian stumbled forward, up a hill, the ground nothing but smooth grass. As he crested the summit, the trail closed behind him, the trees creaking as they returned to their natural place, the earth groaning and shifting beneath his feet.

In the distance, the twin towers of the Fen Gate poked out of the trees. Yet there was no way they could be so close. Even as Ian watched, the horizon shivered and returned to normal.

Fianna stepped up next to him, appearing out of nowhere, without sound, without warning. She sighed.

"That is a sign I will follow," she whispered. "It is sign enough for me."

"And me. Gods be good," Ian answered. "And me."

44

GWEN STOOD AT the lip of the clearing, staring down at the dead, unable to move. Her mind fumbled over the bodies lying in front of her, their faces gentle, their skin cold. Surely the wardens couldn't be dead. Surely she couldn't be alone in guarding the hallow? Surely the gods would not abandon her so?

Elsa shook her out of her reverie.

The bodies were still there.

"These are the witches meant to save the frair's life?" the vow knight asked.

"Aye."

"Well, then," Elsa said, turning in a slow circle, "we'll need… something else."

"I can… I know something." Gwen finally raised her eyes. Lucas looked little better than the bodies at her feet. "This way."

She led them past the killing ground to the base of the sacred hill, to one among dozens of henges that ringed the shrine. Elsa had to support the frair the entire way. When he lay down at the center of the circle of stones, he looked as if he wouldn't get up again.

"Have we made it in time, Huntress?" Elsa said. "I do not wish to bury him here." There was a thinly veiled threat at the edge of her words.

"The ground would not accept him, anyway," Gwen answered, gathering deadfall and starting a fire. "We cannot yet know if we were fast enough—that's for time to tell."

"Have no worry," Lucas said quietly. "I can feel the weight of this place. I have many days ahead of me, Sir LaFey. Many days."

"Come," Gwen said, plucking at Elsa's shoulder. "There's nothing to see, and we have things to do."

"We're simply going to leave him here?" The vow knight didn't move. "You can't be serious."

"It's a ley circle. It focuses the power of life in this place." The huntress frowned. "There are rites, too, and balms, but they are beyond my abilities. The magic of this place might heal him. Or it might corrupt him—but there is no other way for him to reach the hallow."

Elsa just stared at her, then at the corpses.

"Have faith," Gwen said, then winced. "Wrong words. Just trust me—this is as much as can be done. It's not a bloodwright, and it would be better if the wardens were alive to lend their aid, but given his robes, and the faith in his heart..."

She turned and marched back to where the wardens lay. Elsa followed, and they buried the bodies where they lay, dragging stones over their motionless bodies while Frair Lucas slept away his death.

"So what now?" Elsa asked when they were done. "We're wasting time the frair doesn't have, and Allaister is still hunting us out there. We can't hide here forever."

"No," Gwen said, setting the final stone on the final cairn, then swinging her cloak back around her shoulders. "I was hoping the wardens would be able to advise us."

"There's no hope of that now, I doubt even Lucas could visit them in the quiet."

"He couldn't manage it—not here, not even if he had permission," Gwen said. "No, we're on our own."

"Will Allaister be able to get through these wards?" Elsa asked, peering around as if expecting enemies to burst from the deepening shadows. "If the wardens aren't around to maintain them…"

"I don't know," Gwen admitted. "These people must have died in an attempt to build a shield around the hallow. The one who visited me the other night, she said that the gheist was straining the wards. That many had already died. There may be others coming, though. They have ways of speaking… through the trees." She made a frustrated sound in the back of her throat. "I just don't know."

"Then there's something I can say at your trial, after all," Elsa said brusquely.

"What's that?"

"That you don't know much about pagan things," she answered. "Perhaps ignorance will work in your favor." The vow knight snatched up her pack and started walking toward the hill. "Come on. I've no interest in sleeping among the dead."

"I doubt they would want your company, anyway," Gwen muttered. She gathered her things and followed. Mists began to appear in the hallow, forming odd, spectral shapes.

As the first stars appeared in the sky, a voice rose above the trees. The evensong, so familiar, sounded foreign in this wild place of the old gods. No gheists appeared in the darkness, however, and Gwen took that as a hopeful sign. She and Elsa hurried to where they had left the frair, then stopped dead, shock clear in the vow knight's expression. Lucas was sitting up, eyes sparkling in the firelight for the first time since the demon had laid him low.

"I thought you might have been swallowed by the everealm," he said, his voice sounding rough with disuse. He held a handful of wildflowers in his fist, freshly bloomed at the verge of the henge. They appeared to drip blood. "These are fascinating blooms. What are they?"

"They are your death," Gwen said. "Siphoned away and given new life. I... wouldn't advise you to handle them."

"Ah," Lucas said. He dropped the flowers to the side, but his smile remained. "Glad to have you with us, Huntress."

"We were speaking of the wards," Elsa said. "You must know something of the tricks pagans use to hide themselves. With the wardens gone, are we still safe from Allaister's hunters?"

"And it's fine to see you alive and well, Sir LaFey," Lucas said smartly, giving her a look. "Yes, thank you for asking, I feel quite well. It's a miracle I live at all."

"You'll get my sympathy later, old man," the vow knight replied. "Your health does us no good if Allaister gets through."

Lucas stood, dusting the last of the blood pollen from his hands, stretched his back, and took a deep breath of the everam-laced air. The change in him was astonishing. After such a short time within the henge, already he looked years younger. Gwen wondered how old the dead wardens might have been, and what benefits they had reaped from living in such a place.

"He will get through, eventually," the frair said. "I

could, at least, and I'm not sure Frair Allaister isn't my better. These wards are meant to beguile and hide—not protect. Once discovered, they are vulnerable. Without the benefit of Gwendolyn Adair to lead the way, it will take time for him to find the path, but it can be done." Lucas nodded to himself, and looked around. "Wards such as these must be constantly renewed. I'm shocked that there were so few wardens here, considering the importance of this site."

"There were more," Gwen said. "The gheist depleted their numbers considerably." She shook her head. "At least that's what I hope."

"You hope?" Elsa asked. "How do their deaths benefit us?"

Gwen shrugged. "The old gods are fickle, not as well understood as they once were. Lives… are sometimes lost."

"You mean to say that they're not as sane as they once were, Huntress," Lucas said. "Tell the story you like. Years of neglect have taken their toll on your gods."

"And whose fault is that?" she snapped.

"Fault doesn't matter," he said. "You brought us here, Gwendolyn, because you hoped we could help you. You could have left us before now, in the woods between here and there. You could have slipped between the wards and disappeared—but you didn't, and so here we are. In your hallow, saying prayers for the dead of your faith."

"It wasn't really part of my plan," Gwen muttered.

"Nor theirs, I would imagine," Lucas agreed. "Yet the question remains: What do you hope of us? How do you think we will be able to help you?"

"And *why* do you think we will?" Elsa added pointedly. Gwen just ignored her. She stared up at the sky.

"I don't think it matters anymore," she said finally. "With the wardens gone, we'll never prevent the inquisition from finding this place."

"That's no longer an issue," Lucas answered with a smile. "Unless you've forgotten my oath. I'm still faithful to Cinder."

"And yet, I feel you came for another reason. Don't you want to help us hide this site?"

"That isn't my purpose. The time for hiding is past, for good or ill—Allaister and his master, High Inquisitor Sacombre, know what lurks in these woods. They won't rest until they have found it."

"I can't let him destroy it," Gwen said stiffly. "Not while I live."

"Destroy it?" Lucas gave a mirthless chuckle. "No. I believe the high inquisitor means to bend the god to his will. That's why he has provoked this war, why he sent Allaister in secret. If he meant to call a crusade against House Adair, he could certainly draw the support of all of Suhdra, and most of Tener, as well. The northern lords are anxious to appear pious, after all."

"I would destroy it," Elsa said. Lucas waved her down.

"What comes after, comes after," he said. "Our immediate concern is to—"

"No," Gwen said, cutting him off. "What comes after matters—to me at least. I haven't forgotten who you are," she said, her eyes on the vow knight, "nor what you do to pagans when you find them. This lot had the decency to die before you arrived, but I've no doubt their fate would have been the same. Cinder is the god of judges, after all."

"Though not of executioners," Lucas said. "You need to put some faith in us, Gwen, if we're going to be able to help you."

"I brought you here. Isn't that faith enough?"

"Not nearly." Lucas turned to face her. "I know something of pagan lore, Huntress. I know what this place is meant to be, and what it's supposed to be protecting, but I haven't grown up with that lore. Allaister and his men have dabbled in the ancient rituals, as you've seen, and are able to draw some of the everealm's power. But these things are merely means to an end, to them. They know nothing of the deeper arts."

"What does that have to do with me?" Gwen asked.

"You were born into these traditions. Under a façade of Celestial faith, you have been raised in the old ways. Allaister means to come in here and enslave the god at this henge, but he doesn't have the tools. It would be like throwing pottery with a hammer." Lucas raised his hands and moved closer to her. "You have the art, Gwendolyn Adair. You can raise the god he means to tame."

"Raise it, so that you can destroy it?" Gwen demanded. "Or so you can bind it to *your* will, rather than that of the high inquisitor? That's what I need to know, Frair. What do you mean to do with my god?"

"And that's where faith comes in," Lucas said.

Gwen smiled tightly, as if she had eaten something foul but was too polite to spit it out.

"Well, your faith in me may be what's misplaced, Frair. There is very little of the pagan in me, either in power or inclination. My house has been trusted to keep this secret, and given certain abilities to ensure that trust, but we aren't bound to the higher orders. You'll need a true pagan for that." She stood, dusted off her palms, and gestured to the cairns that surrounded them, forming a new and silent henge.

"Unfortunately, we're running short on those."

"But surely you must—" Elsa started.

"You may yet get to kill this god, Sir LaFey, but not with my permission, and not with my assistance," Gwen snapped. She stood abruptly, marched up the embankment, and disappeared into the darkening woods. The mists followed her.

45

"STUBBORN BITCH," ELSA muttered. "We're just trying to help."

"No, Sir LaFey, we're not. Not really—and I'd imagine she's less stubborn than she is frightened." Lucas folded his hands together and sought the naether, drawing it into a crown around his head. "I must think. Keep an eye on her, as quietly as you can. Don't let her get lost." His words slowed as the crown tightened to his brow. "We may still have… need of… her."

Lost in the meditative trance of the naether crown, Lucas's motions slowed to a crawl, and then froze, his mouth hanging open at an undignified angle. Elsa sighed, walked to the old man and pushed his jaw shut with a clap. Then she gathered some food from her bag, slung her sword belt over one shoulder, and went to find the huntress.

Gwen wandered a moonlit trail that led from the clearing to a small brook, and from there to a scattering of hovels that must have been where the dead wardens had lived. The contents of the fire pit had been spread out, and their provisions placed outside the tiny huts, offerings to the wilderness. Something had gotten into the bread, but several racks of meat were still lying in the dust. Gwen foraged a candle and set it on a stone, then gathered up what was left of the food.

"Do they always leave their food out like that?" Elsa asked. She came into the small clearing without preamble, surprisingly quiet despite her armor.

"No, but they knew where they were going." Gwen brought a skin out from one of the huts, brushed the leaves from the meat, and wrapped it up. "They knew they wouldn't need it anymore. They broke up the fire to keep it from spreading, offered their food to the gods and mice, and went off to die."

"Hmm." Elsa toed a haunch of lamb that hadn't escaped some animal's attention. "Always thought they were a bunch of vegetarians. I didn't think they could bring themselves to kill their little totems."

"Are vegetables any less alive than us?"

"I've never gotten into a fight with a cabbage," Elsa said. "Or a conversation, for that matter." She sat on one of the stones that made up the fire pit, then drew the embers together and with a gesture kindled them to a steady ruby glow. The fire lingered in the woman's hand for just a heartbeat, and she winced. The tracery of her veins pulsed bright and then faded.

"Does that hurt?" Gwen asked.

"Only a little, but it's the small pains that sneak up on you. I have meditations to get me through battle, or to ease the ache after a large casting. These small things, though…" She shrugged. "You just deal with them."

"It doesn't make you wonder about Strife? A goddess that burns you alive to harness her power?"

"Everything has a cost. You can't tell me that the wardens back there died peacefully," Elsa said.

"They looked peaceful, at least," Gwen said, looking in the direction of the hallow. She sat opposite the vow knight. "Why are you here?"

"Looking after the old man. Doing my duty to church and creed."

"Not that. Why are you sitting across from me?" Gwen asked. "Why did you follow me? I don't know a better way of telling you that I want to be left alone."

"Ah, the frair asked me to make sure you're safe, and I thought you might be hungry." Elsa took some of the cheese from her bag and unwrapped it. She gestured toward the wrapped meat that Gwen had salvaged. "Unless you'd rather share your meal with the rats."

"Not rats. Wolves, probably, or fox," Gwen said. She laid some game between them, took the offered cheese, and broke it up in her hands. "I'm serious with that question. Strife demands a lot from her followers. Cinder more. Does that seem right to you?"

"She gives in accordance with what she asks. In the greater sense, she gives to all, and asks only from a few," Elsa said. "The sun and summer are for everyone, without cost. If she didn't give to us freely, if the light of the sun only came to those who worshipped her, for example, then our worship wouldn't be honest. Strife wants our love, but she doesn't want to hold us hostage for it."

"And how does that fit in with your power? I've seen your scars. You're burning from the inside out."

"From the bones and my blood," Elsa agreed, "but that isn't truly a cost. Our bodies simply weren't made to contain Strife's glory. A torch can't give any light without giving of itself, yet we never consider the torch's sacrifice. We're just grateful for the light."

"You're more than pitch and wood," Gwen muttered.

"That sounds dangerously like sympathy," Elsa said. "I am a torch—I'm a supplicant, and my god is fire. That is the way of my life."

"The cost seems high, that's all. I don't know how you can trust a god who asks so much."

"Oh, and what of you? Do the gheists seem worthy of praise and prayer? They roam the wilderness like mad animals, tearing villages apart, destroying crops, breaking lives, and haunting the dreams of the innocent. That's a worship I would question."

"It wasn't always that way. We lived at peace with the spirits. They brought us crops, kept us safe in the forests. Our cities never had walls, because we didn't need them. Not until you lot came north."

"Even at their best, the gods of the old ways were fickle. Your stories are full of gheists gone feral, monsters that wrecked mead halls, gods who had to be killed by heroes. Your first named tribesman earned his throne that way, didn't he? Drugal the Godslayer. Isn't that what they call him?"

"It is," Gwen allowed, "but those instances were rare. That's why they're worthy of legends and thrones."

"Not so rare now, Huntress," the vow knight said. "Look, the truth is that no matter what you do or where you pray, the gheists cannot be tamed. You can only ward against them. Kill them, if need be. Worship will get you nowhere."

A strange breeze moved through the clearing. The flames of Elsa's fire guttered, though the candle didn't flicker.

Gwen chuckled.

"You should remember where you are before you say that sort of thing," she said. "The forest has a way of remembering."

"This forest will remember me," Elsa muttered, "one way or another."

"And that sounds dangerously like a threat," Gwen said quietly. "So let's move the conversation. What of the old man? He seems good enough, but even you have to admit that his god is little more than holy murder."

"Cinder is difficult," Elsa admitted. "So is winter, and if we're discussing sacrifice, his was the first and greatest. The world couldn't survive under the gaze of two suns, and so he quenched himself and rose to rule the night and the cold. It was the right choice, but it was the difficult choice. He asks nothing less of his servants."

"But to worship winter… it's a season to be survived, a sickness of weather that leaves the world barren."

"Any farmer will tell you that the barren season is important. An eternal harvest would suck the life from the soil as sure as any blight. And we need time to stop, to rest, to reflect on what has been and what is to come." She picked off the last meat and tossed the bone into the fire. "You won't hear this from a servant of Strife all that often, but winter is both necessary and vital."

"What about those who die, of sickness or starvation? What would they hear from you?"

"Pity, and the promise of spring," Elsa said. "In this life or another."

"It just seems that there should be a better way. A life without sickness, or a world without winter." Gwen stood and looked around the tiny encampment. The sheer domesticity of it struck her, the simple things that marked this place as a home—the decoration of a wall, or an idly discarded object. These people were dead and gone, and their things had been left for the wilderness to reclaim. "The gods use us harshly, if they use us at all."

"You are making a simple mistake," Elsa said. She stared down into the fire, and her voice was surprisingly gentle. "You are trying to understand. Our gods are fire, and the mad wilderness, and harsh death. We are not meant to understand." She stood and brushed off her legs. "Not knowing is part of the bargain. Not knowing is acceptable."

"I'm not comfortable with that. I would rather know. I would rather..." Her voice trailed off.

Something changed. A ripple went across the sky, unseen yet deeply felt. The candle snuffed out, and the flames in the pit flared and then turned to smoke.

"What was that?" the vow knight whispered.

A keening sound went up far behind them, coming from the direction of the river. It sounded like a dirge, the song a river would sing if water was dying. It was followed by a terrible roar, and then silence.

"Something has... something has fallen. Not the wards, but..." Gwen paused, and a hammer fell against her heart. "Something at home. Something with the shrine at the Fen Gate. The god is stirring."

"Which god?" Elsa asked.

"The one who hides. The one I protect." And then Gwen was off through the woods, trees whipping against her face, and fear, terrible fear clutching at her heart.

46

ALLAISTER STOOD AT the edge of the madness and seethed. The rest of the shadow priests cowered in a semicircle behind him. Blood was still fresh on his knife and Frair Abreau's body splayed at his feet, entrails hanging in profane disorder, the scrying of the dead priest's heart baffled by the pagan wards. Allaister turned slowly to his followers and sneered.

"Are any purer of heart than dear Abreau? Speak now, or find yourself volunteered."

The others shuffled among themselves, talking and pinching at shoulders with fingers gone stiff from fear, before Frair Galdt stood forward. She bowed her head to the ground, careful to not look at Abreau's ravaged body.

"The frair was good and holy, and honest to reason. He was gifted of Cinder. No man's blood could be any purer than his," she said.

"Then what of any woman's blood?" Allaister asked. Galdt slid back among her fellows. Allaister shook his head and sighed.

They were a feeble bunch, and dwindling rapidly. His dozen had become five. Allaister had picked them himself from the hosts of Heartsbridge and Cinderfell, young priests primed for zealotry and just loose enough in their theology to be guided. The problem with youth was its proximity to life, and living. They had been unfamiliar with the scrying ritual Allaister demanded, as well they should be, as it was heretical and profane and drawn from tomes so old they preceded the church itself.

Still they had submitted, time and time again. So now their group was diminished, and the wisest of them flinched whenever Allaister drew near. It was a pity. He had once had such hope for them. Or at least, such hope for the power they might provide.

"Enough for today," Allaister said, wiping the blade on a cloth and sheathing it. "Secure our surroundings. Determine Cinder's stance in the sky, then sing your songs and get some rest. We will begin afresh tomorrow."

They scuttled away, two going back to their tents, the other three to the ring of darkstone pillars that surrounded the camp, none larger than a loaf of bread. They had penetrated the wards as far as they could and established this small area of holy ground. The world beyond was madness, the sky cycling through seasons, the forest itself shifting and dripping with profane light, so they had to base their evening prayers on almanacs, determining Cinder's position in the heavens with ink and abacus, a dry progression for a reasonable god.

Without some sign from the gods or a bit of luck, they would go no further.

Allaister turned back to the darkstone pillars. There, between the shimmering trees, just beyond the ridgeline where they camped, he could make out a glitter of water. Water was often used as a boundary for holy spaces in the pagan way. The ancient witches would dribble it around a house before blessing it, or dig a trench and fill it before resting their heads in a foreign land. The oldest henges were built by rivers, the spirit-benders changing the course of the current to surround the holy places.

It was an old practice, familiar to Allaister only by written word and story, not even observed by the common pagans his brothers in the inquisition rooted out of villages in the north. A practice that had been forgotten, or perhaps a practice so holy it had been hidden, buried so deep that even the modern worshippers had lost it.

Allaister knew he was close.

He returned to the center of the camp and assumed a pose of meditation. There was a hollowness in his soul, the place that had been occupied by the god he had summoned in Gardengerry, a brittleness that he was anxious to heal. Being surrounded by pagan wards wasn't easing the process. The gheists that shivered among the trees could sense something in him, something familiar yet foreign. They hungered for him.

The blurring of borders that came with sleep had softened his defenses. Allaister's dreams were filled with yawning gods of the forest. A darkness stalked him, a figure that wore a wicker mask, half covered in fresh buds and tender flowers of pink and white and red, the other half dry, leaves yellowed with autumn as it surrendered to winter's embrace. The figure beckoned to him with hands tipped in bony talons, her breast smeared with blood and dirt.

So Allaister stopped sleeping. He spent the night in contemplation of the winter god, dreaming the judgment he would pass against the north and their feral deities, and the power he would wield once he bent the hallow of autumn to his will.

Something stirred in the darkness. At first, Allaister thought it was the wicker-masked woman. His eyes snapped open. The other priests went about their business, trying their best to avoid him. The world beyond the wards shimmered as it always had. Allaister began to think that he had just drifted into dangerous slumber, and was about to stand when the stirring came again.

Beyond the wards the world moved. It tensed, and as it relaxed the trees seemed to settle into their natural order. Allaister had a moment of clarity. He saw the sky as it really was, stars holding steady beneath the light of the harvester's moon. He ran to the nearest priest, bent over the fragile pages of an almanac.

"What do you read!" he barked. "What is Cinder's phase?" The man cowered away, holding the almanac up, using it to shield his face.

Faith has failed this one, Allaister thought. *He will be the next to give his blood to the rites.* Snatching the book from the man's trembling hands, Allaister made his own reading.

"Shroud descending, Hearts open..." His finger ran along the charts. He realized he was shaking. A smile crossed his face as he found the appropriate entry. "Third of harvesting." He leaned back from the book, turning his face to the sky. The other priests watched in fear. "Third of harvesting," he repeated, then laughed and tossed the book aside. Drawing his dagger he pointed up at the moon. "That, my friends, is the third of harvesting. The sky stands true. Gather your staffs and your faith. The wards have fallen."

While the wards had fallen, the river remained. As he

and his fellow priests approached it, Allaister could see that it was no natural river. In either direction there was a furious current, whitecaps churning over rocks, the banks swollen and fast, but at the place where the shadow priests approached, the water was still. Calm. The river was waiting for them.

"The water is deep and cold, brother," Frair Galdt said. "If this is to be our path, we must find a ford. Perhaps farther upriver?"

"We will cross here," Allaister said carefully. "Lead us, Frair Galdt."

Galdt hesitated, looking first to Allaister, then the other priests who had lined up along the bank. Finally she approached the bank.

"I can't see the bottom," she said.

"It's dark. Let the light of Cinder guide you," Allaister answered. "Or your faith, whichever is greater."

The woman steeled her nerves, then set foot in the water. The rough waters quashed any ripples that carried from her entrance. Galdt was hardly a stride in when the guardian came for her.

The water swelled, as though a fountain formed at its center, and yet the bulge slid smoothly across the surface, directly toward Frair Galdt. The priest gave a shout, but before she could back out, the tide surrounded her and dragged her down. The other priests—all but Allaister—backed quickly away from the banks. Galdt's screams were short and furious, then she disappeared beneath the waves.

"Another gheist," one of the priests whispered, then he turned to Allaister. "Is this the god we seek?"

"No," Allaister said, "but it is the god we will take."

The bulge returned. The dark waters cleared, and a pillar of churning river loomed over the group. Frair

Galdt hung limp in the center of the column, rotating slightly until she faced Frair Allaister. Her skin was doughy and soft, her eyes blank and unseeing, and her mouth hung open. The river shimmered, the column of water flexed, and a spray of mist cascaded off. Inside, the pressure of the column shattered Galdt's bones in a dozen places.

One of the priests stumbled away and began retching.

Allaister nodded.

"God of the river," he said. "I welcome you to this earth. I welcome you to the world of blood and light." He slowly started to disrobe, shrugging free of his cloak, his tunic, slipping his baldric to the ground. "Accept this sacrifice, and be welcome." He stood naked in the moonlight, a blade clutched in his right hand. Across his body were the ancient sigils of a forgotten faith.

The pillar of water churned silently. Galdt's broken body slipped from where it was suspended, disappearing from sight, only to bob to the surface downriver. Her limbs twisted limply in the current. The cascades of mist fell from the column, until a woman of currents and whitecaps stood before Allaister.

He raised arms stitched in runes and the symbols of water, fire, stone, and sky. Then he drew the knife across his palm.

"Welcome," he hissed, "and be bound."

47

THE BLACK WALLS of the Fen Gate were torch-lit and streaming with blood. A massive Suhdrin army, its banners bristling in the fey half-light of thousands of torches, churned chaotically on the fields before the castle's gate.

There was chaos in the ranks, but the only sounds of battle came from the castle itself. The defenders fought on the parapets and along the wall, clustered in towers, but no flights of arrows traveled from there to the ground.

"What is happening here?" Cahl asked. He, Fianna, and Ian had left most of the pagan rangers behind, moving as much through the everealm as the earth in order to travel unseen. They huddled among the close trees of a copse, from which they could watch Fenton unobserved.

"The Suhdra must have breached the walls," Ian said, "though I see no siege weapons, no ladders... some treachery, then—but why doesn't their army press the advantage?"

"The gate still holds," Fianna noted.

"Yes, but the sally gate is broken open. A narrow portal, but one that could be exploited."

"Whose banner flies at the gate?" Cahl asked.

Ian squinted down into the darkness.

"Roard," he grunted. "They hold a line around the sally gate. It's odd," he said with a smile, "but encouraging. If Roard has turned against Halverdt's crusade, there may be others."

"I will not stand with any Suhdrin heathens," Cahl spat. "It's bitter medicine enough to usher the son of the hound through the forests as if he was a lord."

"He *is* a lord," Fianna said quietly, "and he is the true hound." She turned to Ian and raised her brows. "Will you fight your way in?"

"I was hoping you would... you know." Ian shrugged and made a flittering motion with his fingers.

"You want us to spell you in?" Cahl asked with disgust. "So you can run to your father and get back to your prayers?"

"You're the one who said it was an omen," Ian countered. "The hound and all. I'm just doing what the hound has asked of me."

"You do not yet know what the hound asks you to do," Fianna said. "Merely where he asks you to be." Then she turned back to the castle. "However, your faith is enough for me. Cahl?"

"I will not fight," the shaman warned.

"If the wards are as I suspect, the effort of getting us there will be great. You won't have the strength to fight, even if you have the will."

"Whatever we're doing, we need to be quick about it," Ian said. He pointed down the bluff at a small contingent of archers moving in their direction. "They mean to take the hill, in case this becomes a war."

"Very well," Cahl said. He slid down the bluff a short distance, out of sight of the Suhdrin armies below. "The Fen Gate is one of stone, yes?"

"Stone and old iron," Fianna answered. "A gate without blood or fire."

"Stone is friend to water," Cahl said expectantly.

"They have barred the way of water," Fianna said quietly. She peered down at the castle, a touch of wistfulness in her voice. "Gods know why."

"Then I must channel this alone," Cahl said. "The effort may be beyond me."

"The gods ask much, brother."

Cahl didn't answer, but crouched in the middle of the bluff, his palms flat against the rocky surface. He breathed deeply, rhythmically, drawing his shoulders up with each breath, pressing down with each exhalation. Pebbles on the surface of the stone began to rattle with each breath, drawing closer to the shaman, then sliding away. Cahl opened his mouth, and his voice reached into the earth. The bluff blistered under Cahl's feet. Fianna took Ian's shoulder.

"There will be no peace after this," she warned.

"There never was peace," Ian answered.

The witch nodded, and then the two of them stepped forward and took hold of Cahl's shoulders. The result was instant. Ian had the sensation of weight, unimaginable weight, crushing into his lungs and bones, slithering through his flesh like iron snakes, as though his blood had gone solid. The only sound he could hear was Cahl's breathing, heavy and even, sawing through his skull.

Then he spat out the air he had been holding in his lungs and drew in a panicked, painful breath. He stood up and put his hand against the grit of a wall. There was something wet, and still warm. Everything was darkness.

"Where are we?" he asked.

"Beneath," Fianna answered. "Something has happened."

"Such strength," Cahl muttered. The shaman's voice came from the floor. Ian heard him slump over, his flesh slapping limply against stone. "There is a body."

"Yes, I can smell it," Fianna answered. "There should be candles."

Ian felt along the wall, his fingers trailing over spots of something soft and sticky, until he found a candle in a niche in the wall. The wax was warm and soft in his hands. There was a flint and taper next to it. It took several strikes to get the oil-soaked taper burning, but once it was going he was quick to get the candle lit and the taper extinguished. In those brief moments of dim light, Ian had the impression of blood along the stones, and something dark at the center of the room.

He wished they had remained in darkness. A woman lay on her side. She had been opened... no... she had been *unpacked*. Much of her was scattered throughout the room, her lesser organs joined by lines of blackened blood.

Ian leaned against the wall and retched. Cahl watched from his place on the floor, his pale eyes flickering with amusement and anger.

"Witch Maeve," Fianna said, ignoring both the gore and Ian's distemper. "I thought her elsewhere. The secrets we keep from ourselves, eh, Cahl?"

"What has been done here?" Ian muttered, stopping between words to spit the bile from his mouth. "Who would do such a thing?"

"This is the shrine of the autumn hallow," Fianna said quickly, looking around the room, tracing the path of organs, the trails of blood. "It has been made... profane. Broken." Her voice was anxious, as though she had trouble believing what she saw. "I didn't think he had the power."

"Who had?" Ian asked. "What power?"

"The power to expose the hallow," Fianna answered. "The wards will be down. The high inquisitor will be traveling there now. We must go up. Find your father."

"We should have gone to the hallow," Cahl whispered. His face was getting paler, his words weaker. "We should not have been pampering this pup."

"I have made my decisions, Cahl of Storms. I will stand with them. Can you walk?" The shaman only shook his head, settling against the wall. "Then we must leave you. If the guards find you, let them take you. There must be no more blood in this place."

"Does Adair send guards even here?" he asked. "Go. I will greet the baron in your name, Ian Blakley. Perhaps that will stay his hand."

"Come on," Fianna said sharply, taking Ian by the shoulder. He looked back at the shaman as she hustled him up the stairs.

Soon there was no more light. The ascent continued for a long time. The smell of burned blood followed them. The pair stumbled through the darkness, and Fianna often had to stop to correct Ian's footing or to drag him to his feet. After a time, the way ahead turned into gray, and then there was light. They came out in the crypts.

"I've been here. This is just beneath the kitchens," Ian said. They could hear fighting ahead. "More bodies."

"Yes," Fianna said, ignoring the dead. She rushed Ian forward. "The danger is not here, or at least the danger here is not for us."

Ian wasn't sure what she meant by that, but he

drew his sword. The kitchens were empty, but there was fighting in the courtyard beyond. Peering into the chaos, Ian could make out his father, sword flashing, standing with a group of mixed Tenerran and Suhdrin knights. They faced a smaller group of Suhdrin spearmen, and more Suhdrin attackers were gathered at the gatehouse, apparently trying to let the army inside.

Ian surged forward, only to be caught by Fianna's iron-hard fingers.

"Not yet," she hissed. "Dressed as you are, they will cut you down. Let the fighting calm."

"I came to stand with my father. Now that I'm here, I will not watch him be cut down," Ian said. He pulled free from the witch and started to make his way to where Malcolm Blakley was fighting.

The courtyard had seen much fighting. It looked as though some force had thrown open the sally gate, breaking the smaller door and letting this group of Suhdrin knights into the courtyard. They must have been prepared for the opportunity, though why the rest of the Suhdrin army had not followed was a mystery. Perhaps the Roards truly were holding the gate for Blakley. There might still be hope in the house of Stormwatch.

Still, the Tenerrans were holding out. He was nearly to his father when something caught his eye. A familiar dress, torn and bloody. There among the broken spears and fallen knights, Sorcha Blakley was sleeping as the dead. Her face was pale, and blood leaked through the rings of her mail.

Ian rushed to his mother's side, throwing the litter of battle away from her and trying to make her comfortable. All he could hear was the pounding of blood in his ears as the panic of seeing his mother, dying at his feet, burned through his veins. His breathing became panicked.

Fianna put a hand on his shoulder.

"So," she said quietly, "this is why I'm here."

"Can you save her?" Ian asked.

"Gods will it," Fianna said. She fumbled a handful of stones out of her robes and slowly worked open Sorcha's hand, placing one stone in her palm and folding her fingers over it. Then she moved to the other hand.

Impatiently Ian took the stones and pulled his mother's fingers apart. She was holding a small pendant, the edge of it bloodying her palm. He plucked it up and held it to the sky.

"Something my father gave her," he muttered.

"Sweet," Fianna said, "but she's still dying."

Ian grunted, then pocketed the trinket and finished helping Fianna with her preparations. While the battle continued perilously nearby, smooth river stones went in Sorcha's hands, at her feet, and a final one in her mouth. When they were ready, Fianna drew herself to a kneeling position and placed her hands flat against the ground.

"What are you going to do?" Ian asked.

"Ask the river for a favor. For her life."

"There's no river here," Ian said.

"No, but there was."

Fianna closed her eyes and began to sing, low and quiet, her voice carrying eerily through the courtyard. Ian sat back, unwilling to leave his mother's side, but afraid of interfering in the witch's magic. Her song twisted through the air, avoiding the chaos of sound from the fight, joining the natural songs of wind and forest, the quiet hum of earth and stone. Slowly, almost imperceptibly, another song joined them—the heavy, swollen thrum of deep water.

The river came from Sorcha's heart. The blood leaking through her armor mingling with water, and then she was crying. Her eyes fluttered open and pure, clean water flowed out, as though her pupils were fountains and her veins their spring. Water swelled out of her mouth, a pool at first that overflowed, then washed over her face as a clear mask.

Her wound, as well, became a slow fountain—then an inky blackness tore loose from her chest, an oily stain that swirled in the fountain then washed away. In its wake the stream glittered as it babbled over her armor, cleaning the blood and forming a pool around her. That pool grew ever larger until Ian and Fianna both were kneeling in it.

Sorcha blinked and looked around. She tried to speak, but water continued to pour from her mouth. Her eyes fell on her son, and she reached out to him. Ian smiled, leaned forward and brushed her fingers with his.

"What the hell are you doing to my wife?"

Malcolm Blakley stood at the edge of the pool, several knights at his side, the shimmering blackness of his feyiron sword in his hands.

Ian stood.

"Father, she was dying. Fianna is—"

"Ian? Gods be good, you live! What are you doing here?" Malcolm blinked in wonder, his mouth hanging open. Then he looked at the woman still kneeling beside Sorcha, and his eyes hardened. "Get the witch away from her."

"Father, Fianna is saving her," Ian protested. "Mother was dying! Fianna brought me here, helped me get inside, saved my own life—"

"Enough. I have watched my friends die and my land torn apart for fear of these people. I have learned the meaning of betrayal, and paid for another man's heresy. The celestriarch will find only faith in my heart, should he bother to look for it. These pagans have destroyed one house of Tener—I won't have one infecting the woman I love." He turned to a rough-looking knight and nodded toward Fianna. "Arrest the witch. Then have my wife borne into the keep and kept safe until the walls are secured. There are still faithful priests to be found in the north. Bring me one."

"And if she dies?" Ian shouted.

"Then she will be buried," Malcolm spat. "Either way, we'll need a priest." Sir Brennan drew his sword and splashed through the pool. Ian moved to intercept him.

"No," Fianna said to him. "The knight has lost too much today. Leave him his life."

"They can't just take you like this!"

"They can," Fianna said. "They have." She stood and walked toward Brennan. The fountain of water coming from Sorcha stopped. The pool became still, then rapidly disappeared into the muddy stones of the courtyard. Ian's mother lay gasping in the dirt, her eyes wide and white with terror.

Brennan led Fianna back toward the dungeon. Two of the knights lifted Sorcha Blakley and headed toward the keep. Malcolm watched them go, then turned to his son.

"The high inquisitor has betrayed us, and possibly Lord Adair, as well, though his trial belongs to the church." He stared warily at his son. "I thought to be glad, if ever I set eyes on you again this side of the quiet. But instead I find you dressed as a savage, and in the company of a witch. What do you mean, coming to me this way?"

"Sacombre must be stopped. He did something... something awful. In the tombs below the castle," Ian said. "Let me fight with you. Let me avenge what was done to my mother."

"No," Malcolm replied. "You came here in pagan garb, in the company of a witch and moon knows what else. When the story of this battle travels south, it will be a story of Tenerran faith in the face of the inquisition's corrupt persecution. I will not have that tainted by your presence."

"That witch saved my life!"

"Better to have died faithful," Malcolm snapped. "For both of us. The river should have taken you, if this is what you were to become."

"How can you—"

"Stop! We can discuss this later, after this witch has been properly dealt with, by the true inquisition."

"Father, if you reject me now, you reject me forever. I won't turn my back on these people, just because they were foolish enough to help you."

"Then be gone before I return. I won't suffer your mother's wrath for putting my own son on trial for heresy. Leave now. I have a castle to secure."

Ian stood dumbfounded while Malcolm called his knights and marched away. The knights circled quickly around Ian—he recognized many of their faces, faithful knights like Sir Baird and Sir Drugh, dukes like Rudaine, and a rough youth who must have been a MaeHerron. They were few enough, and they looked down at Ian with a mix of spite and pity.

Then they turned and followed Malcolm, leaving him behind.

48

SUDDENLY THE GATE boomed open, and a cheer went up from outside. The Suhdrin army was upon them.

A line of yellow cloaks formed, their backs to the courtyard as the men of Roard defended the sally gate against their own countrymen. At their center, riding a charger of dirty mud, was Martin, holding aloft the banner of Stormwatch and rallying his men. He glanced back at the unexpectedly open main gate. His face flashed irritation, then determination. He wheeled around to face it.

"We must hold the main gate!" he shouted. "Men of Stormwatch! Hold!"

The courtyard quickly became a maelstrom of confused steel. Soldiers of Adair and Blakley went rushing around, trying to organize the defense. Malcolm had disappeared into the castle. Ian grabbed the moment.

"The hound! The hallow!" he yelled. The cheer was taken up in small groups around the courtyard. Slowly, a force began to gather around him. He took up a sword that had been dropped in the trample, and a shield as well.

"They have brought their swords to our gate, but not honestly. They have taken our walls, but not with blood or honor! Men of Blakley, of Adair. Men of Tener—Roard, Jaerdin, MaeHerron! Much has divided us!" More and more were coming to his side, until a copse of spears bristled at his command. Ian waved his sword in the air. "Yet let this join us. Let us find our bond in battle—fight our way to brotherhood, to clan, to tribe and house and honor! Let them remember our blood in Heartsbridge, and honor our deaths at the highest henge. Let us fight, for the gods!"

A cheer went up, and he lunged toward the breached gate.

The army of bonded Tenumbra followed him.

Malcolm heard the gate boom open, and the shout that followed from the Suhdrin massed on the approach. The knights at his side hesitated.

"Get her inside," he said urgently, pushing Sorcha's escort forward. "Somewhere secure. Not the family quarters. I have a feeling Halverdt's men will be seeking their revenge."

"The frair's chambers, then," Sir Baird said. "I will guard her with my life."

"Bless you, sir." He laid a hand on Sorcha's shoulder. Her eyes were closed and her breathing gentle, but a steady course of water streamed out of her mouth and down her cheeks. He couldn't believe that she still lived.

What had the witch done to her?

He turned. "The rest of you, follow me." Then he started toward the courtyard.

The ground in front of the gate was a churned mass of the dead and dying. The thin line that House Roard had won on the approach was clogged with their fallen.

Ian and his companions charged across this ground heedlessly, trampling anything in their path. They crossed the line of yellow-cloaked soldiers and crashed into the Suhdrin forces beyond. The spearmen of Roard fell back to take a much-needed rest and attend to their wounded.

With a fury born of rage, Ian struck the wall of Suhdrin shields. He hammered his buckler into the first face that presented itself, crushing the man's nose guard with the edge of his shield and drawing blood through his eyes. As that one fell, Ian shoved into the gap created by his death, battering aside spears from the deeper ranks.

The Suhdrin forces were so anxious to storm the gate that they were crushing their own lines together, leaving the spears no room to maneuver. He stood in the gap and stabbed out, over and over again, splitting ribs and severing flesh as easily as poking holes in a sheet.

The enemy fell away like wheat beneath the scythe. The Tenerrans at Ian's side pushed forward, widening the breach and reaping the dead. The Suhdrin line peeled open. He pushed and pushed again, driving farther away from the gate.

Then he pushed too far. There were a dozen sworn blades at his side, and then half a dozen, and then three: nameless soldiers of the hound, their colors torn and ragged, their faces desperate as they followed him into the charge. They were surrounded. The Suhdrin force closed around them like fat around a blade.

The four men stood back-to-back.

The man to Ian's left fell. A mace arced out of nowhere, crushing his throat and the first two rows of his ribs, plowing a furrow in his chest and spewing blood from the ruin of his jaw. He was closely followed by the soldier on the right. Ian never saw what killed him, but there was a scream, the sound of bursting flesh, and then a spray of blood that turned the air into red and the taste of iron.

Ian backed up, only to bump solidly into the soldier behind him. The man laughed loudly.

"The moment of our glory, my lord!"

"I will leave the glory for the dead," he replied. "Stay true and we'll—"

A spear tore past Ian's hip from behind. It carried the man's gore on its blade. He felt the body slide down his back, to settle noiselessly at his feet. Then Ian was alone among the blades.

A knight pushed his way through the press. He wore the golden barque of Bassion across his chest and carried a high-hammer crafted to look like a ship's mast, gripping it in both hands. He lifted his visor to reveal a face as red as blood.

"Yield, young Blakley, and we'll give you a heretic's trial," the knight said. The Suhdrin ranks pressed away from him, leaving a clearing around the two men.

"How is that better?"

"You may find redemption under the law of Cinder, and your father may be given the chance to renounce your sins and save his own good name."

"At the cost of suffering a brand down the throat before being drawn and quartered?" Ian shook his head. "I will take the battle, and let the gods judge me."

"As I hoped," the knight answered, then he lowered his visor. He hefted the hammer into both hands, testing its weight. "I declare myself Sir Eduard Leon, sworn to House Bassion and the holies of the Celestial dome. I challenge you to combat, and let the gods be our mercy."

"For certain," Ian said, and he dove forward. His blade skittered off the fine etching of Sir Leon's breastplate, the strike strong enough to push the man back a step.

"Godswind!" Leon howled, claiming the words of his master's house for himself. Then he raised the hammer above his head and swung down. Ian dodged, danced to the side, then was forced to dodge again.

The hammer was too slow to catch Ian as long as he kept moving, but Leon was very adept at its use. Each swing brought it over and around the knight's head, carrying the momentum with it, weaving an endless circle of whistling steel. Ian was hard pressed to stay clear of it, without falling into the mob all around.

The ground they fought across was littered with bodies and discarded weapons, the earth trampled to mud. Ian slipped in the filth and barely rolled aside before Leon's hammer cratered the ground beside his head.

"The hound can dance!" Sir Leon bellowed.

Ian twisted to his feet, kicking at the haft of the hammer and throwing Leon off balance before punching with the forte of his blade into the man's neck. Leon ducked his head just in time, taking the force of the blow on the crown of his helm. It staggered him, but didn't draw blood.

"You have quite a storm in you, Sir Leon," Ian said breathlessly, "but I'm afraid I find it all wind and little worth."

"Lightning need only strike once," Leon answered, shaking his head. He resumed his attack, but there was a wobble to his orbit. The hammer's head kept striking off the ground, crushing the bones of the fallen and digging troughs in the bloody mud.

Ian danced back and then forward, striking hard blows across Leon's chest and the joints of his armor. He had no hope of slashing through the chain links at elbow and neck, but the flesh beneath still bruised, and the joints still stung. It wasn't long before Leon slowed.

"It seems you are all thunder, Sir Leon," Ian gasped, smiling through his own exhaustion. "Have the gods let the wind drop from your sails?"

"Enough!" Leon snapped. Ian dodged forward, planting his feet in the mud just as the arc of Leon's upward swing had begun. Leon stopped the swing abruptly, letting the haft of the hammer slide through his hands. The released weapon slammed into Ian's chest, knocking the wind from his lungs and his body into the mud.

His blade fell away.

Slowly, Sir Leon ambled forward, picking up the hammer and resting the head against Ian's chest. The weight pressed Ian deeper into the mud.

"Enough of this, Blakley," the knight said. "Confess your heresy. Seek the counsel of the gods."

"The gods... the gods..." Ian struggled to get air into his voice. The hammer pushed him back. "The gods damn you, Eduard Leon."

"Sharp to the last," Leon said. "Well, your father would be proud." He removed the hammer from Ian's chest and lifted it high over his head. "A death worthy of the Reaverbane's son."

"I think not," Ian said, then he rolled aside. The hammer buried itself into the mud. Ian grabbed the haft and levered himself up, driving his back into Leon's chest. The knight lost his grip, growling as Ian wrestled the weapon from his hands. Before the man could pull away, Ian slammed the hammer's head into his shoulder—only a short, sharp swing that dented armor, but couldn't break the bones beneath.

Still, the arm hung nerveless.

Ian drew a blade from his belt, then shoved Sir Leon back and to the ground. The knight landed with a terrible thud, his head snapping back. Ian drew the knife once across the thick leather and chain at the man's neck, his full weight behind the short blade, roughly severing the armor and exposing the flesh.

With the knife in both hands, he stabbed down into the neck, once, twice, over and over until the flesh was a ruin of spouting blood, and the tip of the knife broke against his opponent's spine.

Then Ian stood. He was drenched in the knight's blood. His pagan braids dripped red, the runes on his face were lined in gore, the rough leather of his armor slick and bright. He tossed the knife aside and grinned fiercely at the circle of Suhdrin spears all around.

"The hound," he whispered. "The hallow."

They roared and charged at him, reckless in their fury. He closed his eyes and waited to enter the quiet.

The charge was interrupted by the ranks of Roard faithful. The sound of battle erupted around him, and Ian opened his eyes again to see yellow cloaks and the flash of blades. He stumbled back. A hand settled on his shoulder, pulling him free of the melee. He looked up into Martin's mud-flecked face.

"Fall back to the castle," Martin said. "Leave some glory for the rest of us."

"Your son fights well, my lord," Sir Doone said. Malcolm grimaced and spat on the floor.

"He fights like an animal," Malcolm replied. "Like a pagan."

Regardless of Malcolm's disapproval, however, Ian's attack had cleared the space around the gate and broken the brunt of the Suhdrin assault. However the group of Suhdrin fighters that had snuck through the sally gate and broken into the gatehouse was still there. The gatehouse was isolated from the rest of the castle defenses, a tower with its own arrow-slits and heavy door, so that if the walls were scaled the defenders of the gate would be able to hold the gate and keep the courtyard from being flooded. In this case, however, this design worked against the defenders. Now that the gate was open, the small group that had gained the gatehouse was able to repel the defenders who were trying to reclose the portcullis. Cut off from any support, they barricaded themselves inside, and had crossbowmen among their ranks.

"Sir Doone, gather a small group of hard men. Keep eyes on the walls and the sally gate. We don't want to thin our ranks along the perimeter, but I need a number of good swords at my side."

"I can be blade enough, my lord. They're only Suhdrins," she said.

"I like your faith, but I lack it, as well. No more than a dozen should do—and a wagon."

"A wagon, my lord?"

"Yes, with high sides and fine walls. The baron should have something appropriate in his stables. And have them fill it with hay."

"Are we seeking to escape?" Doone asked sharply.

"No. I want only to reclaim the gatehouse."

Sir Doone nodded and disappeared into the press. Ranks of Tenerran soldiers milled about the courtyard. Malcolm sent them to the walls and to defend the lesser gates. He organized a patrol to search the corridors and chambers, as well. There were tales of shadow priests among the stones. He wanted them flushed into the open, if possible.

When Doone returned with her dozen he nodded and led them to the perimeter of shields that surrounded the gatehouse.

"The wagon?" he asked.

"One of Adair's men is bringing it around. Will we need horses?"

"You and I can manage without them." Then there was a sound of wheels on stone. "Ah, here it is."

The crowd behind them parted, and a team of six men pushed a carriage up to the shield wall. In typical Tenerran style it was plain and solid, the only ornamentation an engraving of the Adair arms. But the sides were thick and the leather springs reinforced. The wheels sunk into the mud.

"Well, we may need a hand," Malcolm allowed. He signaled to the men around him. "Back it up a bit. We'll need some speed before we clear the protection of the shield wall."

"You mean to ram the gatehouse?" Doone asked.

"I mean to put those crossbows out of commission," Malcolm answered. "If we can cover the arrow-slits in the door, we can hopefully breach the gate. Now come on."

Together with the men from the stable and Doone's dozen volunteers, they sent the wagon rambling across the courtyard and into the gatehouse. Arrows bristled from its surface, but the dozen men hidden behind escaped unharmed.

As soon as the entrance to the gatehouse was covered, Malcolm called for a torch. The hay stuffed inside the carriage lit quickly, and soon black smoke was rolling up the sides of the gatehouse, choking the occupants.

"They'll be flushed in no time, my lord," one of the dozen said quietly.

"They won't have the time," Malcolm said. "Quickly now!"

With a final heave and under the cover of the smoke, Malcolm shoved the wagon aside just enough to let his dozen men through. He led the way, shield high and sword bare.

Instantly the room beyond was chaos and blood.

49

THE RIVER WAS dying. Whitecaps frothed and roiled onto the banks, and the once calm current had turned into a turbulent chop. Cinder's light was as bright as beaten silver, casting stark shadows and giving everything an otherworldly glow.

The tree line on the hallow side of the river thrashed as if caught in a tornado. Branches whipped against Gwen's face and shoulders, leaving welts on her skin and tearing her tunic. She was glad for the iron of her armor. Stumbling onto the mossy bank, she hefted a spear and scanned the waters for whatever was attacking.

"Don't run off like that," Elsa said from behind. The vow knight had better survived the trip through the trees, but the metal of her armor was scratched, and her tabard was nearly shredded. The remnants of an invocation whispered over her head in an aura of flame. "I thought the wards were down?"

"They are, but the gheists remain—and something is trying to kill them."

"What? I don't see... Oh." Elsa's eyes went wide, and she shifted along the bank, pushing herself between Gwen and the surging waters.

What remained of the guardian gheist was plowing toward them, an amorphous humanoid blob that vaguely resembled a woman, foam and mist cascading off it in sheets of black, infected water. Bound to the fallen god was Frair Allaister Finney. He hung in the center of it, a dagger limp in his hands. Blood leaked from his palms, blood that swirled through the gheist in a veinwork of corruption. He was naked under the water, his body stitched in strange tattoos and blood.

"The Glimmerglen…" Gwen said. "We can't let her fall. We can't let that bastard corrupt her. She can't die like this, not after standing guard for so long."

"Gheists can't die," Elsa said. The vow knight was prowling the bank, testing the grip on her blade and preparing for the fight. "Kill them and they reform in the everealm. I've dealt with my share."

"They can die *here*. Anything can die here. We're too close to the everealm."

"You expect me to wade out into that?" Elsa asked, gesturing to the surging froth.

"I expect you to get out of the way," Gwen snapped. She pushed the knight aside and ran toward the bank, heaving her spear back and letting fly. The spiraling head of the shaft arced over the water and landed with a satisfying crunch against the gheist that rode Allaister. The bloodwrought tip tore into watery flesh, ripping through it.

The gheist flinched, then raised its terrible head and scanned the bank. When it saw Gwen and Elsa, the demon roared with a tortured voice and rushed forward. The river gave one last try at preventing the shadow priest's assault, the fragments of the guardian spirit that remained in the waters binding together to throw up a wall of silent mist. Allaister bulled into it, the mists wrapping around him like a blanket. He slowed, he stumbled, the river strained beneath him.

Then the priest-bound god broke through the barrier. The river burst in a final surge of power, then the whitecaps collapsed, the current slowed, and the river calmed. The Allaister-gheist, withdrawing from the corpse of the fallen god, bellowed its victory.

As the river fell silent, the forest behind them sent up a wail so shrill it threatened to knock Gwen to her knees. The demon hunched forward and continued across the becalmed waters.

Gwen screamed and charged into the water now calm, slow, and shallow. Her boots crunched across a bed of smooth river stone. She drew another spear from her quiver, taking it in both hands and raising it over her head, howling as she ran.

Allaister loomed over her.

She struck. The spear bit into the demon's knee, water-skin tearing and reforming like molasses. Allaister seemed unfazed. He slapped her aside, sending her tumbling through the water, her quiver of spears rattling open, scattering shafts into the current, where they floated away like sticks. The demon reached for her.

Before Gwen could get to her knees Elsa charged forward, invoking the rhythms of the sun and Strife. The heat of Strife's blessing in her blood turned the water to steam at her feet. There was a terrible pressure in the air as she passed, and an intolerable fire. When Elsa brought her sword down on the demon's arm—the arm that was reaching to crush the life from Gwen's body—the sound of the blow echoed like thunder through the valley. The sword severed gheist flesh and sent a great wallop of dead god into the river.

Allaister reeled back, severed arm flapping in the air. The gheist lost form for a moment, its vaguely humanoid shape slipping into a chaotic pillar of water, then Elsa had a brief glimpse of the fallen Glimmerglen, the woman's face startled and angry and alone. At the core of the gheist, Allaister's face twisted in concentration. The body bubbled, sprouted an arm no larger than a child's, then swelled, formed another hand around that one, and then a dozen more in quick succession.

Arms lashed out, a head, the legs split and collapsed and split again. And then the gheist's body was regrown, as whole as it had been before Elsa's blade fell. Allaister smiled in his tomb of water, then crashed the entire gheist down into the river, looking to bury Gwen among the stones.

Gwen was on her feet again, and swung out of the way. A plume of water erupted from the impact, raining on them as they crawled up the bank.

"Cinder and fucking Strife," Elsa swore. The pair of them backed away, seeking dry ground. "This is going to get interesting."

"*Going* to get?"

"Yes, well, the deadly sort of interesting."

Gwen edged along the bank, eyes scanning the water. She fumbled her sword out of her belt—a blade meant for mortal work, for killing men, not fighting the manifest gods of the old religion. The edge wasn't even wrought with her blood.

"My spears are in the river," she snapped. "Draw it away, and I can—"

Allaister surged up from the river like a flood, right at her. Whatever else had been taken from the shadow priest, beneath the corrupted waters of the gheist his hatred survived. Elsa danced to intercept him, but managed little more than deflection. Gwen looked back.

They were nearly at the trees.

* * *

"The river's lost," Elsa said. "The shore as well. Go find the frair, if you want to do something other than die needlessly." She swung through a series of counterstrikes and soft ripostes. Allaister struck with the river's force, great concussive slams that cratered earth. It was only the god-touched power of the vow knight's blade that kept her alive.

Elsa's shoulders wrenched with the effort of deflecting the blows. Her blood burned holy and hot. Tiredly, regretfully, she tapped deeper into Strife's blessings. Her veins flooded with molten power. Ashes filled her mouth and her blood.

"With my spears—" Gwen protested.

"RUN!" Elsa howled. Strife's blessing gave her voice the resonance of hammered bells. Gwen ran.

With the child out of the way, Elsa settled into the serious business of not dying. She had given up her holy mission, her vow to protect the godsroads and domas of Tenumbra. Following Frair Lucas all these years had warped her sense of purpose in some ways, but in other ways she carried with her a clarity that she had never known before.

Here and now, that clarity meant she needed to stay alive. The huntress was no match for this demon, and the frair had higher tasks ahead of him. So it was left to Elsa to stand against the madness that Frair Allaister had become—to stand and to fight and perhaps to die.

The flickering giant that contained the shadow priest lurched to shore. Its footsteps created ripples in the smooth pebbles of the beach, waves of piled stone that washed away from it, as though its very presence created shivers in the earth. Whatever injury Elsa had managed to inflict on the demon was already repaired. It towered over her. Allaister hung limply at the demon's heart, like a hooked fish.

It started toward the forest, ignoring her.

"Hey! Godfucker!" she yelled, waving her sword. Glory wicked off her blade, leaving bright shadows in the air. "This is as far as you're going! This is your grave, you bastard!"

The demon paused, head tilted like a curious dog as it regarded the vow knight at its feet. When it spoke, its voice—a grim parody of Allaister's voice—was as dull and hard as a tombstone.

"Precious Elsa. Far from home, aren't you? What will you say to the high inquisitor when he finds you defending a pagan hallow?"

"What will you say when he finds you summoning gheists and binding them to your flesh?" she asked. "It seems to me you have sufficient heresy to answer for!"

"Oh, Sacombre and I have an understanding. A deep understanding, in fact. And you're right not to worry about answering to Lord Cinder," the shadow priest said. "I am all the judge you'll be given." He stepped forward and almost lazily brought his fist down on Elsa's head.

She sidestepped and deflected the strike so that it buried itself deep into the unyielding earth. Though it appeared to be water, the gheist's form was solid enough. Mist sprang up from the hijacked god's wounded arm, a tiny storm that resolved into a vortex of lightning. Sparks arced from the damage, stitching the earth in ash.

"Great gods, but you're a heavy blow," Elsa muttered.

"The river has its own storms, daughter of suns. You will feel their wrath."

The gheist withdrew the limb and swung again, scything through the air like a reaper. Elsa blocked again, and again, each blow shivering through her bones, pushing her back, her feet sliding on stone and mud as though it was ice. She was forced to draw more and more from her vows, pulling Strife's power out of the sun and through her blood, just to keep moving, just to keep fighting, but the pain of the invocation was taking its own toll. The heat from her body crisped the fallen leaves at her feet and withered the living trees behind her. Even the body of the god began to boil. Light the color of molten gold pulsed from her eyes and veins.

"How long can you burn, child?" the gheist taunted.

"Long enough to end you!" Elsa answered, even as she coughed blood and ash. She tried to press the attack, but the demon's defenses were too much. She fell against a tree. The bark sizzled beneath her shoulder.

"You would break yourself to save the gods you curse? How have you fallen so far, daughter of suns? Is this what they taught you at the Lightfort?"

"They taught me to kill mad gods, and you qualify," Elsa said. She slid to the side, whipping her sword beneath the demon's arcing attack and into the writhing flesh of its arm. The wound was closing even before the steel had left it. Elsa spat and crawled back. "Though you're a little more conversational than most."

"I would never claim to be a god, Sir LaFey. Though I am a binder of gods, certainly. A master of the fallen. The first in a new priesthood." Though his eyes were closed and his body seemingly unresponsive, Allaister smiled. "I like the sound of that."

"The first in a new heresy," Elsa said. She was grateful for the rest, but at the same time the divinity burning through her blood wouldn't last much longer. "The last, as well, if Strife has a say."

"We are in a pagan place, among pagan gods," he replied. "The bright lady is far away. She cannot save you, Elsa."

"I don't need saving," she spat, drawing herself up to her full height, the radiant power of the goddess washing off her armor.

"We will see," the demon answered, then he took up the attack once again. His pummeling fists tore through trees and earth like wet rags. "Pray you live long enough to see the error of your faith. Pray you survive to see the wonders we have wrought. Pray you are blessed with our wisdom, and our knowledge, and our power."

"Pray you shut the fuck up," Elsa said, then threw herself at her opponent. Faster than the hulking god, she was able to gain momentary ground, blade flashing like lightning forged from the sun, her face twisted in a rictus of effort and concentration. The spirit that held Allaister at its heart reacted with a mortal's defense, fighting like a priest, trying to keep fists against blade, careful of its body, falling back as Sir LaFey pressed the attack.

And then the god seemed to remember that it was a god, and Elsa only a fool with a death wish. It slammed its whole form into her, cascading like a waterfall, surrendering the pretense of human form, becoming an arc of thunderous water. The blow knocked her sword from her grip, blistering the flesh along her palms. She fell to the ground, breath torn from her lungs and blood full of fire.

The gheist loomed over her and laughed, a sound like hail on stone. When Elsa looked up, her mouth gaping like a fish out of water, she could see the slightest sliver of Allaister's eyes, barely open.

"There will be little left of your prayers soon enough, Sir LaFey," the gheist chuckled. "It's been a good game."

"How do you know her name?" Frair Lucas asked. He appeared at the edge of the trees. The gheist turned to him.

"A daughter of suns, and elder son of moons," Allaister said. "The old war can begin, can it? Will you finish her while I watch, or do we have a debt to settle?"

"You *don't* know her name," Lucas said. "Frair Allaister does, but you don't. Which means there's more of him than you."

"Not for long," the gheist said, then it turned back to Elsa. "If you won't help, then you must watch her end." It raised its fists in the air, ready to strike the life from the vow knight's flesh.

"No," Lucas said, shaking his head. There was a glimmer of darkness in Elsa's eyes, the glowing veins of her face twisting into shadow, and then her body came undone like a knot, blood and bone turning into mist, a skein of darkness that snapped toward Lucas's upturned hand like a falcon called to roost.

The shadows dripped and reformed like wax from a candle, and then Elsa was standing beside the frair, moved by shadow magic and Lucas's will. She bent forward and vomited bile and sparks.

"I fucking hate that," she said.

"You would hate dying more," Lucas said softly. "Go find the child. I will deal with this one."

"It doesn't cut proper," Elsa warned.

"I am not the cutting kind," Lucas said. He gestured toward the depths of the forest. "Fly. Gwen will need you before this is done."

"My place is with you."

"Your vow is to the goddess, and Lady Strife needs you alive. There are more important things to do than die bravely. Now go, before I get angry and force the issue."

Elsa grimaced. Her sword still lay by the gheist's feet, and there was no retrieving it now. She limped into the forest, then stumbled, then broke into a run, bolstered by the glowing remnants of Strife's blessing. The trees trembled at her passing, holiness stinging the air, her falling sun damaging the sanctity of the pagan night.

When she was gone, Lucas turned back to the gheist. The creature started lumbering toward him.

"You do not show your fear, son of moons," the demon rumbled.

"Neither do you, gheist."

"What do I fear from mortal blood, no matter how tainted it is by the ashen god?" the gheist asked. "Do you know the god you face? The futility of winter standing against spring?"

"No," Lucas said. "Do you?"

The two fell together, and the world bent around them.

50

ELSA FOUND THE girl among the wreckage of her hidden hallow, crouching between the cairns of the dead wardens. As she approached, the huntress made as if to bolt, but settled when she saw the vow knight.

The sky was turning into thin pewter, a precursor to dawn.

The night can't be done already, Elsa thought.

"I thought you were dead," Gwen said as she approached.

"Disappointed?"

"No. Just surprised." She twisted herself around into a seated position and looked at Elsa. "Allaister still lives—I can feel his corruption in the air—and you're here. I thought you would fight until he was dead, or you were."

"Frair Lucas stepped in. He sent me to find you."

"Where's your sword?"

"Lost. What are you doing?"

"Preparing," Gwen said, then turned back to the nearest cairn. Elsa came around the edge to watch. With a pin dipped in her own blood, Gwen was scrawling a rune across the stone. The knight looked around and saw that each cairn had a similar rune hidden somewhere on its surface.

"What is this?" she asked.

"Saying goodbye," Gwen answered, "and giving them a quicker path into the everealm. If Allaister gets past your frair, I hesitate to think what he might do to these dead." She leaned back to examine her work, then stood. "I would spare them that horror."

"We should be gathering our strength," Elsa said grimly. "Frair Lucas is paying a heavy price. If we have the ability to save him, we should be about it."

"There is no further defense," Gwen said quietly. "Allaister has crushed the last of the wards, and our only hope of survival is an old inquisitor and a vow knight without a sword. Even if we win," she added, "the best I can hope for is a trial for heresy."

"It's better than dying," Elsa said quietly.

"If you insist."

They fell silent, and the sounds of battle wrenched the air below like thunder in a gorge. Gwen went to the last cairn, drew a line of blood from her palm, then set to work on one of the stones. When she was finished, she stood. Elsa took her by the shoulder and looked her in the eye.

"So you're going to give up?" Elsa asked.

"No," Gwen answered. "I just have a peculiar way of fighting."

"Peculiar indeed. What are you waiting for?"

Again Gwen didn't answer, so Elsa stared up at the sky.

"How is the sun already rising?" she asked.

"Be glad for it," Gwen answered. "Perhaps Strife's ascent will give you the power you need to die with glory."

"That chance has passed," Elsa said. "Besides, I think I'm—"

Gwen grabbed her by the shoulder and dragged her down so that the grass closed over them. Elsa struggled, but Gwen put her lips to the vow knight's ear.

"Quiet," she hissed. "There is something among the trees."

They lay still and listened. Something shuffled past, twenty yards distant, voices speaking in hushed tones. When they were gone, Gwen crouched in the grass and looked around.

Four priests of the winter court were working their way onto the top of the hill in the center of the hallow. They were chanting now, some sort of incantation, the shadows of naetheric icons floating around their heads.

"They're looking for the entrance to the shrine," Gwen whispered.

"I still marvel that Allaister was able to corrupt so many of the faithful with his heresy," Elsa whispered.

"You're lying next to a pagan, sir knight. So you may not be in a position to judge." Gwen eased herself into a kneeling position, staring intently in the direction the priests had gone. When they didn't reappear, she motioned with one hand. "Come on."

"Where are we going?"

"If they mean to find the entrance, I mean to beat them to it."

Gwen scampered down into the woods as quietly as she could manage. Elsa cast a glance up the hill at the trio of priests, then followed suit. When they reached the trees, Gwen slipped off at a run, circling around and climbing the hill to the east until she came to a stone pillar, nestled into the slope as though the earth had washed up to bury its base. Elsa clambered up a few minutes later.

The sounds of the battle could still be heard, even at this distance.

The pillar was gray and soft, the edges worn smooth by erosion. The base was ringed by inscriptions in some forgotten or forbidden language, the letters disappearing when they came to the loam. Elsa knelt beside it, running fingers over the carvings. Gwen stood beside her, staring first at the pillar and then to the east, squinting into the rising sun.

"This is the entrance?" Elsa asked.

"One of them, yes. The one the priests are looking for," Gwen said. Then she crouched down. "They'll find it, eventually."

"Then we'll defend it," Elsa said. "You have a knife. I have the sun."

"And what of Frair Allaister? If he's strong enough to bind the Glimmerglen, he's certainly strong enough to destroy us."

"Leave Allaister to Frair Lucas," Elsa said, grimacing at the distant sounds of battle. She turned sharply to where Gwen knelt. "What now?"

Gwen didn't answer. She tore some grass from the ground and rubbed it between her fingers, greening her skin. This she rubbed on her temples. Then she bent down and tore more grass, smearing more stain over her face.

"Why are you doing that?" Elsa asked.

"Because there's one thing I *can* do, and it will help to have as much of this place on me as I can when I do it."

Elsa plucked a strand of grass and held it up to the sun.

"It looks like grass to me. Do you mean to smear the everealm all over yourself?"

"No, the real world," Gwen said. "Tener. Suhdra. All of Tenumbra. It would be better if I'd brought some soil from outside the hallow, but that's not practical."

"What do you intend to do?" Elsa asked.

Gwen hushed her and knelt. There was a rustling at the top of the hill—the priests had arrived. Concealed behind the pillar, they talked angrily among themselves, then one broke away and hurried down the hill toward them. Then he stopped.

Something else filled the air.

Silence.

There was one sharp, tearing shriek, and then nothing. All of them waited, Elsa and Gwen straining for the sound of Lucas's voice. Nothing happened. The battle was over.

The closer priest laughed, a rolling, bitter sound that carried down the hill and into the trees. He shouted something back to his fellows, then continued toward the pillar.

Elsa gripped Gwen's shoulders.

"What can you do?" she hissed.

"No time to explain. Watch," Gwen whispered. "Stay here, and watch." Then she turned to the pillar and pressed her cheek against the stone. The gritty rock pressed back, then it slid aside like sand. Gwen's face, and then head and shoulders, and finally her entire body disappeared into the smooth, worn surface of the pillar.

Elsa watched, until the stone was smooth and quiet again, and there was nothing to be seen of the huntress of Adair.

"Gods damn it, child," she swore. Then she tore great clumps from the ground and began smearing the cold mud and crushed grass on her face. The dirt stung when it touched the blistering wounds on her cheeks, and she blinked back tears of pain and frustration.

"Gods… fucking… damn," she said, then pressed her face into the pillar and felt her breath and her skull disappear in an endless depth of gritty, stony sand.

51

THE DOOR WAS broken, but three Suhdrin men with shields stood in the way, spears pointing out into the corridor. The dead of Tener lay at their feet. Malcolm knelt at the end of the hallway, a half-dozen men behind him, all waiting for his word. The rest of the gatehouse was secured. Only this final room—and the mechanism that controlled the portcullis—remained.

"What hope do they have of holding out against us?" he muttered.

"They have the stubborn will of doomed men," Sir Doone answered. She had been champing at the bit to put sword to Suhdrin flesh, and when the alarm had sounded, she had been the first to answer. "I will be glad to free them of it."

"In a Tenerran you might call that bravery, Sir Doone," Malcolm answered. "Though it seems like foolishness, either way." The men at the end of the hall shifted their spears. A face peered out from between the shields, pale skin and hair beneath a chain coif, disappearing before Malcolm could react. He raised his voice and addressed them.

"You have no hope of relief," he said. "Surrender, before we fetch the oil, or the dogs."

"Bring your dogs!" a voice answered. "We've

grown fond of killing pagan dogs."

"My lord, we must secure the portcullis before it is too late," Doone growled. "Let me…"

Malcolm gestured for silence.

"Do you know who stands against you?" he called down the hall.

"The heretical gods of the north, and the heathens who grovel at their feet! It is the true gods of Suhdra who stand with us. What do we fear?"

Malcolm sighed, then slowly stood, pulling himself up with the wall, his knees creaking and grinding every inch of the way. He gestured for Doone to hand him her shield, his own lying abandoned by his bed, left behind in the clamor of the alarm.

"No, not heathens," he said, "but true and faithful Celestials. Men and women of Cinder, and of Strife."

"You bleed like pagans. You die like pagans," the voice answered. "And you smell like pagans."

A small chorus of laughter came from the room. As he marched down the corridor Malcolm twisted his grip on the sword, swung the shield to his side.

"Then you must make my acquaintance," he boomed. "I am Malcolm Blakley, duke of Houndhallow, lord of the Darkling March and true heir of the Hunter's throne. But men and gods and a legion of the dead know me as Reaverbane!" He began cutting the air with his sword, letting the sound of its feyiron blade sizzle through the hall. The tip of the blade clattered off of a wall, striking sparks and cutting stone.

"I stood with Tomas Bassion at the defense of Heartsbridge. I fought beside Castian Jaerdin to retake the ports of Galleydeep, as I fight beside him today. At the end of this blade, I have drawn the heart's blood of a great host of enemies, Suhdrin, Tenerran, reaver, and god!"

The men didn't answer, but closed the gaps between their shields and pressed their spears farther into the hallway. Malcolm batted aside the spear tips with disdain, cutting through the ashwood shafts and then kicking the nearest shield. A gap opened, and he thrust his blade into it. Someone screamed, the shield wall slipped more, and then they fell back, drawing swords and trying to make room in the crowded machine room to fight.

"The hound! The hallow!" Sir Doone shouted from the other end of the corridor, and then she and the rest of Malcolm's men rushed around their lord to flood the chamber with their blades, their blood, and their anger.

The Suhdrins in the machine room died quickly. There were only four of them, and all showed signs of having been previously wounded.

"They had no chance," he muttered. "The fools died for no purpose."

"Close the portcullis," Sir Doone yelled, drawing the remaining soldiers to the great windlass and counterweight. Malcolm grabbed her arm.

"Not yet," he said loudly enough that they all could hear, then he ran up the winding stairs to the gatehouse roof. He leaned between the crenels, Doone's shield still in his hand. Arrows rattled off the metal and pricked the stone around him.

On the field below, Roard's tight fist of spears and swords continued their hopeless fight. Malcolm shouted down at them.

"Stormwatch! We have the gate!" He continued

shouting until he got Lorien Roard's attention. The duke of Stormwatch nodded, then called the retreat. His men, Martin among them, fell back into the courtyard. Malcolm returned to the stairs and shouted down into the gatehouse. "Sir Doone, eyes on the murderhole. When the last of Roard's men is inside, drop the iron!"

A handful of breaths passed, and then the windlass and chain released. He could feel the great weight falling beneath his feet, and the portcullis landed with a crash. Outside, the Suhdrin army surged forward, crushing themselves against the iron grate. With the gates still open, it would only hold them for a time.

Malcolm ran to the courtyard side of the roof.

Someone… his son Ian was organizing the defense. He was covered in blood, dried gore flaking around his face as he commanded the men of Blakley and Adair. They were dragging wagons and other barricades in front of the gate, to keep the Suhdrin archers from firing through the grate and turning the courtyard into a killing field. It was the best that could be done, for the moment. Malcolm ran back down into the gatehouse.

"Secure the walls," he snapped at Sir Doone. "Get someone to prepare my mount. We will need to be ready to ride."

"The castle is not secure, my lord," Sir Doone said. She motioned to a page standing in the doorway. The boy was as pale as a ghost. "Priests of Cinder have been seen inside the walls. Inquisitors."

"We do not fight the church, Sir Doone. That is of little concern to us."

"These priests were responsible for breaching our walls and opening the gates," Doone persisted. "They are not acting alone."

"Meaning?" Malcolm asked.

"The high inquisitor is still in the castle—he was seen in the crypts first, and most recently in the great hall. He is using the powers of Cinder against any who oppose him."

"But…" Malcolm looked from the terrified page to Sir Doone. She was red with anger and the fight. "Those powers are meant to defend the realm against gheists. Surely he wouldn't bend them against mortal men?"

"I can only report, my lord," Doone said, "but it would appear that, whether you wish it or not, our fight is with the church."

"Or at least the inquisition," Malcolm muttered. "Fine. Speak with Duke Roard. Offer my thanks."

"Where will you be?"

"In the great hall, apparently," Malcolm said. He handed Sir Doone back her shield, made the sign of sun and moon, and sheathed his feyiron sword. "To speak with High Inquisitor Sacombre."

The battle was still fierce when Colm Adair left his men in the courtyard and rushed to his chambers. Wounds puckered his skin, blood seeping into his robes and matting his hair. Blakley might still retake the gate, but Colm didn't want to take the chance. That, and he had felt Maeve's death. The walls were no longer relevant. The true threat was already inside. His long deception was discovered, his heresy found out.

He moved swiftly around his chambers, hiding the icons. Then he turned to his wife.

"Elspeth," he said, "take Grieg and a blade. You must run."

"Surely not yet?" Elspeth answered. "Blakley will secure the walls."

"The walls are irrelevant. The high inquisitor has made his move. I felt the witch's death in my blood. Our worst fears have been given form." He pushed a pack into her arms, then threw a robe over her and led her to the door. "A servant has prepared Grieg. There is food in that satchel. Make for the hallow, and pray that the wardens can help you."

"Don't be foolish, Colm," Elspeth said. "I'm not going to leave you here. Surely you know that."

"I am not asking, love—you must do as I say. We don't know Gwen's fate, and mine has already been written. That die is cast, and now I must answer for it, but you and Grieg can escape. The secret of autumn must be kept. Go."

"Love..." Elspeth pulled away from Colm's insistent hands, dropped the pack, then turned back to him.

"Quiet," he said. "Quiet. We will meet again, in the everealm or elsewhere, gods be good. Elspeth, don't make this any harder than it is. Go, quickly, before the shadows find you."

She nodded, and they hurried into the corridor beyond. Grieg stood outside his room, a servant at his shoulder. Colm dismissed the woman, who fled down the stairs. The sounds of battle raged in the courtyard below. The portcullis fell with a resounding boom, but that would only buy so much time, and the high inquisitor didn't care about gates and walls, anyway. At the end of the hallway he pulled aside a tapestry of Cinder's ascension to reveal a hidden door. Colm took a deep breath, then turned to face his wife and son one last time.

"Now, bravery. Strength. Remember the iron in your blood," he said, struggling to keep the tremor out of his voice. He tousled his son's hair, pinched his nose. He stood and looked gravely at his wife. "Keep him safe, but keep the knife close, if it becomes necessary."

"How can you ask that of me?"

"You know that the inquisitor can use our lives to scry the location of the hallow. We must not fall to the church," Colm said quietly. "None of us. Better that the hallow be lost than our living blood lead Sacombre to it."

Elspeth blinked back tears, squeezed her husband's shoulder, took her son by the arm, and disappeared into the hidden passage. Colm let out a huge breath, then turned his back on the door and started walking back to his chambers. To prepare to fight.

Then he froze.

The scream from the passageway was sharp and short and full of terror. Grieg never called out, though Colm felt his death as sharply as Elspeth's. A thread in his heart snapped. Something crashed against the walls once, twice, the sound of bones breaking and flesh bursting like soft fruit. Colm stood in the corridor, unable to move, to act.

The door at the end of the hallway creaked open. Sacombre stepped out, wearing the blood of his wife.

"Lord Adair," the high inquisitor whispered. "We must have words before you leave."

"Go to hell," Colm hissed, then drew his sword.

"Hell is for the fallen," Sacombre answered, drifting down the corridor like a gheist. "I am rising. Rising, forever risen, forever…"

The rest of his words were lost as Adair threw himself at the priest. His roar of pain and anger filled the air, only to be lost in the sound of metal breaking as his sword shattered, then his armor.

Colm Adair gave his blood and his soul to avenge his dead. He fell against the walls, his body scattered about the room like leaves in the wind.

52

THE SANCTUM WAS in silence. The ceiling was tiled in bone and root and the jagged underside of stones as old as time itself. The floor was covered in a scattering of dead leaves so dry that Gwen's footsteps turned them to dust. She stood just inside the entrance and took a deep, rusty breath. The air scraped her lungs clean and dry. Jade-green light filled the room, leaking from veins of luminous quartz in the ceiling.

The center of the space was a tomb. There was a cairn of smooth stones, each the size of a fist or larger, piled in subtle patterns of natural order. It rose to the height of Gwen's forehead. Each stone was scribed with one or more runes that swirled from rock to rock, forming a continuous loop of blessings and bindings that served to keep the god in place. Ancient hands had formed these spells, ancient voices spoke the promises that buried the god of autumn under this hill, during the waning days of the crusade.

Gwen placed her hand on the nearest stone. It hummed at her touch, a song that carried through her blood, seized her heart and washed through her brain with honey-sharp beauty. The dead leaves scratched away from her across the floor, as though a gust of wind whipped from her skin.

"Is this what we're meant to be?" Gwen asked the air and the god who rested at her feet. "Have we forgotten too much?"

The stones of the cairn creaked in response. It brought her impatience, not enlightenment. A chill flowed into her skin, numbness she hardly noticed, so caught up in the thrill of communion with the god her family had protected for so long. When it began to sting Gwen snatched her hand away, shaking her fingers warm.

"They've fallen," she said, hoping for some kind of response, some denial. "The wards, the wardens, my family—I'm the last one. This isn't what I wanted. I don't know what their plan was, the wardens, back when they brought you here and sang you down, but this couldn't be it.

"I wanted to keep the secret," she continued. "*Your* secret. But I can't anymore. So tell me what to do. Tell me what the wardens would have done, if they hadn't died."

Nothing. Gwen sighed and began to pace. The carvings on the tomb swirled under her eyes. They were as much story as spell, recounting the names of the god they hid. The dual nature of its identity and season, the transition from summer to winter, the gifts of comfort and bounty given by autumn, along with the warnings of what was to come. The advent of winter and the death of warmth.

"Father never revealed that you were the god of autumn, though it's so obvious now. The fact that the Celestials grow in power at the solstices, die away at the equinox. It never occurred to me that the same sort of pattern would hold for the pagan powers. I see that now." Gwen brushed the flaky residue of a crushed leaf off the cairn, wiping it with her fingers until the grit rubbed into her skin. "But if you're autumn, there must be another. Spring, right? What became of spring?"

The cairn shifted ever so slightly, a realignment of the spiral stacks of stone, more of a flexing than a settling. Gwen nodded.

"You must know," she said. "Dead, I suppose, or maddened. That might even be why they hid you away. Watching your twin fall to the crusade must have been terrifying. I can't imagine. But your history is forgotten to us—even those of us who think ourselves faithful." Gwen finished her circuit of the tomb, returning to the place by the entrance where she had begun. "Faithful. Such a strange word. What is faithful, now?"

She took a knife from her belt. Bloodwrought and wicked, with a blade thin and barbed at the end. She carried it to the hunt, in case her spears failed and the gheists got too close. Her last resort. She held it out over the cairn, her hand shaking.

"Will they find you? Yes. Will I defend you? Until my last breath, with the last scrap of my soul." With her other hand, Gwen began to remove a stone from the cairn. "I'm the last warden, and I can't let them take you."

A small avalanche of pebbles clattered into the room behind her. She whirled around with a stifled cry. The entrance—a stone column as smooth and featureless as a stagnant pond—was crumbling into scree. A hand clawed free, then a shoulder, and finally Sir LaFey tumbled into the room. She fell to the chamber floor and vomited a pile of gravel. She knelt there coughing dust for a moment before looking up at Gwen.

"Tunnels should have doors," she croaked.

"You shouldn't be here," Gwen said.

"The rocks appear to agree," Elsa said. She slowly got to her feet, her hands on her knees as she gathered herself. "Gods, but that was unpleasant."

"I'm serious," Gwen said, an edge of panic to her voice. "I don't know what your presence will do to this place. You're a damned knight of the winter vow! This is a sanctum, it's holy. You could upset the whole balance of—"

"Enough," Elsa said, finally standing to her full height. "You've been to the Celestial dome, you've knelt at the throne and said your prayers in Cinderfell. That didn't kill you, nor did it bring the Celestial church tumbling to the ground. Have some faith."

"You shouldn't be here!" Gwen said again. She took Elsa by the arm and pulled. It was like trying to shift a statue.

Elsa laughed, though her voice was rough and quiet.

"You keep saying that, but what's the worst that could happen?" Elsa said. "I could get killed. So let's get to it, before those priests find their way in here." She turned to face the cairn. "This is the god?"

"This is its tomb," Gwen said, "and its prison."

"So you mean to free it?" Elsa asked, turning a curious eye to Gwen, then looking down at the knife in her hand. "Or something else?"

"I... I hadn't decided... haven't decided. I'm the last of the wardens. After me there's nothing. No last defense, no other help coming, and what Allaister did to the river guardian... I can't let that happen here. Whatever happens, I have to do it. And I'm not sure how much more I can do."

"Well, I'm here," Elsa said, arching an eyebrow. "Lucas is here—I can't believe that bastard has killed him—and there are more, out there. Last I heard, Blakley was fighting a war to keep your family safe."

"For all the good it has done," Gwen sighed.

"Maybe, maybe not, but you're not alone. We may be in a bad spot." Elsa shrugged. "Worse than most, in fact, but you can't give up now."

"I'm not giving up," Gwen said sharply, and she held up the blade. "But this might be the only way forward. Those priests will find their way in, and if they have the same powers as Frair Allaister, they might be able to bend this god to their will."

"Maybe they intend to kill it. So if you go there first, you'll be doing their job for them."

"If that was their intention, why didn't they bring vow knights? Frair Lucas travels with you. The inquisition doesn't act alone against the gheists. Why would they be they acting alone now?"

"Who's to say? Maybe Allaister thought he could handle it on his own. One thing's for certain, though." Elsa reached down and twisted the knife from Gwen's hand, as gently as her strength would allow. "If you kill it now, there's no going back. Sacrifice this god, and so much will fall."

"Odd words coming from a knight of the winter vow," Gwen noted.

"Frair Lucas has shown me things. Taught me things—and so have you. There's a connection between these gods and our land. Suhdra is struggling through terrible times. I can't blame my gods, Gwen, so I must blame yours."

"Or the lack of them," Gwen added. "It's not like Tener is overrun by the pagan faithful."

"The inquisition has seen to that, but there are remnants. People like you, and others, hidden in the forests of the north. Enough to keep the world going, it would appear."

"If this is how you feel, how can you keep hunting them? You were at Gardengerry. You hunted that gheist into the Fen, and helped me kill it."

"They come back. Even at our best, we can't destroy them. The individual manifestations are corrupted by madness, but their essences flow back into the everealm, only to bubble up again somewhere else." Elsa shrugged. "Then I'm forced to hunt down and kill that manifestation, before it destroys too many farms. It's a cycle."

"Like the seasons," Gwen said, nodding. "But why shouldn't I plunge my blade into this one? If they come back, as you say, wouldn't that be a way to free it from its prison, and let it manifest somewhere else?"

"Perhaps. But remember what you said yourself: we are too close to the everealm, and gheists who die here die forever. If this truly is the god of autumn, then where does it go? It's not merely a manifestation of the everealm, it *is* the everealm. There's a reason your ancestors hid this god away."

"To protect it from the inquisition, and the vow," Gwen said, snatching the knife from Elsa's hand and spinning it around. "To protect it from you."

Elsa held her hands up and backed away.

"If you say… but think carefully on what you're doing. You may free it, but what happens then? If it comes back just as mad as the gheists I am sworn to hunt, who will protect the farms? The villages? Hell, everyone and everywhere will be at risk."

"But what if I *don't*?" Gwen protested, despair in her

words. "If those priests make their way in here, and do whatever they intend, who will protect it from *them*?"

"Why do you think I'm here?" Elsa asked.

They were silent for a moment, staring at one another, Gwen clenching her god-killing knife and scowling, Elsa as silent and tired as the dead. Finally, Gwen tossed the knife to the ground and kicked the stones of the cairn.

"I don't know! I don't know *what* to do! I'm supposed to protect this fucking thing, but I've failed, and you've failed, and we're all completely fucked! My father would know, or his father, or even Frair Lucas, but all I've got is me, a vow knight without her sword, and a knife that might not be enough to do more than piss off a gheist.

"How am I supposed to know what to do?"

"You aren't," Elsa said calmly. "None of us do, at the important moments. We just do what we can, and hope that it's enough."

"That's *terrible* advice," Gwen said, her voice weak and scratchy, tears gathering in her eyes. "I can see why you became a knight and not a frair."

"I haven't got the best death-bed manners, I know," Elsa said with a weak smile, "but I washed out of seminary well before that." She walked to the cairn, found the stone that Gwen had disturbed, then pried the next one off and tossed it aside. "At least I know how to move stones quickly. Come on."

"What are you doing?" Gwen asked.

"Only thing I can. Whatever you decide, you're going to have to move these stones. We might as well do it together."

Gwen watched her for a few heartbeats, then plucked the knife from the floor, slipped it into her belt, and bent her back to help. In moments they had a small pile of stones, more than a few scrapes on their knuckles, and sweat in their eyes. Slowly they made a dent in the tomb.

"This isn't so bad, is it?" Elsa offered. "Losing yourself in the work?"

"Doesn't make the decision any easier."

"No, but it delays it a bit. Why, if we stop to eat, we might not have to make up our minds for most of the day…"

Abruptly there was a rattling of stones, and a pool of pebbles grew at the base of the entrance pillar— slowly at first, then faster. They both froze, staring at the rapidly expanding avalanche.

A hand came through the entrance, ashy dust lining the palm. It clawed at the air, and then a shoulder appeared, and a face.

"We're done," Elsa snapped. She hammered her shoulder into the cairn, shoving a huge pile of rock onto the floor. Something glimmered in the quartz light, a long, stone figure carved to look like a face, and hands, and the barest impression of wings formed of leaves folded over the chest. It wore a half-mask of dry wicker, laid over its face and somehow undamaged by the stones of the cairn. An icon of the old religion—or perhaps the old religion itself. The vow knight grabbed the knife from Gwen's belt and slapped it into her outstretched hand.

"Raise a god, or kill it," she snapped. "It's up to you!"

Gwen stared helplessly at the blade, then the priest who was slowly entering the sanctum.

She glanced at Elsa's worried face.

Then she leapt on top of the cairn, raising the knife.

She plunged the blade into the icon. The tip, forged in her blood and the temple of Strife, struck the stone figure just above the clasped hands, driving sparks into the air.

The blade bit down.

The stone parted.

Autumn filled the air.

53

THE SKY WAS breaking in strands of black and green—war weather, the promise of violence thick in the air. The sun and moon hung on opposite horizons, occasionally visible between the scudding clouds and flashing lightning.

The trees that lined the river stood like broken spears, their bark splintered, their trunks as raw and jagged as a giant's teeth. Frair Lucas stumbled into the forest and ran toward the clearing where the dead wardens lay buried. His robes were torn and bloody. An aura of naetheric energy crackled around him, trace remnants dissipating with the wind. Despite his haggard appearance, however, the frair moved with firm intent.

"There must have been one," he muttered as he entered the circle of dead bodies. "All these good pagans, one of them must have…" Lucas trailed off as he knelt beside the closest cairn, pulling stones from the pile and tossing them aside.

"Would it be the children? Or the men? Surely the wives wouldn't have carried such a thing." The body slowly appeared, revealed stone by stone. Showing more strength than his years should allow, Lucas grabbed the dead flesh of an arm and pulled the body free. Stones shuffled off, sparking as they struck together, piling up at the frair's feet.

This one was a child, her lips curled back from her teeth, the first desiccation of the grave showing around her hollow eyes. Lucas dropped her unceremoniously to the ground and began to search her clothes. Thunder, close to the ground and ominously loud, sounded from the direction of the river. Lucas glanced up long enough to wince, then redoubled his efforts.

"Not here," he said, moving to the next cairn. This one was larger. A strange moss was already forming on the stones, as if the earth were anxious to swallow it. Lucas's fingers slipped on the stones as he started pulling them away. "The women, then. What was I thinking... of course the women."

He had the next body in hand when the trees behind him shivered and split, like a curtain thrown aside. Frair Allaister walked into the clearing, the slithering water of his bound god flickering with shadows as sharp and fast as lightning. The priest no longer hovered in the belly of the gheist. He had reclaimed some semblance of motivation, stalking forward with the river spirit wrapped around him like a cloak—a cloak made of water and shadow made solid, twisting and dancing and crashing around him like a storm tide.

Lucas bent over the corpse of the witching wife.

"You're as quick as a rabbit, old man," Allaister boomed. The gravel in his voice had grown. Even in this diminished form, the gheist that possessed him cast an aura of sheer power. "But the time has come for the hound to hunt, the hunter to sup, and the prey to stop running."

"I'm not running," Lucas muttered. He turned the limp and rancid body of the warden, running fingers over her knobby backbone, pinching her hair aside. His hand paused at a cord of iron and brass, looped around her neck and leading under her arm. He laughed. "And I'm not a rabbit, either."

"You fought well, brother," Allaister said. The clearing distorted, the air growing close, the trees crowding together under the turbulent sky. He gestured, and the gheist that hung around his shoulders swung in a series of short arcs, striking the ground and causing it to shake. "I didn't think you could diminish me so. There is more to you than the inquisitor's way should allow."

"I have my tricks," Lucas said, "as do you. You haven't exactly followed the true path of the inquisition." He clutched the cord in his fist and pulled. A small triangle of iron, three bars joined at the corners, came free from the corpse and flew into his hand. He whirled around, and the body fell tangle-limbed among the rocks. "You've strayed farther from Cinder's pure light than any pagan I've ever judged."

"The god of winter will weigh my soul," Allaister responded. "The path I walk is illuminated by his pale face. His highest servant has blessed my knowledge, and begged for understanding."

"So Sacombre knows of this heresy," Lucas said. "Of course he does, and I'm sure you both believe in your own purity. Zealots and heretics are cut from the same cloth, with the same knife, and to the same pattern."

"Revelation demands zeal." Allaister loomed forward, carried by the tide of living water under his feet. "It brooks no weakness. I am sorry to be the one to judge you, Frair Lucas—you had potential. After all the time you spent in the north, Sacombre thought you could be bent. But now you must be broken instead."

"Test me, heretic," Lucas said. "See that I am the rock you will not be able to break." He backed away from the god-bound priest. "I will carry your death to the high inquisitor, and lay your apostasy at his feet."

"Do you know what lies beneath these hills, Frair Lucas? Has cruel reason given you that insight?" Allaister glanced down at the dead girl. "Even in death you defile them. Why are you surprised when they rise up against you?"

"I will apologize to her spirit the next time I'm in the quiet house," Lucas said. "As for what's beneath this earth, well, I would rather *not* know. I think it's better that way."

"You'll learn soon enough," Allaister said. "I can feel the girl—the huntress. She is reaching out to her roots, finding the heart of what was buried so long ago. It's like that last taste of summer, inquisitor." He breathed in deeply, closing his eyes in pleasure. "Like the earth shuffling into the grave."

"I can't wait," Lucas muttered. He hid the pendant behind his back, turning it over and over in his palm. "Though I think we have some business to conclude first."

The Allaister-gheist chuckled and stalked forward, spreading his hands, palms up. The angry tide of the bound god crashed around him.

"Why do you fight me, frair? The high inquisitor formed me, the god of winter guided me, and ancient truths opened my eyes. I am the scion of your faith. I am the revelation, and the light."

"Only the mad can believe that—and I have a history of killing those who are mad."

"Alas, I'm afraid that I am the end of your history," Allaister said. He spread his arms, wrapped in twisting cords of shadow-tainted water. "Look at my glory, man of the reasonable god, and know fear…"

"That isn't my way," Lucas spat. He brought the pendant around, quickly coiling its cord around his staff, clasping it and the staff in both hands before him. "I can do nothing for you, frair, but perhaps I can save your captive god."

"You will need to save yourself first," Allaister bellowed. He rushed forward, a tide of madness and white water cloaking his form.

Lucas stepped aside, focusing a very tight dissolution around his staff. The body of the gheist evaporated in the face of the binding, allowing the staff to pass untouched through the tidal cloak and strike Allaister directly. Lucas slashed the iron triangle across Allaister's forehead like a short dagger. It left a minor scratch, but blood welled up, drawn toward the pendant like a crimson lace snagged on its rough iron.

Lucas stepped back, pulling the blood with him.

"This is your mistake, Allaister: you depend on gods you barcly understand."

"You know nothing of my theos, priest," Allaister spat. "You did well in reducing me to this body, but there are no tricks in the court of winter that can end me."

"That is why I employ other methods," Lucas answered. He held the pendant up, letting it dangle at the end of its cord. The blood glittered darkly on its iron. "The wardens of this place understood what you were becoming. That's why they died to keep you away."

"For all the good it did them," Allaister growled. He charged again and Lucas swung his staff, battering his opponent back but not penetrating the shell of solidified liquid. Allaister swung a fist, striking rock with a blow that echoed off the trees. They grappled, neither gaining an advantage, and when they fell apart, Lucas was diminished, his frail arms shaking, though he held the pendant high.

The gheist laughed.

"You have your precious jewelry, priest. Would you like me to bury you with it? Or should I give it to that bitch huntress?"

"You shouldn't speak like that of your betters," Lucas gasped. He was winded, the battle wearing through his thin reserves. Most of his energy had been spent by the river's edge, tearing the gheist from Allaister's body scrap by nightmare scrap, until only the core remained. It would swell again, fed by the everealm, drawing the essence of the hallow into Allaister's body. If that happened, Lucas wasn't sure Elsa and Gwen could stop it.

"She can speak for herself, when I find her," Allaister said. He circled the trembling priest, stalking among the graves of the wardens. "Though if she continues along her current path, that won't be necessary. She'll find me."

"Gods help you if she does," Lucas said.

"Your gods won't have anything to do with it," Allaister answered, a cruel smile on his face. "Enough talking. Come, bring me your trick so we can end this thing."

"I don't have a trick, demon," Lucas said. "I just wanted your blood. Allaister's blood, actually."

"Are you going to curse me, inquisitor?" the gheist said. "Scry my name?"

"Something like that," Lucas said. He held the pendant in front of him. A crown of spinning runes formed around his head, etched in the air with naetheric power, glowing as it settled on his temples. His voice slowed down. "Something... quite like that..."

A look of understanding swept across Allaister's face, coupled with newfound fear.

"Wait!" he screamed, jumping forward.

Time slowed. Lucas's mind separated from his body, and the forest fell away. With the pagan pendant—an icon of summoning and perception used by the witching wives to sift the spirits from the material world—combined with his own talents, Lucas was able to observe and manipulate Allaister and his gheist.

Allaister and his bound god hung in mid-step, cloaked in circling runes of naetheric power, glowing as they rotated slowly in the air at the holy points of Cinder's art—the heart, the head, the hands. Other, rougher runes, drawn black and flickering against the sky, hung above his shoulders like scrimshaw wings.

The gheist's body was formed of greenish webs, bright lines of everam that were sharp at the bounds of the crashing tide, mingled with skeins of shadow at their core, tangled with the runes that circled Allaister's spirit.

Indeed it was a guardian spirit, bound eternally to this hallow, feeding on its proximity to the everealm to strengthen the wards that kept the shrine safe. Lucas could see its relation to autumn, the aspect of a river slowly surrendering to ice, the final harvest before winter claimed its place. The spirit of the god was shredded, damaged both by Allaister's rough binding and Lucas's efforts to tear them apart. It was shot through with shadowy tendrils, the priest's will bending the god's spirit.

Whatever magic Allaister was using to bind the god, it was foreign to Lucas. It read like an ancient language, certain words and structures familiar, but the whole was incomprehensible. Elements of the casting reminded Lucas of Elsa's blessings, binding the god's power to the blood of the vow knight, and drawing divinity through her flesh. Yet it also had the taste and tremor of the pagan arts—some kind of blending Lucas had never before seen.

He did not need to understand it in order to destroy it. He raised his hands and drew on everything that remained—his heart and his mind, every scrap of blessing that Cinder had given him. Pushed all of that, his life itself, into the heart of the god and the mind of the priest.

The web of naether and everam frayed.

Lucas faded.

The Allaister-gheist slammed into him, sending Lucas reeling and his mind snapping back into his flesh. The shock of transition sent spasms through his bones. He lay on the ground, sprawled across the rough stones of the warden's cairn, her cold corpse splayed next to him like a forgotten lover.

"A valiant attempt, priest," Allaister hissed, "but you have failed, and now you must die."

"A reasonable price," Lucas murmured, barely able to raise his head, "but not one I have yet paid. Would you like me to shrive you, when you are gone?"

"I am not going to the quiet house today," Allaister said, looming over his enemy.

"No," Lucas agreed. "I don't think they will have you."

Allaister's death first appeared at his heart. The color left his naked body, and a gush of water splashed out of his chest, beginning as a trickle that leaked from his skin, becoming a torrent that grew and grew as the priest lost control of the river spirit.

Lucas dragged himself back and up. The bowl-shaped clearing filled with water. At the center, Allaister struggled to regain control, unable to stand when the swirling maelstrom took his legs away. He summoned naetheric runes, stitched the air with dark invocations, but the god would not bend to his will.

The furious water churned the ground and undid the cairns of the dead wardens, releasing their limp bodies to float to the surface. Bleeding from nose and mouth, Allaister spat arcane wards and blasphemy into the air, then cried out as the currents smashed him against the rocky hillside, breaking his arm.

"It will do you no good, brother," Lucas yelled. "That was your final mistake. The gods do not bend to us."

"No, I do not—" Allaister fought to the surface one last time, fear and fury in his eyes, his skin already swelling. Each time he opened his mouth to speak, water crashed over him as if to cut him off. "It cannot end! I will—"

Then there was silence as the river washed over him, and he disappeared. The surface of the newly formed lake fell into a heavy chop. A dozen heartbeats later it calmed, choked with branches and bodies and other debris, contained by the will of the guardian spirit.

Lucas stood at the edge and raised his hands.

"I have no argument with you, goddess. Return to your banks and your purpose. The house of Cinder will trouble you no more today."

The swirling pool of divine water waited for a dozen heartbeats, then sluggishly flowed into the forest, away from Lucas. The bodies of the wardens went with it, bumping lazily into trees, snagging in the underbrush before being carried by their god back into the hallow.

Of Allaister there was no sign.

The sky cleared, the storm melting away until only the sun and moon remained, and the stars pricked the veil of heaven to surround Cinder's silver face. Lucas sighed, leaning forward on his staff. He was withered, his age fully claiming him. He turned and started the painful walk toward the shrine at the hallow's heart.

54

THE HILL ABOVE the god was as smooth and green as a river stone, slick with moss and the cold current of the stream. The sky was clearing. The first light of an eternal dawn spread across the grass. The air was crisp as an apple and just as sweet.

In an instant it began to change.

The trees that surrounded the hill shifted in the breeze as their leaves slithered together, a velvet-smooth sound that rasped drily through the air. The colors of autumn appeared, radiating outward from the hill and through the forest. Greens became gold, red, yellow, and white with the last jubilation of summer's warmth and the approach of wintry death.

A whirling breeze swirled through the grasses, twisting each blade into a pinwheel for a few brief seconds before rushing on to the next one, the next tree, and on into the sky. Then the breeze turned into a whipping column of air. It mounted the hill, bringing with it a hissing torrent of millions of leaves, painted like gems and freed from their branches.

Autumn roared into the world.

The hill itself split like an egg, rock breaking with deafening cracks, the grassy crown peeling back to reveal a heart of muddy roots and broken stone, grinding open like a tomb. From that tomb rose the god of the harvest, second holiest of the pagan rites, and the one true guardian of the everealm.

It shimmered in a cloud of golden dust, a vaguely human shape that towered over the hill, growing larger as it moved. Its face was featureless but for a pair of eyes that burned like twin suns. A wicker mask bristled around its face, rising from its head, composed of dry twigs wrought in summer's light. The cloak of swirling leaves swarmed like butterflies around its shoulders. Even the sky seemed to dip toward it. The clouds rolled aside.

In the midst of the autumn god, there was a child—a girl dressed in leaves and grasses, in light and retribution. When autumn had erupted at the tip of her knife, Gwen lost her name, her life, everything that made her the daughter of Colm Adair, child of the Fen Gate, child of flesh and scion of blood. All she had now were her primal senses. The only things that she remembered were her title and her prey.

Huntress… and Sacombre.

Slowly, inexorably, she moved into the forest, already towering over the trees as they transformed. The butterfly cloud of autumn leaves followed. The first taste of winter's chill wafted behind her.

Elsa stumbled from the wounded earth, her hair and clothes choked with leaves, sticks, roots, stones, and dirt. Her skin was crisscrossed by dozens of cuts. The wind that filled the tomb at the moment of the god's release had blinded her.

Her last sight of Gwen was of the huntress spread-eagled on a pillar of leaves and amber light. When she had recovered, Gwen was gone and the sky was spilling into the chamber. The priests had been turned into ragdolls of flesh and tattered cloth. Elsa hadn't given them a second look.

Now the sky was trailing banners of golden light flecked with amber. Both god and girl roared over the hallow with the fury of an autumn storm on their heels.

Elsa sighed.

"She came to a decision, then," Frair Lucas said. Elsa turned to find the man, much reduced, leaning against his staff like the totem of old age.

"She did, or the god made it for her," Elsa answered.

"And what of us?" Lucas said. "What is to become of us?"

The autumn god answered. Violent winds whipped at them, filled with leaves, dry and brittle. Elsa rushed to Lucas's side, shielding the frail figure with her bulk. He clung to her as the fury grew and grew, the wind louder, the leaves sharper, until Elsa was sure they would die on that hill, far from the blessings of Heartsbridge.

Without warning, the storm abated. The god was gone, and Elsa and Lucas as well. The hill lay barren and empty. The sky was clear, the sun bright.

Maeve's wretched shadow lurked in the darkness. The spirit of death had taken everything from her, her blood, her soul, even the trace remnants of her memory. She was nothing but a stubborn echo of pain and loss, drifting between realms.

The room that held her remains was dark and broken. The sacred lines that defined it were scattered. Abstractly she wondered what it had once been, before the spirit of death came. Before her undoing. She wondered how long she would be here before someone came and shrived her soul.

Even her lone companion had abandoned her. The shaman lay in a pool of his own fury, confused by the profane dimensions of their captivity. She tried to approach him, but the fool only lashed out. Finally, he gathered himself and melted into the rock, taking his anger with him.

Alone, she witnessed the first leaf fall, somehow visible despite the blackness. It appeared in the blood that streaked the ceiling, emerging damp and gory from between the stones, like a jester's sleight of hand. It plopped to the floor. Another leaf followed, and another, each less bloody, more whole, until a cascade of autumn leaves tumbled from the ceiling. Something stirred in Maeve's memory. Hope.

The floor opened, and a season breached the world. It grew in a furious tornado of autumn color, leaves and dripping sunlight, warm and amber. An entire column of leaves snaked through the shrine and up the stairs, twisting and wailing as it fled the profanity of its sacred heart. The sound was overwhelming.

When it was past, two figures huddled in the black. A man and a woman, shadow and flame, winter and sun. They exchanged frightened words as they hurried up the stairs, following the last vestige of light that had preceded them. The woman nearly had to carry the man. They both looked on the verge of death.

Maeve settled and waited. They would be back. Death would always bring them back.

The god that hung over the Fen Gate was unlike anything Ian had ever seen. It transformed the world in its wake. The forest stirred with gheist-ridden life, the trees groaning from their roots, their limbs uplifted in supplication, their leaves flying like flocks of golden birds.

In his limited time with the pagans, Ian had learned to sense the hidden spirits of the world, had grown accustomed to the subtle touch of their force. Now his skin was alive with burning swirls of energy.

From his position on the parapet he watched in awe as the god gathered into a storm above the castle. It loomed over the ruined village, bent, ran a hand the size of a horse over the wreckage of one building, then another. It seemed to be feeling its way forward, and as the god bent to the earth, Ian saw that there was a seed at its core, a human figure wrapped in light and curled into a fetus. It looked to be a woman, fists over her face, hair floating around her.

The god stood and roared, a sound that echoed through Ian's bones and blistered his blood. The wreckage at its feet shuffled away like a pile of leaves scattered by a child, flakes of stone and timber drifting up into the air, and then disappearing completely. Wherever it moved, clouds of leaves spun in rings in the sky like multi-colored mist, pinwheeling around their host.

The wind tasted of dust and autumn.

"What in the sweet hells…" Sir Brennan muttered. He was standing near Ian, helping organize the defense. All around, men stopped whatever they were doing and stared, slack-jawed, at the gargantuan sight.

"Get everyone inside," Ian barked. "Tenerran, Suhdrin, everyone."

"But, the walls…"

"Forget the walls. Forget everything." Ian grabbed the knight by the shoulders and pushed him toward the great hall. "Get as many people as you can into the crypts. Perhaps the stone will provide some protection."

A tendril of swirling leaves spilled from the sky like a tornado, falling into a courtyard. Everyone it struck was ground into bones and rags of flesh. The courtyard filled with screams as all who survived—knight and priest and page and lord—ran for cover. Barrels of pitch overturned, wagons shuddered, and in places the walkways along the walls buckled at the violence of their retreat.

Ian waited until the worst of the surge had passed, then he turned to the walls and started to climb to the god above. Wind battered his face, and heavy, wet globs of sunlight spattered against him as he made his way up. Pausing at a landing, he looked down. The fields beyond the walls were in chaos. The autumn god was scattering the Suhdrin forces like leaves in the wind.

The war was over.

It was destroying Tenerran lives, too. The castle was coming apart in bits and flecks, jagged stones that joined the wind to cut flesh. Ian's armor was tattered by the time he reached the highest tower in the Fen Gate. Shielding his face from the worst of the assault, Ian peered up at the looming form of the Fen god. It was massive, a pillar of divine light cloaked in bands of autumn leaves, its eyes as bright and amber as the setting sun. There were other figures, warped and strange, gheists moving within the body of their god, and…

His eyes went wide with surprise and recognition. From this vantage, he could see who hung at the center—who was at the heart of the monster.

"Gwen!" Ian bellowed, but his words were lost in the maelstrom. Clinging to the wall, he thought back to the way he had felt when the hound had passed him, trying to emulate the pagan unfolding of heart and mind that had led him to this point. He tasted the storm, and knew its fury. "Gwen!" he shouted again.

"Stop! You're destroying everything—your home, your family, those you love… you have to stop!"

Suddenly he went rigid, unable to move or speak.

Despite the roar of the storm, the Fen god had noticed him. It turned and bent toward him, and reached out with a huge, amorphous hand.

Then there was silence.

55

HIS EYES OPENED to a world of honey-smooth light. He was floating. Layers of amber clouds hovered in a sky flecked with brighter gold, and the endless sparks of butterfly-like life that fluttered through the yellowing air.

Gwen hung close by, still in the fetal position. Her hair had grown into a ragged bush twined with leaves and pebbles and scraps of leather. Her skin was the color of beaten copper. Her fists were clenched and angry. Ian wasn't sure she could hear him, wasn't sure she was really here, really herself.

"Gwendolyn?" he said tentatively. "Gwen?"

"That name is dead," the sky answered in a voice that was near and far, that echoed and came from inside his head. "The guardian house has fallen."

Ian tried to understand, and suddenly he knew. Somehow Colm Adair was dead, and with him his wife and child. Yet...

Sacombre.

"Gwendolyn still lives," Ian said. "The iron is still in her blood."

"Iron is the earth's harvest. Iron and stone." Gwen shifted in her glowing nest of hair. "Iron does not bend to the barking of dogs." At that Ian found himself floating away from the huntress. He bent his will and moved closer.

"What are you doing, Gwen? What do you hope to accomplish in destroying your home? Your people?"

Only silence. In the quiet, Ian could make out a distant, grinding roar, and realized that at the limits of his vision he could see the storm wall and its stone teeth, tearing through the castle. He tried to focus on slowing the destruction, and for a second he could *feel* the edge of the storm, but then lost it. He was reaching to try again when Gwen spoke.

"Do not," she said, and she looked up. Her eyes were twin sparks of golden light, burning in her face. "You are here as a guest. Do not interfere." Her mouth didn't move, yet he heard her.

"There are people dying out there."

"Are you one of them?" she asked, and the sky echoed her words.

"It's your family that's dying," Ian said. "The people of Fenton, of the Gate. Your father's loyal men. The people who left their hearths and homes to defend your name." He paused, clenching his fists against the weight of wind that pushed him away. "The people your family betrayed, Gwen. We thought you faithful!"

The air tensed around him, and a wrinkle formed on Gwen's brow. She turned to face him, and a storm arose at his feet.

"We are the only faithful," the sky answered. "The last faithful. You are the betrayer, Ian of dogs. These deaths are on you! Your father! Your blood!"

The storm that lashed his skin was bitter and cold. Leaves as sharp as steel cut his face and hands. He bore down, dragging himself closer to Gwen and her nest of living hair.

"That's no excuse!" he yelled. "We have died to protect you! My father has waged a war to honor your name. Too many of the faithful…"

"Do not speak of faith," the sky replied, and there was a hint of thunder in its voice. "The tribe of hounds was the first to bow to the new gods. Your hallow is empty, and your gods are absent."

"No, that's not true," Ian insisted. "I have seen the hound. It led me here. The hound brought me to you."

"To stop me?" Gwen asked. "To rob me of my vengeance? Do you mean to stand with Sacombre, Ian of hounds?"

"Sacombre will pay for what he's done, but not if you destroy everything around him. Not if you kill the very people who looked to your father for protection!"

"I have no trust in the justice of your ashen god," she snarled. "I will count the cost and exact the payment myself. You won't stop me. No one will stop me."

She curled away from him again. The storm redoubled. Ian found himself pinwheeling through the air. Behind him, the churning wall of destruction crept closer. If he was thrown out of the towering god now, he would be torn to shreds.

"I can't… let you… do that!" he gasped. He bent his will against the sky, and found his heart lacking. He was floating at the whim of the storm, spinning madly through the air. Ian became just another piece of flotsam in Gwen's destructive maelstrom, and flew over the castle like a discarded puppet.

He looked down at what remained of the Fen Gate. The stone walls were falling apart, shuffling into the air like cards of stone, the roofs of the outbuildings torn away. Far below, the bodies of the dead and dying tumbled close to the ground, smashing against the buildings that still stood, breaking into horrible rags of flesh and bone. The god was burrowing into the doma, cracking the shuttered dome like a shell and scattering the holy instruments of the Celestial faith into the wind. Ian shivered to see such destruction. This was not what he had expected of war.

This was not what he expected of his gods.

Movement near the central tower of the castle, miraculously intact, caught his eye. A familiar scrap of robe flashed past a window. Ian recognized his father, and a half-dozen others, moving carefully through the upper chambers.

They were hunting.

Ian twisted in the storm. He whistled past the window where he had seen his father, scraping along the stone wall to bump unceremoniously against the windows of a farther chamber. As he struggled to right himself, he peered inside.

Sacombre stood over the body of Colm Adair, his hands spread in benediction, the heart blood of the dying baron smeared on his face.

"Gwen!" Ian yelled, though the storm tore his words away. "I've found your justice! There is your priest!"

The storm guttered like a torch, then Ian was snatched up into the sky once again. He felt for a moment the wiry grasp of fur between his fingers and the stone-hard knobby spine of the hound against his chest, but the image passed.

The wind died down, and he was standing beside Gwendolyn Adair. She seemed more herself, though there was still a feral madness to her hair, her eyes, the bright glitter of her skin.

"The high inquisitor…" she snarled.

"My father hunts him. You can end this, Gwen.

There is no need to destroy the castle if you can strike Sacombre down."

"Yes," she murmured. "Yes…" A crown of lightning and wicker graced her head, bright light dancing along the whip-thin branches of the mask, and she was arcing down toward the castle.

The god of storms followed in her wake.

56

SPLINTERED SHARDS OF stained glass littered the interior of the doma, the icons of faith scattered around the stations of sun and moon. The chimes used to denote the hours of Cinder's ascension were dashed against the wall by a howling wind. The bodies of the choir eternal lay scattered among the pews.

Malcolm hurried through, scanning for any sign of life. He thought the high inquisitor might be here, preparing the sanctum's defense against the pagan god, but there was no sign of Tomas Sacombre or his attendants. He took the priest's door at the back of the doma, traveling through Frair Humble's meager lodgings, then entered the labyrinth of back corridors and servant halls that formed the guts of the castle.

Just as he exited the doma, he heard a tremendous crash behind him. The sanctuary collapsed, the wreckage lifted into the air by the storm outside. Malcolm found himself on the ground, his ears ringing.

"Gods bless," he muttered to himself, then crawled forward and into the deeper chambers of the castle.

More bodies, more silence, the only sound the distant hammer of god against the walls. He continued on to the family's corridors.

The great hall was choked with the dead and dying.

They were lined up in tidy rows along the walls, attended by the remnants of the doma's clergy and guarded by knights of Adair and Blakley. Sir Brennan paced quietly near the door to the courtyard, sword in hand.

"My lord," the knight said. "Have you seen your son?"

"What is happening?" Malcolm said, ignoring the question. "Where is Lord Adair?"

"The baron is missing. I have sent messengers to his rooms, but none have returned. I was about to organize a search party."

"I will lead that," Malcolm said. "Do you know anything about this storm?"

"No, my lord. It seemed to rise from the stones themselves."

"Something is buried in this place," Malcolm grumbled. "Something best forgotten, I suspect. What force do you still command?"

"A dozen knights of the banner, mostly of Adair, a few of Blakley. Jaerdin and Roard have reinforced the gatehouse. Hopefully Halverdt's men will be less likely to attack their own blood. The rest are spread throughout the castle, trying to hunt down whatever is killing our servants."

"What other danger is there?" Malcolm asked.

"There remain blades in the shadows. Whether they are spies sent by Halverdt, or some darker emissary, we do not know. The corridors are far from safe." Brennan motioned to an icon of Strife that hung about his neck, hastily formed from the wreckage of the doma and a length of rough cord. "The men have taken to wearing charms, my lord."

"Charms," Malcolm spat. "Soon enough we'll be hanging wicker men from the mantels and touching stone whenever we get a chill. Where are these men you've called to search Lord Adair's chambers?"

"Here, my lord," a knight answered. He stood at the head of half a dozen lesser blades, men in chain and bucklers, with swords hanging from their belts. "Sir Merret, if you please. It will be an honor to repay you for leading me out of Greenhall."

"Don't speak in haste, sir—it's an honor often granted shortly before pointless death," Malcolm replied. "You know this castle?"

"I have served House Adair for a decade, my lord."

Malcolm nodded. "You will lead us, Sir Merret."

"My lord!" a voice called from the far side of the hall. Malcolm turned to see a priest of Cinder and a vow knight making their way between the dead. Malcolm recognized Sir LaFey from their time in Greenhall.

The inquisitor spoke. "I would go with you."

"You will forgive me if I don't find comfort in the company of an inquisitor," Malcolm said.

"I would join you in that," the vow knight answered, "but Frair Lucas is worthy company."

"Sir LaFey and I have had a strange day, made stranger by finding ourselves in the Fen Gate," Lucas answered. "We would like to see the end of this business, and help if we are able."

"The word of a vow knight is sufficient for me," Malcolm answered. He turned to Sir Merret. "Lead us."

The host marched silently through the grand hall and up a winding stairway. Merret headed the column, followed closely by Malcolm and the two newcomers. The rest of the soldiers trailed behind.

"The storm is not so fierce here," Malcolm said.

"It shows a particular hatred for the doma," Merret said. "There are few of the clergy remaining."

"She has been treated poorly by the church," Lucas muttered. "Hardly a surprise."

"She?" Malcolm asked. "You know this gheist?"

"I have spent the last month walking with her. She is no less than Gwendolyn Adair."

"Well," Malcolm said quietly, his expression a mask. "That complicates matters significantly."

They reached the top of the stairs and spread out into the corridor. There were bloody footprints on the carpet, leading from a door at the end of the hall and disappearing at the opposite side.

"Where does that door come from?" Malcolm asked, pointing to the origin of the prints. Merret shook his head.

"There should be no door there, or at least, I was not aware of one."

"A hidden door? More things are revealed every moment," Malcolm said. He pointed to the opposite side. "And that way?"

"The baron's suites," Merret said.

"Very well," Malcolm said grimly. "I suspect this may be a short search, then. These other rooms?"

"Belong to Colm's son and the family's servants," Merret answered. The doors were open, and though the storm raged beyond, the windows remained unbroken. A strange stillness dominated this space. It seemed almost sacred.

"Search the rooms, but be quick about it. Sir Merret, Frair Lucas, Sir LaFey," Malcolm pointed toward the baron's suite. "Come with me."

The lesser soldiers spread out and started knocking through the rooms, moving with reverent silence, as though the occupants might be sleeping. Sir Merret crept to the baron's door, pausing to listen.

"There is movement within," he whispered. Malcolm nudged him aside. He glanced at the inquisitor and the vow knight.

"Sir LaFey, where is your sword?"

"I will be the blade," she answered. "Or at least the shield."

"She wants badly to die a noble death," Lucas said with a wry smile. "Don't let it bother you."

"As you say," Malcolm said. "Stay close and stay down. Whatever we find inside, try to hold your courage."

"If you knew the things we had seen…" Lucas said, shaking his head. "We will do our best, my lord. Pray that your own courage holds."

Malcolm tightened the grip on his feyiron blade, then crouched and put his shoulder to the door. He rushed inside, the other three entering behind him.

Malcolm's heart nearly left him. Sir Merret gasped, and Lucas and Elsa succumbed to anxious prayer.

Colm Adair lay at the center of the room, his life gone. His mortal flesh was unfolding bloodlessly on the carpet. Crouched over him was what remained of Tomas Sacombre. The high inquisitor had his back to the door. At the sound of Frair Lucas's muttered prayer, however, he slowly turned and faced them.

Malcolm had seen a host of demons in his day, gods of the old court and the new. Sacombre's eyes were lined with ash, and his fingers were cracked and dry, the veins of his skin black and pulsing. Blood trailed in lines from them to the body. Madness filled his eyes, and his face was smeared with blood, as well. When he saw Malcolm, the priest let out a laugh, sharp and short and full of rage.

"My lord!" Sir Merret screamed. He rushed forward, sword drawn.

Sacombre struck him down without thought or motion. A black tendril flickered into existence, its barb sinking deep in Merret's chest. The knight, Suhdrin born, Tenerran sworn, honest and true to death, fell beside the body of his baron.

"You found me, thank the gods." Sacombre limped forward, shaking free of the tangle of blood that linked him to Colm Adair's fallen form, stepping gingerly over Sir Merret. "You needn't be afraid, Houndhallow. I am not the man you knew."

"I know a monster when I see it," Malcolm hissed.

"Ho, yes, I suppose you do. A good, holy monster, at that." He let out another cackle. "And now you've come to kill me?"

"If I must," Malcolm said. "I would rather drag you to Heartsbridge and let you face the celestriarch's will."

"Wouldn't *that* be a coup? The Reaverbane, bringing the high inquisitor of Cinder to trial. Quite the show." Sacombre chuckled. "Well, I can't allow that, of course. I have a history to protect."

"You could humble yourself, and beg forgiveness," Frair Lucas said. He looked up from the baron's body, a weight of pity in his eyes. "Make amends for the deaths of Colm Adair and his family."

"They were heretics," Sacombre said, grinning wickedly. "You know that now, don't you?"

Malcolm grimaced but didn't answer.

Sacombre laughed again. "Heretics, yes, and heretics must die."

"What of you?" Lucas asked. "What's to be done with the corruption in your heart, High Inquisitor?"

"Well," Sacombre said, peering first at Lucas, then at the others gathered before him. He smiled. "I suppose you'll have to kill me."

Malcolm rolled his tired shoulders, threw his shield to the ground, then swung his feyiron blade in a wide circle and held it in a double-handed guard. His bones creaked and his muscles burned from the days in the saddle, the months on the run, the weeks at war. His mind was clouded with thoughts of his son's betrayal, his failure at protecting his beloved wife.

"Gods will it," he said sharply. "Being faithful to the church sometimes means drawing a blade and cutting out its corruption!"

"Then come, cut!" Sacombre yelled. "I wait for your steel, Duke Hound!"

Before Malcolm could move, however, a glow lit the room.

"I am steel enough for you," Elsa LaFey spat. She raised her arms and drew the sun from the sky, a golden disc that alighted on her shoulders, glittering brightly off her armor. The veins of her face pulsed brightly beneath her skin.

Frair Lucas drew up next to her. He shook his head and with his hands wove the sign of Cinder.

"The powers you wield are not the powers of the true god, Inquisitor," he said. "I can not allow you to claim his name, or desecrate the orders of Cinder."

Before he could complete his casting, the chamber windows burst inward, and autumn filled the room. A whirling cyclone of leaves cut through the tapestries that hung on the walls and whipped the curtains into shreds. The wind howled and screamed. Sacombre's laughter echoed over the tumult.

"The pagan seeks to purge you, Frair Lucas!" he shouted. "But she will have to wait. The god of winter has many faces, and death is among them!"

A silvered fog joined the storm, leaking from the

ruin of Colm Adair's body, wisping like ink in water, then drew in toward Sacombre's open mouth. The high inquisitor closed his eyes and breathed in the black tendrils, the soul of the dead baron. The lines of his face and the veins of his arms took on a silvery glow. He drew his hands together and pushed.

A storm came out from his chest.

Malcolm's blood went cold.

57

Gwen's fury screamed through the room. The priest and the knight standing against the high inquisitor burned brightly against the storm's tumult. Their power flickered... and went out.

"You'll kill them all!" Ian shouted.

"I will kill the one," Gwen answered. "Others may die."

The high inquisitor laughed. There was an echo to his voice, something that tore through the air, filling a space that was neither voice nor thought. Darkness lurked behind him, through him, shot through his veins like a disease. Sacombre raised his arms and winter filled the room.

The ice that cut the air and froze the wind quickly pushed Gwen's presence from the chamber. The windows froze shut. The power of the autumn god was denied by winter's final judgment.

"No! No, no, no, *no*!" Gwen hammered against the tower, frustration and anger boiling through her voice, the fury lashing stone and whipping the sense from Ian's mind. "I will not be stopped. My justice will not be stolen from me!"

She drew back, tugging Ian with her like a fish on the hook. The autumn god pulled away from the castle, the storm of his presence swirling in the air like a hurricane. Gwen descended in a tornado as wide as the tower, a wedge of hatred that tore stone and cratered earth. The walls tumbled.

The innocent died.

"You have to stop!" Ian yelled. He hung helplessly in the air above the destruction, watching in horror as the castle crumbled below. "Those people are trying to help you! Can't you see that they want to stop Sacombre just as badly as you do?"

"What does it matter what they want? I wanted justice for my family. I wanted peace for my lands, and freedom from the shackle of House Halverdt. From the church. What has that yielded?"

"And what will *this* get you?" Ian asked.

Suddenly, Gwen was before him. She hovered in the sky, her hair a writhing mass of graceful light, her eyes burning like torches. The glow that came off her skin was as sharp as lightning.

"Peace," she said. "This will grant me peace."

"It will grant you death. For you, your family, for everyone you ever cared about. Is that the legacy of House Adair? Is that the story we will tell of your passing?"

Gwen paused, staring down at him with those terrible eyes. Ian nodded toward the tower.

"Look," he said. "Look at the faithfulness of Blakley. Look at what my father does to protect you."

Together they turned and watched. The tower was coming apart, and at its crown stood Malcolm Blakley. Darkness moved around him, darkness given the form of Tomas Sacombre.

58

THE STORM FROZE, beginning with the air itself. Slowly at first, a crisp of ice forming, fragments of leaves clumping together, then wheeling away, only to freeze again.

Frair Lucas screamed and stumbled. Elsa fell, the guttering flame of her conjured sun bursting through the sudden blizzard, only to fail, flicker, and snuff out. With a gasp she fell to her knees, and then there was silence, the wind gone, the windows frozen as solid as stone.

In the center the high inquisitor seethed. The light that wafted from his skin seemed too sharp, the edges cutting the air and his skin. His flesh boiled under his robes, and streaks of black ash smeared his cheeks. Flecks of darkness floated in his eyes, and blood mingled with the sweat that poured down his chest.

"So it is with all the blind," Sacombre growled. His voice left his chest and became a chorus of stones and breaking bones. "Such is the fate of fools."

"What has become of you?" Malcolm asked.

"I am *becoming*," Sacombre hissed. "I am winter itself. The very heart of purity. It is but an aspect of Lord Cinder's power, and I will be its greatest avatar."

"Even if it means heresy?" Malcolm asked.

"Heresy and revelation… what is the difference? What is fear, but an opportunity not taken?" Sacombre drew himself up. His flesh was shuffling off, and something purer, darker, something profane was coming through. "The church will not stand against me. Nor the north."

"It is not the north you should fear, nor the church." Malcolm stepped forward, walking past the fallen priest and vow knight, the limp body of Sir Merret. "They were doing their duty to the Celestial throne. To their lords."

"The duty of the misguided," Sacombre rattled. "The church locks the souls of its dead away. I would free them, as I will free you, Malcolm of Houndhallow." He stretched out a claw-tipped hand, beckoning. "Free you from the flesh and the worries of this world."

"My wife will be quite disappointed if I leave my flesh, I think. My thanks for the offer." He dragged the tip of his feyiron blade across the floor, splintering the ice that Sacombre had summoned, leaving a runnel of water behind. "How ever can I repay you?"

Sacombre snorted. He was growing, height given by twisted legs, his shoulders hunching with the burden of new wings, ribs of stone and bone sprouting from his chest to enclose the pulsing heart of shadow that glowed through his skin and robes. Claws erupted from his malformed feet. What remained of his skin was pebbled with foul growths. Shadows whispered from his open mouth, trailing a stream of fog in the air.

The high inquisitor rose to his full height and spread those terrible wings. They scraped against the ceiling, brushing aside tapestries rimed with frost.

"Enough nonsense." His voice boomed now.

"Come and die like a hero, Malcolm. Come and prove your faith in sacrifice!"

"An excellent invitation," Malcolm hissed, then he ducked his head and charged forward, howling, throwing caution aside as he slid forward on the ice, sword raised above his shoulder.

Sacombre buffeted him with his wings, stealing the breath from Malcolm's lungs and freezing his skin. He fought against the blows, but as he did the high inquisitor charged. With his wings and claws, he was able to find purchase on the ice while his opponent struggled to remain upright, delivering a series of harsh blows that drove Malcolm back into the corridor.

There he fell, sword skittering away, his spine screaming in pain as he hit the ground. Sacombre bent and came through the door, his form clenching and then unfolding into the greater space of the hallway.

"So you see," Sacombre whispered as he loomed over the fallen duke, "there is little hope for you. Your men are dead, your son has abandoned you, and your wife lies dying."

Malcolm pushed himself to hands and knees, then to his feet. White-hot agony blossomed through his chest, radiating from his hips up to his ribs and heart. He winced and spat blood.

"What do you know of my wife, or my son?"

"I have eyes, Malcolm. Eyes everywhere. Yes, things are going well. Your death will rally Tener. My heresy will divide the south. There will be war. Pure, winter-blessed war. Horrible." Sacombre lifted his hands in benediction, sighing contentedly. "But let's make a show of it, shall we?"

"You'll kill me either way."

"Of course. But I don't think you want to die

as cattle do," Sacombre said. He nodded to where Malcolm's sword had fallen. "Go on."

Malcolm sighed. He just wanted this done. The demon was right. Without his son beside him and his wife to guide him, he was a ship without a sail. In truth, he might be ready to die—but he wasn't willing to be slaughtered where he stood. At least he could die fighting.

He went to the sword where it had struck the wall, feyiron cutting stone as easily as wood. He drew it, then faced the creature that had been the high inquisitor.

"You're a heretic, a murderer, and a bastard," Malcolm said, "and I'm here to bring you Cinder's judgment."

Sacombre laughed, long and hard, then he swooped down, wings beating and claws grasping. Malcolm ducked aside, rolling and falling as the creature crashed into the ground. He rolled through a doorway, coming up among wooden soldiers, a playroom decorated in a child's fantasy of war. Sacombre crashed into the doorway, crumbling the frame, freeing a small avalanche of stones as he broke through. Fissures ran through the wall.

Malcolm scrambled to his feet, backing away as Sacombre approached. The gheist that wore the high inquisitor's body flapped those terrible wings, breaking walls and ceiling. A part of the tower slid away. The storm outside leaked in, filling the room with its tumult. Malcolm swung, only to miss and be battered aside by claws that drew blood. He swung the sword back and drove it into the demon's chest. Ribs of rock and shadow sparked as he struck them, but he couldn't find flesh.

A rain of stones signaled the ceiling's collapse. Malcolm squinted through the gravel, shielding his face from the scree. For a second he thought Sacombre had been buried in the wreckage, but then the creature burst from the gray rubble, shaking free of the detritus, spraying knife-sharp shards of stone across the room.

There was a strange peace in the sky. The storm had withdrawn. Two figures hovered in the distance, watching.

Malcolm shook his head.

"Gods damn all of the heretics," he swore. He scrambled up the wreckage of the room to what remained of the tower's roof. Splintered planks of wood lay haphazardly over the yawning chasm of the tower. He skittered to a stop at the chasm's verge, staring down at the courtyard far below, and the fields beyond.

The god was nowhere to be seen.

He saw the terrified faces of Suhdrin and Tenerran alike, eyes upturned to see where the avalanche had originated. An audience to watch him die heroically. He gave a laugh. Sharp pain snagged his ribs, and his lungs protested the wasted breath. That only made Malcolm laugh harder.

There was a crash, and he turned to watch the bound god approach. Sacombre clambered up onto the roof. He stretched his wings, triggering another avalanche of debris, then twisted in strange, impossible ways, surveying the landscape.

"The pagan god has abandoned you, Malcolm," Sacombre said with a leer. "Gwen Adair has stayed her hand. Even she accepts defeat."

"Maybe she ran before I could get to her," Malcolm said. "I'm going to have some very cross words for her when this is over."

"You will have to speak them from your grave, old fool!"

"Oh, will you fuck off with the lofty threats," Malcolm spat, then he raised his sword above his head, and charged.

"He will die," Gwen whispered.

"What does that matter to you?" Ian challenged angrily. "This is all our fault, isn't it? We betrayed your precious gods, bent our knee to the church. What do you care if one of us dies?"

"Your father is throwing his life away," Gwen said. "He cannot hope to stand against Sacombre."

"So kill them both. Kill everyone. You seemed so keen on it a moment ago. Or have you remembered what it is to be human?"

Gwen turned slowly to face him.

"I can help him. If you'll accept a pagan's help."

"No," Ian said. "I will not make that choice for him—and I know what he would decide, if asked. My father is a faithful man."

"Even if it means his life?"

"Especially if it means his life," Ian said.

59

SACOMBRE STRUCK MALCOLM in the chest, throwing him back to slide across the roof. His shoulders came to rest suspended over open air. The tower was slowly falling apart. The roof groaned and shifted, the surface tilting dangerously toward the courtyard far below. Malcolm scrambled up the incline, toward the peak where Sacombre waited, lazily flapping the abomination of his wings.

The high inquisitor was still changing. The ribs now pinched his body, and a gnarled growth of spine had separated from his back, holding him like a spider holds its prey. His legs dangled limp beneath this horrible growth, and the twisted, bird-like legs of the gheist descended from the spine and gripped the stone with talons as black as ebon. Either it was tearing free from Sacombre's body, or Sacombre's soul was so corrupted that it was discarding the human flesh.

"What do you fear, Malcolm Blakley?" the creature asked. "When I end you, what will be your last regret?"

"Not killing you sooner," Malcolm spat, then he charged, sword ahead, heart in his throat, lungs a ragged banner of his scream. The gheist pounded down at him with the talons of one leg, but Malcolm slid aside, rolling and coming to rest beside the other leg. Sacombre swept his wings back, preparing to take flight. Malcolm leapt to his feet and put the blade into the fine webbing of the wing, severing inky tendons and the cobweb-thin folds of demon-flesh.

Sacombre howled, spun, grabbed Malcolm in his claws and squeezed. Malcolm felt the plate of his armor wrinkle and crack.

"I will find Ian next," the creature whispered. "I will have your son do my work for me."

Malcolm writhed in Sacombre's grasp, then raised his sword and began to hammer down with it. Each blow was like striking stone, the force of it shivering up Malcolm's arms and numbing his shoulders. The pain in his chest grew and tore, until red-hot delirium bled into his eyes.

"Will you shut…"

The sword bounced off Sacombre's skull, peeling flesh and bone away, though the gheist didn't seem to mind.

"The fuck…"

Another blow, this one into his shoulder, and the stone-black blade struck the ribs that held Sacombre's body close to the gheist's spine.

"Up!"

One final swing, again onto those ribs, and this time the ebony bones shattered, first one and then the next, crumbling into ruin. Sacombre howled and released Malcolm, throwing him aside like a rag. He hit the debris-strewn roof and bounced.

Sacombre's legs flailed against the ebon bones of the gheist. His arms, corrupted by the demon's bones, shot through with stone and foul growth, fought with the wings that were now trying to smother him. There was a sound like silk ripping, and one of the gheist's arms tore free of Sacombre's flesh, spraying blood and bile into the air. As soon as it was free of the host body, that arm gripped him by the chest and started to push.

And like a stillbirth, the form of the high inquisitor slowly slid free of the gheist, flesh tearing and reforming, bones screaming as they tore away from the growths that had claimed them. Another skull emerged from the back of Sacombre's head, as though the man was an egg. Sacombre's limp form fell to the stones, and the gheist rose.

The old god of winter and death, black and frozen and horrible, drew itself to its full height. It was a skeleton of black ice, wings like fog and ink, claws and jaws as sharp as the coldest wind. It hung at the top of the broken tower and peered down at Malcolm.

"Will you kill me as well?" Malcolm whispered. "Or has your season yet to start?"

A storm answered Malcolm's question.

The sky descended on the tower's roof, filling it with cutting leaves and a wind as strong as stone. The god of death howled against the tumult, but golden light wrapped around its inky wings. Gwendolyn Adair, greatly changed and divinely wrought, appeared before him.

"I can hold this one for a while," she said. Her voice was like a clamoring bell. "I have a debt to settle with you, Malcolm of Houndhallow. A very old debt, but it must keep for a while."

The storm withdrew. Autumn stole from the shadows, the tremendous cloud of roiling leaves disappearing over the horizon as quickly as it had appeared. In its absence, Cinder's silver light bathed the destruction of the castle in sharp whites and blacks. Fires were burning in the village below.

Two figures lay huddled on the roof. Ian, arms crossed and face bleeding, lay as though asleep in the midst of the battle. His chest rose and fell in gentle rhythm. Beside him was Sacombre, somehow still alive, his wounds leaking shadows and the ichor of a fallen god.

Malcolm fell to his knees, laying his sword next to the unconscious form of the high inquisitor. He succumbed to a fit of weeping that came from deeper than his heart. And when he was done, he bound Sacombre hand and foot, then crawled back into the broken ruin of the Fen Gate.

He left his son behind, to find his own way.

EPILOGUE

THE DRY SCRATCH of Malcolm's pen filled the room. There were sheaves of paper stacked on the camp desk, hastily set up in the ruin of the Fen Gate.

For the last week the shattered remnants of the Suhdrin army, devastated by Gwen's mad god, split by Halverdt's death and the heresy of the high inquisitor, had been trickling into the damaged castle to parlay with the reinforcements the northern lords had finally sent. Tensions were high.

"How long will you keep me waiting?" Ian asked. He had been sitting by the door for nearly an hour, staring silently at his father. Malcolm sighed.

"Long enough for your mother to wake up, if I can. Perhaps she could talk you out of this," he answered, then dropped his pen into the inkwell and gathered up the letter. "Will you take this to Houndhallow, at least?"

"I'm not going that way. At least, not directly."

"You don't know *where* you're going," Malcolm said, frustration clear in his voice.

"I'm going west," Ian replied. "Sir LaFey promised to lead me to the witches' hallow."

"If there's anywhere we know she *isn't*, it's the hallow," Malcolm said. When they had cleared and burned the great pile of forest debris, the bodies of

Gwen's family were gone, though no one had seen them being spirited away. The assumption was that the autumn god had taken them.

"Give me Fianna, and I can shorten this search considerably," Ian said. "I only need…"

"The witch is not going with you. She's not going anywhere other than Heartsbridge. She and Sacombre can stand their trials and face justice."

"That isn't justice," Ian spat. "You would really betray her trust this way? She saved my life! She saved Mother…"

"Go into that room and tell me your mother has been saved!" Malcolm said, standing sharply. "Whatever the witch did to her, it did not restore her to anything like life! And she is a pagan, Ian. A witching wife confessed and witnessed! Be glad that I'm not giving her over to the inquisition directly."

"Only because the high inquisitor stands accused of the same heresy. The entire court of winter is in chaos, and they don't suffer disorder well. You know you're simply sending her to her death."

"If anyone can find mercy, it's the celestriarch. Cinder's law is not mine to break, Ian! If the church grants her mercy, I'll respect and celebrate that decision, but no faithful Celestial can ignore the laws of winter just because they find them distasteful."

"Are you calling me a heretic?" Ian demanded.

"I don't know what's in your heart, son," Malcolm said carefully, "and honestly, right now, I don't want to know."

"Why is that, Father," Ian asked. "For fear you would be forced to bind me and send me south with Fianna?"

Malcolm didn't answer, but returned his attention to the papers.

"I have work. If you must go, then go."

Ian didn't answer. Without looking at his father again, he went out the door, slamming it behind him.

The wagons that were to take them south were bound in iron and arcane symbols. A handful of Suhdrin soldiers joined them, along with the injured who could not be treated in the field. They left behind the tense lines of Suhdrin lords who were digging in around the Fen Gate, the war on hold in light of the high inquisitor's heresy, and the incredible devastation wrought by the god of autumn.

Sacombre sat quietly in his cell. There was hay on the floor, and two buckets sat in the corner. The only light came through cracks in the wood. He had half the wagon to himself. The other cell was just as graceless, just as dirty, just as quiet. Its prisoner sat huddled in the corner away from the former priest.

He watched her shadow closely.

When they were well down the road, he stirred and slid across the jostling floor of the moving prison, leaning his head against the bars that separated them.

"What a pleasant surprise," he whispered. His voice was dry, his throat made rough by the god that had torn its way free from his body.

"Hardly surprising, my lord," Fianna said quietly.

"It seems you did well."

"Well enough," she said. "He was a fragile vessel."

"Still…" Sacombre leaned back from the bars, seeking some comfort in the straw floor. "You gave him what he needed. Molded what could be shaped."

"Yes," the witch answered, smiling grimly in the darkness of the iron-framed wagon. "The hound is ready for his hunt."

When night was gone and morning threatened, Malcolm returned to his chambers. His son was gone, and not enough of his wife remained. Tener was fractured. Suhdra was twisted against itself. Sacombre's words hung in Malcolm's mind, about the south being split, and the north united. There was so much work to do, and little rest to be had.

He touched flame to his lantern and loosened his armor, his body creaking like a weathered bridge. He, along with most of his men, had taken to wearing some measure of protection at all times, both mundane and holy. The bound icons that hung from his neck clattered as he set them on a night table. The feyiron blade went beside his bed. Malcolm didn't bother taking off the rest of his clothes—he fell atop the covers and stared at the ceiling, waiting for sleep that didn't come.

When the servant hammered on his door some interminable time later, Malcolm sighed and stood, with not a moment of rest under his belt. The knocking turned urgent.

"Yes, yes, what is it?" he asked with irritation.

"My lord," the servant said, coming in. It was one of Jaerdin's men, filling the role of page when most of the Adair household had fled for fear of inquisition. "You must come immediately."

"An attack?" Malcolm asked, snatching the sword from his bedside.

"No, my lord. It's her. She is awake."

Malcolm stood still for a heartbeat while the information filtered into his brain. His blood leapt. He was about to put away the blade, but thought better of it, then looped the gaggle of holy icons around his neck and rushed out of the room.

Sorcha's chamber was at the end of a darkened hall. Two guards stood nervously by the door. Malcolm could hear his wife's voice.

"How long?" he asked.

"Just now. We sent for you right away, my lord."

"And the priest? Have you sent for a priest?"

The guards looked nervously at one another. They shook their heads. "We weren't sure we should."

"No," Malcolm said. "No. I don't suppose so." Cautiously, with sword in hand and holiness on his neck, Malcolm walked into his wife's room.

Sorcha sat on the bed, propped up on a mountain of silk pillows. The window was blocked by heavy curtains, and there were no lanterns here. The unconscious lady of Houndhallow had shown sensitivity to the light of sun or flame, whimpering in its presence. Yet there was light aplenty in the chamber, flowing from her eyes, her skin, from the cold water that poured through her veins. She was still his wife, just as beautiful, just as fine—but she was strange now, as well.

When Malcolm crept into the chamber, Sorcha turned to him, her eyes the color and transparency of deep pools of clean water. Her hair floated from her head, as if she were drowning, or swimming. Or as if she were water itself. She looked at her husband and smiled.

"Husband," she said.

"My lady," he answered. "How are you feeling?"

"Divine," she answered with a wide smile.

"I'm… I'm glad," he stammered.

"Malcolm?"

"Yes, love?"

Her eyes turned cold, her features grim. The soft current of her hair became turbulent.

"Where is my son?"

ACKNOWLEDGEMENTS

THE PAGAN NIGHT has been on my mind for a long time. I started sketching the cosmology eight years ago, and wrote my first outline for this series two years after that. It's been through four complete rewrites and, by my count, an additional six heavy revisions.

Without a doubt, this has been the largest project of my writing career so far, and the most challenging task I have yet completed. The road has been long, but I haven't walked it alone. This book wouldn't be in front of you without the tireless support of my wife, Jennifer, the patient guidance of my agent, Joshua, or the perceptive and sometimes backbreaking insights of my editor, Steve. I don't envy any of these three the task of putting up with a writer like me, but they've been heroic in their efforts, and indispensible in their support.

Thank you all.

ABOUT THE AUTHOR

T IM AKERS WAS born in deeply rural North Carolina, the only son of a theologian, and the last in a long line of telephony princes, tourist-attraction barons, and gruff Scottish bankers. He moved to Chicago for college, and stayed to pursue his lifelong obsession with apocalyptic winters.

He lives (nay, flourishes) with his brilliant, tolerant, loving wife, and splits his time between pewter miniatures and fountain pens.

Tim is the author of the Burn Cycle (*Dead of Veridon, Heart of Veridon*) from Solaris Books, as well as *The Horns of Ruin* (featuring Eva Forge) published by Pyr Books.

His web site is http://www.timakers.net/.

For more fantastic fiction, author events, exclusive
excerpts, competitions, limited editions and more:

VISIT OUR WEBSITE
titanbooks.com

LIKE US ON FACEBOOK
facebook.com/titanbooks

FOLLOW US ON TWITTER
@TitanBooks

EMAIL US
readerfeedback@titanemail.com